Praise for Atticus Lish and

The War for Gloria

"Ambitious. . . . Lish is a sensational literary craftsman, using the words in his tool belt to construct narrative that is at once coolly dispassionate and red hot with emotion."   —NPR

"Dangerously absorbing. . . . A remarkable portrait of a sensitive boy forced into a life of hardness and violence. . . . [Lish is] a superbly original talent."   —*The Wall Street Journal*

"An epic coming-of-age tale filled with pain, heartache, fear, and undying love. . . . Compelling."   —Associated Press

"Masterful, cinematic in the best way. . . . Lish's sentences are carved out of granite."   —*Harper's Magazine*

"*The War for Gloria* is the finest novel about American millennial masculinity I've ever read."
                    —Matthew Shen Goodman, *The Paris Review*

"Brutally devastating. . . . *The War for Gloria* is an unrepentantly American novel—a big, unwieldy beast about the white working class, the travails of masculinity, Boston, and the ever-present ghosts of the past. . . . Lish, the kind of writer who doesn't just put his characters through the wringer but slowly and methodically destroys them, makes clear that this is a novel not of quiet epiphany and triumph but of American devastation."
                    —*Washington Examiner*

"Lish captivatingly reminds us how much fiction can speak for those who rarely get opportunities to speak for themselves."
—Oprah.com

"A painfully yet beautifully detailed history of Corey and Gloria and their journey through her illness. . . . You have to admire Lish for pushing his vision to the limit, and some of his sentences are so powerful they seem to have been forged in some kind of roaring foundry."
—WYPR

"Lish specializes in bringing hard-knock characters from the rough and forgotten corners of big cities to life, using a concise prose style that owes a great debt to Ernest Hemingway."
—*Pasadena Now*

ATTICUS LISH

The War for Gloria

Atticus Lish is the author of *Preparation for the Next Life*, which won the 2015 PEN/Faulkner Award for Fiction and the 2016 Grand Prix de Littérature Américaine.

ALSO BY ATTICUS LISH

Preparation for the Next Life

The War for Gloria

The War for Gloria

ATTICUS LISH

VINTAGE BOOKS
A Division of Penguin Random House LLC
New York

FIRST VINTAGE BOOKS EDITION 2022

Copyright © 2021 by Atticus Lish

The Library of Congress has cataloged the Knopf edition as follows:
Name: Lish, Atticus, author.
Title: The war for Gloria / Atticus Lish.
Description: First edition. | New York : Alfred A. Knopf, 2021.
Identifiers: LCCN 2020057124 (print) | LCCN 2020057125 (ebook)
Subjects: LCSH: Mothers and sons—Fiction. | Fathers and sons—Fiction. |
Abusive men—Fiction. | Amyotrophic lateral sclerosis—Patients—Fiction. |
GSAFD: Bildungsromans.
Classification: LCC PS3612.I827 W37 2021 (print) | LCC PS3612.I827 (ebook) |
DDC 813/.6—dc23
LC record available at https://lccn.loc.gov/2020057124
LC ebook record available at https://lccn.loc.gov/2020057125

Vintage Books Trade Paperback ISBN: 978-0-525-43321-7
eBook ISBN: 978-1-5247-3233-2

Book design by Soonyoung Kwon

vintagebooks.com

Printed in the United States of America
10 9 8 7 6 5 4 3 2 1

—Alewife Station, 1990, Beth Diane, eighteen,
my fistful of flowers

—In memory of Barbara Lee Works

CONTENTS

The War for Gloria

Woman, Earth, Sun and Richard Feynman

You never think about nerves and breathing. You take breathing for granted. You take the nerves under your skin or under the skin of another animal for granted.

His mother loved him. Gloria said, "You make me laugh." He had a sense of humor about their lives, apparently. She was a single mother and he helped her collect her library off the streets of Boston and never complained about it. They went through crates of books together and shared what they found. Her boy was never bored, even living in her car.

She came from Springfield, which she called her shitty little city. She had come to Boston to go to college. She wanted to stand on the shoulders of Germaine Greer, the author of *Sex and Destiny*. She gave birth to Corey at Mass General during what should have been her final year of college.

She crashed in Cleveland Circle, Jamaica Plain, Mission Hill—just her and her son—and her ever-changing roommates. For a time, they stayed at a triple-decker house in Dorchester and he went to a school where a good half the other kids were from the Cape Verde islands. Corey showed his mom the islands on the map, Boa Vista and Santiago off the coast of Senegal, telling her that he'd be sailing here someday when he grew up and went to sea.

He had learned about the concept of a vessel from living in his mother's car. He had fastened on the concept early. Maybe it was always in his head, one of the basic concepts he was born with—woman, earth, sun, boat.

Her full name was Gloria Goltz. In his mind, she was always a bright blonde. He saw her as having a glass jaw that she kept putting up and it kept getting cracked. But when it came to him, she was stalwart. Once, she took him to a KFC and the manager didn't want to give her another biscuit with her order, but she demanded it because Corey loved biscuits—he had read that sailors ate hardtack and salt pork—and the manager, with his thin arms and striped shirt, relented.

"Mom, you're always giving me things."

"You never ask for anything."

Gloria and Corey cut the biscuits on their brown plastic tray and had them with butter and honey.

"Will you mind it when I become a sailor?"

"Oh no. But I want you to be a smart sailor. I don't want you to be dumb."

"But will you mind it when I have to leave home?"

"I'll have to accept it."

"I'll come back and visit. Voyages usually take about three years. Whaling voyages can take seven."

There was a pattern between them of her getting blue and of him helping her. She got blue because of herself. She had not fulfilled the ambition she'd had at seventeen, smoking a cigarette in front of her concrete dorm building at Lesley College in the shadow of Harvard—in the literal shadow of its tombstone-shaped ivy-covered law library—to think and write and shock the world, to condemn it, to synthesize all the available evidence—art, history, movies, negative images and messages in the media, her upbringing, her body in the mirror, her own thoughts, even the smallest things down to the cigarette in her mouth—into a single scream of rage against the patriarchy. Instead she'd been a waitress, a bar-maid taking bottles off a counter after the bar was closed and the band was unplugging its amps and it was too late to do anything but sleep the next day away. And this had gone on for years—years of telling herself that she was finding her voice, that she was getting ready—years of reading not writing, of groggy afternoons, a feminist book in her hands on the T, *Sex and Destiny*, Doc Martens on her feet, reading at the Au Bon Pain, jumping up from her wire chair and standing on the red leather toes of her boots to hug the street musicians who drifted in with the pigeons, carrying guitars, wearing bowler hats and German army trench coats, the wet stink of the bathroom around the corner and the weird men playing chess all day; the hoboes from Seattle, skinheads in suspenders saluting in the street, a dyed Mohawk the size of a circular saw blade from a lumber mill atop a gaunt bald head, kids from the wealthy towns of Concord and Lexington exploring new identities as bitter waifs, at night a wolf pack of multiracial youths from Dorchester, one a white boy wearing a shirt saying That Funky Cypress Hill Shit, there to sell drugs. Her skinny legs. She had dropped out of school. She had hung out in The Pit at Harvard Square, sitting cross-legged in striped tights on the granite wall, her eyes mascaraed, her mouth painted black, debating with her fellow anarchists, giving the finger to the square—the bank, the bricks, the Coop, the clock, the privilege and hypocrisy. The scream of rage was at herself.

So sometimes as the years passed, she'd look at herself and the weight of the time and the evidence of who she was would hit her and she'd get high and ask, "Will it ever be okay?" And for some reason her son would tell her, "Hey, Mom, don't be sad. You're great. You're greater than you know."

Gloria didn't just gather things; she left them behind too. She couldn't keep things as they moved. They lost his toys, his clothes. She cared more than he did, because of the stupid money. She did a self-portrait when she was painting and left it in a closet in Jamaica Plain. Poems too. On the white wall of a room in a house that someone else was renting, she had written in paint "Forgive. This Is the Unimpeachable Voice of God. Let Your Seeing and

Your Listening Come from Total Self." She had lost and gained. An exchange with the city. A coming and a going. The word was *many*—jobs, roommates, beds, ideas—so many it took a historian to remember. Each year was a miniature history enforcing nonattachment and surprise. Her obsessions and searches for solutions lasted a while and burned out, and they were legion too. And then she returned to them like she might return to a used record store in Allston. She might write a song or pick up paints again, and the feeling she would temporarily have would make her think she never should have dropped this, that doing so had been her worst mistake; here was the answer after all.

As her son grew, he began developing a sharp boyish face. To her, it evoked a primitive axe-head, chipped from flint by, say, the Algonquin Indians. He had a small, round, aerodynamic cranium, like a cheetah. The front of his face—his nose, maxilla, sinuses, jaw—projected forward like a canine skull—what an anthropologist would call prognathous. His blond hair grew in a short, tight cap on his head, like Julius Caesar or Eminem. And he had freckles.

Here was her poem, she thought. How had she forgotten?

She was already a thin woman, as if she had already had the fundamental things taken away from her, like food or love when she'd needed it. But that was how she chose to eat; she was vegan. She gave the usual double-headed reason: It was healthier for her/better for the planet. Cattle ranching destroys the forests, pollutes the rivers, adds to the greenhouse effect. Her cool blue world of wind, air, forest was in retreat from the hot red screaming dying blood-reeking slaughter world.

Was she afraid of her father's anger or his body? Or was it her hatred of her own blood and meat that was at the heart of it—that drop of blood on the bathroom floor? Or it could have been genetic. She was flat-chested and narrow-shouldered, built for yoga.

Yoga, she knew, was an Indo-European word that meant "to yoke"—to yoke the body and the spirit together by means of the breath. The breath contained the energy called *prana*. The prana circulated through the body like an ocean current. The circling of the prana-current made the body healthy, just as the circling of the ocean currents made the planet healthy. If you stopped the tide, the earth would die.

The circulation was like the blood but was not the blood. The energy flowed through silver meridians and a sun that was not the sun glowed in the sacral plexus. It was a moon. To her *sacral* meant "sacred," the sacred female moon.

Eggs were okay to eat as long as they were harvested humanely. These were some of her beliefs as she approached the end of her life.

She had long white legs, and when she put on her leotard and did yoga, you could see her rib cage and the bones of her spine counting up her back to her skull, housing the anterior horns of the cervical ganglia.

His memories were fragmented and out of order. If he reached across his sea of memories, he found a scattering of islands, like crumbled cookies, with no first one, in no chronological order.

In one of his earliest memories, he saw his mother in a kitchen and he could smell smoke and burning cheese. She was wearing giant overalls. Her arms were bare, her armpits were unshaven, you could see the sides of her breasts. She was cooking tofu pups in a skillet. Her blonde hair was covered by a bandana like Aunt Jemima on the pancake box. Brown paper grocery bags stood on the floor, filled with tea leaves and carrot peelings. You could smell the wet brown paper of the bags.

She sat down on the floor with him and put her legs in the lotus position. A panting dog came in and licked the pan while they were eating, and she hugged it and fed it a tofu pup.

They were living with musicians, who had blond curly beards and blond dreadlocks and wooden plugs in their earlobes like the Gautama Buddha. They looked like the Spin Doctors from the "Little Miss Can't Be Wrong" and "Two Princes" videos—tall, lanky white men who said they dreamed of ending racism.

They lived in a bad neighborhood—the apartment must have been in Mission Hill—and they were worried about getting robbed. Corey slept alone in a back room where the musicians stored their instruments. His cot faced a window with a security gate; the window faced an alley. Someone had climbed the fire escape and tried to break in and steal the musicians' guitars and drums while his mother was in the house alone.

Corey got sick and had to stay in bed for a long time. While he was lying there, his mother came in and climbed on the windowsill and stood on her tiptoes, stringing up Tibetan prayer flags over him. She hammered nails in the ceiling and tied the string of flags to the nails. The sun was flooding in the gated window and shining through her dress.

She got a TV from the musicians and put it at the foot of his bed. He watched a cartoon show called *Action Man*. The super-heroes were extreme athletes and they were after an evil scientist who had a luxury yacht armed with a nuclear missile. The hero water-skied behind a rocket-powered speedboat, which turned into a submarine. It shot underwater and sped around a coral reef. It blasted out of the water and turned into a fighter plane. Careening through G-forces, the hero went through every medium—water, air and land—his wake pluming up behind him. His success depended on acrobatic physical control. Accidents happened; race-cars spun in circles, planes got wrecked, and he'd have to eject. When the hero got injured, he said his arm was *tweaked*. He'd use his one good arm instead to save the day. "Go for it, Action Man!" his team said. Corey loved the way they talked. Their voices were so positive and strong.

There was something that spoke to Corey in the way that Action Man talked about his injured arm as if it were a piece of machinery that could be fixed. The word *tweaked* isolated the damage, confining it to a limb, unlike the phrase "I'm hurt," which potentially meant the entire person and all the suffering they could feel, including loneliness and fear.

He'd had a dream while he was sick, one that recurred throughout his childhood. He imagined he was trapped in a wooden closet; he was very small and he could not get out. His mother was on the other side of the closet door, which had been slammed shut and locked, and he couldn't get to her; he was locked in—or out, rather—locked away from her. There was a suffocating silence. He tried to climb out the window but couldn't reach the sill. He knew his mother was in trouble because he could hear her muted voice pleading—but whomever she was speaking to wouldn't listen to her. The house was made of lacquered pine, which could catch fire and burn them to death in an instant. The air was combustible with turpentine vapor. They were in the remote countryside, miles away from help.

The dream would not go away. It felt like a memory. He assumed it was something he had imagined, brought on by fever, but he was never sure it wasn't real.

There had always been something he should have known but somehow didn't. There had always been a sea he couldn't cross inside his mind.

He remembered his mother taking him to a first communion in the basement of a church when he was small. The church was where, he couldn't say; somewhere in the Boston area, like Saugus maybe. He remembered asking his mother what a communion was and Gloria telling him, "It's a Catholic religious ceremony." She put on high heels and lipstick for it. They met a man at the party. Everyone was standing by a table with bowls of potato salad and platters of sandwiches and helium balloons except the man, who stood at the back of the party, not like a guest but as if he worked there like a janitor. His mother told Corey to say hello, not to be a stranger. The man spoke to him and Corey didn't understand what he was saying. The man explained it was because he was talking to him in pig Latin.

She invited the man over to their house to play chess with her. Later, Corey asked who he was and she said, "You know him. That's your father."

The man who was supposed to be Corey's father acted more like an uncle or a family friend who would see them for the occasional weekend. Sometimes, he'd drop in wherever they were staying and meet Gloria's roommates, who tended to be shocked by his intellect. Sometimes, Corey and Gloria would have to drive to meet him. Gloria would navigate out into the rural suburbs of farm stands, cornfields, office parks and the commuter rail, to a highway strip mall—and there he'd be, wearing tinted sunglasses like a Mafioso, waiting to buy them ice cream.

Gloria had met him when she was still in school. He was an East Boston man who worked at MIT. Corey grew up addressing him by name, as Leonard.

There were many interesting things about Leonard. His last name was Agoglia, but his driver's license said DeCarlo. As a child, he had lived, he said, in an apartment above a gumball factory and taken showers at an East Boston community center. Leonard's mother had been on state assistance. He'd had seven brothers and sisters, but all the boys had died. His father had been a drug addict, a heroin junkie, a neighborhood figure who belonged to the streets. Leonard would see him sleeping outside Eddie C's, waiting for Tripe Wednesday. Allegedly, Leonard's father had shot a man in Malden on orders from the local faction of La Cosa Nostra. In high school in the mid 1970s, Leonard had denounced the Vietnam War. The other kids, whose fathers wore American flag stickers on their hardhats and followed longhaired protesters onto the Boston Common to confront them with violence, had labeled him a communist.

"I was more of a Workers Party socialist. I was highly aware of economic injustice. When our check ran out at the end of the month, my sisters and I would dig for clams on the flats. Otherwise we wouldn't eat. When I was fourteen, I lied about my age to get a job as a machinist."

Leonard's mother had been a strict woman. Leonard had told Gloria a number of memorable stories about her. Corey heard that she would wait until the market was closing on Friday to get the fish that no one wanted. "Once, I touched a fish in her pan," Leonard said, "and a worm came out and wrapped around my finger."

Gloria shuddered and Corey was amazed.

But the most interesting thing about Leonard was that while he was working there as a campus security officer, he was also studying physics at MIT.

· · ·

Everything had been stacked against Leonard from the start, said Gloria, who was his biggest champion. He had to wear expensive aviator glasses for his headaches, a curse that made him suffer. And don't forget that all his brothers died. The East Boston schools were no good: a throwaway education for throwaway kids, the idea being that they were going to grow up to pour concrete, and here was this special young person with nowhere to turn, with no one to recognize his gifts, no nurturance—it was something she could relate to.

"And then he's working as a security guard at MIT, and he starts reading Springer-Verlag textbooks on quantum mechanics."

If you listened to the story of Leonard's life as Gloria told it, apparently Leonard had discovered his gift for scientific thought much the same way Siddhartha had found enlightenment one day beneath the banyan tree.

Corey had no frame of reference for how hard physics at MIT was, but everyone said it was hard; it was as hard as anything could get intellectually, and to go there while working as a campus cop had to be unheard-of. More than once, Corey had heard his mother and her friends comparing Leonard to Good Will Hunting.

For years, Leonard had been saying he was working on what physicists called a *result* of some kind. He talked at length about his intellectual work, about why he wasn't having much luck with it: He needed to get away; he needed time. Our capitalist society stood in his way; he had to make a living like a peasant. As the years passed without a result, she worried for him. Was he getting bitter? A professor to whom he submitted a paper had failed to respond. She listened to Leonard's diatribes about the man; they lasted months. She grew afraid to ask him about science, even in the most general way. A safer subject was union politics (the campus cops were unionized, he said—and they were all screwed up). He made it sound as if he was busy all the time. He said he planned to become a millionaire. He was always away, always disappearing, always occupied, always involved in something, but she had a feeling it was nothing after all.

When they first met, she recalled, Leonard used to talk to her in an endless stream of science metaphors. There had been no question in her mind that he was a genius. To make herself more interesting to him, she'd tried reading popularized science books. Usually she retained nothing from these efforts, but James Gleick's *Chaos: Making a New Science* had made a lasting impression on her and changed the way she saw the world. It described the fractal geometry of nature, the patterns in random, unpredictable and turbulent phenomena, like storms and weather.

Trees, lightning, river deltas all shared the same geometry, a self-replicating fractal pattern where the large-scale structure was repeated on the small scale, on the smallest scale, no matter how far down you went. This endlessly reiterated self-dependency could amplify the tiniest disturbance—the flutter of a butterfly's wing—into a hurricane that took down houses. If you looked into a storm deeply enough, a complex tapestry emerged, often of fantastic beauty. She thought the Mandelbrot set looked exactly like a Tibetan mandala.

Nature could not be understood, not ever. To experience chaos, she saw you didn't need a storm. All you needed was the right man. Leonard always left her. He was like her inspirations. She never knew when he would call on her again. She recognized the faucet turned off, but not quite all the way, inside his head. And hers as well. If you plotted his visits on a graph, the self-similar beauty would emerge. The minutes with him would look like the weeks, and the weeks would look like the years. All the essays she'd never written and never would. It would make a fractal, Gloria was certain. It would bloom like clouds or be a starfish or a tree.

Once, when Corey was ten, he and his mom had driven out to meet Leonard at a D'Angelo's sub shop off Route 2 near the town of Ayer. Pine trees rose above the restaurant, which was next door to a dry cleaner's and a quiet grocery store with a long brown roof— and all around them there were trees and the suburban silence and the sun falling silently into the wells of greenery below the stone- gray highway.

Gloria was wearing a hippie dress and round blue sunglasses that made her look like a thin, blonde-headed Janis Joplin. They had finished eating and each now sat before an empty paper plate that used to hold a sandwich.

Leonard wiped his hands and cleared his throat. "I've got it now," he said and began telling them the structure of the universe. "Some people think the universe has seven dimensions. Some people think it's expanding like a balloon. Some say it's flat. But I know now that those models are wrong. The evidence points to multiple universes."

Gloria was thrilled. Multiple universes reminded her of a Tibetan mandala. "Worlds bubbling into existence all around us. Bubbling up and vanishing!" She sighed. What excited her was to see the convergence of Eastern and Western cosmologies, as suggested in *The Dancing Wu Li Masters*, a book on the haunting similarity between traditional Taoist views of the universe and modern physics, which she was trying to comprehend—with difficulty!

"That's not a good book," Leonard remarked. "It's been discredited"; and she stopped talking.

"Anyway. Multiple universes: That's the model. My intuitive starting point. I still have to prove everything. And then after I prove everything, I have to prove it to a peer review board, if I want to get credit for it."

"The good old peer review board," said Gloria. "We know about them."

"They're very capable of putting professional self-interest before the search for truth."

"So if you were flying up there in a spaceship, what would it look like?" Corey asked.

"It would look the same as it always looks to people in spaceships."

"What *would* it look like?" Gloria asked.

"What, the universe?"

"The multiple universes, all the bubbling worlds. Or is that a dumb question?"

"It wouldn't look like anything. You can only be in one bubble at a time. It would look the same as this one."

"Why couldn't you break out of one bubble and fly to the next one?" Corey asked.

That same year, he had tried to build a vessel of his own. He had gone exploring with the neighborhood kids in Dorchester in an abandoned field beneath an overpass. Venturing into the trees, they discovered a clearing in the center of a spiral mazelike thicket: a mattress, rusted beer cans, a rain-sodden roll of toilet paper, someone's clothes, a shit smell—one of the greatest discoveries of his youth. This would be their base. "We can build a ship here and go anywhere we want."

Despite their island origins, the Cape Verdean kids didn't seem to realize that Boston was a port city, that there were seaways all around them. One boy told Corey to watch out, yellow hair attracts bees.

In the sweaty summer heat, they dragged boards and junk into their base with a general construction project in mind: either they would build a spaceship or a submarine. On paper Corey used a crayon to draw a vessel with a propeller and a tube for oxygen. He enlisted the others to bring back parts that they could use. They went out and found ropes, chains, strange but indispensable gizmos—broken toasters, a hollow pipe with a divider inside it like a nasal septum. Carlos, whose father fixed cars, recognized it as a carburetor.

One of the boys handed Corey a rusted D-cell battery.

"Is there any juice in this?"

"No, we were throwing it out."

Corey looked at what they had in their coffee can of nuts and screws, conscious of a dilemma.

"I think maybe we have to stick with a submarine."

"Why?"

"I don't think we have enough parts for a spaceship."

But it wasn't long thereafter that, by opening his mother's copy of *The Flower Ornament Scripture*, a sixteen-hundred-page book, he had encountered the mystery of Vairocana, that being of empti-ness and bliss who had overcome his animal nature through seated meditation. Corey was gripped by the idea of the mind as a vessel gliding on an endless inner sea, entering a trance and coming out of it refreshed and empowered, able to reach into secret stores of mental and physical strength. He aimed to learn tantric practices, to remake himself as a shaved-headed disciple in a bare room with his gaze turned inward.

What would his vessel bring back if he sailed as far as he could go? He imagined super strength, an iron body, immortality, the ability to slow his heartbeat down so that he could survive being buried alive.

At dawn, he came out of his room and sat on the bare wood floor, as the book said to, and fixed his gaze on the shadowed wall in front of him. He drew his breath into his lower abdomen, pressed it down, and blew it out. This made one round. He did 48 rounds. The last breath he held. As he held it, he counted his heartbeats. The technique of heartbeat-counting was called a Tour. Seventy-two heartbeats made a Small Tour, 108 heartbeats a Grand Tour.

By the time he got to 20, the pain began. He heard a voice that rationalized, saying it wasn't worth it, urging him to give in. He held on, focusing on the count. The agony set in at 30—31, 32, 33 . . . He experienced his first convulsion. His mouth wanted to open, and he clenched it shut. At 40, he was entering the deeper waters of anoxia. The spasms came every beat. He was making choking sounds. In between, the pain turned almost pleasurable and he felt himself sailing in a dark blue world. His thoughts were growing panicked and incoherent. He tried to focus on the count. If he could just make it to 60, he thought, the rest would be possible.

He bucked in place as if he were going to vomit. His eyes rolled back. His head was filled with noise. A voice in his mind cried, "Please, please, let me breathe!"

The pain of not breathing overrode every effort at self-control. He was going to give up and then he wasn't and then he was—and then he opened his mouth, and it was over. The vacuum in his chest sucked the air in. He experienced primal relief. There were tears in his eyes.

He could barely remember what the count had been. Sixty-eight? Everything had gotten very confused at the end.

Why couldn't he have held on for just a few more seconds? Something deep down in his neural matter was defeating him, short-circuiting his will.

The purpose of the exercise was to have enlightenment come rushing from the belly up the main channel of the body like mercury rising in a thermometer and flower at the crown of the head.

. . . .

In 2007, Gloria had taken her son and moved to Quincy, a suburb ten miles south of Boston, in time for Corey to enroll in junior high. She rented a run-down, teepee-shaped mini-house with a sandy concrete driveway just big enough to tuck her hatchback in. A concrete seawall stood chest height on the road. The ocean— Quincy Bay—lay to the east. She took a social service job, a forty-hour job that was more like fifty when you added the commute up 93. At home, she lay down on their futon, a piece of secondhand furniture that used to belong to a graduate student at Harvard Medical School who had left it on the sidewalk in Jamaica Plain. And she lay there watching TV.

The job was to pay the rent. They were there for the school system, which was better than Dorchester. She'd done it for her son.

The move to Quincy—it isolated her. Four years. The loneliest time of her life. She hadn't expected this depression, how it cropped up when everything was fine, just from small things being wrong. First World problems—sadness. Her friends lived back in JP. They were all gone now. Here, the neighbors were Boston Irish, and Gloria said they scared her: "They're too tough for me."

Once, she confessed her distress to a neighbor lady who helped her look for the electricity meter. An older, square-jawed woman with her white hair cut short around the column of her head and a small billow of white on top, and the patchy, sun-spotted skin of a sailor—a woman who herself was Boston Irish—the kind who went to Star Market and if the checkout girl didn't know what something cost, said, "That means it's free, right?"—even she agreed with Gloria that the neighborhood men were hard.

But Corey had grown up here, and once in a while he went out with them on small construction jobs, to hang drywall in the back room of a local business, like the Rent-A-Center, or fix a broken sidewalk by pouring concrete in the broken part. They gave him a shovel and a wheelbarrow. He chopped open a bag of Sakrete and mixed the powder with the water from a hose. "You don't want it runny," they said, and turned off the water. Corey had a lot of fathers—he found them everywhere. He did odd jobs for them and they taught him to change the oil.

Now he was in high school and, as always, he was still her friend. When he came home, thumping up the steps and burst in swinging his arms, she thought he sounded as if he was going to knock the place down and put up a better one for her.

Recently, he had taken a ride with a carful of local kids up 93, across the Neponset River, all the way to Central Square in Cambridge, her old stomping grounds. They listened to a live ska band play at the Middle East Café in the company of coeds from Boston University, and he had come home talking about college girls.

Watercraft were everywhere in Quincy, but Corey had never sailed. When he started high school, he was a virgin; the flower that bloomed above his head held the glowing body of a woman. Her face changed with the faces of the girls he went to school with. He let his breath-holding meditation lapse because it wasn't helping him with the major questions now: Did you make the team, get the grade, get the sneakers, get the girl? Have you tried X? Are you hip? And does she like you?

On the outside he looked like every other townie in an NFL warm-up jacket, smoking a cigarette with some other kid holding a pit bull on a leash. He told no one how, in quitting his secret Buddhist regimen, he felt he had betrayed himself.

Freshman year, a classmate named Mark Fahey and his dad took him out on a one-masted Mercury off Wollaston Beach. Mark's father, dressed like his son in cargo shorts and shoes without socks, had just completed a hunger walk for his church. Both Faheys used the boating trip to try to get Corey to open up. He admitted he really liked sailing but that this was his first time on the water. They told him the thing to do was "to get involved more." Corey should join the Navy.

Corey's skateboard was his substitute vessel. He found *The Norfolk Bible of Seafaring* at the local library. In the summer, he rode his skateboard in traffic down the Adams Shore, his hands black from climbing trees, stopping at garages, looking for a job pumping gas, dreaming of a Mountain Dew.

In the fall, he turned into a sophomore. Someone gave him OxyContin and he took it.

. . .

It was possible that Gloria owed their move to Quincy to a friend. Over a decade ago, before the turn of the millennium, she had been living in an apartment in Cleveland Circle—an apartment of many rooms, stone-hard plaster walls, cracked paint on the radiators, few windows, an old cooking smell in the stairwell with its mosaic pattern of tiny marble tiles—and a racing bike in the hall that belonged to her new roommate, Joan, a short strong woman with broad shoulders and trim waist, who was an as-yet-unknown quantity. A pleasant but tactfully distant accord obtained between her and Joan—until one night when Leonard came over to speak to Gloria in his characteristic way about science. He sat on their velvet couch and began discoursing on Feynman diagrams. Gloria was kneeling at his feet, playing with little Corey.

Joan came out of the shower and strode into the living room, wearing a short black kimono, her wet hair smelling like strawberry shampoo, and interrupted.

"*Feynman*—what's that mean? Is that like, 'Yo, she's *fine, man*'?"

"Not exactly. It's named after Richard Feynman, who was a genius. Probably one of the greatest geniuses who ever lived. And the Feynman diagrams have to do with quantum mechanics."

"So it's not like the *finest silks, man*? The finest silks a lady can wear?"

"No."

"It's not like, 'Yo, my bitch be lookin' *fine, man*'?"

"Not at all. You're way off."

"I guess ya can't fool a fool. Are all your boyfriends so smart?"

"You have other boyfriends, Gloria?"

"See, I think women totally blow men out of the water when it comes to who's lying and who's telling the truth."

"What are you saying!" Gloria exclaimed. "You're going to get me in trouble! Corey, she's silly! She's getting me in trouble!" She held the toddler by his arms. She looked up at Joan and used his hands to wave at her.

Corey was wearing faded cotton pajamas with a rubberized image of Spider Man on the chest, which was peeling like a fresco of an early Christian saint on a temple wall in Italy—exploding out of the halo circle of his landing site in rings of red and white.

"Blowing people out of the water at lying—that's what I'd call a dubious distinction," Leonard said.

He must have wanted to be invited into Gloria's room that night. From where he sat, he could see down the open throat of her shirt to her breasts as she played with her son, catching him, lifting him, so the boy could run in place. But Leonard was disappointed; Gloria didn't invite him in.

After Leonard had left and Corey had been put to bed, Joan, still in her kimono, invited Gloria into her room to listen to a rock song on her Walkman. She put the headphones on Gloria's head and pushed Play and watched her eyes.

Gloria soon found she had a friend in Joan, someone in whom she could confide. In the evenings, they made dinner together and learned each other's histories, lying side by side on the carpet, flipping through Joan's notebook of pencil drawings and song lyrics: an unabashed nude self-portrait showing Joan's small-breasted, short-legged body—she looked Mayan; a poem or song about roses and their thorns.

"How are you so creative?" Gloria exclaimed.

The answer lay perhaps in Joan's interesting life. She hailed from San Francisco. As a girl, she'd run away from home and grown up on the street, sleeping in cars, getting hassled by cops, making all the wrong friends, cutting school and surviving on her own. A girl gang at her all-black Oakland high school had forced her to shoplift. "This bunch of big loud screaming black girls comes charging in the store, getting security all freaked out, and I'm over here shoving these designer jeans inside my bag . . . They told me what to steal or they would beat me up."

She was half Japanese, half Irish-Italian, one thirty-second Portuguese, and one sixteenth Hungarian, however that worked math-wise. Of her Japanese side, she said, "We have a sense of honor." She had a temper. "I grew up having gutter fights." She was a tough girl and didn't feel right unless she was practicing karate. She lived a high-risk life. "I'm a very promiscuous person." She'd had more than one abortion. "You come in me, I'm pregnant."

She had strong tan legs with full calves. Those legs had powered her bicycle up the hills of San Francisco. "Flying down the other side is like a video game, weaving in and out of cars." The momentum of that breakneck ride had carried her down east.

Boston was chump change compared to Oakland—not at all as dangerous. Her first job here had been as a dishwasher in Methuen.

After hearing Gloria's story, Joan volunteered to screen Leonard's calls, to meet him at the door and check with Gloria before she let him in—to be her first line of defense. The next time he stopped by, Joan changed into jeans and sneakers—fighting clothes—and challenged him to chess.

She wasn't afraid to open up her heart any more than she was afraid of getting hit by a car. It wasn't long before she told Gloria, "You're one of the best people I've ever met, a doll." And she loved Corey. "If I was a boy, I'd be just like him."

She bought Corey a birthday present and gave it to Gloria to give to him—a book called *How to Bake an Apple Pie and See the World*. Gloria was moved. She sat with her son, holding the book, looking at the drawings, contemplating each of the pages in turn. At each page, Gloria waited for him to study the picture. The book was about a girl who rode a hot air balloon around the world, gathering the ingredients to bake an apple pie.

"Why is she a girl? Why isn't she a boy?"

"Because girls like to go on adventures too."

One night, Joan pulled her into her room and made love to her, and Gloria let her do it. Afterwards, sitting by her side on the velvet couch where Leonard had once sat, Joan put her head—she had coarse black bangs—on Gloria's shoulder and said "Aww" as if this vulnerable-looking gesture wasn't to be taken seriously. To Gloria, she said, "I hope I haven't perverted you."

Their romance became the start of a war with Leonard. Joan said he was a creep and fraud and if she had to, to protect Gloria, she would bite his face off.

For many years, Joan and Gloria had remained close, sometimes intimate, friends. But they'd fought and nearly lost their friendship over the fact that Gloria would not renounce Leonard despite everything Joan insisted he had done to her.

Ironically, Leonard was the one relationship that survived Gloria's move to Quincy. He still saw her sporadically. As always, there were such long gaps between his visits that Corey kept thinking he was gone for good. Boston lay between the South Shore and the North Shore, his father's country, the land of Chelsea, East Boston, Malden, and Revere, making it almost possible to forget that Leonard walked the earth. Then, as ever, he'd drop by. His tie to Corey's mother had stretched and attenuated over the miles and years like a strand of spiderweb, floating invisibly in the atmosphere until it touched the face.

2

Entry into the Realm of Reality

It started in the fall of 2010, a month after Corey's birthday—his fifteenth birthday, his sophomore year at Quincy High. The sensation was somewhere in Gloria's body, she couldn't tell where exactly, somewhere in the flesh between the body and the mind. It felt like an animal coming alive inside her, a spring awakening, but it was out of season.

Her son was growing. She found a sex site on the laptop's history that he'd forgotten to delete. She was aware of him masturbating. In his flushing face, she read the waves of embarrassment and anger that she thought belonged to menstruating women alone. His skin was breaking out and he was growing sharp gold whiskers on his upper lip.

She didn't know how to describe what she was feeling, it was making such a subtle entrance. She wondered if it was her youth returning. Could this be what she had been waiting for, for this strange power to come to her?

She took it as a sign to write again. She took out her books and turned on the laptop and started making notes. "There is so much information out there!" she said, wearing her robe and reading glasses. The sun was coming in her windows, a cup of coffee cooling on the table. She was almost forty. She opened a new file and tried to put something on that blank white page.

Sometime later, she reopened the essay and reread what she

had written. It was actually promising! Wow! she thought. Not bad for once! I mean, this was big.

As always, her subject was everything—all of life. Her beginning ran three pages without a break. As she reread it, she felt it touching one idea and veering off to another, as if she was running through the world naming all the things she wanted to take with her wherever she was going. But go with it! she thought. It had been years since she'd felt this inspired. When she hit her writer's block, she would write about that too. It was all part of what she was exploring, her fear itself, going down to the root, to the fact that men can impregnate women, fill them full of shame, make them mutilate themselves, make them lie against themselves.

All of a sudden, all she wanted to do was write. That was when she noticed that the thumb on her left hand had stopped obeying her. There was no pain, just a loss of motor function.

The winter landed on the Northeast. At Christmas, over wine, she thought sentimentally of calling Joan.

On New Year's Day, she woke up to snow covering everything except the ocean, a frightening foam-skinned body with a gray marble interior. Ropes of foam netted over the heaving body, stretching and tightening.

At her annual checkup, Gloria laughed with her doctor. She'd had trouble opening a jar of peanut butter to make lunch for Corey on New Year's Day. "My son probably wishes I would cook."

She drove through the snow-drifted streets to work, past a tool and die factory, an AutoZone, a Planet Fitness, a moving company. She worked at a private company that had a social service function, helping people who had been in drug programs find work. It was a strange company; for profit. It didn't matter that she didn't have a college degree; she could still be what they called a counselor. She didn't know how the company made money. Probably by applying to the government. The goal seemed to be to sign people up. That was the model, almost like sales. It was one of those things where you didn't know what you were selling, and the customer didn't know what they were buying. The pace of work was slow. When she entered a new name in the online system, no one rushed her if she typed slowly due to the mysterious weakness in her fingers. It didn't seem to matter. But she received a paycheck and insurance.

Her manager didn't object when Gloria had to take time off to see a specialist in Brookline. Having noted atrophy in her left hand, the specialist gave her physical therapy to do.

"Carpal tunnel?" her manager asked, seeing Gloria squeezing a rubber ball.

"A pinched nerve, supposedly."

She took a sabbatical from her essay to read a terrific book by a woman who had started a career as an oceanographer late in life, after a bad first marriage, and who believed that the earth could still be saved.

In April, the snow melted away but it stayed raw and cold. A bill came in the mail from Aeron Medical Partners, and she was dumbstruck to see she owed $1,200. She called her insurance and complained. She was sure that the Brookline doctor was trying to pull some kind of medical billing scam.

"It sounds like a made-up name: *nerve conductivity test*."

"It's not made-up."

"Why would they give me that?"

The customer service rep said she couldn't speak to the doctor's medical decisions.

"Unbelievable," Gloria said. "You don't get a break."

The spring came and the weather became beautiful.

Midnight on a spring night. Out of the darkness came the rumble of skateboards. A series of long sweeping kicks. Now the wheels were speeding this way, faster and faster, louder and louder, racing downhill. It was Corey coming, steering with his balance, arcing right up to the house, which abutted the seawall. He jumped off, running with the board, kicked it up and caught it, and ran up the steps of his house all in one motion.

He had another skater with him, a friend from school. They had gone to hear a thrash band—kids their own age—a drummer, a guitarist, a singer with acne. The audience crowded around the band, face-to-face, no stage, no barrier. Everyone was screaming at everyone else and everyone was dressed the same, in black ski hats and white high-tops. Corey had insisted on leaving early. He had a problem with conformity. He called it "the single biggest problem that human beings face."

Corey led his friend through his house, past the open door of Gloria's bedroom, making no effort to be silent despite the hour. He flipped the light on in his room, and it fell on the scarred wood floor outside his door, suggesting the apartment's empty lack of furniture. His friend sat on the bed holding his skateboard between his knees.

"This is what I wanted to show you." Corey handed him *The Norfolk Bible of Seafaring*. "It's all here: maps, charts, rigging."

Pete looked at the black-and-white pictures of yachtsmen who had soloed around the world.

"Won't a boat like this cost a bunch of money?"

"Not if I build it myself."

"Are you going to build a motor?"

"I'm going to have oars."

"What about food?"

"I'm going to catch fish."

"Won't you get sick of that?"

"I'll go hunting when I get to land. I'm going to pick oranges when I get to the equator so I don't get scurvy. I'll get my water from the rain."

Corey took a rigger's block and tackle out of his closet. There was some thirty feet of seaweed-y rope running through the pulleys—he had found them on the beach. He hooked one to an eyebolt in his ceiling and the other to his bed frame. Heaving on the rope, he lifted the bed off the floor while Pete was sitting on it. The roof beam creaked, the eyebolt started out of the joist. Pete held on. Together they looked at the flying angle of his bed. Corey let go the rope and the bed dropped like a lowrider at a car show.

A voice spoke from somewhere outside the room.

"I think that's your mom."

"Hey, Mom." Corey said to the dark doorway.

Across the wall, someone could be heard getting out of bed and shuffling towards them. Corey's mother came into view. She wore an oriental shirt that came down to her knees and a pair of belly dancer's pants, and she looked tousled.

"Hey, kid. Who's this? Are you Josh?"

"This is Pete from my grade."

"I hope we didn't wake you."

"Oh no. There're no bedtimes here. I smoked a jay and couldn't sleep." She rubbed her face and yawned. "Are you looking at the ship book?"

"Yeah. Corey was showing me some stuff."

"But it's great, isn't it? Corey likes to discover things. It's all about the magic of what's out there."

Pete had to get home. He shook hands with Corey and left. They heard him skate away.

Gloria asked, "Was it raining?"

"No, I don't think so."

"I must have dreamed it was. I had the most lifelike dream. Can we go see what's in the fridge? I've got the munchies."

He followed her to the kitchenette, smelling the pot on her, clinging to her cotton clothes.

She opened the refrigerator and they stared into it together.

"I didn't get groceries. What's my problem? I'm so stupid."

"It's fine. Look." They had half a jar of peanut butter and three slices of bread. He took a knife and made a sandwich and gave it to her on a paper towel.

"For my mom."

"Share with me. You're growing."

"I'll be fine. I'm going open-face."

"Look at you with the last slice of bread. Jeez, Gloria, time to shop. There was no milk in there, was there?"

"No. We've got water, though."

He filled a plastic cup with tap water and sat with her while she chewed.

She swallowed. "I can get with water." He watched her.

"Are you all right?"

"I didn't go to work today," she said. "I spent my day getting stoned. I didn't do anything. I didn't write."

"You did something: You dreamed."

She shook her head.

"No, really, Mom. You did."

"I did manage to read," she said at length.

"What did you read?"

"Germaine. Her masterwork. It's such an achievement. I think she was thirty when she wrote it."

"You're barely forty, Mom."

"I gotta stay positive, right?"

"Of course you do! Forty's young! Siddhartha didn't even begin his quest until he was your age!"

He walked her back to her bedroom and said goodnight. Tomorrow was a new day, they agreed.

"Come on, Gloria! Get it together!" she told herself as she crawled into her bed and got beneath the covers. He heard her setting her alarm.

A week went by and she stayed positive more or less. On Friday, she was going to see a neurologist who had examined her test results and had the expertise to make a ruling. The morning of her appointment, Corey gave her a Mother's Day card before he left for school. She put it in her woven purse and took it with her.

Beth Israel Deaconess was a modern tower built like a space station. She went to the eighth floor. The sun was shining in the waiting room, it was a cloudless blue-skied day, and all around she could see monuments to learning outside the window. Harvard University owned the buildings in the Longwood Medical Area. The very architecture told you what the mind could accomplish with enough discipline.

Two months had passed since the vernal equinox, the pagan day in March when spring begins and the two halves of the universe, dark and light, are in perfect balance. She contemplated the blue sky and thought about what she'd like to read. She wanted to open her son's card, but would save it. Her heart was calm and she knew she would feel like writing when she got home.

The nurse called her, and Gloria followed her to a private room. There was a woman in a red turtleneck waiting in the room, who introduced herself as a social worker. Gloria didn't understand why she was there, but she said hi and shook her hand. A few minutes later, the doctor hurried in and took a seat and crossed his legs. He opened her file and said, "Okay, we've got some things to talk about." He looked at her intensely and gave his diagnosis.

It took a while to explain, and she had to ask some questions.

"Well, that's a hell of a note," she said when she had heard his answers.

The social worker would take over from here. She had a number of resources for her. She wouldn't let Gloria go. She marched her from floor to floor making appointments.

When the woman finally let her leave, Gloria went outside and sat on a bench on the redbrick sidewalk under the blue sky and took her son's card out and opened it. He had drawn the card himself: a three-masted schooner with all its complicated rigging, sailing for the horizon, and put her at the helm. He had written "Fair winds and following seas to you, Mom!"

She called his cell and left a message. "Corey, I got your card. It's so beautifully drawn! Thank you!" She controlled her voice. "You're my bodhisattva."

She took the trolley to Park Street and changed to the Braintree train, hiding her face from all the people on the T. The city ran like clockwork. It had never been more enlightened. All of Boston was a college town today. On the stroke of the hour, the bus left from Quincy Center and took her out to the shore. The spring day was still bright when she saw the ocean. The neighbor kids were playing, little girls and moms in tank tops, just visible through their wooden fence, their voices carrying sharply. The sea of marsh grass that rose behind them hissed and twittered, birds making short flights among the reeds. Gloria closed herself in her house.

When Corey got home he found her in a leaden apathetic state, her eyes red and wads of Kleenex lying around her on the couch, and he found out about the horrible thing that had happened.

"ALS—what does that mean? I mean, what are you telling me?" he asked. What was any of this? What was the meaning of her slumped posture and all these tissues? She was sitting on the couch acting like a little girl who had been yelled at. Where had his mother gone, the person he had seen this morning? What did neuromuscular degeneration have to do with them? And why did she keep crying?

"I'm going to die!" she screamed.

He brought her a glass of water with his hands shaking and kept whispering, "I'm sorry."

She got up and walked away leaving the glass on the table next to the pile of literature she'd brought home from Beth Israel. The top pamphlet was called *ALS: What's It All About?*

He went to his room and listened to music on YouTube with his earphones in. An hour later, he heard a disturbance in the kitchen. It was his mother making dinner. She asked him if he wanted tofu, as if nothing had happened, and he said yes.

When they were eating, he broke the silence and asked her if there was anything he could do.

"Just help me wash the dishes."

She put a piece of tofu in her mouth. He looked at her and saw tears running down her face.

After dinner she wandered back to her room, and he went to his room. In the middle of the night, he got up and found that no one had turned the lights out. It was three in the morning and a kind of absolute silence prevailed. Her medical papers were strewn across the coffee table. Her door was half-open as if she hadn't had the energy to shut it all the way—a mouthlike shadow-gap through which he listened for the sound of her breathing.

The weekend was forty-eight hours long and it passed like one endless day, a day on another planet, one with a longer orbit, interrupted by periods of darkness during which neither of them really slept. On Monday morning, he had been awake for hours when he heard her getting ready.

"Mom, are you going to work?" he asked through the bathroom door.

She came out wearing her flowered wraparound skirt, her face artificially smooth and young, surfaced with blush and lipstick. He followed her out to the car and watched as she backed out and accelerated away in her small underpowered vehicle.

The greater-than-mankind vista of sky and bay, the saltbox houses across the street, boats in the yards, and the city skyline across the bay catching the morning sun, trees cooling the road which curved out of sight, behind him the marsh grass glowing orange in the sun, heating, giving off the smell of grass and salt: It was, he could appreciate, what you would normally think of as a beautiful day.

He was supposed to go to school. He went back inside and his eye fell on her pamphlet. He sat down and read it.

Late in the morning, he caught the bus to Quincy Center. Except for the heaving engine, they drove in silence, swinging side to side on the curves, up the road past the dark brick apartment buildings backed by trees, the historic graveyard. The man ahead of Corey had the emblem of the New England Patriots tattooed on the back of his neck. Hardly anyone else was riding. The town had emptied after the morning commute and the T station was desolate. Construction workers on a city project sat on the ground in the shade eating their lunches.

Sitting in a pizzeria, he spent an uncertain length of time quietly aware of the sunlight shifting outside the shaded windows, the noon intensifying, shadows drawing back under doorways with For Rent signs in them. The day was becoming an outdoor version of what he had been doing indoors all weekend long: wandering from place to place without any idea why.

Sometime in the afternoon, he found himself on the other side of the Burgin Parkway in Star Market's huge asphalt parking lot, under a flat blue sky. A woman with a chipped tooth was smoking a cigarette the mandated forty feet from the supermarket's entrance, wearing an employee's vest and name tag. Behind her, big plain words said: Pharmacy, Liquor, 1-hr Photo.

Corey asked her if the supermarket was hiring for the summer.

"For what, the front end?" She told him they had a website he could check.

Corey asked if he shouldn't go inside and talk to someone.

"You could."

"That's not a good idea?"

"They're just going to tell you to go on the website."

In the evening, having skipped school that day, he hiked back along the parkway to the T station. It was attached to a multilevel parking structure. The commuter rail ran beneath it. On the steps out front, a scattering of people waited for buses, some nurses in scrubs; others, backpack-toting day students returning from community college; all looking at their phones.

A park adjoined the station: a lamppost, three benches, and a memorial to Quincy's Men of Honor, who had served in wartime. A well-trimmed lawn. A clutch of drunks had gathered there, slurring and cursing over some injustice perpetrated by the cops. A freckled woman with a cheerful red ponytail was busy putting makeup, not on her face, but on the crooks of her elbows, where the needle marks would be. The street people milled between the park and the station. A youth wearing a backwards Bruins hat sidled through the commuters, casting his chilling gaze on adults as the subway coughed them up.

Corey went inside the station past placards bearing route maps. An older woman in a transit worker's blouse was leaning against her bulletproof booth watching the turnstiles. To justify his presence, Corey pretended to buy a subway pass at an automated vending machine, pressing the touchscreen, bringing up the options, repeatedly hitting Cancel.

His mother would be heading home now too. She had taken her disease to work, and now she would be bringing it home. He thought he should be there to meet her.

As he turned to go, the T agent cocked her head at him, and he went over to her dutifully.

"Having trouble with the machine?"

"How do you know if a Charlie Card will save you money?"

"You'd be eligible for a student fare. Hasn't anybody explained this to you?"

"I have a student pass; I was going to get a card for my mother."

"Where does she go?"

"She works in Fields Corner. Once in a while she also likes to go to JP. She can drive, but she just got diagnosed with Lou Gehrig's disease."

"Oh, I'm sorry."

"Yeah, she's feeling really bad, so I'm just seeing what I can do."

"I've heard about that. That's a bad one, isn't it? Lou Gehrig?"

"Yeah it's really bad. It's also called ALS."

"Is that the Ice Bucket Challenge?"

"I'm not sure."

"I think I saw something on that. It was terrible. My sympathies to your mother."

"Thank you."

About fifty years old, the transit worker was skinny and pale as if she'd been surviving on potatoes and fluorescent light. Her bones weren't big enough to hold up her uniform, but she had a long hard jaw.

"Tell you what I'll do: I'll give you a card for her."

The woman took a Charlie Card out of her wallet and handed it to Corey.

"You can charge it up. Tell her to keep it with her cards for when she rides the T. All she has to do is tap it and she can go through."

"Thank you! Are you sure?"

"Go on, take it!"

"And that'll be better for her, right?"

"That's way better: two ten versus two sixty-five every time."

That night, he presented the Charlie Card to his mother. She put it with her medical papers and it remained with them well into the summer before getting lost.

The first word in *amyotrophic lateral sclerosis* means "no-muscle-nourishment," from the Greek. The motor nerves start in the brain and run down through the spine like a telephone trunk line and branch out to the extremities to control the voluntary muscles. When a motor nerve dies, the muscle dies with it. Symptoms include fasciculation, spasticity, weakness and atrophy, and are progressive, meaning they get worse. Weakness often begins in the hand and moves to the arm, the leg, the opposite leg, and the opposite arm. The pattern of spread follows proximity in the motor cortex. Each point in the motor cortex maps to a location on the body, like an acupuncture chart. There is a map of the body in the brain.

Fasciculation, a new word to most people, refers to tremoring, a sign that the nerve is shorting out. The patient may feel as if her muscle has been hooked up to a battery. She may be tricked into thinking that she is coming into new life.

No one knows exactly what causes ALS. An unknown chemical event triggers a chain reaction that destroys the motor system. The ALS patient will progressively lose function until she is almost completely paralyzed. Death usually comes within three to five years, by way of respiratory failure.

The rational approach to managing this disease is based on looking ahead. At each stage, the goal should be to slow loss of function and maximize quality of life—and to prepare as much as possible for the next stage. Immediately after diagnosis, the patient should make certain she has and understands her medical insurance. She must plan ahead for when she cannot work or care for herself.

In the early stage, the patient can still walk and perform activities of daily living (eating, dressing, bathing, hygiene, housekeeping), but these functions will decline. To maintain independence, she can substitute Velcro fasteners for laces, zippers and button closures on shoes and clothes; use specially designed tableware that is easier to grasp; and open jars using a clamp device. Myriad innovations are possible. To remain ambulatory as her strength declines she will need a walker. Orthotic foot support is recommended to prevent tripping due to toe-drop, a condition caused by weakening shin muscles. After a certain point, she will graduate from a walker to a wheelchair. Equipment might not be available when the patient needs it; orders can be slow, and getting insurance company approval can add to wait times. All equipment should be ordered in advance.

In the middle stage of the disease, the patient is wheelchair-bound and can do little, if anything, for herself. She will have to rely on others to shop for her, to feed, bathe, dress, and groom her, to clean her house, control the TV and take her outside. Who will these others be? They will have to be patient, loving and willing to help. She will be losing the ability to speak. To communicate with those around her, she can resort to various technologies, from a letter board to an iPad that reads eye movement and sends output to a voice synthesizer.

As chewing and swallowing muscles progressively weaken, feeding becomes a challenge. Caretakers should prepare—and she should try to eat—soft, pureed foods. Foods with about the same viscosity as mashed potatoes are easiest to swallow. (Water and tough foods like steak, respectively at opposite ends of the viscosity spectrum, can both cause choking.) She'll need a food mill or Cuisinart. A sippy cup helps reduce mess. Mealtimes will be hard on both the patient and her caretakers. She will choke on her food and spit up. Some patients rely on a motorized suction device to clear excess salivary secretions, another symptom of this disease.

A healthy person moves involuntarily, redistributing pressure on joints and body surfaces. Severe discomfort results from sitting/ lying too long in one position without moving. The ALS patient will have to rely on a caretaker to move her, especially at night. Given that by now she cannot speak, only moan, a baby monitor next to her bed can tell her caretaker when to come and help her.

At the end stage, the patient will have the option of receiving two surgical interventions: a feeding tube (PEG), and a breathing tube. These interventions can keep her alive. She must decide if she wants them. She can decide in advance by means of a living will or advance directive. She can also appoint an agent to make these decisions on her behalf. Law protects the patient's right to change her mind, as long as she can make her wishes known. Intubation creates the risk of a locked-in state, being kept alive against her will. It is important to remember that the disease will continue to progress no matter what she does.

ALS affects the voluntary motor system. This excludes the heart and the smooth muscle of the digestive system, which function autonomically. It is commonly thought that breathing is autonomic, but consider: You can hold your breath. Therefore, ultimately the disease will spread to the patient's diaphragm, taking away her ability to breathe.

When they are diagnosed with ALS, some patients are willing to face the disease and plan ahead for it. Others only face it when they are forced to.

3

The Hibbards

Corey's school year ended in June. Star Market hired him for the summer. From the parking lot where he chased down grocery carts, he could see the back of more one-story shopping center construction—loading docks and dumpsters, rooftop ventilation. White clouds moved across the blue sky like shipping traffic overhead—low over the suburban roofline, following the wind out to sea.

One afternoon, a white Ford pickup with a Knaack Box in the back swung in off the parkway. The driver parked and came this way on foot, wearing shades and a biker's do-rag. Corey watched him come. Six feet tall, slow-walking, he carried his keys in his hand. There was something grudging in his bearing as if he were angry and wanted to be left alone.

Corey called out a greeting, which the man returned. His name was Tom Hibbard and he was Corey's friend. The hint of surliness that smoked off him from a distance had a tendency to vanish up close, buried under careful decency.

"What's going on." He shook the boy's hand gently. Tom was a tin knocker. He had an unusually strong hand.

Corey followed him into the market. Lifting his shades, Tom planted his boots and stood like a lighthouse, looking back and forth. "There's the beer." He made a cleaving motion with his thick hand, as if he were showing a line along which he would cut—through the intervening aisles, if necessary—and then set himself in motion along this line.

Corey followed Tom while he picked up a case of Sam Adams.

The checkout girl, an energetic young woman who knew the PLU code sheet by heart, was so experienced she told managers what to do as it pertained to her job—coupons, bad meat, returns. Handling the customer ahead of them, without bothering to look up, while dragging cans of cat food over the barcode reader, she knew exactly where Corey was and where he was needed.

"They need help on eight."

"I'll go to eight. Just let me get this to his truck."

He pushed Tom's cart outside.

"Hey, kid, I got it from here. I don't want you to get in trouble."

"It's no problem."

"Nothing against any job, but you wanna work in there? I've worked on supermarkets, but I've worked *on top of them*. See that building? I forget what they have in there, a T.J. Maxx or whatever, but I did the air for them. All those rooftop units, those are us."

Corey looked across the parkway with admiration.

"Give me your number. I might know a guy who could use a helper."

Corey insisted on putting Tom's beer in the truck for him. He strained himself lifting it over the tailgate.

He had met Tom the year his mother had brought him out to Quincy—on a summer day. Eleven years old, trudging up the Adams Shore, carrying his skateboard, Corey saw a Viking-bearded man working on a ladder inside Quincy Steel & Welding and thought he was a sea captain visiting dry land.

The man saw him looking.

"We're putting a fan on the roof. We're gonna use a crane to put it up there. You wanna see the crane? Come on, I'll show ya." And he walked the boy outside and pointed at the crane and the rooftop fan that would sit on the pedestal he had built for it.

"It has to sit like this." As he spoke, Tom used his hands to form planes—cleanly vertical or horizontal—the right angles Corey would learn he insisted on—chopping them carefully out of the air. He showed widths with his fingers; described mechanical actions with his hands. To put the bolts in, they had to come in from underneath—and he corkscrewed his hands up like a pair of surfers shooting up the inside of a curling wave.

Thereafter, Corey said hi when he saw Tom around town. He hung around him, watching and listening as he worked with other men. He met his young relations, his many nephews, in the playground. They skated away the summer days, sometimes seeing the man from a distance and discussing him.

He learned Tom got up every morning at four, put the bandana on his head and drove out to work, the Knaack Box in the flatbed loaded with his tools—power saws, metal blades, hundreds of feet of mud-spattered extension cord, extra water in the summer.

Sheet metal can be razor sharp and installers cut themselves when handling ductwork no matter how careful they try to be. More than once Tom had sliced his hands severely. But instead of getting stitches, he taped his cuts with duct tape and kept working. He had been cutting tin for twenty years, six, eight, sometimes ten hours a day—however long the job took—using nippers, the constant squeezing blades through metal building up his naturally big hands until they were unusually powerful.

In his youth, Tom had been mean and rowdy. Once, pissing out a bladderful of Coors in the bathroom of a bar in Keene, New Hampshire, he had interpreted a look from the guy at the adjacent urinal as a homosexual advance. Tom had whacked him in the chin and knocked him out cold without breaking his stream. But now he was an older man and he hardly ever made a fist anymore except to wave at his young white-haired nephews as a joke.

Ductwork is assembled in sections, which fit together like tin cans. If the craftsman doesn't do his work with care, the sections won't line up fair and square but will form an unsightly angle where they join, called a dogleg. Stand beneath Tom's ductwork and you would see it running straight and even.

There was a thoughtful quality to Tom's speech, a need for correctness. It was a speaking style that popped up occasionally in Boston. But Tom had spent years out on the New Hampshire border; maybe that was where it came from. He gave you the letter of every syllable. He pointed at his ductwork in the ceiling of the job site and said, "It's got to work perfect and look perfect," enunciating each and every *t*.

Soon after meeting Tom, Corey had met his daughter, Molly, who was a year ahead of him in school and had developed. He thought of her as "Molly of the long white limbs" and admired her greatly.

He learned she was the woman of Tom's house, the one who did the cooking and cleaning, not her father who, at most, threw his jeans on the washer jammed in the garage with his conduit. When she was a girl, having learned to microwave his dinners, the On-Cor chicken nibblers, she'd climb on Tom's lap, pull his biker beard, pinch his nose and say, "You're ugly!"

He'd tell her to play nice and hold her. "How'd you get so mean?"

"Because you're stupid!"—and they'd fall asleep like that when she was a little girl.

In school, she played volleyball, track, hockey, soccer, basketball. She had a strong, well-rounded body. Men told Tom she was a great athlete, and he said yes, she was, "but I have to keep my shotgun ready."

In junior high, Corey saw her go running by his house in tights on her statuesque legs, wearing a hooded sweatshirt in the winter, a sweatband holding back her hair, leading the way to adulthood.

At the age of eleven or twelve, he had wanted to move to Houghs Neck to live near Molly and her dad. The Hibbards lived on Winthrop Street, which came from Manet Avenue, which came from Sea Street, which went inland and bent back towards the water like a spoon. "They're just like us," Corey told his mother. "It's just the two of them." People had left Tom and Molly too. Tom hung his head and slouched as if he didn't think much of himself—his father had left him when he had been a boy in Lowell; Molly's mother had left him also. Corey asked his mom if she'd ever consider marrying a man like Tom. Gloria said, "I don't think so!" and gave a howl of unhappy laughter. "So we can't move out there?" Corey said, disheartened.

. . .

And so, in those days, to be near the Hibbards, Corey had gone out to Houghs Neck to play—behind the Church of the Sacred Heart—it had a weather-beaten statue of Christ—near a ball field, general store, and tavern.

Two sunburned blond boys in long swaying shorts and plain old shirts from the bargain lot were dribbling a basketball in the playground. They flung it, hitting Corey in the chest. He flung it back and they let him join in shooting baskets. Their friends wheelied bikes in the street. When he knew how to ollie, they taught him to grind. They went to the general store for ices where the counter girl said "one sixty-nine" and thumped your change on the wooden board. She looked young and old alike, dead in the eye, the same as her big sister on the grill. Landscapers a year out of high school came in and got cheesesteaks.

The houses on Houghs Neck were built the same as Corey's, a door in the middle, a room to sit behind the door, like, he thought, sitting in your low-roofed car with your elbow out the window, watching the wind blow in from the ocean when you were old enough to drive. A four-leaf clover hung from a knocker giving out a Warm Irish Welcome.

Super Duty trucks barreled down Manet Avenue—huge, lifted, covered in rivets, union stickers, political statements, skulls and crossbones, and lights. They said Gagny Landscaping and Rock Island Lobster and Salt Life. In their trucks, the men had sideburns and beards without mustaches like Celtic fighting elves. And behind the wheels of their secondhand cars, the big women with their long straight reddish-gold hair sweeping down their broad shoulders faced into the sun, wearing black aerodynamic sunglasses like soldiers in Iraq.

Corey would be balanced on a bubble of asphalt on his skateboard and a pickup truck would roar in and stop, the grill almost touching his face, a guy would leap out and say, "Hey, do me a favor and scream when I start driving so I don't run you over," and dart in for a sub.

The mothers rounded the corner where the boys were hanging in the street—sharp-faced mothers with a bunch of girls in tow—vigorously, doggedly pushing their strollers, telling the girls, "We look for cars, then we cross the street. It's safe. Okay, run." The girls ran across the danger area. They had heavy feet and tan skin—they were already growing little bellies—their fathers black or Latino.

"I want to play with you," a girl in purple shorts said to a long-legged boy on his bike.

"Play with me later. Go with your mom."

Skating with teenagers, Corey ran into a pack of nine-year-olds running wildly from house to house, who ambushed them with a Super Soaker.

Corey knew women too, the dyed-haired mothers who ran the stores. "I've been up since before five. That's my life. What can I get for ya?" He knew old men who, if you asked them what day it was, would look up at the blue sky and say, "It must be Sun Day."

When he skated down the Adams Shore, the houses on the east felt like the beach was hiding just behind them. It was. A powerboat was thrusting its bow over someone's white fence. The blue sky dropped down between the houses, and the only thing below it, just out of sight, could be the water. In the lots behind the houses on the west—always the dark trees, which surrounded the marsh. In the backyards—tree houses, inflatable pools, a purple plastic princess house for a little girl.

He saw a flag on a lawn that said Gather Friends Like Flowers.

He would always remember the sight of Molly standing in front of her house in the summer light when he was a boy of thirteen and she was wearing cutoff shorts. The sun had been pouring down on the grass in the rutted yard, turning it verdant electric green. A beach blue sky soared overhead above the points of the treetops. Below the cliff and beyond the trees lay the sparkling ocean.

Charcoal smoke suffused the air. Pickup trucks were parked all over, on the street and on the grass. Rock was playing on a radio—eighties hits—"Putting on the Ritz" and "Pink Cadillac" by the Pointer Sisters. Tom's friends and family from New Hampshire were lounging around the yard, drinking Coors and Mike's Hard Lemonade. A cousin manned the grill—so drunk he would laugh hysterically every time he had to ask somebody if they wanted cheese. Tom was standing with his feet planted apart, smoking a cigar. "It's the kind of day when you don't worry about anything. Didja get a beer? Have one." At his back, Tom's house—screen door, sagging porch, dirty white paint—was slouching forward, careless but solid, on stilts that held the roof up. A driftwood board covered a hole in the foundation. A ladder lay in the driveway. A child's Lego box covered an upstairs window instead of a shade. Trees, canted over by storms, leaned like older brothers on the roof, casting down a medley of leafy shadows on the siding. Kids were running around with a plastic gun that fired strings of bubblegum, and aunts and grandmothers were sitting on lawn chairs discussing the affairs of a nineteen-year-old niece who was getting married to a boy in the National Guard.

A band of preadolescent kids was running over the hill and back, past the stop sign on which, the year before, Corey had stuck a sticker from the Fast Wheels Skateboard Shop, to the end of the street and beyond.

A group of older male construction workers stood in a line, staring contentedly out at the street, saying nothing. Like Tom, these older guys wore their work clothes even to a cookout—bandanas and reflective lime-green shirts with witty slogans: "J. Clavella Rigging—We get it up in a hurry"; "Bay State Scaffolding—Topping off." A few were in their fifties. Many were heavily tattooed, like bikers or ex-cons, their skin leathered by sun and work. You could see invisible responsibility hanging on them—payments for vehicles and homes, children and women. Steadied by weight, they were further restrained by a shared sense of the right way to act; they had to work with each other. There was no wildness; they were ships with ballasts and keels. When a truck gunned down Winthrop—Powers Heating—driving way too fast, one of these older guys yelled, "Slow down!" It honked and sped onward—driven by a Celtic fighting elf in Carhartt overalls with bushy sideburns. Tom's buddy cocked his beer can, but didn't throw it.

But as for the young men at the cookout, aged sixteen to twenty, some unsettled need kept them apart. Restless, angry, glowing, strong and fit, a line of bone white at the napes of their necks from new haircuts, some were white, freckled, and thickset with big-boned chins, college wrestlers and volunteer firemen with the faces of Irish politicians and cops; others, equally forceful, and in some cases giant, had the olive skins of Italians. A range of young men of different sizes, all a bit tense. You heard them rumbling, deep voice-boxed with deep vocal folds in their throats—round tattoos on their biceps—crests, flags, American eagles—asking for a burger with nothing on it. "What can I say?" said a seventeen-year-old. "I'm a simple man."

The young women in shorts and high ponytails came out to them, bringing them hamburgers on paper plates. The men took the food and said thank you, and the young women, in groups of three, bore the plates away and went off laughing, their pony-tails shaking behind them.

The young women and men kept apart from each other; they ignored each other—or so you would think—and then suddenly you'd hear laughter out of nowhere, a voice raised in dramatic protest, and a girl would be arguing with a guy, challenging him. He'd throw a paper plate at her like a Frisbee and smirk. Or you'd see a girl sidle up to a couple of guys and pretend to talk with one of them, while fixing her hair. She'd lift her arms and redo her scrunchy and her shirt would lift above her silver belly stud. "What's that?" a guy would ask. "Oh that?" she'd say, and explain it to him. Molly was at the center of several such conversations—stretching her back and looking casually up at the sky, seeming to forget the males and rediscover her girlfriends and go off with them again. They danced, did gymnastic moves on the lawn, and the young men forced themselves not to look, or made fun of whatever they saw, burying their deep yearning.

Tom's nephew had a toy called the Green Hulk Fist, a giant superhero fist bulging with knuckles and veins, made of heavy foam rubber, that you put on your hand like a glove. It took double-A batteries and made a crashing sound when you hit anything with it. He'd been hitting Corey in the legs for the last ten minutes, and Corey was telling him to hit him again. "I'm tweaked but I'm not dead. Come on!" The aunts and grandmas turned in their lawn chairs. "Give him another one, kid. What'd he say? He's tweaked? Finish him off!"

The kid hit him below the belt, nailing Corey square in the gonads—or so it seemed to the onlookers, who did sympathy flinches. Two men shouted out as if they were watching hockey and had seen a foul. One of the aunts yelled to the grill man, "I know you felt that, loverboy!"

"Did he get him in the nads?"

Corey swore he was basically fine. "It was off-center. I shifted."

From across the yard, Tom shook his head at him. "You're weird. No you're not. Just kidding. Yeah you are!"

In the middle of being pummeled, Corey had been watching Molly with the older kids, thinking she'd never notice him. Miraculously—or maybe because her mind was in tune with her father's—she turned to Corey and thrilled him by saying, "You boners are so lame."

That afternoon, after finishing up at Star, Corey skated out to the Neck alone. Between the Manet Bar and the general store, there was an island with a patch of green and a planting of two or three trees, which happened to be pines. A woman lurched out of the bar, meandered to the island, threw her purse down and started gathering up pinecones. She had a ton of black hair, she was wearing a turquoise and silver necklace and turquoise and silver wrist bands and rings, and a tank top. She had her sunglasses on top of her head, but they were falling off every time she bent down. She was very tan, she was about fifty, and she had a big, well-structured face.

Corey put his foot down and skidded to a stop and asked what she was doing.

"I'm picking up pinecones. I'm an artist. I use them. I do all kinds of things with them. Big ones, little ones. You gotta check the bottoms.

"They're so good. If you have a slice wound—which I've had— you can use the resin to hold your skin together. Look—see what I mean?" She made a white line down her tan forearm with her thumbnail, then clutched him by the wrist and made a line with her nail down his arm while he watched her. "A slice." Then she rubbed his arm in circles with her fingertips while staring in his face. "It heals it.

"I've been working my ass off," she continued, "for thirty days straight. I'm an industrial cleaner. In those big-ass fuckin' tower-ass buildings—who do you think cleans those? It's my first day off in thirty days. That's why my breath smells like alcohol—excuse me. I don't like my job. I can't even look out the window—of those big fuckin' buildings, are you kidding? It makes me want to throw up. The height does! I wanna get out of it. If I can just make money from my art!"

"Well, take it easy."

"Oh, I will! Don't worry." She turned away and began picking up pinecones again. He started to drop his wheels but turned back. Her purse was lying on the ground. "Make sure you don't forget it," he told her.

"There it is!" She lunged for her purse and picked it up. She felt for her glasses on her head, took them off, shook her great black hair, and put them back on like a tiara in her magnificent hair.

"You dropped your money," Corey said.

"Where?" she shouted.

Corey pointed it out to her lying in the grass.

"Oh, aren't you a sweetie!" She staggered over and picked it up—a folded five-dollar bill—and put it in her big bra, while eyeing him. "I'm gonna put it in my boob. You're too young, I know. That's where ya gotta keep your money in the city. I keep all my money there." She poked her breasts. "I call 'em Savings and Loan. My husband used to laugh his ass off when I said that." She sidled up to Corey.

"You remember that."

"I will."

She grabbed his arm.

"I know you will. You'll remember me the rest of your life."

She let him go. He lingered, but she had turned away. "Good-bye, honey," she said, and he skated obediently back to the mainland.

A little while after putting Tom's beer in his truck, Corey got a text from a carpenter named Darragh who said he could use him on a roofing job, putting in an attic and a dormer. Corey wrote back that he was ready to work and had his own hammer. The carpenter replied that, based on the fact that Tom had recommended him, "I'm shore your all set."

4

Dark Green Leaves

The last time Gloria had spoken to Leonard was in the fall, before her diagnosis.

After some thought, one night in June, she placed a call to him. The phone rang and was answered. She heard him say her name.

"I'm the woman you met when I was young and dumb. You put a baby in me. It's the same old Gloria, and I'm terminally ill. I thought you should know. Laugh. And how are you?"

Later, she would be unable to remember his reply. He must have expressed concern, a quiet request for further information. Whatever he said, it was something smoothly forgettable. At least he had picked up and was listening. It was all she had wanted. The floor was hers. She caught him up.

"I spent all winter going to these stupid doctors hearing I had a pinched nerve. And then it's this dreadful thing. If I could have the time back, I wouldn't even have gone to them. There's nothing they can do about it anyway. Just when you think you know everything, here comes this thing. And I spent all that time wondering if I should write a book. I don't want to talk about it. I don't. Corey's fine. He took it like this little champ. We did something right. I know you've never bonded—I'm just being honest. Because I care about you, Leonard. Yes, I care about everyone now. That's what it's teaching me. And I want you to love him.

"How could this happen to me?" she asked. "What did I do wrong?"

After their call ended, she put her head against the pillow and shut her eyes. At one in the morning after she had drifted off, her cell phone rang and woke her up. It was Leonard again.

"There can be many causes," he said into her ear. He had already done a great deal of research. "It can be sporadic, or it can be familial. Familial would mean that someone you share genes with has it too. I'm assuming no one in your family has it. You would have told me. Your father died of heart disease, I think, so he's absolved. I'm not sure about your mother. Sporadic means it just pops up. There's a higher rate among smokers and Gulf War veterans, neither of which would be you. So that means there's something in there that we're not seeing, probably a tiny molecule that goes bad. Something in the environment sets it off. The thing that's fascinating is that, mathematically, there has to be a single domino that starts it all. One domino goes down, and it sets off a pyramid effect that takes out everything."

The turtleneck-wearing social worker had given Gloria a folder with her appointments in it and told her she needed to mark them on a calendar. She had to follow up with the neurologist and her primary care doctor in August. She was going to meet with a physical therapist beforehand. She had a note to contact the patient services department to ask an important question, but she couldn't remember what the question was and had to find where she had written it down; she had a Post-it somewhere. Also the social worker had strongly advised her to contact her insurance company to learn about her coverage. Did she need a letter from her primary care doctor? Did she need referrals? Did her insurance cover DME, which meant durable medical equipment?

It struck Gloria that the story of her death was beginning as a homework assignment.

At school, she'd dropped out in stages. She'd seen the end of her schooling coming; she'd watched it happening. All throughout this progressive breakdown, she'd taken the position that the school was an unreasonable authority and that she was trying to do something that mattered more than her assignments. Wasn't it possible, she liked to think, that her bad grades and run-ins with teachers and administrators were part of a larger story, the formation of a rebellious and independent mind? When a college counselor warned her that she was headed for trouble, Gloria sat through her lecture and promptly headed outside to smoke a cigarette, aware of herself as a misunderstood and embattled figure in the story of her own life. If a fellow student asked why she'd failed a paper, Gloria would say, "I had to work. I had fucking rent. I'm sorry if Mister Ivory Tower Professor doesn't get that."

But she would live to repent her choices. Sometime after dropping out of school, she'd painted a picture of a woman: face, arms, shoulders, ribs. Under a shower. Mouth open. Arms held up under the chin in a cringing, self-protecting posture. Forearms flattening the breasts. Hair dripping blue paint. The oil paint applied to the canvas with a knife. Clumps and streaks of dark oils—black, gray, purple—thick pigments visibly laced with threads of crimson. A woman emerging from the swirl through hints of contour, nakedness, falling water. The eyes blotted out by the shower falling on her head.

The painting was a self-portrait. Naturally, the woman in the shower, made of oil and canvas, couldn't speak. The point of her seemed to be to express through her physical bearing a suffering that rendered her mute. But if she could have spoken, she might have told you that all she could think about was dying as a way of escaping sadness.

But this was long before Gloria knew that she would die of ALS.

Rather, it was after meeting Leonard. She had met him on a crisp fall day in 1993 when she had been supposed to write a paper. Fleeing from her assignment, she had ventured onto the MIT campus by accident, partly abetted by a wish to trespass on the elite university, marched into the student union, put her Doc Martens on a chair and tried to read *The Female Eunuch*. Seconds later, a man had told her, "I find you very attractive," and her life had changed forever.

His fascination for her consisted in all he knew. A security officer with the keys to all the rooms, he let her into things she'd never thought of, like approaching the humanities from the standpoint of mathematics. What if there was a formula for feminism—or for her self—and, through him, she could figure it out?

They broke up very soon; they didn't even last six weeks. He simply dropped her, as if she were defective, which she knew could not be completely true. Then she spent the whole next year thinking about him, which meant that there was something to him even if he'd broken her heart. She dreamed about having him and the formula, if it existed.

The baby, the fetus, she didn't want and had that taken care of. And doing so, alone, at the women's health center, made her angrier at her mother and father, who were traditional and religious, than at him.

In 1995, she ran into him again while working at a coffeehouse in Central Square, where everyone from MIT came for coffee, which she had known when she got the job.

They fell back together immediately without courtship, waiting or flowers. She didn't believe in those things. She believed in the truth of her feelings, which were as real and valid as anything in the Bible.

They began their second affair in the winter. Sometime that spring, before the end of the semester, she dropped out of Lesley, where she had been hanging on so long now by her fingernails, for good, thinking this was the ultimate rebellion.

That fall, after some psychological trouble, she had Corey, alone, at Mass General.

She lost school, love, family, pride, trust in human beings, her apartment in Mission Hill. Her man from Malden had misused her and ditched her yet again! The portrait of depression dated from this time.

But if she thought she'd gotten rid of Leonard, she had another think coming: Now that she was a single mom, he came around to see her. They didn't live together—she lived in Mission Hill, Cleveland Circle, Dorchester, JP, and other places, including her hatchback—but he was part of the city and kept coming, at times of his own strange choosing, to sit in her chair and discuss the origin of the universe while she breast-fed her son in front of a changing cast of roommates, one of whom was Joan.

Finally, she had moved to Quincy in oh-seven, had been here since.

It had gone like this with him all throughout the time that Corey had been alive, fifteen years now, and Leonard was ingrained in her.

❧

Corey resigned from Star Market and, the next day, hiked up the hill away from the water with his hammer and met Darragh at a house on Albatross Lane. There was a thirty-yard dumpster out front where the roofers were throwing out shingling and a one-ton stack of pine two-by-fours in the yard.

It was seven a.m. and Darragh was hauling tools out of his truck. When he saw Corey, he said good morning and took him to the stack and explained: He was going to pull each two-by-four, measure half its length to find its balance point, mark it with a pencil, hook a rope around it, and let the roofers pull it up. Two boards were already leaning up against the house as skids to protect the siding.

Darragh gave him a tape measure and a carpenter's square-tipped pencil. Corey tried tucking the pencil behind his ear. It fell out right away and he put it in his pocket. He laid his hammer on the grass.

The house looked like a pretty house with blue siding and white trim. The walnut front door had a shiny knocker. Through the living room window, he saw a ship's lantern and other nautical motifs. Only the roof had been taken apart, giving the effect of a human face with the skull open for brain surgery.

Carrying the boards exhausted him. They were very long and heavy. In his fatigue and inexperience, while turning away from the pile, he struck the house with the end of a board and came within an inch of breaking a window. He looked up at the roof and saw Darragh staring down at him.

"If you can't do it, just say so. I'll get someone who can."

"I can do it."

When they took their break, Corey trudged up to the DB Mart alone. He was standing in the parking lot eating a ham sandwich, his arms and shirt filthy from wrestling the boards, when Tom drove up in his Ford and hailed him.

"How ya making out?"

"Great!" Corey hurried over and shook the hand that Tom extended.

"What's he got you doing?"

"I take these two-by-fours and tie a rope to them and they pull them up on the roof."

"You been up on the roof yet?"

"No."

"I wonder how fast he's going. He tells me he doesn't have the best crew."

"I hear them. They sound like they're having a good time. I'm down in the yard by myself."

"He says they're slow. Ya never know. It could be him. He's a touchy guy. How is he—Darragh? You getting along with him?"

"Oh yeah!"

"He's got a way of losing his cool sometimes."

"Really?"

"It doesn't mean anything. He comes around eventually. I always used to think it was funny to see him lose it when me and him worked together. One time, I seen him take a guy's snap line and throw it across a fence."

"His snap line?"

"The string they use to snap a line."

"Oh yeah. Right. Why'd he throw it?"

"Because it was the wrong color. It's supposed to be orange. It's a carpenter thing. Whatever. Ha!"

"Why does it have to be orange?"

"So they can see it better. They make them other colors, but you're only supposed to have orange. The guy had green or something. Darragh's like"—Tom grabbed an invisible object from Corey and tossed it—" 'Fetch!' We were laughing. He's all right, though. I never seen him miss a day of work."

That was commendable, Corey agreed.

"Thanks for getting me the job."

"I'd rather see you work than some kid who doesn't appreciate it."

Tom went into the minimart and came out a minute later with a shopping bag of wet, cold Gatorades and Dasani waters from the cooler. He mounted his truck and plunked them in the footwell.

"For your guys?"

"Yeah. We're in the rafters today. It's a sheet metal shed, so it's hot as balls." He cranked the ignition. "Going back to work?"

It was his way of saying goodbye. Corey promptly nodded yes and went back down the hill.

Back home after work, Corey was taking a shower, the white sunlight coming through the small window, half-open to a wilderness of backyard marsh grass like the hairs in a giant lion's mane. His arms showed up very tan in the bathroom, contrasted against the tub, the white vinyl tile. The tile was peeling, the porcelain discolored, the faucet encrusted with salt, soap scum, mildew. The green shower curtain with frogs on it was attached by cheap plastic rings to the bar, some of the rings tearing through the plastic. The water ran coolly over him, and he felt very alive and cool after working in the hot sun.

He heard someone arrive when he was in the shower. He turned the water off and listened through the wall. It was Leonard—visiting their house for the first time in quite some time. He was having a long talk with Gloria about her disease.

Corey walked out in a towel to get his jeans. Leonard had his back to him, and Corey saw his sallow face in profile.

"You're all alone out here in Quincy, aren't you?" Leonard said. He looked out Gloria's window at the distance to the Boston skyline up the coast. He glanced around her sun-filled house and listened to the tranquil silence of the marsh.

He left around four o'clock, saying he had a shift. He wasn't in uniform, though he could have been planning to change at MIT. He was wearing a pair of charcoal slacks, a fedora like a detective, and a white undershirt. Corey followed him outside. The daylight was coming from the west but still beamed hot and bright on the shore. Leonard's polarized sunglasses responded by darkening, making his eyes impossible to read. The glasses were expensive. Corey would see them on sale at a LensCrafters in the Braintree mall for $350. His father's car was waiting on the roadside. He drove a Mercury Sable, a shadow widening under the wheels on the graded asphalt. The kind of gym bag a lot of cops carry sat in the front seat.

He asked his father what he would be doing when he got to work.

"I'm doing a plainclothes investigation. There's been a string of campus burglaries."

Corey noticed that he was carrying a set of police-issue hand-cuffs.

It was the time of year when the days are long and you can't see the evening coming. When you did, it was just a brief pretty postcard as people went off to the bars before an aggressive summer night began.

Leonard got in his car.

⋘⋙

Her car was a red hatchback from the 1980s. The red had faded out. She called it "Scarlatta" as in *Scarlet*. The day after Leonard's visit, she took it north along the shore, across the bridge into Mattapan, a ghost town. She passed a Baptist church and saw huge dark trees behind the sunlit wooden buildings and not a soul in sight. The road became the Arborway. She reached Jamaica Plain.

It was Sunday and everyone was holding hands in Jamaica Plain. A rainbow flag hung outside this church. Couples in sunglasses and straw fedoras were licking ice-cream cones together in the sun. Mop-headed children in hand-me-down dresses ran through the crowd and drew chalk spirals on the sidewalk.

Gloria parked and joined the throng. She had a burlap shopping bag with a heart on it. She went into an organic grocery.

Yesterday, Leonard had told her to consume antioxidants. "That was my instinct all along! The yoga diet! And now to hear it from a science perspective!" she had marveled. He said she could beat this disease; it depended on her willingness to follow the correct solution, even if it hadn't yet been ratified by conventional science, which was corrupt.

She went to the vegetable bin and weighed a sweet potato in

her hand. Her eye fell on lush wet greens brimming from a cooler. Did they have dinosaur kale? She went to check. On the way, she found powdered wheatgrass. They had lucuma powder too, a natural sweetener with a caramel taste that reinforces the immune system. The lucuma fruit has green skin, yellow meat, a large pit like a mango, and grows in Peru.

"I miss your store!" she told the checkout girl, a woman wearing a kerchief in migrant-worker style.

After paying for brown rice pasta and a dry pint of raspberries, Gloria took another turn through the market to see if there was anything she had missed. Past the vitamin aisle, there were books on alternative medicine: She read the titles on the spines.

A bulletin board at the back of the store issued calls to action: protest the war; protest Harvard University's expansion into Allston; protest Whole Foods, which was displacing minorities; protest the police, the city council, gentrification; join the Socialist Workers Party, create a fair and decent world, one that would not be ruined by our animal natures.

The market had a back door. It led her into a high-ceilinged, blue-walled space. A wide staircase with an ornate balustrade led up. She climbed the stairs, carrying her burlap bag. A wood-carved golden lotus hung above the landing—a picture frame, which, instead of a painting, held a mirror in the center, like a third eye. A cold spicy, incense-y smell filled the air. On the next floor, past saffron curtains and a cubby full of shoes, she found a yoga studio with hardwood floors—a whispering place.

She saw an advertisement for a spiritual retreat run by a guru—a Caucasian with a shaved head who had given himself a Hindu name. His flyer said he was a Harvard-educated doctor. You could spend a week with him in Telluride, Colorado, meditating and praying, hearing him lecture—full immersion, $3,500 for ten days.

The girl behind the counter at the yoga studio looked like a twelve-year-old boy. Gloria went to her, smiling, and whispered, "This looks so fantastic!"

The girl whispered, "It is!" and gave her a brochure.

"Can I take this home and look at it?"

"You should!"

She drove home, both hands on the wheel, centering herself, filling herself with serene breaths at the stoplights, the small engine running under her.

Gloria's summer went on—it wasn't over yet. The date passed when Leonard had said he'd check back without any word from him. Corey kept going to his job at the house that needed a roof and coming home, suntanned and scraped-up, dirty and hungry and sleeping in his room across the wall from her. At his job, he heard the carpenter's crew clowning on the roof. Day after day, she applied her makeup and drove up 93—to help people who had checked out of America with their drug problems check back in—now knowing what she had always claimed to believe, that there really was something far bigger than workaday life: death or life itself.

A week into August, she went to her clinic day at Longwood. The neurologist held Gloria's hands as if he wanted to dance with her and compared her limbs with his eyes. He slid his hands up her bare arms to the shoulders. She was wearing a gown. She thought she smelled his breath. He noted a pathological hardness in the thinning muscles of the left forearm beneath the soft bag of her skin. Spasticity, a classic sign. She looked away from what he wrote on his chart.

In Gloria's mind, she had a bad hand and a good hand. The disease was in the bad hand, the left one. It was now visibly, abnormally thin—and weak. She could barely generate any pressure with her thumb, her weakest digit, which severely limited what she could do. Her fingers were a little better, but not by much. She placed things in her bad hand instead of picking them up directly. Paying for groceries, she dropped her bank card on the conveyor belt and was unable to pick it up. She told the impassive checkout girl, "I'm sorry, I have a bad hand." At home, unpacking vegetables, she ran cold water over her hand at the kitchen sink.

"Will that help at all? Icing it?" she asked the neurologist.

"It might not hurt." He held her atrophied hand in both of his and studied the dent that had formed in the adductor pollicis, the triangular muscle between her index finger and her thumb.

She had fasciculations in her bad hand, and the tremors were climbing up her forearm. But, so far, just the forearm, the muscles connected to the fingers—the flexor sublimis digitorum, had she known the name. The internal sensation which had first crept over her—that manic feeling in the flesh—the electric energy—she was waiting to feel where it would happen next.

She bought *The Book of Ayurvedic Healing* at Whole Foods. She bought a book on essential oils and aromatherapy. She bought a book by the Maharishi. She bought a set of metal spheres, so-called Kung-fu Exercise Balls, in a red velvet box; they were to be rotated in the hand to build dexterity and health. They contained little chimes, which warned the user if she wasn't manipulating them smoothly. They cost her $45 in Chinatown. They were too heavy for her bad hand, so she never used them. But of the chimes, which Corey said were girly, she said, "Don't you understand? I need them so much." And he was so sorry for laughing then. She racked up five hundred dollars on her credit card buying healing books published by Singing Dragon Press and the Higher Balance Institute.

A twenty-one-year-old associate at the market, who considered herself "a passionate expert in healing," told Gloria she "absolutely had to had to" get clary sage oil.

Labor Day was almost upon them now.

Gloria returned to the yoga studio in JP and bought a month's worth of classes. They were expensive. The instructor wore green-and-orange tights, which made her think of tropical fruit—and the rain forest, where chemical compounds with extraordinary properties have developed over the millennia. The instructor put Florence and the Machine on the sound system, arched her ripe flexible body and lifted herself into a handstand, her legs projecting sideways like a break-dancer above the polished maple floor.

"We're not here to show off," she said. "Try it if it serves you. This is the Eight Angle Pose."

"I'm out of practice," Gloria said.

"There's no such thing."

At home, Gloria faced her son in the kitchen. "My yoga instructor said I'm the most focused student she's seen in a long time. I try everything, even things that are too hard for me. I tried a really hard one today and fell on my face: the Astavakrasana. Your mom's no quitter."

She had stopped at the Purple Cactus. She took a wet bunch of Paleolithic kale out of her reusable shopping bag and put it in the refrigerator. She unrolled her mat on the kitchen floor and kneeled and bowed in a posture of obeisance to something greater.

The next day she was too tired to execute a Cobra. She couldn't rotate her biceps forward, lock her arms, point her toes and lift her heart. By the third week, she didn't want to go to class. She moved her mat to the back of the studio and limited herself to Downward-Facing Dog until she could get her strength back. She caught the instructor eyeing her; she wasn't her favorite anymore. But even Down Dog got too exhausting. She spent the rest of the hour in the half lotus, whispering *ong namo guru dev namo*, telling herself that golden streams of prana were flowing through her hands.

The instructor suggested that maybe Gloria should try something less intense than Vinyasa Flow.

A few days later, she dropped a fork. She and Corey looked at each other across the table. She had been holding it with her good hand. "Oh no," she said.

The dormer got built, Darragh didn't need him anymore, and the summer ended.

The first week of school, the principal met with Corey's class. The students sat in the bleachers in the indoor basketball court, looking at how each other's bodies had changed over the summer—the shoulders, the hair, the girls leaning forward on the bleachers, the tattooed butterflies and roses that had appeared on their lower backs.

"Welcome back," said the principal, Mr. Gregorio, who wore a yellow dress shirt and black slacks and a laminated ID card. "This is going to be a special year. We did a lot of work over the summer to make this an even more outstanding year than last year. I want to remind you of your opportunities at this school. Football, basketball, volleyball, wrestling—you literally have everything. In other districts, it's not the same. Take Braintree. If you want to try welding, they make you go to vo-tech. Not here. We let you decide on your major as late as senior year."

It was all made possible by block scheduling, he said. He held up a schedule card.

"You all need to have one of these. We've spent a lot of time on these, so that you can avail yourself of the opportunities."

His staff stood at the wings of the court. The men were dressed like him in ties and extra-large dress shirts to contain their chests and shoulders, tightly buttoned at their necks and wrists.

After Mr. G spoke, out came the guidance counselor, a straight-backed Chinese woman with a Boston accent, who told the juniors it wasn't too soon to start thinking about college.

Corey went to his scheduled classes, shook all the same hands as last year, ate his lunch and did his bit of homework. But the semester seemed to get underway without him. He saw Molly with the girls' volleyball team, wearing warm-up suits and white towels and running stairs. Because of their different schedules, he only saw her at a distance. He tried to wave. He heard she was busy applying to UMass. He went home to his empty house in the afternoons.

On Saturdays throughout the month of September he helped out a friend of Tom's at a construction site in Milton—organizing a job trailer, creating order, sorting screws and nails and tubes of silicon, putting each thing where it went. It was the high point of his week, but the job ended.

Tom was under the gun with a new project and it was best not to bother him until further notice, so Corey looked for his next job on his own. He didn't try that hard to find one.

One day after school he turned on the computer and Googled his mother's disease. He found a website hosted by the National Institutes of Health and watched a video of a thing that looked like an X-ray image of a leg bone—a whitish transparent pipe with a bulbous end. It converged on a pink striated cable made of bundled strands, almost touching it. Golden flashes of light pulsed in the gap between the transparent bulb and the pink striated cable. With each flash, the pink cable contracted like a beating heart. The pipe was a nerve, the cable was a muscle. The pipe started changing color, shriveling and turning gray, blackening like a dying tooth. The flashes went dim, like a bulb burning out. The pink cable stopped squeezing, and then it changed color too, darkening like unrefrigerated meat.

After watching the video, he sat for what seemed like hours with his head in his hands.

When he looked up, he noticed the rigging tied to his bed, which had been there since Mother's Day last spring. He sprang up and pulled apart the knots and threw the ropes and pulleys and all his nautical books away in his closet and closed the door on them forever as far as he was concerned.

The sky projected a gray movie down on the shore, the color of concrete, the color of the sea—and he watched it, watched it like a woman on a widow's walk, frozen into inaction except for pacing with her eyes on the horizon waiting for her husband's ship. The autumn winds picked up. Out on the Cape, a squall was hitting the boats that weren't in yet. Sitting alone in his room for how long he didn't know, he listened for Scarlatta. He stood up when she came in, the night having fallen. As she came in out of the black outdoors wrapped in her winter coat, he looked to see if she was doing badly or not, if there had been more bad news.

Sometimes she made dinner, sometimes not. She didn't want to talk about what was happening. They didn't hear a thing from Leonard.

As the weeks passed, the fall turned very dark. To Corey, it seemed as if an invisible hand was turning down the lights of the world. His mother went out at night, and Corey didn't know where she was going, that she was sitting by herself at the Half Door, while a local DJ played early eighties breakbeat and the young electricians and landscapers drank around her. They wore heavy black hooded sweatshirts and plaid shirts.

One night, a guy watching Gloria at the bar signaled his friend. He had seen her wrapping both her hands around a beer bottle in order to lift it. They watched her drink. The men smiled at one another.

She would have looked so small at the bar with her short blonde hair and her spine beginning to hunch from loss of muscle.

"Want me to hold that for you?"

"I bet you could."

A few days later, through her bedroom wall, Corey heard his

mother talking on the phone, saying maybe she ought to shoot the moon and go to Thailand while there was still time. Not Lhasa— the hippie trail, China Beach. Get a boyfriend. Get her groove back.

The conversation frightened him.

"Right!" he heard his mother say. "OD on China White. I should."

Adrian Thomas Reinhardt

The next day, he asked his mother to give him Leonard's number.

"Take it. I don't think it works. He hasn't been answering. Maybe he'll pick up if he knows it's you."

Corey went outside to dial. The number went to a generic voicemail.

"It's Corey. My mother's not okay. Is there anything we can do? Are you there? If you get this, can you call me?"

Kids weren't allowed to bring cell phones to Corey's school, but the security guards didn't inspect backpacks, and he was able to sneak his phone in without much trouble. He had a Samsung smartphone with the screen smashed in one corner. It had fallen from his jeans when he jumped his skateboard. During the day, he checked it in the bathroom stall six or seven times. After twenty-four hours without any word from Leonard, Corey took the subway forty minutes north to MIT.

He walked from Kendall Square to Mass Ave, to the university's main building. From the outside, it evoked a Roman temple. Corey climbed the stone steps and walked beneath the entrance columns. He hauled open a bronze door and stepped inside a high domed lobby, which echoed like a train station or a museum. The sunset cast a rectangle of orange on the marble floor. The rest was shadow. The silence had a sacred character. It felt like a place to fly in—a giant cranium, expanded by thought. A mason had chiseled everything the granite brain knew on a ribbon of stone around the brow: Architecture, Agriculture, Industry, Engineering, Mathematics . . .

He'd seen those words before. Many years ago, his mother had brought him here along with Joan to show her where she'd met Leonard. They'd been on a tour of places related to Gloria's failed romance. "Look at that," Joan had said, squatting down to Corey's height and pointing up at the workmanship of the dome. "Trippy! I feel like I should light a candle."

But they hadn't seen Leonard that day. Corey had never in his entire life seen his father at his job.

Crossing the lobby, he started down the Infinite Hallway, passing the admissions office, the office of student life, and so on, the names stenciled on frosted-glass doors in understated elegant capital letters like headlines from an old newspaper.

He saw a restroom that said Men on the glass. A laser-printed notice tacked to the antique doorframe asked "Do you want to find a gender-neutral restroom on campus?"

The hallway became a gallery of posters for everything you could do at MIT. He stopped to look at a photo of a boat cutting through bright choppy water, white sails taut, coming straight at the camera, the bow wave foaming, young people in sunglasses and life preservers sitting on the rail.

"Interested in sailing?" he read. "Come to the Sailing Pavilion on Memorial Drive."

Interspersed among the flyers for folk singing and rocketry, he saw several notices that asked "Are You Depressed?"

Further on, he came to a laboratory on display like an open kitchen in a fancy restaurant. Closed for the night, its microscopes rested in shadow on immaculate graphite tabletops. Fume hoods climbed to the ceiling. In the back loomed a giant industrial drill.

Wandering on another floor, he stumbled across a very quiet set of rooms. The door was open and he went in, but he knew he shouldn't be here. In the kitchenette, a coffeemaker shone with a cobalt ready light, and a handwritten note on the cabinet said, *Coffee today, Nobel Prize tomorrow.* It looked like a psychiatrist's office, trimmed in blond wood and carpeted in cooling gray tones. Around one corner, he had a distant view through multiple glass walls into the heart of the building, distorted by layering and refraction. Blackboards were arrayed in a Stonehenge circle and in their center was a ring of soft chairs, the same cool muted buckwheat as the carpets. Scientists would sit in them to contemplate the blackboards. They were covered in six-foot-long equations. A warning to janitors: Do Not Erase. It was quiet as a chapel.

A raw concrete pillar rose through the floor, giving the effect of stone, as in a church. An open staircase led through the ceiling to a higher floor that promised an even more extreme silence and an even cleaner light.

He beheld a set of papers displayed on a wall. The center one was entitled: *Dark Matter and Non-Hilbert Space with Implications for Black Holes.*

Taped to a door, he saw a cartoon: "Physicists make bad parents." It depicted a man, woman and, in the background, a child, the woman saying, "We can ignore Charles because he's small."

A corkboard by the exit held photos of the department's members, Polaroids. They smiled shyly or looked tousled, frozen behind their glasses, some young, some old, mainly male. He saw no more than three women—Chinese or Israeli. The names weren't Boston Irish but were full of *t*'s and *v*'s and *k*'s. He examined the faces, seeing one liver-spotted scientist in a cardigan treating the camera to a knowing laugh. Corey went down the line of portraits until he realized: Leonard wouldn't be in any of them.

Another piece of humor caught his eye: "Having abandoned my search for truth, I am now looking for a good fantasy."

In the hall outside, he looked back and saw the place he had just been in was called the Department of Theoretical Physics.

Nearby he saw more flyers: Are you feeling down? How about looking for God?

In the basement, he saw acetylene torches, kilns, signs of researchers but not the researchers themselves: their fans, coffeepots, ten-speed bicycles and socket sets. Nowhere did he find a security guard or an office of campus security, just laboratories and an endless stream of flyers for clubs, activities, internships, stress reduction and the search for God or meaning from the department of community wellness. He walked miles of internal halls. Sometimes the walls would change, plaster to concrete, and he would know he was in another building. Sometimes he could see outside and tell where he had moved in relation to the neoclassical structure where he had started.

Eventually, he backtracked and found his way back through the antiseptic white tunnel of the gynepathology research center to the physics department.

Along the way, he stopped before a series of giant laminated posters called The History and Fate of the Universe. The stars looked like the distant campus safety lights he had seen outside the window. Next to a gray planet, he read: *The moon and its seas. The atmosphere on Venus is extremely dense. Absolutely no water is present.* A thin red line cutting through the nuclear fireball at the heart of space showed the boundary between our universe and a universe that collapsed under the force of gravity and imploded, crushing everything in existence back down to the size of an atom.

One floor lower down, he met Adrian Thomas Reinhardt.

As he exited the stairwell, Corey passed a stadium-style auditorium whose door had been left ajar. The hundreds of seats were empty, but on the stage, there was a figure standing underneath the lights. From a distance, Corey thought he was a young professor in a motorcycle jacket writing on the blackboard. Sensing that he was being observed, the professor turned around and his eyes found Corey in the doorway.

"What are you drawing?" Corey asked.

After the two of them had finished laughing, their conversation took off right away. The young man wasn't a professor at all; he was just a high school senior with five o'clock shadow taking AP Physics at Cambridge Rindge & Latin. He was applying early action to MIT, which explained why he was here; he'd been meeting with a professor—some old guy upstairs—who was giving him a recommendation based on an independent project he had done on the chemistry of high explosives.

"Basically, I looked at these explosive formulas with nitrogen and phosphorus, and I said if these things are explosive over here, then these other things should be explosive too."

Within half a minute, the precocious young man was talking

about improving memory, training the concentration, using the mind at its peak potential to go infinitely far into intellectual space. You have all these connections in your head, he declared. You want to have a *sense of power*. He said his name was Adrian, and Corey listened. He talked in terms of neurotransmitters rather than prana. Serotonin came from bananas. The chemicals degraded, so he ate them every twelve hours. In addition to being a physics honors student, he was a 190-pound bodybuilder. Strength began in the psyche before it reached the biceps. You could train your brain to output a higher voltage to your muscles. Through arousal, it was possible to unleash superhuman forces.

Corey couldn't believe what he was hearing. He told Adrian, "I barely know you, but I've wanted to be you all my life."

"Oh wow," said Adrian. He was so pleased to be admired.

He lived on Mount Auburn Street in Cambridge with his mother who, in a bizarre coincidence, had brain cancer.

"My mom's sick too. This is crazy. Are you on Facebook? How do we stay in touch?"

As a first act of friendship, before they left together, Corey erased the picture that Adrian had been drawing on the blackboard when he came in.

"What'd you do that for? That was beautiful."

"I don't want you to get in trouble."

"No one's going to know it was me."

Corey lasted less than a week before he emailed Adrian. In the afternoons when Corey got home from school, where he was bored and depressed and driven half-mad by attacks of longing for the tan, dark-haired girls in his class, he had a habit of borrowing his mother's laptop—he got home an hour before his mother—and he used the time to do an online bikini search. He looked at an image or two—or three or four or twenty images—of bikini models—it was sometimes hard to stop—while listening for the sound of his mother's car arriving. After relieving his tension, he cleared his history. On this day when she got home, he was, as usual, sitting a healthy distance away from the laptop innocently doing his homework. He asked her permission to email his new friend.

"You don't have to ask my permission. You know that."

He wrote Adrian and asked him how physics was going.

Sometime later, while he was away at school, a reply appeared in Corey's inbox. Adrian said he studied seven days a week until ten at night. He was doing an exhaustive review of basic mechanics and could use a study break. Corey took the Red Line north to meet Adrian in Harvard Square.

Corey saw him waiting at the top of the long escalator that led out of the T station.

"Hey, man." Corey smiled and grasped his hand. Adrian fumbled their first attempt at a handshake.

"I guess I don't know what I'm doing."

"You're fine."

"Is it a high-five or a shake?"

"It's just a dumb convention."

"I guess conventions are dumb," Adrian said.

Adrian took him to the Harvard Coop bookstore. Corey looked at the book selection in awe. The store smelled like espresso. Adrian said he spent a lot of time in Philosophy and Psychology. He led the way to the P's.

On the way, Corey noticed the Harvard women sitting in the coffee bar. They were writing papers amid their shopping bags, purses, bags of candy and open laptops, drinking cappuccinos, flipping through magazines, consulting iPhones, checking Facebook. Corey said, "Hey, how's your homework going?" to one girl—she had chestnut-brown hair and Arabian eyes—but she gave him such an alien look that he apologized for disturbing her.

"That chick was gorgeous," he told Adrian. But Adrian claimed he hadn't seen her.

In the P's, Adrian started telling Corey about the theory of plyometrics. The goal was to build explosive power by taking advantage of the muscle's stretch reflex. You hurled the weight ballistically and exerted all your force in the opposite direction until you overcame momentum, which could be colossal. As he spoke, he stared at himself with extreme interest. He seemed to freeze in midsentence, losing himself, charmed by his own body. He expanded his hand over his bicep without touching it, as if it were even bigger than it was. He treated himself as if he were a massive piece of expensive lab equipment.

Tall philosophy graduate students, aggressive in their own

rights, didn't know how to get around him to the Heidegger. Adrian didn't move an inch for them. He didn't know they were there. He kept on lecturing in his droning nasal voice, which he seemed not to know how to modulate. He was the only person talking in the store and, if anything, he was getting louder.

"The animal with the most explosive muscle in the world is the panther. It has a seventeen-foot standing vertical leap. If I could get some panther muscle, I'd graft it into my own body." He mimed doing surgery. "I'd connect up all the nerves. It'd be so awesome. I'd run right outside and jump up on a building."

He gripped his arm, showing it was a unit that could be replaced. His enthusiasm filled Corey's heart with hope.

Everyone could hear him—all the Harvard girls efficiently planning their weekends.

The motorcycle jacket fit him tightly. There was, at most, room for a sweatshirt underneath it. Adrian refused to wear a hat. He left the Coop with his black, leather-clad shoulders hunched up around his ears. The temperature had dropped very low that night, and the asphalt roads were streaked with frost.

Corey, in a forty-dollar bubble jacket from the Burlington Coat Factory, asked, "How come you don't get yourself a parka?"

Adrian stopped on the redbrick sidewalk, pressed his hands together and flexed his chest to stop himself from shivering. "The cold gives me a simple thing to overcome."

Instead of sneakers, he wore last season's tattered wrestling shoes, a thin piece of rubberized plastic between his feet and the ground, which offered no insulation or support. He made a heaving throat-clearing noise to deal with his phlegm. He had a cold. "It's an infection," he smiled. He was unshaven. "I like having bacteria in my throat."

They hiked down Mount Auburn Street to the house where Adrian lived alone with his mother. His parents had gotten divorced when he was a very little boy.

"I love making everybody sick."

. . .

His house was the color of cocoa powder with brown trim. It was inventively designed—a set of different-sized boxes put together to form an un-box-like shape—certainly not the kind of simple, peaked-roof house a five-year-old would have drawn with eye-like windows, a sun in the sky and a dog in the yard. Corey saw a rearranged face, à la Picasso, with eyes, nose and jaw stirred in a circle.

The boys went inside. Adrian's home boasted hardwood floors and a cathedral ceiling, and a kitchen with a breakfast nook and barstools. A cast-iron woodstove crouched on a platform in the living room. Everything was open plan. The axes of the different rooms were set at surprising angles to one another. The walls were very white.

No one was home. Adrian led him up a spiral staircase. It was open too, and the climbers were suspended in midair above the living room before they went through a ceiling. As they climbed above the second floor, the staircase and the walls—the house itself—seemed to tighten around them like a fist.

In the narrow quarters, Corey thought he smelled an animal.

"Do you own a pet?"

"That's just me," Adrian said, and the two of them started laughing.

Adrian had his bedroom on the fifth floor. His room was laboratory-neat. The first thing you saw when you walked in was the desk against the high white wall cut by the angle of the roof. He had a skylight, which showed the night. A physics textbook rested on the desktop. It was positioned in the center of that surface. A pen lay next to it, parallel to the spine. The book was closed. Corey had a clear vision of Adrian sitting there, his muscular shoulders hunched over his physics book until precisely ten at night.

He had a lamp with a flexible neck that clamped to the edge of the desk.

The bed hardly looked big enough for someone of his size. You would have thought a fifth-grader slept in it. A copy of *The Basic Writings of Nietzsche* sat on the bedside table.

Despite the wealth in the Cambridge apartment, Corey picked up a strange sense of deprivation here.

He asked to see Adrian's Nietzsche. The book was full of handwriting—in the margins, between the lines—in all block-capital letters. He saw mathematics and the language of self-help psychology all jumbled-up together in the form of strange equations. Certain phrases leaped out at him as he flipped the pages. One was *Develop Self Esteem*. Another one was *Happiness Equals The Integral of Power*. The handwriting was so strong he could feel it in the page like Braille. He jumped ahead a hundred pages and found still more of it, blacking out the margins—an astonishing amount of obsessive note-taking, which spilled over onto the blank sheets at the end of the text. On the very last white space of the book, the inside cover, he came across a calculation and stopped to read it, his eye having picked up the number 2070, which he correctly identified as referring to a year. It took him a minute to figure out what he was seeing. It appeared that Adrian, using high school probability and statistics, was predicting the date of his own death.

"I've never been comfortable with science," Corey said. "But you are."

"To me, it's a way of overcoming problems and controlling the universe."

"What's the biggest problem in your universe?"

"My mother."

"Me too," Corey said. "Me too."

And Corey spoke to Adrian at length about his mother's illness. It struck him that Adrian listened with remarkable sensitivity—or interest. His precise words to Corey were "I'm sorry you're going through that."

"I'm sorry your mom has cancer. That must be rough," Corey said in return.

Adrian frowned. "It has its disadvantages. Obviously you don't want someone else to suffer. That would be immoral. But if somebody uses her illness to take advantage of you, that's immoral too."

As Adrian talked, Corey began to gather that his new friend felt very differently about his mother than he did. Adrian described his mother as "controlling." After speaking in philosophical terms for several minutes, he concluded by saying, "I feel morally absolved from worrying about her."

. . .

Adrian wasn't just smart, he was funny too. He was always talking about his own ass. He farted loudly—explosively loud, cracking farts, where one could hear the muscular sides of his buttocks reverberating—and he would do it in public. He would do it right next to a woman standing at a bus stop, and Corey would die laughing.

It was almost always night when Adrian could see him. Corey had to work around Adrian's inflexible self-improvement schedule. They studied together in Adrian's white room. They read books together in the Coop when the rest of the world was getting ready for Thanksgiving. He followed Adrian on meandering walks through Cambridge, listening to him talk relentlessly, using physics as a metaphor for everything. They hiked all through the dark hours of the night. Corey texted his mother at three a.m. to tell her not to worry, he was learning to develop himself. They broke into Adrian's high school gym together so he could watch Adrian working out. Adrian played his violent workout music, and Corey listened. He watched as Adrian refueled his giant muscles by drinking gallons of milk.

Corey told his mom that he had found a real-life Vairocana on which to model himself.

In view of Adrian's greatness, Corey had to see his drawing on the blackboard at MIT as something out of character. It was the same cartoon one sees on every shithouse wall: a disembodied female genital display between a pair of open legs.

6

Holiday

At her November clinic day, she told them at the hospital, "I've got a refrigerator full of kale and I'm only getting worse."

Gloria's physical therapist had been planning to teach her range-of-motion exercises to unfreeze her progressively stiffening limbs: Lie on back, bring knee to chest, exhale.

"That's a lot like yoga, only easier. What else you got?"

"We could try some weights." The physical therapist—speaking in a soft western accent and projecting a calm that seemed to come from somewhere beyond the professional realm, like a trail guide who refuses to raise her voice out of respect for nature—brought out a pair of rubber-coated dumbbells and, kneeling in her olive cargo pants, showed Gloria how to use them. Gloria went home and started working out.

She changed into an old Lesley College athletic shirt and sneakers, previously unworn. Up to now she'd always been a sandals-and-boots woman. She moved her holistic healing books out of sight behind her bed, stacking them on her art books, the rumpled pages of her abandoned essay, put on music from her bar-maid days at the Rathskeller, bent down and rowed the dumbbells to her belly.

The therapist had also recommended that Gloria begin taking a protein supplement, one that was *complete*—contained the essential amino acids. So she went to Whole Foods and bought a canister of protein powder and set it on the kitchen countertop. She started drinking one scoop three times a day in orange juice.

Corey would see his mother's little tub of protein every time he went to the kitchen—it had a vanilla bean on the wrapper—and he'd associate it with the spirit of self-development and progress that he was absorbing from Adrian, who was dedicated to building himself up from the smallest possible molecule.

Throughout the rest of the semester, he would watch her standing on her yoga mat, pushing the small weights up in the air, her white legs bare in gym shorts, varicose veins in the backs of her knees, sweat dampening her shirt, hair sticking to her forehead, the radio playing Hüsker Dü while she did her sets—the strange sight of her in sneakers.

He stopped his brain from seeing certain things. The dumbbells weighed eight pounds each. They hung from the last joints of her fingers. They were a hair away from falling. She couldn't close her hands. The only thing that stopped them was friction between the rubber and her skin. She would graduate to five-pound weights, then threes, before she had to give them up completely.

At night, to avoid the electricians, she had stopped going to the Half Door. She went to Acapulcos Mexican Family Restaurant & Cantina. She was there on Thanksgiving, eating dinner alone. She hid her body beneath a long down coat. The Greek fisherman's hat she wore was a size too big for her skull. One would have seen her short blonde hair and the stalk of her neck, the disease rounding her spine, giving her a hump back, as she sucked Long Island Iced Tea through a straw. It was getting late.

Her son texted her, "r u ok?"

"I'll be home soon," she wrote with her weak fingers, the software in the phone finishing the words for her.

She hadn't made him dinner. She declined the bartender's offer of a refill and ordered a fifteen-dollar entrée and took it home to Corey in a round aluminum foil container with a cardboard top.

One night that same Thanksgiving week, she had a run-in. After the bar discharged her, a man saw her crying on the shadow side of the street. He approached and asked what was the matter.

It was midnight and she was a little drunk. She told him she was dying. He said he could cure her for ten thousand dollars. He must have expressed concern. Or certainty. He offered to walk her to the Bank of America ATM on the corner.

When she got home, she woke Corey up and told him what had happened. Her son stared around the house in alarm. "Did he get anything from you?"

"No. He followed me."

"What do you mean?"

"He followed me until the bus came. I waved at the driver and he took off."

"What the hell did he look like?"

"I was scared. I didn't look at him."

"What did he look like, Mom? I want to know."

"Just a man."

The episode triggered a childhood memory in Corey's head:

Joan was wearing a short black silk robe. She made him spaghetti and opened a jar of Prego.

The year was 1999, Corey was four years old, and Joan and his mother slept together at night. They all lived together in the apartment in Cleveland Circle, which had plaster walls, wood floors, lots of rooms, few windows, shelves full of books and CDs, a basket of VCR tapes, and a TV. It faced the living room couch, which was dirty, soft and velvety. Joan sat next to him on the velvet cushion and gave him food.

"Can you eat it like a big boy? You're wicked mature."

The remote didn't work. She got up and turned on the TV by hand, bending over in her short robe, and flounced back down again and her leg touched him.

"What's this? *Yo, MTV Raps*? Snoop Doggy Dooooog! Bow wow wow, yippeeyo yippeeyay. I love Snoop. I think he's a braciole. I'd let him put me in his dog pound. Nah, that's messed up."

"What is?" asked four-year-old Corey.

"Guys thinking they can be big mac daddies. What gives them the right? You'd never do that, would you? Dog a girl?" She looked down and adjusted her robe over her legs. "You'd never two-time your girlfriend, would you?"

No, he said. He'd never do that!

His mother was leaving. "Bye!" she said. She squatted on the floor and spread her arms and he jumped off the couch and ran into her embrace. With his eyes closed, he felt his mother's cheek against his face, the hard cheekbone and jaw, the thin pad of her cheek. A mother's face feels just right to her child.

She stood and Joan, who had strolled over bare-legged, put out her arm for Gloria. The women kissed. Corey looked up at the women talking, saying goodbye. Their legs were at the level of his eyes. He embraced them like trees in his play forest.

He knew that everything was not okay outside the door of the apartment. A man was out there in the city and he was making problems for them. Of course—as he would appreciate when he was older—"the man" was just Leonard—but as a child Corey had believed that Gloria was in danger every time she left the house.

But Joan said not to worry, she would kick him where the sun didn't shine.

When Joan was alone with Corey, she put tapes in the VCR and they watched movies. She went into his fantasy life, steering him towards Indian maidens with black hair, tan legs, buckskins, beads and leather fringe—women who looked like her—and he dreamed about them when she put him to bed.

Together, he and Joan saw *Billy Jack*, a movie starring Tom Laughlin as a denim-clad 1970s-era Shane figure who defends the multiethnic runaways at the Freedom School from small-town bigots, using the Korean martial art hapkido. Billy Jack goes through a Native American rite of passage, sitting with a rattle-snake inside a ritual ring of stones, allowing the snake to bite him. Corey admired the ascetic Laughlin.

There was a scene in *Billy Jack* that disturbed Corey. The leader of the Freedom School, the heroine, a blonde pacifist who looked like Gloria with longer hair, lay in a desert canyon to sun-bathe. There she was discovered by Billy Jack's nemesis and raped.

But in a later scene, Billy Jack kills the rapist, getting revenge with his bare hands.

On a Friday night in mid-December, Corey got home from hang-ing out with Adrian and encountered Leonard in their house. It had been months since Leonard's visit in the summer, and Corey was mildly astonished to see him. Gloria was sitting at the end of the futon next to the scavenged end table, a space between her and Leonard, with her body turned so she could listen to him talk. She had hidden herself in a long, thrift-store dress, fisherman's hat and woolly sweater, and retracted both her atrophied hands up inside her sweater sleeves. There was a wineglass on the end table.

When Corey entered, they were having a discussion. Gloria had stated that the aim of sculpture was to overcome the inherent rigidity of the material and make it appear flowing, dynamic, alive, changing, like a child becoming an adult, or any of life's evolutions. Leonard was replying to her view. He said, "I don't know anything about art—and I think most of it serves an economic agenda by elites, where you have people spending millions of dollars for something a five-year-old could draw—but when I look at sculpture, like so-called Mother Mary in a church, I think the sculptor is freezing reality so we can see it and hold it. Sculptures don't grow into adults. They don't evolve. They get bought and sold."

When she saw her son, Gloria's face lit up and she raised her half-hidden hands in her lap. "Yay! It's Corey, the man of the hour!"

"Me?"

"We were just talking about you. About what a super kid you are. Man—young man—you are."

Corey went over and hugged her. He greeted Leonard. Leonard was dressed in so much black, from the fedora on his head all the way down to the black soles of his shoes, that it made Corey appreciate as never before this color's ability to separate a figure from the world around it.

Leonard nodded at him. "You've grown since I saw you last."

"I've been working out."

"Have you?"

Leonard produced a joint and lit it for Corey's mother. "I'm afraid I'll drop it," she said. Leonard put it to her mouth. She leaned over and dragged from it, making the pot crackle and the resin bubble, her eyes squinted under the wool brim of her too-big hat. A knot of smoke hung in her oral cavity giving her a thick white tongue. She inhaled and the smoke was whisked away into her breathing passages and vanished.

High, she talked with him on subjects ranging from sculpture to impressionism, to Darwin, to eugenics. Leonard argued that Hitler was a rational agent in a world of limited resources, but that communism is both rational and moral. Corey lay on the floor and took a book at random from the milk crate—*Democracy and the Market: Political and Economic Reforms in Eastern Europe*. He let his eyes take up the words while he listened to their talk, experimenting with letting his brain work on two tracks at once.

"We're bad parents," Gloria said, waving at her pot smoke.

"No, you're not."

"I'll have myself to blame if you turn into a stoner on me."

Corey said he was armored against bad influences because he was only motivated by ways to become "more *overcoming*."

"*Overcoming* isn't an adjective," Leonard said.

Corey said that he was drawing his ideas, and his vocabulary, from a new friend, a highly original young man who was teaching Corey to dedicate himself to amassing physical and intellectual power.

"I think I detect a little recycled Nietzsche."

"You're starting a new chapter in your life. There's such excitement ahead for you!" Gloria said, her eyes shining.

Later, when the adults decided it was time to wrap the night up, Gloria asked Corey to open the futon so Leonard could recline.

For some time now, since meeting Adrian, Corey had been expressing a sudden ambition to work hard in school, to study subjects he had previously ignored, like math and science, and apply to MIT—just like Adrian—or, failing that, UMass—just like Molly. But at any rate to actually try to go to college and study hard wherever he went—and build, within the neurons of his own brain, an enormous structure of knowledge and deductive ability—whole libraries in his head, a hierarchical structure—stacks to shelves to books to the parts and chapters in the books themselves. He envisioned an intellectual spectrum with math at the foundation: calculus, the language of the physical world; physics to chemistry to biology to psychology; from force and magnetism to molecules to neurotransmitters to language and love and anger to all the literature of the world; the history of all civilizations—all the farming, rebellions, wars and paintings.

Leonard visited them again a few nights later to consult with Gloria about her disease. His late-night visits created a mood of holiday, coinciding, as they did, with Corey's winter break. Generally, Leonard's tour was midnight to eight, but his schedule seemed to migrate through the hours. Sometimes he stayed past midnight and left at two or three in the morning. He'd knock on their door in the dead of night and Gloria would tell Corey to let him in. They'd stay up watching videos and eating macaroni and cheese.

"What are you watching?"

"Horseshit," they told Corey in unison. They were watching *Robocop*.

They were living in a bubble—in one of the bubbles in Leonard's universe, Corey thought. He joined in the togetherness.

Leonard urged him to try pot. "Just one puff." Corey took a hit off Leonard's joint.

The camping-out feeling lasted several weeks. Sometimes they didn't sleep at all and Gloria called out sick. Before the break had even begun, Corey had missed some days of school and one important test, Biology.

During the Christmas holiday, Leonard didn't have money. Gloria would say, "Don't worry. You can eat on my dime." And they'd put a meal on the credit card because she didn't want to face cooking. Corey would take her card and drive to Acapulcos and get two or three entrées—burritos, enchiladas with sour cream, guacamole— the corn chips stale. "I don't care what it costs," Gloria said. "Let's enjoy it."

They'd position themselves on the futon, Leonard on one end, Gloria on the other, Corey on the floor between. His mother—in a rare moment of playfulness—kicked him lightly in the back of the head. "You don't have to sit down there."

"I don't mind. I'm a floor person more than a couch person." Sitting on the floor, he was close to the laptop so he could control the mouse.

"He's the remote," Leonard said. "Down in front, remote."

"He's low enough. How low do you want him to get, for heaven's sakes?"

"It's fine," said Corey, scooting lower. He touched the mouse. The movie started playing, then actors, sound effects, and drama broke out on the screen, and they were diverted for a while. This was how they got through Christmas.

But after several nights of this, there began to be a hangover effect: the waking up late in a messy apartment, the day half over, no chores done, crumbs on the floor. The daylight was unforgiving. Corey prayed for another night and another movie. He worried his mother might be regretting how she spent her time. It was a relief when she asked, "What'll we do to have fun today?" because the answer was another movie and something fun to eat.

Then there were the long silences while Gloria, wearing bifocals, hunted for a video they could stream for free. She was interested in a story about a woman who, after a romantic misadventure, returned home to live with her parents, bringing to light unresolved family tensions. Leonard said *Road Warrior* had a political substructure that made it more worthwhile. Corey wanted to see it too. They watched it and Gloria said, "I don't understand why men revel in cruelty so."

"Women are by far the crueler species," Leonard said.

"That's topsy-turvy. Look at history. Who's always declaring wars? Your species, Leonard."

"Hey, it's Christmas," Corey put in. The movie played out.

"Well, we got through that one," they laughed. But it was late and now they needed another movie more than ever. Gloria said she didn't care what they watched; the men could decide. "Come on, Mom, don't say that!" He found her female drama and put it on. Leonard turned on a light and read his math book. They couldn't see the screen. Corey pushed Pause and took the laptop to his mother's bedroom for her to watch alone. And it took a long time for her to emerge the morning after Christmas. She'd been up late. He'd heard her through the wall.

7

Trees Don't Hit Back

Except for his parents' movie marathons, Corey's break from school was completely lacking in structure except for that provided by the weather: All the days but one were very cold, and it was very warm, to the point of being an anomaly. He didn't have homework and he wasn't working. The moratorium on calling Tom was still in effect. He was at loose ends. As much as possible, he went to see Adrian, who was on his break as well, though as always, Adrian was frequently occupied with his studies and couldn't be disturbed, so Corey only saw him twice.

The first night he went to Cambridge, he found Adrian alone. Mrs. Reinhardt, who had an active schedule despite her cancer, had gone to visit friends. Both boys were happy to be unsupervised. Corey experienced a giddy sense of freedom as he stood in the big dark cold house with his friend looming above him on the stairs and the entire nighttime city awaiting them outside.

He said they ought to go to Harvard Square to look for girls.

Adrian said that, for once, he didn't feel oppressed by the need for a woman because the first thing he'd done when his mother left the house that night was masturbate.

"Thanks for sharing."

"Oh, that's right. You don't like to talk about that." Unlike a lot of guys, Adrian admitted that he masturbated. He talked about it openly—incessantly—until it became an uncomfortable form of comedy. "I don't see how anyone can resist it. Don't you jack off?"

"I can't deny it. But I want a real woman. Don't you?"

"Well, if you could meet those needs another way, wouldn't it be more efficient?"

"I'm not thinking about efficiency, I'm thinking about a girl-friend."

"But how can you guarantee you'll get one?"

"Of course I'll get one."

"How? You can't just snap your fingers and make one appear."

"I don't know how. I'm just gonna try. I'm gonna get lucky."

"I wish that would work for me."

Corey was reminded that a few weeks ago, Adrian had told him that he knew a girl at Rindge, a big girl with a big rear end. She was five-foot-nine, she had full lips and long hair. In Adrian's words, she had a "big beefcake" and he wanted to "pop it." Adrian had heard through the grapevine that she was into him. People were saying she thought he had a hot body and was waiting for him to ask her out. What should he do? Corey had told him to go for it. Adrian had agreed (reluctantly, it had seemed to Corey) that maybe he should. But he didn't want to mess this up. He knew what he was going to do: He was going to write down everything he was going to say to her beforehand.

"I'll get three-by-five note cards and plan everything out."

Corey had said he didn't think that was a great idea.

Adrian had turned on him and glared. "Why not?"

It was the first time his friend had ever been angry at him and he didn't know what to say. He wanted to say that scripting your date with a woman sounded like a surefire way to turn something alive and unpredictable into something dead, and above all, why would you even think of doing such a thing? But he held his tongue.

"No," Adrian repeated firmly, as if Corey wasn't even there, "that's exactly what I'll do. I'll plan everything out beforehand."

Shortly thereafter, Adrian had informed Corey that he had asked the girl out and she had accepted. But since then, Adrian hadn't said a word about their date. Remembering it now, Corey asked him how his date had gone.

"Oh, that. Not well."

Adrian had picked her up after class and they'd taken a walk to Inman Square. On the way, he worked through his preplanned conversation points. It was going well, he thought, but then she changed things; she wanted to get pizza, so of course he had to say okay. They went into a pizza place. She ordered a slice and they sat down. She crossed her big legs and ate her pizza. He tried to adapt to the situation by talking about the pizza place, but there wasn't much to say. "I could tell she was losing interest. It got really awkward." She wiped her fingers and her big mouth with her napkin and said she was ready to go back to school; her friends were waiting. He had to walk her the four long hedgerow-lined blocks back to their high school campus. When they got there, she was just like "Thanks, bye." Adrian had waved at her as she walked away from him, saying, "Happy trails"—speaking to her thick rear end.

"How do you know that's bad?" Corey asked. "She might be waiting for you to ask her out again."

"No, she isn't. I got shot down."

"Don't let it get you down."

"I don't. I don't set high expectations so I don't get disappointed."

However, Adrian was not a virgin.

"I am. I'm counting the hours till I do it. It's gotta be incredible. What's it like?"

"It's better than jacking off because you're kind of like—unh!—on top of her. But it doesn't feel as good as your hand. There are all these grooves in your hand."

"Shit, it's gotta be way better than your hand."

"No, take my word for it. It's not."

Instead of going to Harvard Square, Adrian suggested, Corey could watch him hit the bag. He took his G-Shock watch and led the way downstairs, unlocked the garage, turned on the light. A sledgehammer stood on its solid metal head among shovels and rakes. On the concrete floor rested an Everlast punching bag. It was very hard to move, as if it had absorbed weight from the earth. Corey bear-hugged it and walked it out and dropped it in the driveway.

They hung the bag on a tree growing out of a grass-covered patch on a traffic island between Mount Auburn and an intersecting road. Adrian began preparing, wrapping his hands with long bloodstained strips of elastic cloth that resembled Ace bandages.

They reeked with the urine-stink of dried sweat. His knuckles were perpetually scabbed and bleeding. Because he never gave them time to heal, they had developed fleshy wartlike growths.

Corey wandered around on the black grass in the freezing New England night, trying to stay warm.

His eye fell on Adrian's big red boxing gloves. He tried them on. They were damp and cold inside and full of fungus. He stood sideways and raised the gloves. They felt huge on either side of his head. He closed in on the hanging bag and started hitting. The bag gradually tilted away from the pressure of his punches. When he relented, it swung the other way.

He tired himself out after a minute.

"How'd I do?" he asked.

He took off the gloves and held them for Adrian. Adrian shoved his fists inside. Corey clipped the iPod that played death metal to the headband of Adrian's black ball cap, took his G-Shock watch, hit the timer, yelled, "Go," and Adrian exploded.

The eighty-pound bag folded when he hit it where your face would be. The bag jumped as if someone had thrown it and came down on its chains. The report of leather hitting leather cracked across the street and flew above the trees. Adrian's other fist hit the bag, folding it the other way.

He did three rounds, separated by a minute's rest, during which he stared at the pitch-black treetops, the music chugging in his ears. Cars went by, no few of them driven by people associated with Harvard University—often lone women with Quaker haircuts. But towards the end of Adrian's workout, a construction worker's truck stopped at the light, and the man at the wheel called out to the boys, "Trees don't hit back!"

The light changed and he drove away.

"Let me see how hard you hit," Corey shouted.

Adrian took off his iPod. "Did you say something to that guy?"

"He was saying 'Trees don't hit back.'"

The boys guffawed together.

"Have you been in a lot of street fights down in Quincy?" Adrian asked.

"No."

Adrian said he loved street fights. He turned his ball cap backwards on his head just to talk about them, but he hadn't been in any either.

He went back to Quincy, where the movie marathon was still ongoing. Leonard and his mother were sitting on the futon, staring at the laptop. Corey ate his mother's leftovers, sitting on the floor in the space between them and watched whatever they were watching until he fell asleep.

The next day, the meteorological fluke, he went back to Cambridge and sat with Adrian while he studied physics at his desk. The skylight was filled with blue sky and the room was filled with shining white radiance—and, gradually, as the morning passed, with heat. It was a beautiful warm day outside. Corey told his friend, "We've got to get out there."

Adrian finally agreed they could leave the house. But first he had to solve another physics problem, which took another hour, and then he couldn't leave until he had gotten dressed a specific way: in kneepads, wrestling shoes, cup and jockstrap, sweatpants and leather jacket. Corey was surprised by everything he had to wear.

By now it was noon and downright hot. They headed towards Belmont, a direction Adrian chose at random—it was difficult to steer him—then turned and cut at random through wooded side streets. Sweating, Corey carried his jacket. Adrian walked with his large head down, armored in his leather as if he didn't feel the heat, talking about ideas. At the Alewife Brook Parkway, they turned south and hiked down Mass Ave. They walked for hours, circling through the district until after sundown.

They arrived at Harvard Square. The Pit was full of people. Skate kids sat on the ring of granite around the T. The night air was soft and thick with mystery and excitement. The trees thought it was spring—they were budding—and girls and women had come out on the street in skirts and heels.

Corey stopped. Adrian halted next to him like a terminator robot with his muscles flexed.

"What is it?"

Corey had been stricken by the sight of a brunette with a

shapely solidity. The fullness of her legs glowed through her stretched black stockings.

"Man, I really want to talk to her."

"Oh sure, that's a good idea. All you're going to do is feed her ego. Then she's going to tell you to get lost and laugh about it with her friends."

"I gotta do this. Just look at her."

"Take my advice: Don't."

"Be right back."

Corey went across The Pit. The woman was polite enough to let him say hello. Her face reminded him of Joan's, only better cared for. She didn't think it would be a good idea to give him her number because she had a boyfriend. Corey told her she was beautiful. She saw how young he looked, his blushing and his freckles, the Patriots jacket tied around his waist. She wished him luck. He told her she was beautiful again and walked away.

Adrian had disappeared.

Still smiling, Corey bounded up on the stained granite wall where the skaters were sitting and looked around. He finally made out the black-jacketed figure of his friend standing stock-still, as if mesmerized by something inscrutable, on the outermost edge of the square, facing into traffic.

Corey ran over. "Hey, man."

Adrian took hold of a traffic sign. "Hmm, let me see. What would the forces be? Is this a rigid body? No, not quite. I can bend it. Now, I can exert a force of about eight hundred foot-pounds. Convert to newton-meters. Measure the length of the lever—" He measured off a length of the signpost with his forearm. "Say, one meter. Torque equals force times l. If the impact comes from this angle, let's see, mass times velocity, an inelastic collision . . ."

"You were right. She didn't want me."

"What did I tell you?"

"But she was really nice. What are you doing?"

"I'm seeing what would happen if this hit someone in the ribs at one hundred miles an hour."

"What should we do now?"

Adrian suggested they go down into the T. "So soon?" said Corey; he hadn't planned on going home yet. But Adrian said they could talk down there; they could watch the trains. They did, and Adrian was happy. The subways gave him such a sense of power. "Ahh! Listen to that!" he said when the Red Line T roared in. He delivered a slow-motion left hook to an invisible target in the air in time with the train's arrival, a faraway look in his eyes, full of wonder and beatitude.

After Corey had left to see his friend that morning, Gloria found herself alone in Quincy. By nine, the house was growing hot. She opened a window, which was hard with her weak hands. Leonard wasn't there to help. He had gotten up before everyone and driven away, presumably to work. She thought he was coming back, if for no other reason than to discuss her disease. It engaged him, he assured her.

"Let's see the power of the rational approach," he said of her illness. "I'm a great believer in the miracle of science."

"I want to believe in a miracle. I need one."

Then he had gone, leaving her brooding about their history:

That cold clear day in the fall of 1993, he had told her she was attractive. She had closed her book and followed him out of the student union, through the lobby, up a stair beneath a skylight, down a hall, a checkerboard of black steel doors, the silence absolute except for purring ventilation. He had thick workingman's forearms and the keys to all the doors. She swung along next to him in her ragamuffin dress and riot girl boots. They went into an empty laboratory and he showed her an equation.

Afterwards, she straightened her dress and they went for a drive in his economy stick shift. He drove very fast through streets she'd never seen. He took her for an Italian sub soaked in vinegar and oil at a deli called a *spa*. Peppers squirted out of her sandwich when she bit it. "Are we in Somerville?" she asked. She didn't know where they were.

Their romance involved a lot of driving. It was a time of blue maritime skies and windy days, hard rock on the car radio, dark nights, streetlights and perpetual motion. He knew all the byways, all the one-ways. He drove bent over the wheel, looking up through the windshield at the signal, hand on the stick, rolling through the stop, checking sideways traffic, going early against the red—complaining how the city was run: in a manner that interfered with common people and catered to elites. She sat in the passenger seat, sunk deep, impressed with him, and smoking.

He gunned them through an endless maze of houses—seemingly undifferentiatable—no commerce except the odd corner store. She didn't know how he told his way. He took her through East Cambridge up the Fellsway north of the Mystic River along an industrial route from Everett into Chelsea, to an Italian restaurant in East Boston that smelled like frying garlic.

When she was with him, she never quite knew where she was. They'd be speeding over a bridge, then suddenly the familiar city would appear again like magic—the student/tourist part—the Prudential and the Common, Copley Plaza, the Charles River, the CITGO sign in Kenmore Square. He took her home to Mission Hill, where she was staying among poor blacks and white bohemians.

On their excursions, he told her the inside story of the city, the Boston lore—the dirt on the universities, on Mayor Menino, the union contract disputes, the way the city really ran. Stephen "the Rifleman" Flemmi, Raymond Patriarca—there were names you couldn't say out loud in certain places. The president of the State Senate was the brother of Whitey Bulger, the crime figure who had killed his underage girlfriend with the help of Kevin Weeks.

Leonard killed her with possibility.

❧

One night in 1993, Leonard drove Gloria to a spot behind the Blue Line train tracks in Revere and pointed in the darkness. "See that?"

"What?" she asked. The ocean was crashing on the shore. He said nothing. They sat for quite some time in silence. The train went by on its way to Wonderland.

"This place gets dangerous at night."

She asked why they were here.

Had she heard about the woman who had gone missing? "Her name was Marie."

"What happened to her?"

"Do you really want to know?"

When she said yes, he drove her to Malden and stopped outside a house like any other on a street that terminated in a public park.

"The guy who lives in that house killed her. His name is John Nunzio. He's my neighbor."

Over the course of their affair, Leonard brought Gloria to Malden and showed her the place where he lived across from the murderer on several occasions. The street was cluttered with houses—turquoise, white and brown like a collection of hen's eggs—showing signs of disrepair. One had a flat roof, its neighbor a pitched roof. The street itself zigzagged side to side and up and down, giving the vista a jumbled, chaotic appearance. On the outside, Leonard's house was no different from the others.

He brought Gloria inside. It was empty and large. There was only one room that had anything in it—his bedroom. He slept on a mattress on the floor. He had a desk, chair, dense books full of math. In his closet, there were uniforms. A mimeographed study guide for the police test lay on a Formica table in the kitchen, a room of blistering paint over rotting cabinetry, which smelled like earwigs and termites. He turned out the lights so she could see. She looked out his blinds at his neighbor the murderer's house across the street.

The woman had been killed that summer. The cops' efforts to tie John Nunzio to Marie Sacramonti's disappearance were failing due to lack of evidence. They knew he was guilty but couldn't prove it. John had an alibi. On the night of the crime, he had been at his job in front of witnesses. But Leonard assured Gloria that Nunzio was far from innocent. You only had to look into his eyes to see he was hiding a terrible secret. There was no question. But he would never serve a day in jail because he had hidden Marie's body so well the cops would never find it.

Sooner or later, said Leonard, when the heat had blown over, John was going to move away, all the way out to the suburbs, away from all the police and the people of the neighborhood who thought ill of him. He had a place that no one knew about that belonged to his family, out west of the city.

. . .

As the nineties elapsed and Gloria's relationship with him went through changes, eventually settling after Corey's birth into a pattern of receiving visitations from the father, Leonard continued, from time to time, to raise the subject of the crime.

"We used to socialize," he once said of Nunzio. "Obviously, there were limits to what we could talk about. If you tried to talk to John about ideas you'd lose him, but within the confines of his intellect, we had a good relationship. It helped that we were both Italian. The shared heritage meant we could both go to the café and order an *espress'*. We knew what was going on. Things like pizza and cannolis were standard fare to us. Now the rest of the world is just catching up and exploiting them commercially. But we could go to the old neighborhood and enjoy the culture because we were of it.

"His girlfriend, Marie, was a classic Italian beauty from the eighties era—the Stallone era. She had the heavy metal look they had back in the day. It's too bad she was two-timing him. John was a very dangerous man—very sick and dangerous. I warned her, don't get in a relationship with him if you aren't one hundred percent sure of yourself because he'll be able to tell."

As years passed, Leonard revealed steadily increasing knowledge of Nunzio's crime, claiming to see it in its entirety. He said he understood the killer.

"Knowing John, Marie's death was more agonizing than it had to be. That's what I lament."

It seemed to Gloria that Leonard's insight was so acute that he ought to share what he knew with law enforcement.

"Don't forget, I *am* in law enforcement," Leonard said. He had a statutory obligation to assist the investigation. He had fulfilled it by speaking to his contacts at other agencies, though he couldn't make them act on his recommendations in an intelligent manner. If they ever did, they would crack the case.

"I've given them everything they need to do their job. The rest is up to them."

The case remained infamous throughout the decade. Leonard was still talking about it at the turn of the millennium when Gloria was living with Joan in Cleveland Circle. By then, it was clear that Nunzio wasn't going to be convicted for his crime, unless new evidence emerged—DNA perhaps.

In a bizarre coincidence—and proof that Boston is a small city—Joan once met someone in Revere who knew Nunzio and confirmed he was guilty. John's evil—and the travesty of his having escaped justice—were the only things that Joan and Leonard ever agreed on.

8

Chiralities

To break out of the lassitude of the vacation, Corey roused himself and hiked around the shore with his hammer in his backpack, looking for contractors. He stood on the wooded streets, misty and gray near the ocean, and searched for trucks and vans with ladders strapped to the roofs. Naturally, he didn't see anyone; it was New Year's Day. Since he couldn't call Tom, he called his old employers—Star Market, Darragh, men he'd worked for in the past—but this was also unavailing.

The winter semester began. At school, Corey looked for Molly to ask if her father had a job tip, and beyond that, how her break had been, but didn't see her in the swarming kids. He went to the principal's office. This semester, his biology class was doing human physiology, an advanced course. Thanks to his poor performance last semester, he wasn't eligible to take it. Corey petitioned Mr. Gregorio to let him take it anyway. He said he was going to make the winter better than the fall. Gregorio gave him permission. After school, Corey crossed Route 3A and wandered down the long hill back to the seashore. On the way, he stopped at the DB Mart and bought a new notebook for 99 cents, planning to fill it with notes.

When he got home, he discovered to his surprise that Leonard was still there. He had imagined that his father's sojourn with them was tied to the holidays, but apparently it was continuing.

Several of their books from their milk-crate library were open on the futon. Leonard had pulled out one of their Noam Chomskys, the *Great Open Heart of Sadness*, a Shambhala book with a torn cover, Elmore Leonard's *Freaky Deaky*—all books that Corey and his mother had found together years ago. Sitting on the futon with his feet on the coffee table, Leonard looked especially sallow in the gray light. He had football-shaped calves, blanched white skin the color of a dying Jesus in a Caravaggio painting—his loincloth was a pair of boxers—and banana-colored bruises on his knees and shins as if he'd been laying tile. Corey stood in the middle of the living room floor, his schoolbag trailing from his hand, regarding Leonard. They were alone.

"I remember the first time you told me there were multiple universes."

Leonard looked at him. "Do you?"

"We were in Ayer. Don't you remember that?"

"I don't know if we were in Ayer."

"We were on Route 2."

"I see."

"We were at a D'Angelo's. Do you remember?"

"You're going to make me remember every time I had to buy you lunch?"

"No. I was just thinking about it. My mom was okay back then."

Leonard kept reading.

"You like science a lot, don't you?"

"*Like*'s really the wrong word. That reduces it to entertainment."

"Do you work on physics at home? When you're not at work?"

"That's what I'm doing now."

"No, I mean at your own home."

"When you enjoy something, you do it in your free time."

"But where do you live?"

"In Malden."

"Is that where you've been this whole time?"

"It depends what time you mean—but probably. I've always lived in Malden."

"And you just got curious about us?"

"Your mother called to tell me she was sick."

"Back in August."

"July."

"Right. July. She called you, and you're here now?"

"She told me she was sick, and I did some research for her. I tried to make sense of her disease. I thought I could explain it to her better than an article in *Nature* magazine. Without jargon."

"I'm trying to do the same thing, make sense of it."

"It's fairly complicated."

"Is there anything you could tell me?"

"To what end?"

"So I can help her."

"If you want to help her, get a job."

"I have a job."

"No, you don't."

"I work. I have worked. I'm gonna work. But I have a mind too. I want to know what's wrong with her. If I were this friend of mine who's good in science, I'd know everything about it already down to every molecule. That's what I want to know."

"To what end?"

"So I can help her."

"Help her do what?"

"Live, obviously."

"You can't."

"Why not, because it's a terminal illness? No, what I'm saying is, she's alive *now*. I'm saying, I want to help her *now*. Like, what if there's stuff she can do so she doesn't get sick as soon? Maybe there's a medication she could take. Is there anything like that? That's what I want to know."

"What do you want me to do?"

"Isn't there stuff you could tell me about research, like what to look at? Like websites?"

"You turn on the computer . . ."

"Okay."

"You type in a search term . . ."

"Okay."

"And you hit Enter."

"Okay. I will. I just thought there was more to it."

"What more to it do you think there could be?"

"I don't know. I just thought you'd know something special."

"I do know something special: It's that if you want to learn something, you learn it."

"Okay."

"You could put me next to someone from an elite school—a Harvard, an MIT—and if I'm doing the work, then I'm the one who's developing knowledge of the discipline. The pampered kid could just be sitting on his ass. Science doesn't care about your family tree. That's the beauty of it. The greatest mind of the twentieth century was a working-class kid from Far Rockaway. A Jew. He didn't have any advantages. He didn't have affirmative action. But he beat everyone."

"That gives me a sense of power."

"Science was his elevator to the elite level. He gets up there, and who does he meet? Newton, Aristotle. You can't deny him. That's what's beautiful."

"That is beautiful," Corey conceded. But he continued to press Leonard on ALS.

Leonard declared that Gloria could halt the progression of her disease by consuming large amounts of dark leafy vegetables for their antioxidant effects.

"She was trying that."

"Maybe she should keep going. It would be interesting to see if I'm right."

"Is yoga like an antioxidant, because you hold your breath? She was doing that as well."

"Yoga reduces stress, and stress breaks down antioxidants, but holding your breath isn't the same as an antioxidant."

"But they're related."

"Maybe if you insist. At the high school level."

Corey laughed, flattered to be made fun of.

"Is pot bad for her?"

"Pot's good for practically every medical condition," Leonard said. "Pot's the least of her worries. It's way better for her than plenty of things she could be doing. Like taking Rilutek. Don't let her give her money to GlaxoSmithKline. That's the one responsibility I'll charge you with. Don't enrich GlaxoSmithKline."

"Why not? Isn't that the only drug for what she's got?"

"It extends survival. That's all it does."

"Isn't that good?"

"*All* it does is keep you alive."

"You mean, when she may not want to be?"

"Exactly. It's an example of a bad drug. Like chemotherapy for stomach cancer. There're lots of drugs like that. You sell them to people if you're amoral. They're worse than crack. Did you hear about the kids at MIT who fell asleep and never woke up?"

"No, what happened to them?"

"They thought they were taking Ecstasy. Something else was in it, and they died."

"What was in it?"

"How should I know?"

"I don't know."

"The only person who would know that is whoever gave it to them."

"Did you catch whoever did it?"

"If you were to ask me, do I know who the drug dealers are on campus, I have my sources."

"So, you know?"

"We have a lot of rules in our legal system, probable cause, and so on. So maybe I know who's a problem. That doesn't mean I can go and crack heads. If these were *moolies*, as we used to call them, I could deprioritize their civil rights. But these are rich kids, so maybe I 'know,' but I have to pretend I don't know."

"So you actually know?"

"Oh yeah. Twenty years in law enforcement, they're not hiding shit from me. You'd have to get up pretty early."

"It'd bother me to know that they'd gotten away with doing something that bad, though. Haven't you ever wanted to take the law into your own hands?"

"I have to uphold my vows as a peace officer."

"Isn't that frustrating?"

"I have to uphold my vows as a peace officer."

"Are you telling me something?"

"Listen to how I'm saying it: *I have to uphold my vows as a police officer.*"

"So you might have done some head-cracking?"

"I would deny that in court."

"Holy shit."

"I would never do anything in my official capacity to violate my legally mandated duties as a peace officer in the Commonwealth of Massachusetts. Official capacity. Listen to the words. *Official. Capacity.*"

"But in your unofficial capacity . . ."

Leonard deadpan-stared at Corey.

"I really respect that."

"I don't know what you're talking about," Leonard said.

"You must have stories . . ."

"Who knows?"

"But you can't tell me."

"Every relationship is a proof, you understand?"

"Uh . . . not really."

"A proof. A mathematical proof. You want to prove a theorem, you have to demonstrate it. If A then B. A relationship's the same."

"You have to prove yourself to another person. I have to prove to you that you can trust me."

"He catches on quick."

"I would never tell on you to anyone. You're making the world a better place. If you fucked up a drug dealer who was hurting kids, why would I tell anyone?"

"Corey?"

"What?"

"Relax."

"Okay. Sorry."

"Little by little. When you are ready. Have you ever fucked a girl?"

"Uh . . ."

"That's an eloquent answer. I take it the answer's 'no.' Well, it's like fucking a girl. It's when she's ready."

"Okay. Good metaphor."

"And don't try so hard."

"What do you mean?"

"To impress me. Just calm down."

"All right. I'm calm." Corey reddened and laughed at himself. "Is there anything else you can tell me?"

"About what?"

"About ALS."

"I could tell you a lot about it if I wanted to." Leonard basketed his hands behind his head and looked up at their low ceiling. "The question is, what are you capable of understanding? There's no diagnosis for ALS. You can't see it in the body until someone's dead. All we have is a name floating around until you're lying on a table in the morgue. A long time ago, a French scientist did an autopsy on a patient and found these hardened neurons in the spine, and gave it a name. His sole contribution is a name. To me, that's not science; that's taking a nature walk. It's like if I went out and pointed up at the night sky and named a star. As a result, he got his name in the history of medicine. Ironically I can't remember who he was. Thanks to this, now we have all these different models of the disease: glutamate toxicity, autoimmune disease, protein misfolding, or the genetic explanation. We know the pharmaceutical companies are developing drugs for each one. I see a corruption of the scientific method, because of the profit motive. As a physicist, I feel there has to be a single cause, ultimately, if there's a single disease. Otherwise it's not a single disease; it's bulbar palsy or prion disease or radium poisoning or dot dot dot. My personal feeling is that it's going to be the genetic explanation. It's not going to be autoimmune or prions; when they get to the bottom of it, it's going to be the gene, the most elegant explanation. A nucleic acid that should have been right-handed is going to be left-handed. We have all these chiralities out there, and they determine what happens in the universe. It's quantum logic: right hand, left hand. On or off, sick or well, friend or foe. This is what's telling the body what to do, basically. Just this."

Leonard held up his hand and turned it palm out, palm in— and Corey watched it turning.

9

Springer-Verlag

That weekend, Corey found a building site a half mile from home, on the broad hill that came up from the water via the wide asphalt causeway with its steadily curving centerline. The site was chaos—workmen everywhere, saws screaming, wood falling and clattering, the muddy lot chockablock with trucks.

The man running the show had a stern, rugged face: big bones, sunken eyes, hollow cheeks, a Joseph Stalin mustache. In turtleneck sweater and boots, he looked like a woodsman who cut down trees all day with an axe. His pale skin was healthily lit from within, and he had an active man's impatience with chitchat. In a Slavic voice, he told Corey, "You're too young. I can't use you. If you cut your thumb off, what am I going to do? Sew it back on?"

They were standing in a hallway from which it was possible to see through several doorways at once, as if into the multiple chambers of a heart—a busy crossroads point. Construction workers in heavily loaded tool belts were tramping by on the creaking plywood which served as decking underfoot. One doorway let into a gutted kitchen, where only the cabinetry remained. Two men in kneepads crawled on the floor, laying tile. In the adjacent chamber, sheets of drywall leaned on a cart with swivel wheels.

One fellow passing in the hall had a lighter step than the others: He wasn't wearing a tool belt. He had a drill gun in his hand and a drywall screw in his mouth like a toothpick and traipsed past as if he were headed to the bar to spear another olive for his drink.

Corey recognized him from Darragh's roofing crew. His name was Dave Dunbar, and Tom had dismissed him as a joker.

"Hey, Dave! It's Corey. You remember me from the summer?"

"Hey, chief, what's crack-a-lackin'?"

"Can you vouch for me with him? I'm trying to get a job."

"Yeah. Hire this kid. He's good."

"What can he do?"

"He can do everything. He's a mad-dog killer."

"Okay," Blecic said. "Come." He led Corey to the kitchen. "The ceiling. You see it's black? You're going to clean it. Take the spray."

"Thank you!" Corey said.

The boss returned to the crossroads from which he could see everyone.

From the other room, Dunbar called, "Yo, Blecic, you better hire him."

"Don't give me any more bullshit today."

"I'm not giving you any bullshit," Dunbar said innocently. He resumed chatting with a buddy, tacking up drywall. Blecic watched obliquely, using a line of sight that, if it had been a bullet trajectory, would have made them duck for cover.

Corey went up a ladder with a bottle of degreaser and a roll of paper towels and spent the day spraying and wiping holes in the grime on the kitchen ceiling.

An hour into the job, Dave rolled through beneath him with the drywall cart, felt his head and looked up.

"Sorry. I think it dripped on you."

"What're you doing up there, washing it? What's he making you do that for? They're going to tear that whole thing out anyway. Don't do that."

"I've got to do it. He's giving me a job."

"No, you don't. Tell him he's a snapper head. You could be chilling with us, throwing up drywall."

It was quitting time at three. The men began gathering their tools. Corey came down the ladder and set down the emptied spray bottle. Blecic paid him from a roll of cash and told him to come back.

Corey walked out with the other workmen, leaving the smell of plywood and concrete, amid shouts and laughter, the rattle and bang of toolboxes slamming into truck beds, the crunch of tires as they rolled out, stereos kicking on, engines revving as they peeled away. It was a relief to not be craning his neck after several hours. The fresh air was cold and the sun touched the shingled roofs of modest houses among the wintry trees. He followed the road with its white centerline down to the ocean.

When he got home, he showed his mother the cash and told her he'd gotten a job.

"Corey, you're a take-charge guy."

He hugged his mom, then asked where Leonard was so he could tell him too.

Thereafter for the entire day on Saturdays and half a day on Tuesdays, when his classes let out early, he worked for Blecic, and studied physiology in school. He was having intense conversations with his father almost every day. This period of close involvement would last approximately a month before it ended for all time. Later, Corey would realize he and his father had talked more during this brief period than they had in their entire lives. He was so captivated by Leonard during these early days of the year, he told his mother he felt as if the man was taking him on an amazing journey, which challenged everything he thought he knew.

Gloria said she was glad they were connecting. "That's good for you. I give thanks for that."

At the peak of his enthusiasm for Leonard, Corey defined him as an unsung hero of theoretical physics. "I see him as a tragic figure. He's gotten cheated out of credit for his discoveries due to class bias. I want to fight for him in my own work!"

She heard out his appraisal of his father without comment.

So far, the subject of fathers had only come up once between Adrian and Corey, when Adrian asked what Corey had been doing at MIT on the night they met.

"I was looking for my father. He works there."

"What's he do? Is he like a professor or something?"

"He's a cop."

"A cop?"

"He works for the campus police. Supposedly."

"You don't know?"

"I think he does. I've never seen him at his job. But he's been doing stuff at MIT since before I was born. He used to, like, go there."

"He did? What did he take?"

"Physics."

"Physics? That's really interesting. Does he have a degree?"

"I don't know. Like I said, I'm not that close to him. I didn't grow up with him. My parents didn't live together. I don't call him 'Dad.' I call him by his name."

Adrian said he wasn't close to his father either. When he was four or five, his father had divorced his mother and gone to live in Cincinnati. Mr. Reinhardt was in real estate. He was in superb physical shape. He'd been in the Air Force and now ran three-hour marathons and played a lot of tennis.

For Adrian's fourteenth birthday, Mr. Reinhardt had taken him on a hunting trip. On the way, they'd gone to a whorehouse to get him laid. The whorehouse was in a trailer outside the city limits. It was here that Adrian had lost his virginity. A few days later, he had started having trouble urinating.

"It was like pissing razor blades. I didn't know what was wrong with me. My father and his hunting buddy started going, 'Adrian's got the—'" Adrian clapped his hands.

"I don't get it."

"They were saying I had the clap."

"What's that? Gonorrhea?"

"Yeah. Unfortunately."

"And your dad was laughing?"

"He can be a mean SOB."

When Mr. Reinhardt was in the Air Force, his unit had held regular boxing smokers behind the mess hall. If you didn't like someone, you were encouraged to call them out and settle it with the whole platoon watching. Mr. Reinhardt had fought a lot of matches. Once, he fought a man he especially disliked. After whipping him, he picked him up, stuffed him in a trash can and rolled him down a hill. Years later, in a bar, Mr. Reinhardt heard another patron telling everyone how, in the service, he'd seen a man get beaten senseless and rolled down a hill in a trash can. Mr. Reinhardt said, "I did that! That was me!" And the storyteller declared, "That was the meanest fucking thing I ever saw anybody do!" and bought him a drink.

"What happened with the gonorrhea? Did you tell a doctor?"

"Yeah, I had to see a doctor and that wasn't too fun. She was this big mean psycho bitch who hated men. She gives me this look and goes, 'Take off your clothes.' Then she took a Q-tip and stuck it in my dick. It was the worst pain I've ever felt, and I could tell she enjoyed it. She was getting off on it. She was smiling."

"Oh my God."

"I felt so violent, I could have ripped her head off," Adrian whispered.

Corey didn't know what to think or say. He was troubled. "Why didn't your dad tell you to wear a condom?"

"My dad says there are some things you have to find out for yourself."

But he could be a great guy too. After they had bagged a deer, Adrian had wrestled the animal onto his back and posed with it draped victoriously over his shoulders. His father had taken a picture of him with the vanquished deer and Adrian had always kept it.

In mid-January, Corey learned that Adrian had gotten into MIT. In fact, the early-action letters had gone out six weeks ago. Corey couldn't imagine why his friend hadn't told him sooner. He was thrilled for him! He congratulated him. He had an idea: He wanted to introduce the two men he most admired to each other, both of whom were now linked to the same university. He invited Adrian to Quincy.

But tonight Adrian wanted to study. But Corey kept after him until he finally sighed and relented.

"I'm happy you're coming. You're not annoyed, are you?"

Adrian said he was used to tolerating his mother's unreasonable requests.

They boarded the train at Harvard Square. Adrian persisted in talking about his studies, as if to prove that, though Corey could take him away from his books, he couldn't interfere with his intellectual development.

As they traveled south, and especially after JFK/UMass, from which point on they moved along the open coast, Corey found himself overmastered by a grand sense of the voyage of their lives against the great map of the earth. He saw the earth from space, the arc of the coast, their movement along that arc from Cambridge down to Quincy, from port to port, as it were, and tried to express this idea to Adrian. "I can see us sailing down from Cambridge. We just as easily could be coming this same way in a boat. We'd be out there in the ocean." He pointed out the window at the offshore blackness.

"Yes, we could easily be in a boat." Adrian burst out laughing. And he began to lampoon Corey's statement in the first person: *"I'm in my boat! Don't bother me!"*

Corey tried to clarify what he'd meant, but made no headway with his friend.

At their destination, they debarked and walked out of the empty, white-lit station, into the night.

"This is where a lot of stuff goes down," Corey said. "Usually there's a cop." Adrian turned his hat backwards.

"There's nothing but bars down there. Come on." They descended the hill.

"That's my school." It was a clean modern structure fronted by a dark lawn and a granite statue of an apple. They stopped and looked. Lights shone deep inside the building. A digital signboard scrolled the words *Quincy High Pride.*

Adrian could tell a lot of street fights happened here. He began to talk about mechanics. The key to delivering a maximally destructive blow was twisting around the axis of your trunk. Physicists represented the quantity of angular momentum using the variable *omega*. He stood in place describing how to calculate it. Corey wanted to get them moving again, but Adrian wouldn't move until he finished talking.

As they were crossing the Southern Artery, Adrian caught sight of a Burger King and wanted to stop and feed his muscles. He laughed when Corey said it would slow them down. Corey waited while his friend consumed a double cheeseburger.

They continued down the shore, passing between the police station and the cemetery named after a Captain Wollaston, an old field gun on the rise amid the graves. They passed the turn for

Corey's job site, but he didn't point it out because he didn't want his friend to seize on any more distractions.

"It's only a half mile to my house."

But Adrian had seen the sign for Grumpy White's and stopped. "Are you telling me that's their name? That's the funniest thing I ever heard!" He began whooping with laughter. He pretended to hold his stomach, as if to demonstrate he was in such pain he couldn't touch it. "I'm going to be *grumpy*! That's so like—" and he began one of his analyses.

"They've got an awesome sub," Corey interjected. Adrian overruled him. He said the owners of Grumpy White's were stuck in the anal stage of development.

"What do you mean?"

"It's like a little kid who has to shit himself to show he's mad."

But then, to Corey's relief, they reached the bottom of the hill.

"Oh look! My father's car is there; you'll be able to meet him." The Sable, a shadow, was parked behind his mother's hatchback. He led his friend inside.

The inside of the house looked like a walnut—glossy dark brown. You couldn't see anything in the shadow, which inundated the premises. It felt like a small cabin. A single lamp sat on the end table, and yellow light was escaping from the top of the lampshade leaving a glow on the wood veneer wall in the shape of a thumbprint. The room was empty. A book lay on the futon: *Mathematical Physics*. But the place was silent as if no one was there.

"Just a minute." Corey left Adrian hulking in the center of the floor, crossed the room, tapped on his mother's door. "Mom?" He opened her door just enough to slip in and closed it behind him. He found his mother in bed with her laptop. She was looking at images of slender flexible women doing yoga poses that made their bodies look like Sanskrit on a changing series of landscapes. He asked if she knew where Leonard was. Gloria didn't know.

As Adrian stood in the living room, Leonard walked out of the darkened kitchen and said, "Hello."

Corey heard voices commence speaking behind him. He said goodnight to his mother and closed her door carefully.

In the outer room, Leonard was kicked back on Gloria's futon with his foot on her coffee table, in mid-discussion with Adrian.

"This is Adrian," Corey interrupted. "He's going to MIT."

"He knows already," Adrian said. "So what you're saying is, to account for the cosmological constant, you take all this energy you have lying around and divide it up into all these different worlds. That takes care of the infinity issue . . . hmm. I see that. That could work."

"Can you tell me what I missed?" Corey asked.

"Four years of high school physics," Leonard said.

"Well, basically, we're just saying, if you have this big thing that's super huge that's sitting in your equations, if you chop it up into enough pieces by using infinitely many equations, you can make it disappear."

"I can follow that."

"Have a look at the math and see what you make of it." Leonard handed Adrian his book.

Corey tried to see the text over his friend's shoulder. Adrian said the p's and q's had to be world states. Leonard said, "Very good." Adrian began to explain how he had guessed effectively. It had to do with making leaps based on what he already knew. He explained how his brain worked. Leonard simply watched him through his amber glasses.

Adrian handed back the text. Corey intercepted it.

He'd never looked in one of his father's books before. He saw nothing but mathematics—a blizzard of p's, q's, x's, y's, Greek letters, calculus, symbols from a strange arithmetic, including an upside-down delta operator. There was no English he could see. The rows of equations looked like the remains of sentences from which all the vowels had been vacuumed out.

Leonard had marked the page up thoroughly, just like Adrian had his Nietzsche. Unlike Adrian's relentless block capitals, Leonard's handwriting was irregular, jumping with internal disruptions. His words were different sizes, some big, fat, loopy, cursive; others small and tight and jagged and bent in one direction, as if written in a gale, then bent back the other way like grass; then screaming straight up and down, crushed together, and scribbled higher and higher like a spiking EKG. Corey couldn't read a single one.

He began to grow self-conscious. He closed the book and tried to hand it to his father. But Leonard didn't move to take it, and Corey set it on the table at his feet.

"You're a wrestler," Leonard said.

"How'd you know?" Adrian exclaimed.

Corey listened to them talk about wrestling and boxing, how it all came down to basic mechanics—to omega.

"I'm wondering if I could move us to the kitchen. I don't want to wake her."

"She's not sleeping," Leonard said.

Corey waited for the right moment to interrupt again. He told Adrian he wanted to show him something in his room.

"It looks like Corey's getting anxious."

"Yes, it looks like I have to go now. You've given me a lot to think about. I'm going to want to look into this type of mathematics."

"Do that. You'll have fun with it. I hope to see you at MIT."

"That'd be great."

Adrian followed Corey to his room.

"What's this you have to show me?"

Corey took his block and tackle out of his closet.

"Look at the mechanical advantage of this!"

Adrian forced a smile. "Very good."

In the aftermath of Adrian's visit, Corey wanted to know what his father had thought of his friend. He announced that Adrian was getting the best grades in his high school AP Physics class. Leonard said that didn't exactly qualify him for the Manhattan Project but acknowledged that he had seemed intelligent. Raising his eyes from his Springer-Verlag text, he added, "He's eccentric. I think I smelled him."

"He doesn't like to wash."

"He won't do very well with the opposite sex if he doesn't wash."

"But he understood your book, didn't he?"

"Yes, he seems remarkable," Leonard said, returning his eyes to the page.

Later, in Cambridge, Corey told Adrian, "My father likes you." Adrian's dimples appeared. "That's awesome." He smiled and made a stilted, self-conscious cheering gesture with two tentatively clenched fists, like a robot saying hurray.

10

Palm of Saint

Gloria had not been sleeping. While looking at women doing yoga poses, balancing on one leg, she had been contemplating what had happened earlier that day. Upon arriving in Fields Corner, she had parked her car by the Planet Fitness, put money in the meter with her disobedient fingers and begun walking the hundred feet or so to the building where she worked. Her route passed in front of houses with bare trees jutting out of yards, silhouetted against the cold pale sky. The morning light was changing, the earth was tilting, the days starting earlier. It was already brighter than December. She had been having this thought when her legs stopped working and she fell.

It was her first fall, and it was utterly disastrous. It happened just outside her job—within grabbing distance of the steel tube railing on the concrete handicap-accessible ramp. But she hadn't had a prayer of grabbing it. She hadn't been able to get up, had lain on the sidewalk weeping. Emotional shock, public embarrassment— she had felt slapped by her father, a man long dead. Strangers had helped her up and she had pulled herself together, refusing further assistance.

Now, with her blonde head on the pillow, she remained awake deep into the night with her knees curled up. Her eyes kept opening and she kept closing them. She didn't drop off until two or three. She woke up again and saw it was four already on the bedside clock, the lamp still on. She was still in her clothes, yesterday's slacks, and it was nearly time for another day. And in the day that was to come she'd continue to keep her accident a secret. She wouldn't tell her neurologist, wouldn't tell her family—her son, that is. She'd keep it a secret, pretending it had never happened out of real fear about what it meant.

But as the month played out, Corey would see his mother's gait was changing. At the same time, he would become aware of a disquiet that centered on his father.

A few days after Adrian's visit, Corey was alone with his father after school and Leonard got on the subject of Richard Feynman, the working-class genius of immigrant parents who had contributed both to quantum theory and the atomic bomb, against all odds whether intellectual or economic.

"You have to understand science is a human pursuit, therefore it's an economic pursuit, therefore it's subject to competitive economics. Consider capitalism—" If history was a lie, Leonard said, so was the history of science. Real science was done by armies of exploited workers, common folk whose names were never known. Unlike Feynman, a heroic revolutionary, James D. Watson, Bill Gates, Isaac Newton were robber barons who had stood on the shoulders of money.

"Capitalism teaches us to lie, cheat and steal. Those of us without the silver spoon have to lie, cheat and steal more than the competition just to keep up. Just ask Paul Erdős."

"What did he say?"

"The world is run by women. Paul Erdős was the greatest mind of the twentieth century after Feynman."

Corey said he had an errand to run. He left the house and walked around the neighborhood, thinking. He returned when dusk was falling and told Leonard he wanted to talk about ALS.

His father had made himself dinner while he was gone and had already finished eating.

"You realize, nothing will stop her from dying."

"I know that."

"That's what terminally ill means."

"But we can still help her, can't we? You care about my mother, don't you?"

"Of course I care about your mother. I go a long way back with her. A lot longer than you do. Before you were born."

"I was worried for a minute."

"It's a difficult situation," Leonard said.

Corey bowed his head.

"It's very sad for me," Leonard sighed. "I remember when she was still in college, when she was really still a girl. I took her around Boston for the first time, the real city—not Cambridge. We went to Santarpio's. I remember how it opened up her eyes. Her eyes blew up—Italian pizza! Learning about different cultures, getting her outside the narrow framework she was in. I had never been with someone who was so fundamentally narrow before. She was from the sticks. I remember it forced *me* to take stock. I made the decision to get involved. I mentored her. She was so proud of her education, I remember, and she was actually getting a very bad education at the time, a terrible education, and I had to be the one to tell her: Challenge authority! Question everything! Don't buy what they're selling you! And most of all, grow, grow, grow! I watched her grow a huge amount as a person. I put myself on the line to make that happen. I had to be the one to tell her to quit school. How do you think that went down? Sometimes the student turns on the teacher. I took the heat for that."

"Well, I just want to help her now."

"I know that no son wants to hear about what his mother did before he was born. It makes you uncomfortable. But I'm telling you this for a reason, Corey. There's always a reason. It's because I think you're old enough to hear. Do you understand?"

"I guess so."

"I became very good at surviving. There are lots of things I've learned. Things most men don't know. Things I could teach you."

"Like what?"

"My experience has been very wide."

Corey asked Leonard to tell him what he meant. Leonard said he'd have to wait. Be patient. He'd tell him when he was ready, a little at a time.

As they were talking, Corey had been getting cold. When he went to the kitchen where Leonard had been cooking, he found the reason why: The window was open as wide as it would go like a gaping hollering mouth. Pots and pans lay everywhere and the room stank. The trash barrel was full. The sour greasy rankness of the smell distressed him psychologically for reasons he could not explain. It didn't feel like their kitchen anymore. Leonard's cooking—brown sauce full of chunky stuff in Tupperware containers—had taken over an entire shelf in the refrigerator. Gloria's food was stuffed on other shelves. An empty can of tomato paste sat on the floor, the razor-sharp lid open like a talking trash can.

When he went to close the window, the screen was nowhere to be found. It was lying on the ground outside. He leaned out and picked it up and fit it in the sash.

He started putting the pots and pans in the sink. One was an expensive Teflon skillet that was unfamiliar. There was grease on his mother's protein. The paper towels had been used down to the cardboard tube. Tiny orange grease spores and black cindery dust were spattered in a ring around the stovetop burner, a white hole in the center, corresponding to the skillet, like the hole in the center of a solar eclipse. He took his shirt off and used it as a rag.

The room began to warm, but it was getting darker. He snapped on the light and took the trash out. There was another bag of garbage leaking on the kitchen floor. He ran the bags out to the curb—they were heavy to the point of ripping—and ran back in, barefoot, bare-chested and freezing.

He felt the need to explain himself to Leonard. He said he wanted to get the house in order for his mother: "I know I'm weird."

When she got back that night, Corey told her in Leonard's hearing he'd been cleaning up a mess his father had made.

The next day when he came home from school and didn't see Leonard on the couch, he went to the kitchen to look for him, and he was there. Corey broke into a grin and said, "What are we going to talk about today?"

"How about nothing?" Leonard said.

"Are you mad?"

The man was cutting piles of garlic with a kitchen knife, which appeared to come from the same designer cooking-ware collection as the Teflon skillet. The skillet was green-tea green; the knife's blade and handle were enameled dandelion yellow and modeled on a samurai sword. Leonard had chopped so much garlic with it the tiny slivers formed a mountain you could have scooped up and molded into a baseball. He wore a gauntlet of sticky white garlic slivers as if he'd dipped his knuckles in glue and then in broken lightbulb shards. Skins lay drifted on the kitchen floor. He broke another head of garlic into cloves. The skins stuck to his fingers like sheets of dandruff. He picked up the knife and continued cutting.

"Corey, let me give you a word of advice."

"Sure."

"You can bullshit anybody you want, but you can't bullshit me."

"What do you mean?"

Leonard told him to get lost. Out of nowhere, Corey lost control of himself and started crying in the kitchen doorway. Wiping his face, he began making a full confession. "I narked on you to my mother about the mess. I still want to earn your trust."

Leonard was willing to forgive and forget. "You had a labial moment."

"A what?"

"A labial moment."

"Oh, like labia?"

And so Leonard was willing to talk to him again.

"Look, Corey, you have to understand: I grew up different from you. It was a very different time. We had rumbles. I doubt you know what a rumble is. It's a gang fight where you hit someone with a garbage can lid or a bike chain. Society has changed. If you did half the stuff I did back then, they'd lock you up and throw away the key. You can do anything now of a peaceful nature. You want to do a protest march, they'll let you. We had the Vietnam War back then, and you *did not* oppose the Vietnam War—but I did. I got called every name in the book: pinko, commie. I had these kids in my school who were dead set on fighting me. Their dads were construction workers. My dad was a bum unfortunately. So I said we could fight, but we had to go to this place I knew. We had these marshes, these flats where I dug for clams. I knew exactly how far away it was; it was two miles exactly from where we were.

I thought they'd say forget it and the fight would be off. But they were willing to walk the whole two miles for the chance to beat up a communist."

"What happened?"

"The fight didn't go the way they thought it would."

"You mean, you beat up two guys?"

"I find that when you know boxing and wrestling, you can do pretty well in most fights, and I knew boxing and wrestling."

"That's so awesome," Corey said.

"A boy could never cry, even a young boy. No matter what was done to me, I could never cry, even when I was four or five years old."

"That's great. I have to be more like that."

"By the time I was your age, it would have been unheard-of, even for a weaker kid. But I didn't grow up with a mother like you."

"I thought you had a mother."

"That's what it said on the box, but that wasn't what was inside."

"She was really psycho?"

"I don't like that term *psycho*."

Corey waited for Leonard to tell him a better term, but he didn't. Instead, he told Corey, "You want to talk about everyone's mother but yours."

"I'll talk about my mother! I mean, we both care for her, right? We wouldn't say anything bad about her, right? So of course I'll talk about her."

"You're such a perfect son."

"No, I'm not."

"Yes, you are. Gloria got everything she wanted. No, really, you are perfect."

"She's just going through a bad time."

"Yes, and you want people to say, 'Oh, look at the perfect son helping his mother.'"

"No, I just want to help her for real. I don't care what anyone says."

"The noble son."

"Hey, could we talk about something else?"

"Too tough for you?"

"No, I just feel strongly about it." Silence held between them for a moment. Then Corey said, "You know, I tried to call you back in November. She needed help and you weren't around. You never answered my phone call."

"Oh, Corey, I am so sorry for not getting right back to you. Please give me another chance, it'll never happen again. Would you like me to call you right now and apologize? Maybe I should apologize for creating you in the first place."

"I care about my mother. What do you want?"

"Not much. Not much."

"Did I offend you?"

"Corey, you couldn't offend me if you tried."

"Well, that's good. Look, we started off with you telling me about your childhood. Why don't we go back to that?"

"How 'bout I tell you about your childhood, Corey?"

"Okay. Fine."

"Okay, fine. You were an accident."

"It worked out for me."

"Yeah, and you want to hear the kicker? I talked a certain somebody out of flushing you."

"Your parents didn't like you either, so I guess we're the same," Corey blurted. He was upset and didn't want to talk anymore. He claimed not to be upset and left the room, saying he had homework.

After this, he began to look back at everything Leonard had said to him and question if it was true.

For instance, they'd had a recent conversation about the police. It had started when Leonard had been taking off his trousers because, he said, he didn't want to wrinkle them for work. They were black polyester uniform trousers with a double blue line of piping down the legs. He folded them and laid them on his cop bag. He took out another pair of trousers and put them on. They were almost exactly the same as the original pair except they had a different style of piping: a single crimson line. Corey asked, "Why do you have two different kinds of cop pants?"

Leonard ignored the question, and Corey thought, Did I annoy him?

"I didn't mean to pry."

"Cops! They're a bunch of pigs," Leonard snarled. "The worst are the Cambridge Police Department. They're some of the most despicable people in the world."

Corey was astonished. Leonard told him not to be naïve. "I know certain pigs I'd kill without a second thought."

"In Cambridge?"

"Without hesitation. I'm talking worthless people. Real human slime. The kind where you'd be doing the world a favor by blowing them away."

"But what did they do?"

"They're a corrupt organization. I began independently investigating them for racially profiling minority women. We have a lot of minority women on campus, and when they were going out into Cambridge, they were getting harassed. My investigation found the problem started with Chief Scumbag Joe LaFleur, who was basically giving days off in exchange for traffic stops. This is the caliber of man who thinks that Karl Marx was one of the Marx Brothers. Most of his officers wouldn't understand the concept of being a capitalist stooge if you drew them a picture. So, doing my job as a peace officer working for one of the leading universities in America, I forward my investigation to my commanding officer. I tell him, we've got a problem here. We have a highly diverse campus. Many of our students are off-white girls. They're getting clobbered out there. Let's handle this diplomatically with the higher level of the Cambridge PD. Translation: Get off your ass and tell your golf buddy, LaFleur Fuckface, to quit coming down on these women of color. Next thing you know, I'm facing a disciplinary hearing, loss of pay, loss of rank. I guess I must've struck a nerve. They're coming after the whistleblower. Now, I know where the battle lines are drawn; I'm a lifelong socialist in the line of Chomsky, in that lineage. I'm prepared to plant a bug in the chief's office. I'm prepared to be a dirty trickster. Because these women were innocent! They were girls! And I said to my union rep, I'll go all the way with this. I want to speak the truth, and if I get fired, I'll take that. I begged him, 'Do not muzzle me.' But he said, 'Lenny, forget it. These guys are all best friends, and if you take them down, you're gonna take down a lot of good people with them.' So I walked into that hearing and didn't say a word in my own defense."

"But I don't get it. What was the hearing for? What did they say you'd done?"

"They had me on a whole trumped-up case of stalking these coeds. All my investigation notes, my log, where my car had been— they took everything and creatively interpreted it to say that I was following them. I was actually impressed at their creativity. They must have taken a lot of time building this trumped-up case against me instead of keeping the people of Cambridge safe."

Corey had assured Leonard he completely appreciated that a given thing could look two utterly different ways depending on how you looked at it. At the time, he had taken Leonard's story at face value, as evidence of his colorful life and embattled individualism, and as an eye-opening account of how the world really worked—of how contemptibly misguided and narrow-minded even supposedly good people could be.

But now, he wondered why *did* Leonard have two different sets of uniform trousers?

Corey took his troubles to his friend.

"Just a week ago he was a great scientist. What could happen in one week that would make you turn against him? Think hard." Adrian leaned forward, frowning, wearing glasses. "What are you really worried about?" He pressed the first two fingers of his hand against his lower lip and prepared to listen. "Try and be specific." Adrian knew how to ask these questions. He'd been seeing a psychiatrist for years.

"I don't trust him," Corey said.

Adrian tapped his lower lip, said "Hm," and betrayed the hint of a smile. "That's interesting."

"How so?"

"You're paranoid."

"Really?"

Adrian smiled openly. "I'm paranoid too." He spread his legs and rapped his crotch. "Why do you think I wear a cup all the time?"

"I didn't know you wore it all the time."

"Oh but I do." Adrian said he wore it all the time—not just during wrestling practice, but after practice when his cup was reeking and all day long without washing, and not just during wrestling season either, but year-round. Adrian admitted that it made him stink, but far from minding it, he delighted in it; he was proud of smelling bad.

"But why do you do that?"

"I'm afraid of getting castrated."

"Yeah, but why?"

"It's related to my mother. Freud describes it." Adrian touched the Freud on his desk, a thick chunk of a book that brought together the thinker's major writings—a portable edition like the Nietzsche, which he had finished.

"Can you explain it?"

"It's simple really. Let's say a boy has a certain amount of self-esteem, but it makes his mother jealous. She has penis envy. She wants those feelings of love and esteem for herself."

Even if he couldn't explain it to the satisfaction of his psychoanalytically inclined friend, by the end of January, Corey felt he had gone full circle: from not knowing his father, to thinking he knew him a little, and back to not knowing him at all.

The energy of their relationship changed, but it didn't dissolve right away. Corey still had an appetite for Leonard's stories. Then one sunny day, Leonard gave him a drug without warning, something that wasn't pot. He gave him what appeared to be a joint from his cop bag. Corey lit the joint and the smoke tasted bitter, almost like burning plastic, right away; not like an herb, but like something you shouldn't put inside you.

"Do you want a hit?" he asked his father.

"No, that's for you."

Everything else in the room—the splintered wooden flooring lit by the sun, the battered coffee table, the dust on the books, the beige futon, the woven wall hanging of Buddha Gautama floating joyfully in the center of a flower, Leonard's cheap black trousers, his undershirt and the gray-white meat of his large bare arms, his Jesuit face in spectacles—all was opaque and no light passed through it; it all absorbed the sun, thought Corey. He realized that he didn't feel normal.

"Pot is the drug of the counterculture," Leonard said. "You know who turned me on to pot? I had a girlfriend who used Jamaican marijuana as an aphrodisiac. She'd feel like making love for hours. To please a woman, you stay inside her. You can't go slow enough. You enter her and very gently start to move. You don't go in and out. You stay in and move in a circle. Most men have no idea what they're doing. She taught me all that. Do you know who she was?"

"I feel sick in the head," Corey said.

"Go get yourself a glass of water." Leonard took the joint out of his hand, extinguished it on the table, swept up the ashes, and put it in a plastic bag.

That night, Corey dreamed that he was driving through the desert with his mother. They rode in a beat-up white car with dirt ground into the paint, as if they had been driving for days. They were living in the car and the metallic strip along the door had been broken off. He didn't know why they were in the desert. For some reason, he knew it had to do with San Francisco.

The sky was radiant. There was an ache behind his eyes. Something was tightening protectively inside his head to stop him from seeing so much sunlight all at once.

His blonde-haired mother was showing him the giant saguaro cactus. She wore sunglasses, and he could see the giant cactus in her eyes like the figure of a man.

Saguaro, he knew, meant "palm of saint."

Someone else was there, someone he believed to be the man he knew as Leonard. He saw a building that was a trailer or a gas station. The man came out carrying an armload of food cans. The man was putting a bottle of black oil in the car. He thought they must have been at someone's house, a trailer or a cabin in the woods.

All of them were working, doing some kind of landscaping. To Corey, it was a game of watching out for thorns. The man, whoever he was, was cutting branches using a chainsaw, wearing leather gloves.

They threw down mesquite and bright green creosote boughs that the man had cut, and started a fire, a little quiet flame that began seeping through the branches. The fire caught on and started crackling. When the creosote ignited, the wood made a sound like a blowtorch and a thick unreal-looking curtain of orange flame lifted up ten or twelve feet high.

The fire made him think of a giant genie dancing and flapping an orange rug over his mother.

Corey was fascinated by the churning, bloody-looking fire, licking and billowing. But his mother was upset. She asked Leonard not to burn anything else.

But Leonard wouldn't listen. He told Corey to help him drag more brush on the fire, and Corey did what he was told, but felt guilty about it.

An American Indian woman wearing a cowboy hat came directly up the road to them and asked, "Do you know what you're doing? Ten years ago this entire desert burned up from a campfire. All it takes is a little wind and everything here is going to burn, all these people's houses."

"You see?" his mother cried. "Don't you see, Leonard?"

But the man ignored both women and set fire to the rest of the brush.

There was something in the dream that Corey's mind was hiding from himself, much like the inner mechanism of his eyes shutting out the sun.

11

Scarlatta

A short time later, on the first of February, Gloria was driving to work when she stalled her car opposite a Hess station on Gallivan Boulevard in the middle of morning rush hour. She tried the ignition twice. When she didn't get lucky, she reached out and turned off "Land of the Glass Pinecones" by Human Sexual Response so she could think. Behind her, cars were forcing their way into the other lane.

Chances were, she reasoned, the problem was in her left leg, the one that worked the clutch. She made a special mental effort and pushed the pedal all the way down to the floor. She tried the key again. The engine started. She took her foot off the clutch. Scarlatta started pulling forward.

A big girl in a bomber jacket zoomed around her in a Jeep Cherokee, yelling, "You stupid fucking retard, learn to fucking drive!"

Sealed inside her car, Gloria shouted, "Don't yell at me! You have everything!"

She was only fifteen minutes late for work, but her trouble on the road suddenly hit her with its implications, and she got panicked. From her work computer, she looked up how to apply for disability in Massachusetts.

It was complicated and bureaucratic and would take quite a lot of time. They needed her work history for the past fifteen years, her educational background, and a medical release form for every doctor, hospital, therapist involved in her disease. There were ten pages of medical release forms.

She called the social worker, near tears, and said, "This thing is so enormous."

Dawn Gillespie didn't seem to share her aversion to paper-work. She spoke about the system as if she were explaining it, but it wasn't an explanation, it was a burying in fine print. She sounded like human fine print. She knew so many rules it was amazing. The more she talked fine print, the more overwhelmed Gloria felt, but she was afraid to tell Dawn to be quiet because she was the only help she had.

"All I know is it isn't safe for me to drive. I'm in trouble here. I shouldn't have waited this long."

The social worker kept talking forms until Gloria thanked her and, holding her head with her eyes shut, said goodbye and hung up the phone.

The next day, she asked Leonard to help her out by driving her to work. He dropped her off in Fields Corner and took her little red hatchback for the rest of the day, going wherever he went.

That evening at five o'clock when he was supposed to pick her up, he wasn't there. Gloria couldn't reach him on her cell. She called her son and had him try Leonard's phone, but Corey couldn't reach him either. She waited for an hour on the ramp out-side her job. Finally she went to the nearest bus stop. She took the first bus that came. Then she noticed they were driving through unfamiliar streets. She got up to ask where they were going but was afraid of losing her balance and sat back down. Out the win-dow, she recognized Blue Hill Avenue and, with difficulty, pressed the Stop Request button. As she was getting off, she asked if she could get to the Red Line from here. The driver told her no. It was very cold. A bus was waiting by the park. She hurried towards it, but it pulled away. She hurried to the next one. "Wait!" she called. The driver, a dreadlocked man, waited. After climbing aboard, she clutched the grab bar and asked him how she could get to the Red Line. "You're a long way off," he said, but promised to tell her when to disembark.

She took a seat near the front, behind a sign that showed a man in handcuffs. Assaulting the driver was punishable by a $10,000 fine. Except for two fat girls in tight jeans and gold mascara sitting across from Gloria who gave off an air of secret jubilation, the other passengers maintained a strict reserve. The bus swung downhill onto a forested road sparsely dotted with old houses. The driver let her off at an outdoor train platform. She was confused. "Get on the train," people told her. The train operator, a thin fellow, leaned out of his chair and asked if she was getting on.

"But I'm looking for the Red Line."

"That's where I'm going. Get on."

She took a seat right near him.

"I've never taken this train before."

"This is the oldest subway in the United States," the operator said. "Sometimes I feel like I'm driving history." He had a tattoo of a bird on his neck, his name was Andrew, and he had been working for the MBTA for eight years, working nights. Originally he was from Connecticut. Now he lived in Brockton.

"Do you like it?"

"Nah, Brockton's too far out. I'm a city guy," Andrew said.

"Me too. I'm a city girl."

"Where do you stay at?"

"Quincy. I'm not happy about it. I moved a while ago. For the wrong reasons."

"I know Quincy. Upper-class poor, lower-class rich."

"That's a good description!"

"That's what I call it. Everybody up here is getting pushed down there, and everybody down there is getting pushed up here." They were rolling by clumps of black trees, a nightscape in which it was impossible to make out any landmarks. "Gentrification, so-called. Prices are going out of control."

"Oh my God, they are."

"A dozen eggs used to be two seventy-five. Now it's three forty-nine. That's a high percentage increase. You see it with the consumer price index. Milk, eggs, staples."

"I used to go to Whole Foods, the one at Alewife? It's like the original store; it was called Bread & Circus back then. This was back in 1997, to tell you how old I am! And you could eat natural, whole, healthy . . . food. Like you're supposed to. And it wasn't your whole paycheck. It wasn't a gourmet grocery store like it is now."

"They know how to pick your dollars apart."

"They do!"

Without warning, they pulled up at the terminal stop in Ashmont and her conversation ended.

"Good luck, Andrew," she told him as she dismounted. "Keep on enjoying history."

"Be safe."

"I'm Gloria, by the way."

"Be easy, Gloria."

At Ashmont, she had to wait for the inbound train to JFK before she could catch the outbound train to Quincy, and then she had to wait for another bus to take her out to Sea Street. She didn't make it home till nine. Corey ran to the door when he heard her coming. The trip had exhausted her, and the next day there was still no sign of Leonard or her car. She took mass transit to work, and she had another fall and, this time, broke her cell phone and cut her chin.

Leonard reappeared several days later, on a Friday, and returned their car. He and Gloria talked all evening as if nothing was amiss. Corey waited until after his mother was asleep. He closed her door and asked Leonard for a private word. Corey led him to the kitchen. The window, which Leonard habitually raised, was open, letting in chilling damp air. In the black outside, Corey saw a mass of moving reeds and heard them soughing in the wind. Knowing what he was about to say, he experienced physical fear symptoms. Their intensity surprised him. He felt his body shaking.

"Basically," he said to his father, "I wanted to talk to you about the car. About how you took it."

The fear—call it stage fright—eased once he had started talking. He said, "I value knowing you. I'm glad you've been coming to see us. I think my mother's glad too—she's been lonely. What she's going through is lonely above all. We're alone out here. But you took her car, and she fell. I was mad over that. I'm still mad—I'm actually shaking, and I thought it was because I was afraid of talking to you, but now I think it's because I'm angry. I never told you how angry I was. But I want to get over it, so we can work together. You're the one who told me that we want the same thing. So why would you disappear like that? There're things I don't understand about you—like how you live, these girlfriends, all this stuff. Or these things you've been telling me at your job. I mean, we need you, don't get me wrong. I'm asking you for help. I don't even care about your private life. I just want to see all of us pulling together to help my mother. That's all I wanted to say. I'm done."

Leonard suggested they step outside.

"I'll get my coat."

They left the house. It was after midnight. Leonard began leading him down the shore road.

"Where are we going?"

"Let's see what's down here," Leonard said, choosing their direction: towards a spit of land that jutted out into the water. The homes had boats in the yards, propellers sticking out from under tarps. Security lights shone on the shingled houses, the watercraft. The night sky was drizzling. Leonard walked him down a concrete staircase to the beach, among the stones and broken asphalt. The black seawater came up to the edge of where they were standing. The water was calm and lay in front of them like a parking lot with the light rain falling on it. The dull black surface raced away from their feet to various masses of black, which were islands, and merged with the night sky, which was full of clouds. Industrial lights smoldered in the misty distance of the half-urban landscape.

"I never knew you liked the ocean."

"It's great. Let's go farther."

"I can't see anything down here."

"I thought you wanted to talk to me."

"I do. I'm coming. What are we going to do about my mom?"

"There's nothing anyone can do. We're all living with a death sentence."

"I know, I know . . . I know she's going to die. But we have to help her . . . face death. I mean, what are we going to do between here and *there*? What about her job?"

"Massachusetts has disability for people who can't work."

"She's had trouble with that."

"She has trouble with everything."

"I don't see it that way. She raised me by herself, Leonard."

"She's a real success."

"Why do you hate her?"

Leonard spun around and snatched Corey by the coat.

"Hey, let's get something straight: You don't know anything."

"Okay."

"You know nothing. Nothing. About anything."

"All right. Jesus."

"Don't you Jesus me. Who the fuck are you? Some kid, some punk kid—from Quincy. Some little fucking idiot from Quincy, Mass."

"All right. All right already. I didn't mean to anger you." Corey pretended to laugh. The sight of the nearest houses, which looked empty in the night, filled him with abandonment.

"A dummy. So shut the fuck up. You want to learn from me? You want to get close to me? Lesson number one: Shut the fuck up."

Corey spent the rest of the night in his bedroom with the door locked and his arm over his face. At three in the morning, he heard his mother use the toilet through his wall. Sometime later, he heard the click of the living room lamp going off and the futon settling when Leonard put down his book and went to sleep. At dawn, Corey opened his bedroom door and emerged already fully dressed in coat and jeans. The living room was steeping in the dirty gray light of another day. Carrying his boots, he crept through the house in sock feet, past Leonard's sleeping form, and went outside.

It was six a.m. and the beach was dead and gray. He tied his boots looking at the spot where his father had yelled at him the night before, on the other side of the concrete barrier which was supposed to keep the sea from drowning the road in a storm.

On his way uphill, over the rooftops, he saw the sky going from bluish gray to a pale copper color out on the horizon. He bought an egg sandwich at the DB Mart and waited in the parking lot until it was time for work. Pickup trucks came and went. The doorbell chimed and people came out of the store with coffees. The day got warmer and the ocean chill dropped away. A gold light spread over the asphalt. A white F-150 drove by, but it wasn't Tom. At seven, he went down the side street, lined by trees, to the job site, all the branches having turned gold on one side and gray on the other in the strong horizontal light from the east.

There was a thirty-yard dumpster in front of the house and plaster-dust-covered guys were carrying Rubbermaid trash cans up from the basement, full of broken wood and drywall. They walked into the dumpster, dropped their loads of debris and walked out, smoke billowing from their barrels. Hardly anyone else was there.

Corey asked if they needed him. They lent him a pair of leather gloves. He went down into the basement. There was a tiny window letting in warm white sunlight. He tried to lift a barrel that had been loaded with fragments of a demolished wall.

"That one's a monster. You're not gonna get that one. Take less. Don't blow your back out."

Carrying an armload of wood and plaster trash, he dropped a wedge of sheetrock on the basement stairs and an already fully burdened guy running up behind him caught it and put it on his own pile without breaking stride. They went out into the daylight, nails poking through their sweatshirts, and dumped their armloads in the dumpster.

At nine o'clock they rested. The smell of marijuana reached them.

"Smell that?" one guy said. He went off to check it out. Corey and the other guy stayed behind. It was silent in the sun. In the lull in work, Corey's depression grew.

The first guy came back. "It's some dude blazing out by the porta-shitters."

They ambled back to the basement, and Corey followed.

He asked if they'd seen the boss.

"I don't think he's here."

Corey said he wanted to look for the boss.

The guys shrugged.

Corey went around the site looking for Blecic's truck. He encountered Dave Dunbar coming towards him from the port-a-johns.

"Hey. You seen Blecic?"

"Not me, chief." Dunbar got in his subcompact Nissan.

"Where you going?"

"The hardware store."

"Come on, man," said Corey. "You can tell me. I'm cool."

"I'm breakin' out, kid. Gonna set it off. The boss ain't here. He doesn't know what's going on. His head's up his ass. I've been putting sixty hours on my time; I worked like twenty last week. We're all doing it." He started his car. "What's up, dude? You wanna jump in? Come on."

Corey got in with Dunbar and they drove away.

They drove around Quincy picking up other passengers—two kids from high school and a local man, a hairstylist. At midday they were burning down the Southern Artery. Corey was sitting in the back with the boys in the now-crowded Nissan. The hairstylist sat up front with Dunbar. Dunbar drove bending forward with his head over the steering wheel, looking out the windshield at the traffic converging on him from all sides—converging on him as, simultaneously, he stepped on the gas even harder and shot out ahead of it. And the car swooped forward—and then he had to downshift, engine braking—because there was a slow guy rattling along ahead of him, a pickup in the center lane with PVC and copper pipes sticking out the back over the tailgate like lances. The boys in his backseat, knees and shoulders squished together, rocked forward. Dunbar darted sideways, changing lanes, then crawled past the Chevy, the driver a stolid forward-looking shadow wearing a baseball cap above them, passive-aggressively accelerating at long last now that they were going to pass him.

They drove on, the windshield filled with blue sky and sun, an ad for Jordan Marsh on the radio—Dunbar punching the radio off, driving with an unlit cigarette in his mouth, feeling his pockets, hitting the glove box open, digging for a lighter, and the man, Anthony, giving him one while all the boys in the back asked each other, "You got a lighter?" and had to admit they didn't have one: "Not me. Sorry. I don't smoke."

"I bet you smoke dicks," Anthony the hairstylist said.

Dave torched his cigarette, smoke filled the speeding car and the boys pretended they didn't mind it.

"How youse mad dogs doing?"

Good, they all said.

He willed the car forward, ooching it, imparting it momentum as if it were a becalmed sailing craft instead of a speeding missile on the highway, exited and shot through an intersection, looking both ways, the traffic on either side closing like shark's jaws that just missed him as he squirted out ahead of it—through the ubiquitous landscape of Greater Boston: a CVS on one corner, a sub shop on the other, and if you looked far enough in the distance, a church spire sticking up over the houses. He was six feet tall, Irish but olive-skinned, had his hair cut high and tight—like he was entering the Army, though he never would; he loved smoking weed too much and he wouldn't have wanted to leave his town, or his friends, or his girlfriend, or his job, even though he said they all sucked, which was why he got hammered. And he jammed the accelerator and sped them down a lane of clapboard houses, and parked. And all the guys, all these young, growing males, uncramped themselves and climbed out of Dave's tiny car.

They went into the house. There was a carpet and a kitchenette and a couch facing a bare white wall with an outline, a reverse shadow, a lighter rectangle where the TV had once been, and the cable coming out of the wall with nothing attached to it, just the silver connector and that tiny poking wire. A few other older guys were there with their hats on backwards, and the boys were on their guard. They shook hands all around. One of the men, a tall fellow in a faded sweatshirt, loose around his red wrists, and carpenter's jeans with a loop for a hammer, had an edge. When Corey introduced himself, the guy said, "You said hello to me already."

"No, not me. That was him."

"Yeah you did. It was you."

A battered metal toolbox rested at his feet in battered leather boots, glints of steel toe caps showing through the worn-out leather, the steel battered and bent too. He was drinking a beer from a case of beer on the kitchen counter and spreading waves of approach-me-at-your-peril.

But Dave went through the house, pulling off his shirt as he went, and went up to him bare-chested and clasped his hand and grabbed a beer of his own. He made sure all the boys got beers. He had a Bud Man tattooed on his olive chest, in garish blue and red.

Dave grabbed the radio and ran down the stairs, the music

descending with him—Journey, Aerosmith, Foreigner—the guys following him down, and the boys trooping after the guys. Down they went into the basement: a room like the one they'd just left only smaller, more confined, no natural light, and no carpet or couch: a concrete floor, load-bearing pillars, a breaker box cocooned in spiderwebs, and a weight bench in the center of the space. A pile of rusted iron weights in unusual denominations—no doubt culled from some antique powerlifting gym hidden somewhere strange and forgotten like in a church basement when it was being gutted to make way for a more modern facility.

Dave set the tunes on the sill of a bricked-over window, Boston singing "More Than a Feeling." The guys arrived with six-packs under their arms and set them down, clinking, on the basement floor.

The hairdresser, Anthony, took off his parka and revealed a set of enormous blotchy red-tanned arms. He had black curly hair and wore a black silky jersey and heavy, shiny, black, satiny track-suit trousers and big white Jordans and a gold chain. He put on a thick leather weightlifting belt and a pair of black leather finger-less gloves with Velcro straps and mesh backs. He spent a long time putting his gloves on, adjusting and readjusting them. He was unlikable but immensely strong. He lay down under the barbell and pumped it up and down as a warm-up—twenty times with no sign of fatigue. Then Dave changed places with him, took a swig of his beer, hit himself in the chest, on the Bud Man tattoo, and could barely lift it.

The men lifted weights and drank in the basement for several hours. The hairdresser got mad at something one of the boys said, and got up off the bench red-faced and shouted, "I've taken shits bigger than you!" He walked slowly out of the room with his swollen red bulbous inflamed-looking arms out to his sides. When he was gone, Dave said, "That's what 'roids'll do to you," and a mood of approval went through the room. The boys looked at each other with vindication. The carpenter, lounging on a broken lawn chair, drinking his tenth beer, cracked the barest smile, and sank back into scowling at his raw red hands.

The boys got on the bar when it was their turn. "Youse can do whatever you want," said Dave. "I work different body parts every day. You got your shoulders, your arms, don't forget your trapezius—they're over here—do your shrugs. Your farmer's carry. Ask Anthony. He's the expert—if he isn't being a hard-on. He does his body parts six days a week. He spends one whole day on shoulders."

"He's a fucking weightlifting pussy," the carpenter said.

Anthony stalked back into the basement, and now he put nearly all the weight they had on the bar, and pressed it up and down three times, his body almost bursting—held in by the wide leather weight belt strapped around his waist—a human torpedo arched on the bench.

"Keep talking," he said, breathing hard. "Spoken like a drunk."

"Come to my job. See if you could do my job. Let me see you try paving. And I will keep talking. All you can do is drink wheatgrass."

"Keep talking."

"Fairy wheatgrass."

The hairdresser made a lunge at the carpenter, who dived up out of his chair. The fight got broken up with a lot of pushing and shouting. The carpenter put his finger in the hairdresser's face and said, "I'll kill you"—but then he slammed his way upstairs and took his toolbox and jumped in his truck and left.

The almost-fight provided fodder for discussion for a while. The day went on, got boring. The two high school boys wanted to take the commuter rail home and they did. But Corey didn't want to go home. He kept lifting weights long after everyone had left the basement. Between sets, he drank until he got dizzy-drunk. Upstairs, Dave and his friends were playing some version of hockey in the house. Dave came down to check on him, saw all his empties and said, "Are you hammered? I work out hammered all the time. It's great so you don't feel the pain."

The sun went down. They put their shirts back on and went out to the train tracks in the night and kept drinking. A new crew of guys, new strangers and friends, the train tracks and the gravel ground in the moonlight. The art of speaking when spoken to, but not too much. Not mouthy but not shy. One of Dave's friends asked Corey where he lived, and Corey told him Quincy.

"A lotta ginzos up by you?"

"What's that, Italian?"

"Yeah."

"My father's Italian."

"Sorry!"

"It's okay. I'm not sure if I like him."

The guys loved that. "You're not sure you like him!"

"Yeah. He just started hanging around my house after sixteen years."

"I didn't like my father," the hairdresser said. "I told him he could suck my dick."

Corey got drunk enough to tell Dave "My mother's dying" and clasp his hand. Dave said, "I gotta get this kid home."

But Anthony the hairdresser said, "Let him sleep on the couch." Dave's girlfriend was coming to see him. Whispered adult plans were in the works, cars and keys borrowed, strategies agreed on, a ten-dollar loan for a bottle of wine, a trip to the package store—a swirl of intrigues, all the more subtle to Corey because he was so staggeringly drunk. They walked him inside and he fell asleep on the couch in the TV-less room with the cable coiled on the floor like a root pulled out of the ground.

At two in the morning, he woke up and saw Dave and another man standing toe-to-toe under the watery fluorescent light of the kitchen, slugging each other in the arms and chests—heavy, meaty, smacking, bruising bare-fisted blows that thudded through their feet into the floor. It wasn't a real fight, but it was a rough and painful form of entertainment.

A little later, Corey woke up again in Dave's car, and Dave was driving him home. All around them, he saw a black forest, the car rushing under the trees, spotlighting with its headlights the white houses with their dead-looking windows—behind every mailbox and fence, the dead-black background. Dave scrupulously drove him to his door on Sea Street. The sight of his own house distressed him, a black box against the waving blue sea of the marsh.

"Are you straight? Can you get inside? Okay, be good," Dave said. "Don't tell your mother I let you drink." And he drove off.

Late on Sunday morning, Corey stood in the doorway of his room and held his head.

His mother looked up and asked if he was okay.

He just had a headache.

"Are you sure?"

Were they alone? he asked.

They were, she said. What did he want to ask her?

He approached her with his eyes full of emotion. "Mom, were you planning to abort me?"

"How could he have said anything?"

"Mom, I'm sorry. It's okay. I can put it in context. You didn't know me. I shouldn't have said anything."

"I never would have. Oh, Corey. I rue the day."

"Why is he even here?"

"We need him, Corey. What are we going to do when I can't work?"

"He doesn't do anything. We don't need him."

"Maybe we don't," she said.

In the afternoon, Corey and Gloria sat alone together and looked through a catalogue of prosthetics and assistive devices. He proposed getting her a knob for the wheel of the car, which he could have easily installed. But the stick shift would still be a problem. They thought of trading in her hatchback and getting an automatic, but in the end, they wouldn't do that either.

At three o'clock, he asked for his mother's car keys. He wanted to change her oil. She sat inside reading on the futon while he worked outside. It was cold, the sky was blue and the wind was blowing. Leonard's Mercury wasn't there. Corey fetched a container for the dirty oil and a three-eighths wrench and a new Fram filter and set them on the ground. There was brine in the air. A brownish-green crab shell lay on the roadside, tangled up in seaweed.

He popped his mother's hood, unscrewed the engine cap, stuck his finger in the brass threaded hole, swept his finger in a circle and smelled the hot black oil. It soaked in and brought out the whorls of his fingerprints. He climbed under the car and fit the three-eighths wrench to the nut, gave it a twist, unscrewed it with his fingers—and the oil jumped out, a smooth, heavy, hot, dense liquid. It leaped across the back of his hand and poured into the receptacle.

Standing, he stuck his hand inside the hot sharp-edged engine and tried to unscrew the old filter. The oil made his hand slip. He rubbed his hands with a rag and tried again, made a mighty effort, a moment of isometric tension, gritting his teeth, straining as hard as he could, angry, his arm in the car and his eyes staring at his house. But the heat had welded the metal screw threads. He had to use the filter wrench—a snarelike clamp. A quick mental review of which way he was turning—righty tighty, lefty loosey—and he took the filter off.

He had three quarts of golden black thirty-weight oil. He stuck his finger in the clean oil and rubbed it around the rubber rim seal of the new Fram filter and attached it to the engine, twisting it tight, but not too tight, doing it with care. With a rag, he cleaned the nut and threaded it carefully back into the hole in the bottom of the engine case, plugging it, and tightened it with the three-eighths wrench, cautious of stripping it. Using a funnel, he poured the clean oil into the crankcase.

It was advisable to run the engine for a minute. He got behind the wheel and started her car and listened to it run. The engine made a looping hum. He was convinced something had been done to it, that it had been damaged in some way.

Where had it been driven?

He drove to a garage and dumped the used oil in a steel drum, went home and gave her her keys back. "These are yours and yours alone," he said. Did she want him to hold them for her? Did she want him to keep them safe?

Leonard never offered to drive Gloria again. Nor did he leave. Instead, starting around the second week in February, he consolidated his presence in their house, staying with them every night, as if he truly lived there, exactly like a real member of their family. Now it was a family in which no one talked. The house rang with an inaudible dog whistle of tension. Gloria and Leonard pretended not to know each other. She would wait for Leonard to finish in the kitchen and then, without a word, go in and make her dinner.

Corey stopped talking to Leonard completely. From now on when he saw his father, he put his earbuds in and listened to Theory of a Deadman with the volume cranked.

Rather than going home and facing Leonard after school, Corey began wandering in town, looking to hang with Dunbar or his friends. There were a lot of them. Sometimes they met at a house in Quincy; other times Corey caught a ride to Weymouth. On workdays, he cleaved to Dunbar at Blecic's job site, which meant they often absconded from the job together and submitted phony hours. Dave's friends worked in factories, in warehouses as order pickers or forklift drivers, as sandwich makers or delivery drivers. Some were in jail. The paver was doing ninety days. Someone had pulled a knife on him at a party, so he had broken a bottle and used it as a weapon: "He was in a jam, so he jammed," Dave said. The hairdresser, Anthony, said that standing up for "The Cause" meant standing up for a fellow white boy if you were in jail with him. It was better to fight and lose than to be a punk or bitch.

The guys at Dunbar's house took off their shirts and put on hockey gloves and punched each other in the chest. Corey wrestled on the floor with a kid his size and lost. He crowded in with the guys and watched a video of a cage fight on Dunbar's cell phone and, when one of the fighters caught a kick to the head and collapsed, joined the others hooting, "Aw shit! He got knocked the fuck out! He got merked!"

In the ideal of standing up to anyone no matter what the consequences, Corey heard the echo of Joan, who had followed the same principle. He saw himself living up to her code of valor and winning her approval wherever she was.

Gloria came home with a cane. Her doctor had made her understand she couldn't drive. She was taking the T to work. She gave her car keys back to Corey.

Tonight, she was in the kitchen, making wild rice for dinner; Corey was lingering at her side, the automotive key ring in his hand. The house was tensely silent, Leonard in the other room. She moved around unsteadily, her shoulders rounded, neck thrust forward, face downcast—an Albrecht Dürer face, the German draftsman and painter of the Middle Ages—all well-defined bones—thin nose, cheekbones, jaw, a healing cut under the point of her chin; her forehead swelling slightly, the sign of a mind holding on to things it was trying not to say.

Her bad gait was plainly visible to Corey. Something was obviously wrong. A spasticity in her calves made her want to stand up on her toes. She was as unsteady as if she were walking on stilts; her knees didn't bend. To open and shut the cupboard, turn the knobs of stove and sink, fill the pot with water, and so on, she was using her hands like hooks or mitts with bones in them. Corey was reminded of the plastic claw they used at Family Dollar to grasp a pack of toilet paper from an upper shelf—a clumsy device with scant leverage. She hadn't told him what her commute was like, or what her job was like once she got to work, but he only had to look at her to guess.

She had been holding a Charlie Card to the scanner with both hands, sometimes dropping it on the concrete floor of the station while people behind her said, "Just go through!" Bus drivers waited for her to climb their stairs with her cane hooked on her arm, her weak hands gripping the stainless aluminum handrails, arms shaking as she pulled herself up, and they waited while she got her card out and held it to the reader until it beeped, and they waited while she went back and looked for a seat—and everyone else was waiting too. And then the slow acceleration towards Fields Corner.

He stood by his mother's shoulder at the burner. There was a pat of butter floating on the boiling water, dissolving into a yellow skin. He offered to take the wooden spoon. She let him stir. The bubbling of the water and the stirring of the spoon masked the sound of their voices from reaching the other room. Corey began to talk.

He said he wanted to drive her to work. She said that was out of the question; he'd have to miss school. He said he wanted to quit school and work full-time; he could support them. "You're too young," she said. He insisted that he wasn't. She didn't want that for him. He said he wanted it himself. He could support her and they could live alone.

Gloria lowered her voice to say, "Corey, I don't want you missing a single day of school because of this hateful disease."

"But what are we going to do?" he asked.

"We're going to have to get along with your father."

. . .

They were in the house alone, in separate quadrants of the house; Corey was in his room. One minute, the house was silent; the next, he heard a crash. He started running for the kitchen before he even knew what he had heard. His mother's scream was preceded by a time delay. She must have been drawing breath. The scream began hitting his ears when he was halfway between his bedroom and the kitchen. Everything was knocked over—a table, a chair, a carton of orange juice lying sideways, silverware, a glass, his mother. She was bare-legged wearing shorts, the kind of shorts she wore to exercise. Her mouth was open and her eyes were squeezed shut in the attitude of someone who had fallen from a great height, far higher than anything in this room, and broken her back.

He dropped down and cupped her head. "Are you okay? What's broken?" He couldn't understand her she was crying so hard. "I hit my head," she sobbed. He held her head. "Mom Mom Mom." Her back was soaked in orange juice.

"I tried to jump!" she screamed in anguish. "I tried to jump one last time."

12

Punk Kid from Quincy

The first sign of a change in Corey's personality was that he started getting in almost-fights in school. His physiology teacher was a white-haired New England woman with a pageboy haircut who showed no loss of vigor due to age. At the start of the semester in her introduction to the course, she had told them they would be writing a ten-page thesis. Corey had been sitting in the front row. Behind him, he heard people groan. "Oh, don't start whining!" the woman shouted. "That's nothing! When I got my degree, I had to write *several* one-hundred-twenty-page papers."

Corey looked behind him and did a fast room scan. There was a girl in a knit sweater and leggings who grabbed his attention. She was bending sideways to whisper to her friend and was laughing at something behind her hand. Her shoulder, crossed by the white silk band of her bra strap, showed through the holes in her sweater, and he thought, Oh no, that makes it hard to concentrate!

But in the back of the room, there was a group of kids—a group of guys and girls—who were going to be mocking everything.

The teacher was wearing khaki pants, a teal fleece, and hiking sneakers in brown and green. She had her glasses on Croakies around her neck. With her glasses off, she had small eyes that she held on you fixedly while blinking and talking at the same time. Her eyelids would close over her eyes in mid word and open again and she'd still be staring in the same place. But she never looked at Corey. She seemed to prefer the back of the room, even though they'd been making fun of her. At the front of the room, on her desk, there was a computer showing a changing rainbow screensaver.

She said they would cover the cell, the mitochondria—oh goody, her favorite!—the skeletal system, the muscular system, the nervous system, respiration, digestion, and reproduction. "I will expect maturity," she said. "If anyone can't handle talking about reproduction, they can leave now. We will deal with this subject respectfully. People think the female system is complicated. They don't know what they're talking about. The male system, as you will learn, is *much* more complicated. It's a wonder it works at all."

Someone sniggered. Corey turned around and looked at the source of the laughter. At the very back of the room, there was a lanky girl sitting with the V of her crotch conspicuously thrust forward, glaring directly at him, and by her side there was a guy, her friend, playing with his hat, adjusting it so that it perched on top of his head like a royal cushion, and you could tell that, in his mind, what he was doing with that hat was more important to him than anything else that was likely to happen anywhere on earth all day. And they were shooting looks to a network of associates and sympathizers who sat all around the room.

"Let's let her talk," Corey said.

"What?"

"Let the teacher talk."

"Let the teacher talk?"

The teacher told Corey to turn around. "I can fight my own battles, thank you very much."

Since then, Corey had sat in class every day with his head turned solemnly forward, taking notes in his ninety-nine-cent notebook, but aware of the sideshow going on behind him. Some weeks had gone by. Now it was mid-February, and the students had to announce what they were going to write their thesis papers on. When it was Corey's turn, he said "amyotrophic lateral sclerosis"— the first time he'd ever said those words in school.

"What?" said the hat kid.

The teacher explained that amyotrophic lateral sclerosis was a rare disease similar to MS. Corey heard someone make a retarded sound.

So, after class, Corey found his own friends and told them

that he was having trouble with a kid who had called his mother a gimp. Corey was still relatively well liked. Pete Lucantonio, Kevin Darby, Stacy Carracola, and Josh Eammons all told Corey that he should fight him.

His new enemy, the kid with the backwards hat, came over through the crowd, taking off his backpack as he came. All of them, Corey, his enemy, his friends—they all shoved out through the fire door onto the concrete pad at the back of the school where there was the open sky and the endless weeds like cornstalks and Faxon Field. Pete held the door and looked out for teachers. "He's gonna kick your ass." The kid, whose name was Brendan, didn't seem eager to fight. Corey just stood there.

"Ha!" Pete said, slapping Corey's shoulder. "You chumped him." The combatants shook hands.

But the glaring girl told Corey, "You didn't really do anything."

One day a short time later, still in February, he was in Quincy Center hanging out after school. A bunch of high school kids were sitting under the bus shelter, smoking cigarettes. As he watched them, a short androgynous freckle-faced person in long shorts and a sideways hat came speed-walking out of the veterans park, grabbed her crotch with one hand, grabbed the bill of her hat with the other, pointed at them with two fingers, and shouted, "Yo, if youse disrespect me again, I'll knock your fuckin' teeth out."

She speed-marched away.

"What was that?"

"I'm not sure. I think it was a girl."

Corey went up to them and told them, "She's more of a man than any of you."

"Don't we know you from school?"

"That's fuckin' right."

"Why is that fuckin' right? What do you want? Do you want something?"

"Maybe you'll find out."

"There are five of us."

"I don't care."

"Great. What are you, like, Superman suddenly?"

There was no fight, just sneering, but someone tossed a cigarette. Behind him as Corey was leaving, he heard one of the boys telling the others, "This is the weirdest day."

At school, Corey began to stop talking to people in the old friendly way. He practiced three things: 1. The Deadpan. 2. The Up and Over. 3. The Front-Off. The Deadpan consisted of an expressionless stare. He let you talk without any facial feedback from him. You could be telling him a storm blew down his house: He would give you no reaction—as if all the nerves in his face had been disconnected from his facial muscles. The Up and Over was, after boiling you in his dead stare for as long as you could stand, he allowed his eyes to unhitch from your face, as if you couldn't hold his attention, and rise to a point in the air above your head. The Front-Off was, if you were finally offended by all this and dared to call him a jerk, he squared up with you and made an arm gesture with both hands as if he were throwing down a pile of papers on an invisible desk. The gesture came from the waist, so it looked as if the papers were stored in the groin: It looked sexual and baboon-like. The elbows were out. He was throwing down a gauntlet—or a red carpet that would unroll towards you—a walkway inviting you to your doom if you dared to come at him.

Practicing this new language took a lot of work. Corey had no time to think about anything else. Every day was showtime, moseying around, pretending to be a gangster and wondering when the world was going to call his bluff, and if it did, was he going to play his role to the point that it went from being a role to being real? He spent a lot of time telling people what he would do if other people crossed him. He spat on the ground. He pretended to get angry even when he wasn't.

He drove off everyone who had ever liked him except for Molly. For weeks, she kept trying to get his attention. "Hey!" she said to him in the cafeteria, where the ceiling was hung with international flags and all the tables were little hexagons. Not wanting to break character, Corey didn't smile. "Hey, shorty," he said to her, and went and sat and dead-stared at his grilled cheese sandwich.

His greeting made her raise an eyebrow. She came towards

him through the tables, wearing a Quincy High athletic jacket over a long knit sweater, which functioned as a short dress, cotton tights and old Nikes. Fresh from basketball practice, her still-wet hair was contained under a ski hat. The gym bag hanging from her shoulder was on a long strap and it was hitting her knees as she maneuvered between the tables to his side.

"You seem like something's wrong lately. Are you okay?"

But Corey refused to drop his mask, wouldn't joke with her, wouldn't smile. She kept on pressing him, "What happened? You used to be so chill."

"What, do you need a friend?"

Her other eyebrow went up. She stared at him for a minute. Then she said, "Hey, we're playing Duxbury this weekend. You should come and watch us if you have time."

"Thanks," he whispered.

She didn't give up on him.

He went to see the girls' basketball team play their rivals in the gymnasium. The girls ran and dribbled and jumped and passed the ball, and sometimes they shoved each other, fouled each other and took long skidding falls on the polyurethaned floor, but the only thing he could think about was his mother's car being taken and her falling face-first on a concrete sidewalk.

After the game, he waded down through the parents and friends to tell Molly he had supported her. He didn't even know if she had won or lost. She was breathing hard, flushed and sweating, a towel around her neck, in a crew of tall teammates wearing high-top sneakers, headed for the locker rooms. She put her hand out sideways and touched his hand. Her hand was wet.

"Thanks. You're awesome."

He challenged people to fights without getting into them on the street. He sat next to a guy on the bus, and the guy pushed his knee into Corey's knee, and Corey pushed back. The guy was hairy and French-looking, as if his roots went back to fur trappers in Montreal. He had a bearded face and a skinny body. His knee was hard and it ground against Corey's knee bone, and Corey could feel tension loading up in the man's body like a spring.

"How old are you?" he asked Corey. "I was in the Marines. I was in Force Recon, and I loved it. One thing I learned: If I get in a fight, I won't get off the other guy until they pull me off him."

But Corey didn't stop resisting his leg, and the man, for whom life was overwhelming, got off at the next stop, having decided that he had to avoid the consequences of another conflict. He threw a look at Corey that said, "Kid, if you only knew what I know."

And then Corey spread his legs out all the way and his heart stopped pounding: another fight avoided.

But finally he pulled the pin on the wrong grenade. An Irish kid— white skin, red hair, freckles, a Boston Celtics uniform—attacked him a block away from the Family Dollar. The kid wore a newsboy's hat, a gold chain, and dollar-sign rings. On his fist, he had a tattoo of a bomb with the fuse burning down as in a Tom & Jerry cartoon. Afterwards, Corey couldn't remember what he had done to set him off. There had been an exchange of words between them. He had lost vision of the street, of the parked cars, bystanders, everything—and then the kid himself had disappeared and a painless impact had exploded in Corey's eye. A balloon popped inside his nose and something shot out of his nostril. Then he was hanging on to the Celtics uniform and fists were hitting his head, but he didn't feel anything. They were wrestling. He had a flash image of his enemy, hatless, the chain whipping around his neck. Someone was shouting, "Let him go!" Then he saw a cop car, a black and white, that said Quincy Police on the body. Then Corey had his arm around the kid's neck and was grinning, pulling him close. The kid was still angry.

"Oh, they're friends," a cop said to his partner.

"Yeah," the kid muttered, snatching up his newsboy hat.

All of them went their separate ways, including the police.

At home, Corey found the entire white of his eye was filled with blood. He found dried blood under his nose. His sinus had popped and blood had shot from his nose and hit his shirt. He had to go to the doctor—a forty-dollar co-pay. His knees had gotten skinned badly through his jeans, and he had to soak the wounds in the tub. His scabs hardened up and for several days after the fight he had to go around on crutches because he couldn't bend his knees.

But then he went to school, his eye still swimming in blood, and began to swagger, imitating the walk of the kid who'd beaten him up, and for a little time thereafter wore a newsboy's hat—until he had a change of heart.

He still saw Adrian, but their relationship had changed now that Corey spent most of his time outside school hanging out, going to Blecic's job site but not working, playing hooky with Dunbar, acting out the role that no one could tell him what to do and, at home, bracing for another fight with Leonard—waiting for Leonard to do something to his mother. For weeks now, in front of Adrian, Corey had been talking about how Quincy boys were tough. When the honors student complained about his own mother, Corey would say, "Just overcome your problems, dude." He stopped showing any interest in Adrian's analyses or treating him with deference. Their meetings stopped being philosophical. He would put Adrian through a bro-shake and treat him with aloofness and amusement. He practiced his Deadpan on him. He took over the dialogue between them, rolling through the streets, pointing out the corners where half-imaginary disputes had taken place, referencing a cast of characters Adrian had never heard of.

"That dude looks like Hawk."

"Who's Hawk?"

"Some dude I was beefin' with."

Corey delighted in treating his former mentor in this highhanded way. He told Adrian the world was divided between those who were real and those who weren't—and let Adrian draw his own conclusions.

An irony occurred when Adrian invited him to spar. They looped back to Mount Auburn. New England was having a gray day and it was rainy. They were on the edge of March. The cocoacolored house waited in the wet trees. Adrian opened his mother's garage and invited Corey in. Corey, his clothes damp from the weather and hanging on his lean frame, entered without hesitation, his jeans bunched at the ankles over his big sneakers. All his clothes were oversized, bigger than he was.

The garage smelled wet and moldy. The boxing gloves lay on the floor. Adrian only had one set of gloves, so they would get one each. Corey took the right one: the power hand. At first he thought he had given himself an advantage, but then he wasn't sure how to stand.

Adrian took his leather jacket off and exposed his arms. Unlike some people whose muscles bulge, Adrian's arms didn't expand when he flexed them. They looked like they were made of blocks. The internal parts seemed to slide inside one another. He put the left glove on.

"Are you ready?"

"No, wait. Which way do I stand?"

Adrian told him not to worry about it. All they were going to do was work on their feints.

They put their hands up. The garage had very little light in it. Adrian advanced and Corey backed up into the wall and his back hit the handles of rakes.

"Wait," he said. "I can't see shit."

Adrian waited, bouncing on his tiny wrestling shoes. They started moving again. Corey jabbed at Adrian. He hit nothing but air. The garage filled with effortful scuffing and breathing. No one hit anyone.

I should get closer to him, Corey thought, and took a step towards Adrian.

A shadow ballooned in front of his eyes, covering everything he saw, like a car speeding into his face, blacking out everything.

The shadow was Adrian's left hand hitting him in the face. Corey threw his arms out and fell flat on his back on the concrete floor, striking his head.

He came to sitting up against the garage wall. He saw Adrian standing several feet away.

"What time is it?"

"You've asked me that already."

"What am I doing here?"

"We were sparring."

"We were? What happened?"

"I threw a jab and you walked into it."

· · ·

Corey remained friends with Adrian despite the knockout. A week later, he was back in Cambridge, sitting on the floor of Adrian's room, saying, "I don't care that I got snuffed. I may be smaller than you, but I'm crazy. I don't give a fuck."

Rain was falling on the skylight. Corey was holding his newsboy hat, feeding it through his hands like a steering wheel. Adrian was enthroned at his desk, looking down at him.

"I can see that. You act like you don't care what happens to you."

"I've changed. I don't care."

"That's very interesting. How did you change?"

"Had to. It was time to get some balls."

"Hm . . . So you're really not scared of street fights anymore?"

"No," Corey lied. "It's a mental shift."

"It can be really satisfying to make a mental shift or connection," Adrian said. "That's something I really need to work on. If I could be as fearless as you, I'd be unstoppable. I'd be a killing machine."

"It's all in the mind."

"I should show you a picture I drew for my art class. I bet you'd really appreciate it. It's so violent."

Adrian opened his closet door. Tacked to the inside wall was a sheet of drafting paper. On it, he had drawn a larger-than-life rendition of his own face.

The looming Adrian-face held the viewer with its steady, hypnotic gaze. The picture was astonishing in its detail: Each of the whiskers on Adrian's jaws, each of the hairs of his eyebrows, each one of his eyelashes, each of the hairs of his head, each follicle had received its own pencil line. It could have been a photograph. There was nothing stereotyped about it. It was completely the opposite of the drawing of the vulva that Adrian had made on the board at MIT. It wasn't a token of a thing; it was the thing itself.

There was more: Exploding out of the side of Adrian's head, there was a second figure, a kinetic figure—another Adrian—muscles flexed, swinging a sledgehammer, bursting out of his own skull, like a mushrooming bullet.

The portraits—both the bigger-than-life-size face with its heavy open-eyed gaze and the kinetic mini-man leaping out of the brain—were highly accurate likenesses of the artist. Corey was awestruck. Adrian said that the work had taken him eight weeks of meticulous effort. He'd spent an average of two hours each night in front of the mirror, studying himself, using a ruler the way his art teacher had taught him, to get the dimensions right. He'd sharpened his pencil every ten minutes to make sure all his lines were the same. He'd posed night after night with his sledgehammer to capture all the muscles of his torso. He leaned back and indicated his abdomen and rib cage where the latissimus ties into the ribs, the serratus, not quite touching his own anatomy, but indicating it with his fingertips.

"You can see my narcissistic identification. How I think I'm beautiful."

"You should be proud."

Adrian said he was.

Then why was the picture in his closet?

Adrian said his mother wouldn't let him put it on his wall.

"I don't understand. What's wrong with it? Didn't your teacher like it?"

Adrian said his teacher had given him an A. But his mother had reported the teacher to the principal. She'd threatened to pull Adrian out of school. She'd called his psychiatrist and made sure Adrian saw him twice a week. She'd demanded that Adrian put the sledgehammer back in the garage, otherwise she couldn't sleep in the same house with him.

"But that's crazy!" Corey said. "What is she, afraid you're going to kill her?"

"Yes."

"I really think that's wrong! You do something artistic, she ought to be proud of you! She ought to encourage you! This shouldn't be in your closet! Look, you've complained about her a lot to me and I always thought you were overblowing it. This is the first time I finally get what you're talking about! She's not right, man! You've got to stand strong against her, if that's the way she is! You gotta be you all the way!"

Adrian said nothing.

"You don't seem happy."

"I'm not unhappy. But I know there are things about me that are bad."

"You're not bad!" insisted Corey. What did the picture mean? He saw a man escaping, flying free.

No, said Adrian. Not quite. It meant: His head contained an angry weapon. There was an explosive projection from his psyche, a force that could destroy.

They closed the closet door on Adrian's self-portrait and went downstairs. Gray light was flowing in the windows and filling up the house like a beaker, bringing with it the dismal cast of the rainy blacktop road and the dripping trees outside through a gap in the white, see-through curtain. The house was full of shadow. Mounting to the platform kitchen, Adrian took a jug of milk out of the refrigerator and began to drink.

"That'd make me sick."

"I can overcome it." Adrian belched. Swallowing the entire gallon took some time. It was zero percent fat; just water and protein. He crushed the empty jug and put it in the flip-top trash can.

Corey looked in the refrigerator. "You got anything to eat?"

"Everything in there belongs to my mother."

"You can't eat your mother's food? How 'bout this? What's this? Meatloaf?"

"That's hers."

"Can I have it?"

"I can't give you something that belongs to someone else."

"There's barely anything here. She's not even going to notice it's gone."

"Oh, she'll notice."

"How 'bout if I just take it?"

"It's up to you, if you want to do that. That's between you and her. I'm staying out of it."

"I don't understand what she's going to do. What's the big deal? It's leftovers. It doesn't look like you guys are starving."

"I've made my position clear."

"Fine. Relax. I'm not gonna touch her food. Where is she anyway? Is she at the hospital getting treatment?"

"Maybe. There's a schedule around here somewhere."

"Is this it?" Corey pointed at a sheet of paper clipped to the refrigerator door: a laser-printed table of the days of the week. In one cell of the table, the words "Adrian garbage don't forget" caught his eye.

"Yes, that's it. Let's see: On Thursday she goes to the cancer center. On Wednesday she sees her friends. On Tuesday she has her real estate meeting. On Monday she goes to some other committee thing. She has the whole week planned out for both of us. Mondays, I do the dishes. Tuesday, I do dishes and trash. Wednesday, I—no, Thursday, I see my psychiatrist. Friday, I have nothing to do. Saturday, I get to go out. Sunday, I have to see her. She's got every day of the whole week on her computer. Yeah, here we go: Saturday, she goes to the hospital. She should be back any minute. We should get out of here."

Corey leaned back on the sink, took his hat off and spun it on his finger. "She's your mom. I don't see what she's gonna do to us."

"You'll see. You can stay here if you want, but I'm leaving."

"You're running away, bro?"

Just then they heard a car outside and Adrian said, "Uh-oh. Here we go. Guess who."

The front door opened and a woman's voice sang, "A-drian!"

She bustled in and Corey saw Mrs. Reinhardt for the first time, a winter-coated figure wearing big eyeglasses and a helmet of lustrous chestnut hair. She was carrying a heavy lady's purse, shopping bags hanging from her arms, and a cardboard file box in her hands. Corey wanted to help her, but something stopped him: the fact that Adrian wasn't saying anything. She set her things down. When she looked up, Mrs. Reinhardt saw her son.

"I called you!"

"I answered you. You must not have heard me. You must be going deaf. There could be something wrong with your brain."

"Oh, Adrian!"

She took her coat off. She was wearing slacks and a sweater and a wide shiny belt with a huge square buckle like a buccaneer. The chestnut hair was a synthetic wig.

"Hi, Mrs. Reinhardt. I'm Corey. I'm Adrian's friend."

She didn't respond. Dropping her coat over a flower-patterned chair, she descended to the living room and strode to the white couch, which faced the claw-footed stove. The polished floor of the living room was canted away from the kitchen as if by continental drift.

"Adrian, can you come here?"

"What for?"

"I need your help."

"How do you know it's something you need my help with? Have you tried to do it yourself yet?"

"Are you going to help me or not?"

Adrian sighed.

"What is it?"

"I want you to move the couch for me."

A discussion began. She wanted him to move it an inch. Adrian didn't want to do it. Corey listened to the mother and son negotiating for Adrian's labor as if he were a crane operator and she needed him to hoist a Jacuzzi onto the penthouse roof.

Corey offered to help—"I'll do it with you and we'll knock it out in one second"—but both Adrian and his mother ignored him.

Finally, Adrian bowed his head and moved the couch an inch. He acted as if it made him very tired.

Corey asked, "Is that thing a monster? Is that the kind that has a bed in it? A sofa with a secret?"

"Are you satisfied?" Adrian asked his mother.

By now the windows had darkened and it was nighttime. Mrs. Reinhardt turned the chandelier on. She climbed up on the raised dais above the living room. "Thank you, Adrian!" she called down. "Thank you, boys!" She turned to Corey. "We'll have to have you to dinner. I love having dinners with Adrian's friends! They're fascinating!"

"I'd love to have dinner, Mrs. Reinhardt."

"He doesn't have time," Adrian said. "We've got to go."

He hurried Corey out of the house and walked him to the grassy traffic island, as if seeing him off on his way back to Quincy. But once they were away from the house, Adrian wanted to talk about physics.

"I don't see what's so awful about your mom," Corey interrupted.

"Trust me. You don't know her."

"No, really, I don't see the problem. Why do you care if I eat dinner with her?"

For the second time since he had known him, Adrian turned hostile, stating that he wasn't interested in the opinions of people who didn't know what they were talking about.

Corey said, "I'm heading home." His friend said nothing. The rain had stopped, but when the wind gusted through the trees, there was a hissing disturbance that sounded like water turning into steam. Corey walked away, the ground wet underfoot. Behind him, Adrian said something indistinct—something bitter and sarcastic.

Corey glanced back and saw him in the gloom, feinting at a tree.

On the T, he replayed the exchange and realized that his friend had just threatened to knock him out again.

He went home and asked to borrow his mother's laptop and searched for *Fighting gyms near me*. A map of the South Shore unfolded on his screen, dotted with flags. He zoomed in. The details of the terrain appeared. For some time, sitting on the edge of his bed, he moved his Google Maps eye around the state, looking at the names of mixed martial arts training centers, biting his lip. He drew the coastline in his notebook, filled in roads, marked an X—a place to sail to.

Then he seemed to remember himself. He cleared his history and returned his mother's laptop, saying, "Sorry, Mom. I lost track of time. I was just looking up some bio stuff for school."

13

Welcome Day

Since Leonard's fight with Corey, the two of them had barely spoken. Leonard had been watching the development of Corey's new persona, in silence.

And Corey had been watching Leonard. During the same period, Leonard's pattern was as follows. He was working a day shift at MIT. At night, he parked on Sea Street, came in from the winter's cold, dropped his cop bag on the floor and took off his black nylon parka and other zippered jackets—he dressed in layers for warmth—sometimes revealing a uniform shirt with epaulettes on the shoulders, which was unbuttoned and untucked. Under it, he wore a sleeveless wife-beater undershirt like the neighborhood bookie.

From night to night, the uniform shirt changed its color and cut—gray to blue to white. Once, Corey glimpsed a patch that said MIT Police on the shoulder. But the patch wasn't always there. The shabby trousers' pinstripes flickered from red to blue to nothing. Handcuffs dangled from Leonard's belt some nights, alongside a chrome key chain, and other nights disappeared. He never wore the Sam Browne utility belt that cops carry their guns in. Leonard explained, under MIT police department policy he had to leave his sidearm in the armory at night, but he carried a backup weapon in his cop bag for protection—in case he ran into a crime in progress off the job. He wasn't allowed to show his personal firearm to civilians.

After getting settled, in his open shirt, hat and tinted glasses, he went to the kitchen and cooked for hours. Late at night, he showered in Gloria's bathroom and came out in boxer shorts, the undershirt steamed through and clinging to his white chest.

He'd put the fedora back on after showering and wear it for the trip from the bathroom to the futon.

Around the futon, he'd built a little home away from home of Roche Bros. and Walgreens shopping bags containing clothes and socks, prescription medications, garlic, packages of crackers. He kept everything in bags in lieu of a chest of drawers.

The signs of his presence expanded over time. He left his toothbrush out to dry on the corner of the coffee table. In the beginning, he put it away after it had dried but eventually began leaving it there permanently. Soon his soap, shampoo and conditioner had joined it—Vidal Sassoon hair products in black cylindrical squeeze bottles with gold lettering. The expansion of his campsite meant his possessions floated out in their world and some of their belongings floated into his. Sometimes Corey would see a book from his mother's milk-crate library had been left lying near the futon in among Leonard's toiletries, and he would rescue it.

At night, to sleep, Leonard unfolded the futon—an operation that demanded moving the coffee table. Leonard had soon begun to forget to refold the futon when he was done with it and put the table back. Corey adopted a standing policy of refolding it whenever he saw it open and returning the coffee table to its proper place. Leonard wanted his bed left alone, as he made plain by the rough way he yanked it open after Corey had closed it. This tug-of-war over furniture caused the first conflict between them since the car incident.

"My mother can't close that herself if you leave that open," Corey told his father one night in early March.

"I beg your pardon?" Leonard said. "Excuse me, was I talking to you? Who the fuck told you to open your mouth?"

"Leonard!" Gloria protested.

"No, it's okay, Mom. I don't need protection. Let him talk."

"Get the fuck out of here before you're sorry."

Corey began shaking inside but said nothing more. But he made up his mind to show greater strength around his father. The next night, for Leonard's benefit, he swaggered around the house, deepened his voice and put on a careful show of manhood.

He saw Leonard gazing at him through his amber glasses.

"What is it?"

"What's what?"

"You look like you want to say something to me."

"Want to say something to you? What would I want to say to you, Corey?"

"I don't know. You're looking at me."

"Corey, if I wanted to say something to you, you'd know it."

"I'm sure."

"Is that a smart remark?"

"Take it however you want."

"What does that make you, a tough guy?"

"Tough enough. I ain't a bitch."

"You must be a real success. I bet your life is going really well for you."

"My life's going great. I got a hundred homeboys who'll tell you that."

"Sure you do. Corey, I'd be surprised if you had a single friend."

The day before Corey's spring recess, it rained. That evening, he took his mother to the grocery store—the Stop & Shop in Quincy instead of the Purple Cactus in Jamaica Plain. They entered through the garden center. He got his mom a shopping cart. She hooked her cane on the rail and they moved slowly down the aisle under the yellow ceiling.

She had pages of claims against her private medical insurance. She hadn't gotten disability in time to cover herself from a slew of charges. The amounts were bankrupting. And every time she saw the doctor, someone else billed her. The physical therapist had billed her for the dumbbells she no longer used. Her checking yo-yoed up and down between her monthly pay and zero dollars. She had less than two thousand dollars in savings. Corey knew some of this.

She knew her son liked Subway's, but a prewrapped sub from Stop & Shop was cheaper. She wanted him to have one.

"Mom, I don't need anything. It's okay."

He wanted to buy a jumbo jar of peanut butter, which weighed two pounds.

"You can't live on that, Corey."

"Yes, I can. It's a good investment."

They bought mac and cheese. She chose a pack of tofu. In the spirit of saving, he said, "Mom, isn't there a cheaper brand?" and she got upset and said, "Fine, I guess I don't have to have it. What difference is it anyway, right?"

"No, Mom, I was wrong. I was wrong. Let's keep the good one."

They were stalled in the aisle when a guy in a yacht club sweatshirt with a package of ground meat in his basket tried to push past his mother. Corey put up a hand to stop him. The ship's wheel on the guy's chest ran into Corey's hand. The man's eyes opened.

"What? She's my mom, you know what I'm sayin'?" Corey said.

Gloria apologized: "He didn't mean anything. He's concerned for me, is all. I'm ill."

The man shook his head at him and went away.

In the night, as it rained, Corey stood hidden in the kitchenette listening to her on the phone with the insurance company, hanging up in frustration, trying to reach a real person at the twenty-four-hour number.

"It's all a big mess," she told him when he came out and asked what she had learned. "If this keeps up, we might wind up on charity."

First thing in the morning, Corey told his boss he had the week off school and could work full-time.

Blecic told him he was letting him go for lying on his time sheet.

"What do you mean?"

"Please. I don't have time for bullshit."

As they were arguing, Dunbar strolled up, greeted Blecic and went to work. Corey looked at his boss and said, "I didn't lie to you." The Slav would not relent. Corey had to walk away with the other men watching, get in his mother's car and leave.

Blecic kept Dunbar working.

That night, Corey saw his friend on the street on his way to Point Liquors. He shook Dunbar's hand, embraced him and said, "I didn't rat you out."

"Good looking."

And for the rest of the recess, Corey hung with Dunbar and his boys when they had time for him. He didn't tell his mother he'd been fired. He loitered outside the job site, behind the port-a-johns, pretending to be just happening by, trying to catch Dunbar's attention. When the latter snuck away, Corey would be there to hook up with him and they'd speed down to Weymouth in the Nissan. Dunbar told his friends, "This kid's a stand-up guy."

Corey picked up there were two levels of life being lived among Dunbar's friends. A billboard in Weymouth urged all citizens to call 911 if someone overdosed. Another said: "Save a Life: Carry Narcan." A lot of people, including Dunbar, had normal jobs but also dealt and used drugs. Steroids were popular. Dunbar took his shirt off and demonstrated radically improved muscles thanks to Decabol. His pectorals had white striation lines where they stretched the skin. He told Corey he ought to take a cycle. Anthony the hairdresser was a real dealer who could get you 'roids, meth, coke, Bizarro, X, smack, and oxy. In the wake of his firing, Corey let it be known he was open to selling drugs for Anthony. As soon as he had said this, he felt oppressed by a sense of gathering doom and loss of control.

One afternoon, he cut class and met the hairdresser at an apartment above the salon where he worked, facing the glass-fronted gym where he trained. It had low ceilings, white stucco walls, a sliding door to a patio deck, which overlooked a mass of trees nestled around a white New England church spire. The surrounding streets were a medley of clean, smooth grays and beiges, some cool, some warm, like the khakis they sold at Work 'N Gear by the CITGO plant in Braintree.

There were two easy chairs. Dunbar sat in one, Corey in the other. Anthony came in wearing a Cerucci jacket—a short, black iridescent high-collared garment with the collar turned up and a gold chain around his sweaty purple neck. He took the couch, which seemed like a single chair just big enough for his huge legs.

"So this kid's got a hairy dick now."

"He's a good shit," Dave said.

"You got a driver's license? Put it on the table."

Corey took out his driving license, bearing his full name and address next to the seal of the state of Massachusetts. Anthony photographed it with his cell phone.

"This is like your first day at McDonald's. Everything you do either speaks for you or against you. If this goes right, we can build things up. If you put money in my hand, I'll put money in your hand. But if I catch any heat, Quincy's a short drive. You heard? If I get hurt, you get hurt."

He pulled a ziplock bag of yellow capsules out of his jacket pocket and dropped it on the table.

"What the fuck is that?" Dave asked.

"Don't touch. This is candy, motherfucker. He's gonna sell it in his school. People want this. This product here will sell for a rack and a half, fifteen hundred dollars. Twenty pills, eighty bucks a pill. Here's what you do. You let your friends know you can hook them up with this candy. Everybody gets one piece for free. You give away a couple. Don't double up on anybody. Wait for them to come back for the next one, and then you sell them."

The next day, Corey cut school again. "I'm a hustler," he said, standing under the bus shelter in Quincy Center while it rained.

Yeah, we get it, the others said—a mixture of kids and young adults who weren't going anywhere either, except maybe on the buses, which came and went while they stood around and smoked. Most had dropped out of high school, some were working on it. There was an older guy among them, a twenty-five-year-old, who had stopped when he saw their skateboards, to tell them about his glory days, the risks he'd taken and fears he'd faced doing tricks and jumps and taking painful falls at the Swingle Quarry. He had a piercing in his lower lip, a girlfriend and a baby, which he could be seen pushing in a stroller through the station in the middle of the workday—he was unemployed—on his way to Dorchester to leave the child with its mama's family, while he went to a community center very similar to the one Gloria worked at and asked for counseling and drug treatment and help getting a job.

"I learned to deal with that fear," he told the dropouts. "You will too."

Corey was holding a cigarette while it burned. He squirted saliva through his teeth at the wet pavement, and nodded at the older guy as he left them and went through the drizzle and into the station, passing the cop who was always posted there to watch the truants and street people.

The parking lot faced the backs of stores—a line of connected buildings with dumpsters by their rear exits—a minimart, an always nearly empty Indian restaurant where white people went to drink, a coffee shop–hangout called Gunther Tooties, a law firm in the underutilized office suites upstairs. A short girl opened the back door of the café and ran through the rain to the bus shelter in her sweater and leggings and Uggs, her hair messy, her lighter in her hand. "Yo," she said. "This rain sucks my dick."

She advanced on the cluster of young people, hitching her hip at them, skipping sideways, saying, "Gimme a cigarette! Gimme a cigarette! Gimme a cigarette!" One boy said, "I'll think about it," and gave her one, and she jumped up and kissed his cheek. Another was holding a dark brown pit bull on a chain, and she patted the dog's wrinkled forehead.

Another bus came and went while she talked about her art class. The cop watched them without watching them. He was a tan-skinned colossus in a sharp navy uniform and black boots who had mastered the Deadpan. Corey glanced at him and looked away.

Corey never sold any drugs. He gave away one pill to a black kid named Brian and took one himself and gave the rest back to Anthony. They were opioids. They put a wall between Corey and the world.

But they didn't put a wall between him and Anthony. Through a third party, he heard that Anthony expected five hundred dollars for his two missing pills. Corey tried to get a job, but Dunkin' Donuts wasn't hiring. Someone called his mother's cell phone and told Gloria that her son didn't pay his debts. He went to Dunbar and asked him what to do. Dunbar was broke and couldn't help him out but promised to speak to the hairdresser on his behalf. In the end, Corey borrowed two hundred fifty dollars from his mother and gave it to Dave to give to Anthony. But after that, he heard from others that he could have simply blown the drug dealer off, and he was left wondering if Dave had taken advantage of him. He heard rumors about himself.

The story of the episode came back to him in exaggerated form, with him an even bigger fool, a mark, getting played for even more of his mother's money. His friendship with Dave Dunbar ended.

❧

On the fifth of April, MIT held a welcome day for next year's freshmen. Workers put up canvas tents on the lawn outside the student union. Administrators sat with upturned faces to speak to parents and their children. A sign asked "Want to Spend the Summer in Kazakhstan?" A caterer delivered brisket from Redbone's in Davis Square. Initially, it was sunny. The sun passed overhead, making the tent glow like a lampshade. In the afternoon, however, the weather clouded over and the lampshade went dark. The brisket cooled. Mrs. Reinhardt pushed through the tent flap in her wig, followed by her hulking son, Adrian.

She approached a long-necked woman with a pious face and medieval bowl cut who sat with her hands primly clasped and her fingers interlaced, waiting to be called on to help someone.

"My son's coming here next year!" Mrs. Reinhardt indicated Adrian—the figure in the black leather jacket. He was standing with his feet braced out like a man about to meet a charging herd of horses, holding open a heavy textbook, studying the contents with a look of dramatic fascination on his face. "That's him." And she laughed at the sight of her son. The administrator, either due to innate humorlessness or because there was something that troubled her in the sight of the figure in the mouth of the tent, didn't laugh.

While his mother talked to the administrator, Adrian drifted out on the lawn, repeating formulas, whispering to himself, working out a problem, touching his lip in thought, writing in the air on an invisible chalkboard, looking up at the clouds.

His mother emerged and reclaimed him. She wanted to inspect the student union. It was a public space open twenty-four hours a day: slightly trashed, smelling like old pizza. Anyone could sit for as long as they wanted in the chairs, leaving the stink of their sweat in the fabric of the cushions. She toddled past the young engineers-in-training sprawled out doing homework. At the far end, there was a Dunkin' Donuts–Baskin Robbins, giving off its characteristic confectionary smell—a sugary, creamy, coffee-flavored, vanilla-chocolate goopiness.

"Oh, Adrian, I'm going to have an ice-cream cone!" she cried. Then she noticed she was alone. Adrian had let her go on without him.

She bought an ice-cream cone and went back and got him and made him follow her around the campus for another ninety minutes.

When she was satisfied, she took him to his dorm. It was a redbrick-limestone building with white colonial trim. There was a glass rotunda with a white roof and white vertical elements separating the windows. She took her son inside. There was a guard desk in the lobby but there was no one there.

"Let's go upstairs!" she said. "I want to see where you'll be living!"

"No, that's okay."

"Oh, come on, Adrian! Don't you want to take me? '*Where the boys all go, the girls go too!*'" She sang to him in a show-tune falsetto.

"No, that's okay. I'm not interested."

"If you won't come with me, I'll have to get a college man to show me his room."

"Go ahead. I'm sure that will be very satisfying."

"Adrian . . ."

"Yes?"

"You better not wander off."

"We'll see."

"Adrian."

"What?"

"You better be here when I come back."

"You can't tell me what to do. You're the one leaving."

"I'm only going for one minute."

"Okay, one minute." He set his G-Shock watch. "That's sixty seconds. You're going to have to hurry, otherwise I have no obligation to wait for you."

"I know somebody who wants to go to physics camp this summer. Maybe you better think about that, unless you want to get that yanked."

"You're just countering a reasonable condition with a threat. We went over this with my doctor. For an agreement to be valid, both parties have to have a stake in it. You're acting in bad faith. To be in good faith, you would have to say how long you're going to be upstairs and then you would have to make a faithful commitment to be back here by that time."

The elevator arrived.

"If you're not here when I get back, I'll take away something you want," Mrs. Reinhardt said.

When she was gone, Adrian stood in the lobby, staring at his watch. "That's thirty seconds," he announced to the empty room.

He inspected a science exhibit in a Lucite case: a geode, an egg of stone that had cracked open, revealing fang-shaped crystals of purple and white, like frozen milk. The outer surface glittered with shiny dollops of chrome and nickel. Geodes, the exhibit said, form in bubbles of molten stone within the earth.

The leather of his jacket creaked. His bicep compressed it when he flexed his arm to look at his G-Shock watch, strapped to the joint of his powerful hand.

"A minute's up."

He found a fire exit, which led to a stairwell, and went down into the basement.

Thirty minutes passed, and the security guard who tended the lobby of the dorm returned to his post to find a woman talking excitedly on her cell phone. Her tone of voice suggested delight. But there was something paradoxical about her voice. It didn't match what she was saying. She was saying, "There's a maturity issue! He's not ready to be away from home!" The guard realized she was seething.

The woman got off the phone. "My son's disappeared," she told the guard. "You haven't seen him, have you?"

"What does he look like?"

"You'd know him if you saw him," she said.

The guard offered to put out a call on the radio.

"Don't bother. I'm going home. I've got cancer, you know. He's going to regret this. This is a very nice dorm. I was just upstairs. It's a lovely dorm and I met some lovely people, but he's never going to know them."

She left the building.

The guard strolled through the hallways on the upper floors. Finding no one out of place, he entered the stairwell, tapping his trouser leg with the antenna of his radio, and after looking up and looking down, descended to the basement.

There was a red exit light at the far end of the basement, which was otherwise dark, and it glowed on the overhead pipes—water, sewer, gas, electric—turning them red. The air was humming from a high-voltage generator running in the power room. The guard began to stroll into the throbbing darkness. As he moved, white lights keyed to motion detectors came on and went off, so that a square of white light traveled with him down the tunnel, illuminating the cinderblock walls. The last bank of lights to blink on revealed a human figure standing like a robot absorbing the sound waves coming out of the generator.

"Hello, Adrian."

Adrian turned around and looked at the guard. The guard was Corey's father.

"Mr. Goltz, is that you?"

"Almost. Goltz is my baby mama's name."

"Oh dear, I've committed a faux pas. What should I call you?"

"You can call me Leonard."

"Leonard, what are you doing here?"

"I work here. What brings you down here?"

"I like feeling the energy radiating from the walls . . . I feel like no one knows I'm here . . . I feel violent and powerful . . . I feel like I'm in this big red humming pussy."

Adrian looked inside himself while he talked, following his ideas from one to the next, until he came to this conclusion. Once he said it, he looked up with the air of a sleeper coming awake and registered Leonard and a smile spread over his face at the hilarious strangeness of what he had said. He laughed.

"Don't worry," Leonard said. "That's perfectly normal."

And Adrian laughed even louder.

"You're getting away from it all. I get it. This is my favorite part of my rounds."

"Are you a policeman? Corey told me you were a policeman for MIT."

"I'm a guard. I was with the cops. But the hours are better for me as a guard."

"I don't blame you. I think you're so lucky. I've always wanted to be a night watchman! I'd have time to read and study . . . I wouldn't want to be a cop either, telling people what to do. What kind of person needs to control other people like that? It's like something's missing in them, like they have some kind of penis envy, so they have to wear a gun."

"They're small-minded. They're blinded by status markers."

"Exactly! I hate that! They want to wear an MIT T-shirt and brag about having their kid go here."

"You see it with academics getting letters after their names. I call it alphabet soup: PhD, MS—multiple stupidity, more like; bachelor of science—BS, BS, BS. I've gotten letters after my name too. You think I introduce myself as Leonard Agoglia, PhD?"

"You have a PhD?"

"Yeah, you bet your ass. Got it in 1998. Wrote my dissertation. Did original work. Big fucking deal. Life goes on. I don't need the status."

"Wow! Corey never told me that!"

"That's because I never told him. It doesn't change who I am. It doesn't change the universe."

"Gosh, that's such a noble attitude!"

"People look at the surface and think they know you. They have no idea what you're thinking."

"That's exactly how I feel!"

"They look at me and see Joe Shit the Rag Man. I just laugh at them."

"I think of myself as a proud, lonely boy."

"We're all heirs to the capitalist system."

"In what way?"

"It's the system of competition: the zero-sum game of I-win-you-lose instead of the understanding that knowledge is not property. You can't buy and sell knowledge—even though that's what places like this try and do. Knowledge lives outside the economic realm. And if you look at history, mistakes have happened when people have tried to bring these realms together." He held his hands apart and moved them towards each other until they over-lapped. "This is a problem. Things that are separate should stay separate. This is the problem right here—" and he gripped his hands together, clutching his own flesh.

"Hmm, that's very interesting. I have to think about what you said. I wouldn't have thought of it as capitalism. I guess I was thinking more of it in terms of psychology, like somebody has this expensive house or car, and they want to fight over it, but deep down, the reason they're fighting over it is because it's this part of themselves that they see being taken away, like a penis."

"Capitalism is based on false value—the value of a bar of gold. You can't eat gold. In material terms, it doesn't do anything for human survival. What good is it?"

"You're right! People love to talk about how beautiful gold is: It's shiny; they practically masturbate over it; they fetishize it; they make statues out of it. But it's just a bunch of atoms. You could melt it down to nothing in a kiln. If we can worship gold, why not silver? Or why not shit? I'd like to grind up a gold statue into powder and make a gorilla eat it; then I'd collect the gorilla's shit and make a new statue, and worship that. People would say, why are you worshipping a shit statue instead of a gold one? And I'd say it *does* have gold in it! Here—smell!"

Leonard laughed ha-ha. "Unfortunately, most people worship gold."

"Yeah. I guess that's why I'm doomed to my lonely quest. Nobody wants to smell my shit."

"You never know. Stay hopeful."

"I thought Corey would be a great person to share ideas with."

"I think he's very taken with you. He looks up to your aca-demic success."

"I looked up to him too. He was so hyped-up about ideas in the beginning. I'd never met somebody who was so into the same things as me before. It was incredible. It was like looking in a mir-ror! But he's changed."

"Yes, he has."

"You've noticed it too! It's like he's lost his intellectual side, and he's doing this tough-guy thing, like what matters is being this big man instead of being a friend."

"Yes, it's ridiculous."

"What's been causing it?"

"His mother."

"I thought it had something to do with her! Hasn't she got some health problems?"

"Yeah, she's sick. But everyone's got health problems."

"You must be really bummed."

"I'm not surprised. His mother's destroyed everything she's ever touched."

"Gloria—that's his mother?"

"Yeah. The thing is, he tells her everything, so if you talk to him, she'll hear everything I'm telling you."

"I won't tell Corey anything we talk about."

"I thought I had you pegged as a solid guy."

"That's a sacred trust to me. I wouldn't expect anyone else to understand what we're talking about."

"They probably wouldn't. They probably wouldn't get the whole thing about the big red pussy, would they?"

Adrian laughed. "No!"

"It might be a good idea not to tell anyone we know each other."

"I have no problem with secrecy. It's how I've survived knowing my mother."

"I think I met your mother upstairs. Is she short?"

"She's pushy."

"I was going to say loud, but that fits."

"She's loud. Her voice is so whiny . . . She's awful."

"I know the type: has to get what she wants when she wants it. She wants to know where you are."

"She's stalking me. That's why I'm down here. I'm going to stay until she leaves. I know she's got to get to bed at a set time, so all I have to do is stay out till ten thirty and I can still get eight hours' sleep and be up by, like, seven. I can study the way I want, I can work out, I can lift, I can get stronger; everything's still improving; I'm learning everything for my courses; she isn't defeating me."

"A difficult woman. Is she Italian?"

"Does it show?"

"It shows. Italian women are hysterical." Leonard made devil horns and pointed them at the earth. "See this? This is what my father did when he saw my mother, to ward off the evil eye. You ought to try it."

"I'm not going to be able to keep her away with that."

"Is she in good health?"

"She's got brain cancer."

"Oh, I'm sorry."

"No, it's okay. I hope she dies!" They laughed.

"When did you figure out your mother was difficult? How many days, how many minutes, after being born did it take?"

"It was early. I was like four or five."

"Did she do something?"

"Yeah."

"Something you don't want to talk about?"

"Yeah. How'd you know?"

"My mother was a freak of nature also. I can barely talk about her. She fed me worms."

"That's awful. That makes me feel really violent."

"I have to get back to the lobby," Leonard said. "Keep the faith."

~❧~

Still oppressed by the Dunbar affair, Corey cut school and took the Red Line up to Cambridge, planning to surprise Adrian at Rindge, a campus of green lawns and gray stone buildings that harkened back to churches. Class was in session; the grounds were quiet. Corey could see a teacher lecturing behind a distant window. Then the doors opened and kids with backpacks came out of all the buildings. He looked for a leather jacket. Coming down a path beneath a high stone archway, Adrian appeared, carrying a book under his arm. Corey put himself in his way.

"What are you doing here!" Adrian exclaimed, looking with wonderment at Corey, who stood before him, draped in baggy clothes and hood.

"I cut school!"

"Your rebelliousness gives me such a sense of power."

"Come on! Let's go to Harvard Square! Let's go meet some ladies!"

Adrian thought that was a great idea! He checked his watch and said he'd be free to do that in four hours and seventeen minutes.

"What do you mean, four hours? Let's go now. Come on!"

But Adrian refused—he had to maintain his grades.

"What am I supposed to do, stand here and wait for you all day?"

"I told you my terms. I can see you in—four hours and thirteen minutes, now. All you have to do is occupy yourself for that length of time. Anybody should be able to do that if they have basic inner resources and aren't hyper-needy."

Corey said, "Forget it," and went off to Harvard Square alone. At no point did Adrian mention that he had talked to Corey's father at MIT.

Mr. Gregorio had Corey summoned to his office. An assistant showed Corey in and closed the door, closing him in with the principal and two other male teachers. Corey stood in front of the principal's desk, wearing his newsboy hat, NFL jacket and loose-fit jeans. He had forgotten where his feet were and so he was standing slightly pigeon-toed. All three men were staring at him. He put his eyes down.

"Hello, I guess," he said, and took his hat off.

"Hello, you guess," a teacher said. "What are you supposed to be, a tough guy? Look at him. He gets in fights now."

"Okay," Gregorio said. "We're not here to make you feel mis-understood. If there's a problem, you can tell us. Is there something going on?"

"No."

"I let you take your course. Now Mrs. Clark is telling me you're a disruption."

"I'm sorry."

"I've heard worse than that," one of the other men said. He had a face that went white-to-red in half a second when he was angry, a sharp nose, close-cropped orange hair, a strong voice, and a wedding ring. He was looking at Corey steadily as if he were a nail sticking out of the seat of a chair, which needed to be ham-mered down. "We ought to have security check his bag."

"I'd be up for checking his bag right now."

"How about it, Corey? You have any contraband on you?"

"No." He took his backpack off and the red-faced teacher unzipped it and went through it.

"My daughter goes here. If I heard that somebody was selling drugs to her, do you know how upset I'd be?"

"Here's your bag back. Don't forget your bio book. Wait a sec. Is there anything in here?" He flipped the textbook over and shook it. A piece of paper fell out: Corey's notes on adenosine triphosphate, the energy currency of the cell.

The red-faced teacher's name was Edgars. He coached.

Gregorio said, "We've got a proposition for you, Corey. You go with Mr. Edgars. You work with him, do what he says, go to the games, assist during practice. If he's happy, we take you off probation. That's *if* he takes you. It's up to him. He's no softy. But we want to see a change of heart here. What do you say?"

"What happens if I don't?"

"You stay on probation the rest of the year."

"I'll stay on probation."

"That's what I thought," Edgars said. "I don't want him anyway."

14

Dopamine Reward

Instead of going to class, he went to the cafeteria, which was empty, and sat alone beneath the ranks of foreign flags hanging from the ceiling. Probation meant that he would remain in school but was on thin ice and would have to behave himself or risk further disciplinary action. He fit the page back in his notebook. ATP becomes ADP leaving you with one free phosphate. He resolved to fail everything. He was going to study nothing but one thing: his mother's illness. No more math or English. Maybe they'd kick him out. Maybe they'd hold him back.

At the end of second period, his peers started pouring down from upstairs and lining up to eat. The cafeteria gate went up. Kids rushed in to get to the burritos wrapped in foil.

Through the window, he saw Molly outside in the sun, her long reddish-blonde hair hanging down her back. She was with a big guy dressed in a plaid shirt and slouchy blue jeans like a farm boy—a shot-putter on the track team, Corey thought. They were standing together in a haze of sunlight by the granite apple of knowledge, arms around each other's waists.

Corey went out and hailed them. "Are you cutting?"

The shot-putter turned and squinted. He had reddish whiskers on his chin. Molly shook her head. Out of self-consciousness, perhaps, she didn't give Corey the warmest welcome. After an awkward minute, he said, "See ya," and went back inside the modern school with its dark glass windows.

When school let out, he walked all the way to Houghs Neck. He drifted outside the Manet Tavern and wandered through the churchyard, looking at the setting sun.

He was carrying a tire, which he had picked up on the roadside.

Thinking he was alone, he put it against the fence of a baseball backstop and started hitting it.

When a passerby came down the road, past Sacred Heart, in the dusk, he stopped, ashamed, and flung it in the woods as if he were practicing the discus.

When the passerby was gone, he retrieved the tire and started hitting it again.

Sometime later, he started walking again without any plan of going home—or anywhere. Misty night was rolling in from the ocean, suffused with the glow of streetlights on widely spaced masts—old masts of old ships. The blacktop road was empty. Dark trees mantled the town. The fog smelled metallic. His knuckles were white-hot and bleeding. He had a bruise, which moved like a button under his skin. The rubber had left black vulcanized streaks on his knuckles.

As he was cutting through a gas station, a pickup truck shot by him and stopped. Corey recognized the Knaack Box in the back.

"Tom?"

"Get in," Tom said. "I'll give you a lift."

The truck smelled faintly like Egg McMuffin sandwich wrappers, McDonald's coffee drying in a cup—food-on-Styrofoam smells—vanilla air freshener, and cigars.

"Thanks for picking me up."

The truck began dinging.

"Your door isn't shut. Ya gotta shut it."

Corey reclosed his door. They were zipping into the fog, behind the lances of Tom's headlights. The ball field blipped by. Something heavy, hard and sharp was in the footwell: a circular saw. The guard had slid up from the blade and a tooth was biting Corey's ankle.

"I haven't seen you in forever. How you been?"

"I'm at Home Depot the other day and this guy I know tells me there's this kid dropping my name all over town who's fucking off at work."

"That was me."

"I didn't know what he was talking about. He said some kid is lying on his time card, giving people attitude. When he said it was you, I told him he had to be making a mistake."

"I've been fucking up."

"I heard about you and Dunbar. I said, that's not the kid I know. What's the story with you?"

Corey shook his head.

Tom made a series of right turns and they zoomed back the other way. They seemed to be driving out of the fog into civilization—although a temporarily uninhabited one. Their head-lights picked out houses, then a playground. Here they actually saw a family—a mom in a Boston Red Sox hat, a dad with a Nerf football, two kids running for a pass on a black ball field. They sped by the statue of Christ in robes—young, pensive, bearded, longhaired. The Ford ate up the distance to the seawall, glowing in a snowy pool of streetlight, the bay flat and black beyond it.

"You only got one reputation. Somebody trusts you," Tom said, pulling up at Corey's house.

Corey looked out the window and wept. He dried his face.

"I've been having trouble with my father."

"That's too bad. What kinda trouble?"

"He's a punk. He disrespects me."

Tom remained silent.

"He disrespects my mother."

"What do you mean, he disrespects her?"

"He took her car and she fell."

"She fell?"

"My mom has a disease. It's called Lou Gehrig's. She's getting paralyzed, and she can't drive, so she asked my piece-of-shit father to drive her, and what's he do? He drops her at work and steals her car for a week. So she takes the T and falls, and when I step to him about it, the guy tells me I'm a piece of shit, I'm a little punk from Quincy. You think that's right?"

"No. I don't understand why he'd do that. He shouldn't do that. Some people are assholes. I didn't know your mom was sick. Is she going to the doctor?"

"Yes, she does."

"Is there anything they can do for her?"

"Not really. Once you've got it, that's it."

"What is it a disease of? Is it like some kind of cancer?"

"It's neurological. It starts in the brain and starts paralyzing all the nerves that go to your muscles so you can't move, but you can still feel everything; you can still think; you can still see. You know everything that's happening to you, and you get weaker and weaker until you can't do anything. Right now she can't pick anything up with her left hand. She's having trouble walking. She's got a cane. If somebody bumps her, they could knock her over, and here she is taking the T to work, because that scumbag won't drive her."

"What's your father's problem? What is he, like your stepdad or something? You didn't used to have him around the house, did you?"

"I probably talked to him four times my whole life until this year. We never lived together. Then my mom gets sick and, boom, he just moves in and starts acting like a fucking psycho. He takes her car. He shows no concern for what he's doing. He's a burden in our house. He's a fucking stranger."

"My father was a stranger."

"Did you hate him?"

"I didn't know him enough to hate him, Corey. He wasn't around. I just got in a lot of trouble."

"What kind of trouble?"

"We vandalized some guy's warehouse one time—me and my brothers and my brothers' friends."

They were silent.

"I realize that nothing I've said is an excuse for fucking off."

For the moment, Tom seemed to have talked to his limit on the topic. "Don't worry about it. Life goes on."

"I'm going to apologize to the guy I was working for."

"Who were you working for?"

"Some guy named Blecic. We were renovating a house."

"Didja learn anything?"

"A little drywalling with Dunbar."

"Drywall is good to know."

"They had me cut around some pipes. I learned to cut straight. Dunbar was always letting me do his work. It was good because I learned."

"There's people ya gotta stay away from."

"I know now."

"I had a guy on my site who came in high. I took one look at him and said, 'You're going home.'"

"I acted like a little punk. I'm not blaming anybody."

"The problem with guys like Dunbar is they get you in trouble. My brothers' friends were like that. I was the youngest and they took off on me. The security guard who was guarding the warehouse grabbed me."

"Fair-weather friends."

"You lie down with—what is it? dogs?—ya get up with fleas."

"I've got a few fleas on me."

"Yeah. Get 'em off ya," Tom said. "Put a flea collar on. Haha!"

"How's Molly? We've barely talked since I saw her play Duxbury."

"She's been working hard. At the beginning of the season, her coach told her she was too slow. I think he saw her size and he had some kind of a hang-up about it. He made her do laps around the court or something. That's what she told me. And he was supposedly always making comments about her weighing too much."

"What a jackass."

"He gave her, like, a complex at the start of the season. She was quiet after practice. So finally I asked her what was wrong and she told me. I told her, 'Don't worry about what he tells you. You know what you can do. Don't let this guy get under your skin.' So, she kinda went out there and showed him. She brought home this rope ladder thing and put it in the street in front of the house and did these foot-speed drills. Whatever the guy told her, she did it double. It paid off. He's played her every game, and she's been having a good season."

"God bless Molly! How did everything go with college? Did she get in?"

"Yeah, UMass is taking her. The coach gave her a recommendation. They're giving her an athletic scholarship."

"I'm happy!"

"The thing about her is that she works hard."

"You've got reason to be proud. Like father like daughter."

"I gotta start making it to her games."

It was after eight and Tom rose early for work, so they parted.

Corey climbed out of the Ford and marched up the steps of his mother's house. The truck hooked a U-turn and zoomed away behind him. He went straight to his room and threw his newsboy hat in the closet and never wore it again.

That weekend, he helped a pair of local guys fix up their backyard. The guys, who were putting in a fence, disagreed about when and how to put it together. They argued about everything, including what Corey should be doing. He dug out stones and moved them to the edge of the property while they argued. "You're fine," they told him, "he's the problem," pointing at each other. They bought him a Snapple and a sub both days and, on Sunday, paid him in cash, saying, "This is thanks to all your hard work and the goodness of our hearts."

First thing Monday, he took his money and his notebook and his mother's car to school. The notebook contained his driving directions. As soon as the bell rang, he gassed the car at Hess and headed south on Yankee Division Highway.

As he drove it began to rain. The highway traveled under red granite cliffs in the gray rain. A semi humming next to him sent up fountains from its tires. He passed a Speedway gas station and a sign South to Fall River. His wipers and turn signal thumped and clicked as he took the exit. The area had strip malls with lesser-known stores, and there was an incompletely built nature to the place—the pavement gave way to dirt and trees. He passed a sign for Slice of Greek Pizza and a knee-high New England stone wall, overhung by trees. The grass rose like rain falling upward from the earth.

He drove into an office park of sheet-metal buildings and saw the sign for Mixed Martial Arts by a windowless shed. The parking lot was filled with pickup trucks carrying bikes and fishing poles in the back and bumper stickers saying Fighting's Not a Crime and This Is Sparta.

He parked, jumped over a puddle, and ran inside, wiping water off his head. The first thing that hit him was the smell of feet. The air was hot. There were grappling mats on the floor, Zebra mats on the walls, a row of heavy kicking bags, long as a person is tall, still subtly swinging. An uppercut bag like a plum bob. Title grappling gloves, Ringside boxing gloves, Team Aggression kicking shields, Everlast hand wraps, Fairtex shin pads spilling out of homemade wooden shelves. A squat rack, barbells, and kettlebells. A spit bucket covered in dried blood. An icebox with a sign: Water $1. Trophies on the counter, banners on the wall: UFC MGM Grand, Ericsson Globe Arena, Key Arena, Bell Centre, USF Sun Dome—with endorsements: Wild Wing, Sprawl, Lexani, Training Mask, Revgear, Venum, Headrush, Instaloan, TRX, Versaclimber, Torque, Dethrone Royalty, Alienware, Muscle Pharm, Kill It Clothing, Hayabusa, Jitz, Contract Killer, Pain Inc.

There was a cage in the back of the room and several guys were lying sprawled around it with their backs against the mesh, sweat-drenched, in a state of exhaustion. Their skin was reddened, chafed and bruised. One had a healing black eye. Their knees and elbows and the bottoms of their feet were blackened by the dirty canvas. They sat in their fatigue, picking up water bottles between their boxing mitts and aiming the water into their mouths.

Corey asked if he had come to the right place to train.

"Yeah, but you gotta come back later. The regular class won't start until—when does it start? Five? Come back at five. Eddie should be here."

He went to the Slice of Greek to wait. The drizzle was keeping up outside. He got a slice of pizza. As he ate, he recalled that, when he had come home flush with optimism after talking to Tom, he'd encountered Leonard sitting on their futon, reading a yellow hardcover mathematics text in his fedora and boxer shorts. Corey had knocked on his mother's bedroom door to ask if there was anything for him to eat. Behind him, Leonard had turned a page and said: "What's the matter? You're a big-time drug dealer. You can't afford to buy yourself dinner?"

What Corey hadn't known was that, while he'd been talking to Tom, his mother had been talking to Leonard—about money. She'd somehow let slip she was out two hundred fifty dollars—the amount she'd lost bailing Corey out of his entanglement with

Anthony the hairdresser. The whole story had come out about Corey's abortive drug-dealing experiment. Leonard had said, "I'm not surprised." Gloria hadn't wanted to tell him, but now that she had, she hoped he would "step up," as she put it, "and show Corey a little guidance."

"I'm supposed to help your son?"

"Suit yourself, Leonard. He's your son too," Gloria had said, and gone to her room on her unsteady legs.

Corey had heard the details of this exchange from his mother after the fact.

At the time, when Leonard accosted him about paying for his own dinner, Corey had replied, "I don't know what you heard, but I don't want to talk to you about this."

Through the door, his mother said there was chicken for him in the freezer. Corey turned his back on his father and returned to the kitchen. He was microwaving a precooked chicken patty when Leonard appeared in the doorway, holding handcuffs.

"Do you want to get arrested?"

Corey backed away. "What are you doing?"

"You're going to be wearing these at the rate you're going."

Leonard hung around watching Corey while the chicken cooked. The timer dinged and Corey took his steaming chicken patty out of the microwave and put ketchup on it and took it to his room. Leonard followed him. Corey shut his door on him and sat at his desk to eat. He could hear Leonard outside his door. Outside his door, Leonard flicked the handcuffs and made the bracelet spin around and ratchet into the locking mechanism. Corey heard Leonard moving all around their house, ratcheting the handcuffs, slowly pushing the steel bracelet through the locking mechanism click by click by click.

He went back at five and met the coach, Eddie, instantly identifiable, circling around the mat, explaining technique to early arrivals to the grappling class. "Oh, you want to train?" He excused himself from his students—"Let me take care of this"—and took Corey aside so they could talk.

Lean and heavy-boned rather than stocky, Eddie's torso had

a boardlike flatness. With his muscular neck and clean-cut head, he looked like a swimmer. But his ears, absent the usual cartilage whorls, stuck out like a monkey's or bat's ears on either side of his buzzed head. The bridge of his nose was thickened and his forehead and cheekbones had knobby prominences like bumps on a mace, as if his whole head had become a hitting tool. It was hard to tell his age. He was a professional fighter. He could have been anywhere from twenty to forty. He asked Corey if he had any experience with martial arts, boxing or wrestling. Corey said no: just a street fight he had lost.

Eddie said then maybe he'd like to try a class. He sent him to get a pair of shorts from the locker room. Corey came out, barefoot, dressed in a borrowed pair of Venum board shorts.

On the mat, the class was paired up, one student on his back, another kneeling between his legs. Most were male, but some were women. Some women were paired with men. Everyone was in the guard.

The *guard*, Eddie explained, was the defining position of Brazilian jiujitsu, a grappling system developed by the Gracie clan in the early twentieth century, based on traditional jiujitsu, which Japanese travelers brought to South America. The founder of the art, Hélio Gracie, a physically frail youth, pioneered an approach to combat based on conserving energy through efficient movement with the goal of outlasting an opponent and wearing him down. The guard was where you might wind up after being pinned on your back by a bigger, stronger adversary. You wrapped your legs around his waist like a woman with whom he was having sex. This position of apparent weakness, in Hélio's method, became one of strength. You pulled the top man in, broke his posture, sucked him in, thwarting, smothering, fatiguing, unbalancing, sweeping him over, trapping him in chokes and joint-lock submissions with your legs.

Eddie demonstrated. He locked his legs around Corey's waist, gripped his wrists so he couldn't use his hands, and pulled him in. Corey fell face-first on the wall of the coach's abdomen. Then Eddie shoved his head away, spun on his back, threw a leg across his face and put him in an armlock that straightened out his elbow to the breaking point.

"That's an arm bar."

Eddie let him spend the rest of the class having his body bent and stretched in weird ways by his partners.

Midway through the night, he was matched up with another novice—a guy named Troy who worked at the Finish Line, a sneaker store in South Shore Plaza. Troy tried to bully him, Corey got sore, and the two of them started wrestling in anger.

"Whoa!" people said. "White-belt fight!"

They were head-locking each other. Someone told them to calm down. They didn't listen. Troy twisted and threw Corey on the mat. He fell in Corey's guard. Out of nowhere, Corey shoved Troy's head away, threw a leg over his shoulder, put him in an arm bar and made him tap.

"I can't believe he got me. I'm stronger than he is."

"Troy, you can't leave the arm in there for him."

Corey went home, speeding on the wide nighttime highway going north, listening to Aerosmith's "Big Ten-Inch Record" on WAAF. That night he couldn't sleep. He got out of bed and borrowed his mother's laptop. He looked up Brazilian jiujitsu online and sat in the dark watching videos of submissions.

The next day in school, he invited a hockey player out into the hallway to wrestle around. The jock was muscular and strong but had no idea what he was doing and Corey submitted him easily.

He went back to Bestway. "You're back," said Eddie—"Go on, get out there"—and sent him out on the mat for class. This time he had his own shorts. They didn't talk business until after training. "Did you like it?" Eddie asked. That seemed to be all Eddie wanted to hear, that someone might love what he loved and share its infinite value. There was not so much concern over money. Corey would pay tomorrow or the day after or soon. He'd have to sign a waiver. Since he was sixteen, a parent would have to sign it for him.

This was conveyed in Eddie's unique way: He talked in rapid run-on bursts in which you couldn't tell the individual words apart but could get the general sense of what he meant. Everything was vague, everything but athletic technique. In his obsession with martial arts, Eddie was so fixated on an alternate world, a quasi-mathematical system, that, combined with his relative silence, which could read as shyness, he seemed—almost—like a gamer geek. Maybe he was shy. He didn't like talking. He was from Brockton and his accent was a rural twist on the East Coast Boston sound of dropped *r*'s.

So Corey began going to BJJ class. He gave Eddie a down payment of fifty dollars, all the cash he had saved, and a permission slip signed in his mother's shaky handwriting. Within a week, he was staying late to roll with purple belts who cared more about what they called *flowing*—noncompetitively chaining techniques together, almost a form of partner meditation—than getting up for work in the morning. They would have stayed all night exchanging techniques; they all had Eddie's bug.

Corey flipped a page in his notebook and began keeping track of what he was learning, which he illustrated with human figures locked in combat. There were innumerable techniques and limitless combinations. To master a single thing, you had to embed it in muscle memory by drilling it ten thousand times—or one hundred times a day for about three years. Scoring on somebody, tapping them out, brought an addictive rush of power thanks to the dopamine reward system, a feature of brain neurology that keeps the chess player playing chess and the cocaine addict snorting cocaine—a phenomenon he had read about in physiology, though it was not a topic that Mrs. Clark assigned.

Instead of doing homework, he lay on his room floor at night and did arm bars on invisible Troys. Holding his textbook over himself like an enemy, he reread the chapters on nerves and muscles.

Around the house, his mother saw him perpetually reviewing what he was learning at the gym, twisting on the floor, as if he had a special kind of palsy. Corey announced that he was training in an art that was mathematical and infinite. He said, "When I can afford it, I'm going to go for another month."

His mother called him over and gave him her credit card.

"No, Mom. I don't think it's responsible of me under the circumstances."

"Corey, I want you to."

Finally he accepted. He told his mother, "I'm going to pay you back."

. . .

By the end of April, the trees had started blooming in the rain—
millions of yellow-green buds arrayed in three-dimensional space
throughout the armature of the dark wet branches under the gray
spring sky—and the landscape seemed to shrink, screened off by
foliage. Sunrise featured new and intensely beautiful violets and
pinks, as if the sun were shining through a piece of watermelon
candy. Early one morning, Corey went to his old job site and
found the house had been completely refurbished. He wandered
through, looking for the boss. The interior walls had been plastered and painted, the floors carpeted and tiled. The kitchen ceiling, which Corey had degreased, had been torn out and replaced,
just as Dunbar had said it would be, and was now a brand-new
plane of low-gloss white.

Around back, he found the boss meeting with a group of older
men in clean mackinaws and sweatshirts, holding coffee cups in
hands that wore wedding rings, looking at blueprints.

"Could I speak with you a second?" Blecic turned and Corey
put out his hand. "I made a mistake."

"I don't have anything for you."

"I'm just here to apologize."

The fearsome set of Blecic's strong features relaxed. He didn't
offer Corey his job back but talked with him a little, in a guiding
way, about life and work. In his youth, he said, he had served in the
army in the former Yugoslavia. Mountain training had been ardu-
ous. Wearing a pack and holding a rifle, he could do knee bends
with another soldier, similarly accoutered, on his shoulders. When
he got to the United States, he had worked at a meatpacking plant
for a year—heavy, repetitive lifting. "I lose fifty pounds. I am your
size." Then he had started his own construction company, doing
all the work himself—plumbing, electrical, even finish carpentry—
"beautiful, like antique." He'd built his own house, where he still
exercised with gymnastic equipment as in his army days.

Corey said he was proud to know him. They shook hands and
that was that.

The rain began letting up at the end of April. Corey sought
jobs on Craigslist. He cleaned a homeowner's grill; reorganized

a basement rec room, which was full of hockey sticks, beanbag chairs, sleeping bags, and toys; and disassembled Ikea furniture.

He was too preoccupied with his new obsession to visit Adrian. They talked once by phone before the end of the month, and he told Adrian excitedly that he was taking martial arts.

15

Smoker

Corey began training four, five nights a week in May, thanks to his mother's credit card. The other grapplers at Bestway were high school wrestlers, firemen, bearded jiujitsu hippies in full-sleeve tattoos who worked at the mall, computer programmers, a DEA agent with a mustache, a young sullen Marine with acne, a thick-limbed tow-truck driver and various other guys of mixed complexions, ages, sizes, body odors and temperaments. There was a woman, Cindy, a black belt who was a doctor. People's jobs and identities off the mat mattered little; the only thing that counted was their skill. A guy named Scott was very good. He wore a shirt from the Mansfield Fire Department. He'd been training several years and during Corey's painful tutelage as a beginner made a custom of putting Corey in his place. When it was time to spar, Scott didn't even look at him; he lay back with his hands behind his head as if he were at the beach and talked with friends while toying with Corey with his legs. Corey fought his legs, which fell on him like rollers in a car wash. Eventually Scott would notice him and casually flip Corey over and finish him with a one-arm guillotine.

While he was still coughing from the choke, Scott would ask if he wanted to go again, to which Corey would of course say yes, and with a sigh of boredom, Scott would gather Corey into his guard like a father pulling a baby into his lap and choke him again.

One day Corey tried to use one of the tricky moves he'd picked up online to surprise the fireman. He trapped one of Scott's large clammy feet under his arm, leaned back on his side, and heel-hooked him. A heel hook is a dangerous move that can pop some-body's knee and rip their ligaments. Scott tapped.

"Finally! Thank you, God."

Scott said, "Where do you think you're going?"

"I was gonna take a break."

"Oh no you don't. Get back here. You're not walking away now."

"What do you mean?"

"Get over here now."

Corey came back and kneeled down. They slapped hands, and the fireman scooted into Corey, hooked his feet under Corey's legs, grabbed his elbows, and butterfly-swept him. When he scrambled, Scott took his back, and the relentless process of getting choked began again, a process that consumes the whole body. Corey was gasping, fighting to feed his working heart. Scott worked his arm under Corey's chin. Then the choke came, the massive brain-killing pressure. Grimacing, his eyes rolled back to the whites, Corey tapped his partner's arm. Scott let him go, and Corey lay slumped on the mat, coughing.

"There's a time to play and a time to play."

The same thing happened in Muay Thai, which met on Tues-days, Thursdays, Fridays. The trainees were different from jits; there was a Mexican guy who tied on a headband with a red sun like a kamikaze before they rang the bell. Muay Thai is a striking art and an important component of unarmed combat perhaps best known for its roundhouse leg kicks. Corey felt he had to try it. He crept forward, hands high, bouncing his toe in blind imitation of the others, no idea what he was doing, trying to sock people in their headgear and nearly getting knocked unconscious. Eddie thought he was going too hard, so he had them switch partners so he could spar with Corey himself. With the ball of his foot he kicked Corey in the stomach. The blow knocked Corey on his behind and sent him rolling backwards head over heels like a stuntman in a movie. People thought it was hilarious. "Ong Bak!" they shouted.

Unsmiling, Eddie marched over to Corey, high-fived him and made him finish the round.

To Corey, getting beaten, getting tapped out, getting humili-
ated was a disaster. He got another old tire from outside a Midas
and hung it on the baseball backstop out in Houghs Neck and
cracked it with his fists. Guys playing catch ignored him. In his
room at home, he reviewed the mechanics of how your weight
shifts onto your lead leg, your hips and shoulders twist as you push
off the ball of your rear foot. Outside his brown room door was
his father. The mechanics are: You're slamming a door shut. The
plane of the door is your shoulders. Your arm travels forward, the
hand turning over, the fist tightening on impact, snapping, striking
the target with your first two knuckles. If it goes out at ninety miles
an hour, it comes back at a hundred miles an hour to protect your
face. The Thai fighter has eight limbs: fists, feet, elbows, knees.
Nine, if you count the head—the head-butt—the Irish kiss. He
made his artistic strokes—jab, cross, hook, uppercut, overhand—
learning to raise his heel and twist on the ball of his foot when he
threw a hook, his eyes looking in his mirror over the blurred bar
of his hand.

For Mother's Day, he gave his mom a card. No sailboat this
year. He drew his mother as a fighter with her knee on the belly
of an anonymous man and her arm cocked back to punch him in
the face.

The train to Dorchester is aboveground. It comes on a curve.
The tracks curve and away beyond them, out the back window, is
the South Shore. Then the train stops at the platform. The sun
is shining in the car. The doors open. She uses the cane to stand.
She rocks to her feet. Now she is on her feet and stepping to the
door, carrying a knit bag which has a Sanskrit word on it, the first
syllable of OM. She has fifteen seconds, she has timed it, to get
off, if no one knocks her over. People go around her, chatting, taking e-cigarettes out of their purses. She steps across the gap and
doesn't trip. The doors slam and do not catch her dress, which
is long, loose, linen; she seems not aware of how close it comes
to being caught. It touches the ground around her feet. It drags
on the cement as she goes down the steps. The T has gone away,

north, to Boston. She descends the staircase, one step at a time, using the cane, knit purse on her hip, back bent, head thrust forward on atrophying neck. At the bottom of the stairs—she hasn't fallen yet—she heads down a tunnel, graffitied, that goes beneath the tracks. On the other side, there are stairs again. She rests a minute and then starts climbing.

When she makes it to the street, she sets off through an alley—it's the only way to go—through a maze of concrete barriers and rusted cyclone fence. A littered embankment rises up from a retaining wall to a decaying fortress of brick housing projects. The other commuters have all outpaced her. She travels here alone.

There's a crazed man blocking the sidewalk on Dorchester Avenue. He's there every day saying "Hey, baby" to the office women. If Gloria wants to get around him, she has to cross the street, but the curbstone is very high; it must have been built in the horse-and-buggy days, before sewers, to keep doorways above floodwater and manure. Furthermore, two avenues cross here in an X like a pair of open shears, making a wide distance for her to cross before a car—and the light is short.

She presses on, pretends he isn't there.

Getting to work has become the hardest thing she does. Still, she does it—has been doing it since February—and, as a result, she's fallen. She's fallen numerous times since beginning to take the T. Once, she stood up early on the train to anticipate her stop, the train lurched, and she pitched over sideways. Blacks and Vietnamese ran to pick her up—minorities she'd always believed to be more enlightened, and maybe they were; they were her saints—they gave her back her cane—and she was too embattled to even thank them, for the train kept roaring on—to Savin Hill—and now she had to go back. What was she to do? Change at JFK. Two enormous flights of stairs or an elevator that stank like urine.

Heroin gives people diarrhea. She found the elevator reeking with a sludge of brown shit like pudding batter. There was shit smeared on the stainless steel buttons. Two floors: 1 and 2. She managed to push 2 with her elbow.

"I apologize for that," an MBTA guy told her. The MBTA people were great—Boston's best. She had a new appreciation.

She fell again and again—climbing into buses; in the street

across from Planet Fitness; beneath the Cambodian signs. Her dropping toe, which she tried to raise, caught the ground when her thigh got tired. Shin and thigh grew quickly weary. *Anterior tibialis*. Her arm was too weak to hold her on the cane. She'd begin to twist and lean. She'd scream when she saw the fall coming. She couldn't help it. People looked. She'd pitched over and smashed down on the cement. Her Greek hat fell off, her woven purse spilled open, her keys and lipstick, which she never used anymore, rolled out. The cell phone popped open and the battery fell out.

She couldn't stand up without help. Recently, she had fallen on Dorchester Avenue when a pair of women were walking by. Speaking coolly and with composure from the ground, Gloria had told them she needed help to stand. One woman, in sunglasses, had had a cigarette hanging off her lip. She'd said "Here" in a gravel voice and handed her purse to her friend and tried to help Gloria stand with one hand while holding her cigarette with the other. They'd staggered.

"I can't hold you, honey. Ya gotta use your legs."

"I can't. That's why I need your help."

The woman, who was a drunk, let her fall again. Gloria fell backwards while looking up, like someone falling backwards into the gray ocean with her eyes never leaving the faces of the people in the lifeboat.

"I can't help her," the drunk said to her friend.

Men in newsboy hats hung out at 7-Eleven, drinking coffee and reading the paper. A man put down his paper, ran and helped her up. Gloria told him she needed her purse. He went around the sidewalk picking up her things—lipstick, wallet, keys, a Tibetan elephant charm. The two women had hurried away.

Gloria said, "I can't find my cell phone."

"It's not here. Are you sure you had it?"

"Yes. I know what I had. I've been robbed. Those two women took it. Can you get it back from them?"

"Aren't those your friends?"

"They're not my friends. They're a couple of thieves. Can you call the police?"

"Are you sure?"

"Yes, goddamnit, I'm sure."

She'd lost her phone, money, the last shred of her dignity when she collapsed in front of strangers or—worse—the people at her job. Her most agonizing spill was the one she took on the ramp outside her job and had to let her colleagues help her up.

What was wrong with her? they asked. She had always been aloof, reading art books, taking her lunches apart, skipping the office parties and balloons. Now she was getting her comeuppance. They wanted gossip.

"I'm infirm," she said.

She took to wearing sunglasses to conceal her face in public. When she fell, the glasses flew off as well—another twenty-dollar pair of glasses broken, another trip to Walgreens in her future to look at the sunglasses rack and see her face in the mirror, the butterfly suture on her forehead. She knocked a tooth out in the front of her mouth. It broke her down. "I can't go out like this!" she wept.

Insurance sent her three different bills for the dentist, who had seemed so nice, but it must have been a lie—three steadily increasing amounts. She dried her eyes and read the statements with her bifocals on her as-yet-unbroken nose.

"This isn't right," she said, and prepared to call the insurance company. She used a hands-free device with her new cell phone, a headset with a boom mike, like a telemarketer. It took her several tries to put the jack in with her hands.

Today, she had gotten to work without falling. Now she was seated at her desk in her cubicle, the cane by her side. At the end of the day, she would face the journey home.

At Gloria's clinic day, the neurologist noted she had been diagnosed roughly a year ago. He assessed the state of her body. He tested her ability to generate force with her hands, lift her arms, raise her knees. The flesh was disappearing from her shoulders; a hollow was developing behind her arms at the site of the *teres major*. When he asked her to stand up straight, she had difficulty. Her back was humped. When she raised one foot, she lost her balance. He held her. She pressed down on his hand. Her hand couldn't grip him; she was pressing him with the bones of her wrist.

The physical therapist fitted her with orthotic braces at wrist and ankle—shiny plastic gauntlets that secured with Velcro fasteners. They kept Gloria's toes from dropping. The most significant piece of equipment she got was a walker. She was graduating from a cane.

The therapist showed her how to use it: set it in front of her, take a step with one foot, then the other, then move the walker out again.

The therapist had a practical, no-feeling-sorry-for-yourself way about her that discouraged Gloria from opening up. Gloria kept everything bottled inside until she saw Dawn Gillespie. In Dawn's office, at the first question from her, "How have you been?", Gloria broke down crying. Her temples flushed, the vein in her forehead stood out, her eyes squeezed shut, mucus ran from the point of her thin nose, and she sobbed: "I think I need to talk to somebody." In a few minutes, however, she had pulled herself together.

Nevertheless, Dawn scheduled an assessment of Gloria at her home to see what her "support structure" was like. Shortly, the social worker arrived in Quincy with her clipboard.

Gloria invited her to sit. She told Dawn that her hands were so weak that she was having trouble manipulating a mouse at her job even with orthotics. She was having trouble bathing and performing tasks related to hygiene.

"Toileting?"

"No. Not that, but—I didn't want to say it—tampons."

"I always say, there's no room for shyness," and Dawn explained the basic human fact that we all have body functions. "Is this something we can outsource to an intimate partner?" She looked around as if someone else might be in the house whom she hadn't seen yet.

"Corey's father lives with us," said Gloria.

"He couldn't make it today," said Corey. The social worker looked at him. Corey's mother explained that he was very angry with his father.

"I'm not angry at anyone. I'm just worried about my mom."

"You sound angry," the social worker said. She added that being angry was perfectly okay.

· · ·

Gloria began to take The Ride to work—a free service provided by the MBTA for the disabled. In the morning, a car would stop outside their house and honk. The driver was a grizzled guy with a heavy New England accent. He watched Gloria coming down her steps, Corey walking backwards in front of her, ready to catch her if she tripped.

"Here she comes. Take it slow and easy."

Gloria did not respond.

When she reached his car, the driver made a move to help, but Corey insisted on buckling his mother's seatbelt. "I usually do that. Never mind. Whatever you're more comfortable with." The driver took the walker after Corey had folded it and put it in the trunk, then jumped behind the wheel and sped away with Gloria as if she had put him behind schedule.

The school year ended. Corey sat through his finals.

Surrounded by her peers, who were trading hugs on senior graduation day, Molly ignored him. That is, she tried, but he forced his way into her circle to wish her well at college.

She wished him luck in turn. The implied meaning before their onlookers seemed to be that he was the one who would be needing luck to mend his many faults. Her friends smiled and waited for him to leave.

Corey backed away, went home in the sun, missing the ceremony. He had failed his finals and wondered what would happen.

He got a landscaping job working for an Italian, a short stocky older fellow in a straw hat.

With school out of the way, he planned to devote himself to a pure life of martial arts, paid for by mowing lawns and planting flowers.

June. Corey and his mother hadn't seen Leonard in several days. Now, in the hot weather, they lived in suspense about when he would appear. He'd be gone for days, then, in the middle of the night, Corey would wake up and know that someone else was in the house, and in the morning, he'd see Leonard lying asleep on the futon—a cheese-white shoulder stippled with purple zit scars thrusting up from the blankets; a pile of iron-gray hair. Leonard's hair looked as full as a judge's wig when crowned by the fedora. Without the hat, there was a mangy hole in it as if it had been sprayed with weed killer. The white pate glowed like a shard of bone in the nest of steel-wool hair. His morbidly alabaster calves lay heavily on the mattress opposite the head—they were hairless on the backs and gleamed. The man's hips were wreathed in sheets like a Roman. The rest of his person—his clothes and accessories— lay around like a disassembled body. His black trousers stretched across the coffee table like a tongue. The fedora rested on a bag, creating the impression of a droid which remained awake while Leonard slept and which could zip around the floor fetching math books at his master's whim. The aviator glasses were substitute eyes filming Corey as he reacted to the sight of his father's body, a film that Leonard would watch when he was awake.

Other times, upon opening his door in the morning, Corey's eye would follow the spill of dancing shadows and golden-blue lights that shone in through the blinds across the coffee table to the futon—and there'd be no one there. But he would see the evidence that Leonard had come and gone: His things had been moved; the bed was open; the sheets cast off; the blankets were awry.

His father left his long curling hairs and the smell of his body on the mattress. Corey's first action of the day was to close the futon so his mother could use it as a couch. He hated touching the fabric that had touched his father's nakedness. He smelled the man in the cotton. He rolled the sheets and blankets in a wad and set them in a mound on Leonard's pile of bags.

Occasionally, Leonard left his cop bag behind in the house. Corey thought of looking in it but never did. He shoved it behind the furniture with his foot and went to wash his hands.

Now, in his second month of training, Corey began to realize that his daily defeats at the gym, where he went fresh from landscaping every afternoon with grass stains on his knees, were part of a long slow enlightenment. The experienced guys watched him getting beaten and told him, "You see how you're getting swept? Don't let him control you. The first thing you have to do is win the grip fight"—and he listened. In mid-June, he rolled again with Scott and actually passed his guard. There were extenuating factors— Scott was tired—and Corey's success was short-lived—a minute later Scott nearly crushed his neck with a Peruvian necktie—but the fact remained that Corey had learned something since he'd started. Later in the month, he competed in a submission grappling tournament at Waltham High in the beginner's lightweight division, and won his first match. Other teams sat in the bleacher seats, black guys with their hair dyed blond, drinking Pedialyte after their weigh-ins, jiujitsu girlfriends stripping down to pink Bad Boy shorts and competing too, everyone getting almost naked— the ripped abs, the mixture of celebration and fear.

Everyone filmed the matches on their cell phones.

At the end of June, Bestway held a smoker—a gym fight. A bunch of guys showed up from a nearby school, South Shore Sport Fighting. Moms and wives sat in folding chairs while the competitors warmed up, hitting focus mitts and skipping rope. The sun fell inside the warehouse door. A pair of whirring shop fans blew air across the seats. Eddie had a microphone. "I don't really like talking on this thing," he said. "Anyways, thanks for coming. Our first fight is gonna be . . ."

Corey had bought a mouthpiece for this occasion. He put it in. Both he and his opponent wore visored headgear and shin pads. At the bell, his opponent rushed across the cage and punched him in the face. The punches landed short of Corey's face and Corey didn't move, but the headgear flew off and, Eddie, who was refereeing, ran and fetched it and strapped it back on Corey's head. "Fight!" he shouted, and they resumed. His opponent began walking him down, nailing him with solid, whacking Thai kicks, which came too fast to block, while Corey stuck out his jab and retreated. In a clinch, he got thrown off balance. The pads kept him from getting knocked out. It felt out of control, like being in a car accident but not being hurt.

When the fight was over, his opponent took off his headgear, revealing a sweating head, brown eyes, and a heavy dark brown mustache like a forty-niner panning for gold in Jack London's Yukon Territory.

"You got a lotta balls stepping in with me," he said.

· · ·

The day after the smoker, Corey met Adrian on the Esplanade. When he arrived, he found Adrian waiting at a point directly across the river from MIT. He was impossible to miss: He was wearing a shirt with the sleeves ripped off, heavy black-framed glasses, an all-black baseball cap, tiny shorts, and high-top black combat boots.

Stalled in the middle of the sidewalk and staring into space, he was forcing joggers in spandex bras and clinging tights to run around him.

Corey waved a hand in front of his face. "The cosine of the coefficient of the integral of the square root of the—what's up, buddy?"

Adrian came out of his trance. "I was just thinking of the most beautiful theorem!"

He led Corey along the riverbank. Sailboats were bounding in slow motion over the water. A gentle silence held sway, as if, in this part of Boston, the outdoors was just another wing of the library. College girls sunbathed on the grass.

Adrian said his summer was going well. He was in physics camp at MIT. It was such a great school! He couldn't wait to go there in the fall! He wouldn't have to live under his mother's roof anymore! It was so satisfying seeing his plans work out. He was learning such interesting things! He'd even begun finding ways to enjoy himself. Since he wasn't working, he used his free time to study here on the riverbank. The views were so exciting! It was a perfect place for physics!

"Yep, I can see that," Corey said.

"Yes, it's the perfect place for beautiful ideas."

"Might be hard to concentrate."

They went past the sunbathing women into a natural arcade of interlacing trees which formed a tunnel over the path. Adrian discoursed on the topic of his current studies: relativistic momentum and the fact that the sun is losing mass. With each step, the giant, dense muscles of his legs jumped and flexed as if they were being galvanized with electric shocks. His shorts were so short that you could see the hair growing out of his crotch and spreading down his thighs. Corey avoided the sight of him. He noticed a thin lone man looking at them through the trees.

"Let's go back the other way. My meter's going to run out."

On the way back, Adrian asked what was on his mind. Corey said he had just fought at his gym.

"That's right, you said you were taking martial arts."

"That's right, I am. I told you that a while ago."

"I didn't know how seriously to take that."

"Maybe you ought to take it seriously."

Adrian asked if he had won or lost.

"I lost, but it was a decision. Nobody knocked me out."

"That's good. Even for a crazy person like you who doesn't care if he gets knocked out."

"I'm not crazy, Adrian."

"I'm not crazy! Go ahead and knock me out!"

"I did all right. I stung the guy a couple times."

"Who was the guy?"

"A Thai boxer."

"A Thai boxer. Was he crazy too?"

"Not sure. Couldn't tell you. It was a good day for me. I even stopped thinking about him." He jerked his head at MIT across the river.

"You mean your father?"

"Yep."

"Hmm." Adrian pressed his lip. "I know in the past I've looked at this differently from you, probably because of my mother—well, definitely because of her! But there are two sides to everything. It might help you get it off your chest to talk about what's been going on with your father—if not with me, then with a therapist or a counselor. It could be really good for you. I could tell you how to get a therapist for free—or almost free. You'd be surprised at the insights you can get! Or if you want to, you can talk to me. It'll give me a chance to try to put my mother out of my mind. I can put forth challenging ideas and maybe you can practice being open-minded. It could be really fruitful. Maybe I'll learn something that will spark new ideas with me too. It could be good for both of us."

"I'll tell you: That sonofabitch hasn't been home in weeks. Not in daytime."

"But I thought you didn't like him—"

"Of course I don't like him, but he's supposed to help my

mother. He's just using our house as a hotel. Let me tell you what I'd like to do to his face."

"Go on," said Adrian. "That's very interesting."

They returned to where they had started. Corey said he had to leave; he couldn't afford to get a ticket. Adrian said that was fine; he had a problem set to do. "It was pleasant to take a walk. It was pleasant to look at the babes. That made me feel good. Let's see: It'll be satisfying to think about the interesting ideas in my problem set. I'm learning interesting things. My workouts have been going well. Everything is going well; I'll be very satisfied to stay here and think about the equations for relativistic momentum." Adrian stretched and sighed, bringing his hands to his ears and flexing both his biceps, showing his abundant armpit hair, while smiling down at the sunbathers lying on the grass in their bikinis.

The sigh, the stretch, the secret smile—Adrian seemed to be acting out a show of contentment and satisfaction.

Corey noticed an oiled man watching them.

"Dude, that guy's looking at you."

"How do you know?"

"Because he's looking right at you. It's gotta be your shorts. Why are you wearing Daisy Dukes?"

"I really fill out a pair of shorts, don't I?"

"I have no idea."

"Not just in front; in behind too. I've got big glutes."

"I'd fill out my shorts too if I wore a cup everywhere."

"I'd fill them out without it."

"Guys are looking at you."

"I'm doing exactly what babes do to get attention. It works for them; why shouldn't it work for me?"

"It might not be the same."

"Why shouldn't it be?"

"All right, I'm going."

Corey hiked up the grassy slope to the hatchback, which was parked one block over on an avenue of brownstones, and headed back to Quincy in gathering afternoon traffic—workingmen were getting off work. He looped around the river on Storrow Drive, past the place where he had just been, into the tunnel beneath the city, then out into the sunlight. Shopping plaza. The dilapidated homes of Dorchester. A beach-white causeway. Now a glimpse of blue water.

In the stop-and-go traffic, he was surrounded by trucks filled with disassembled scaffolding, rope rigging, ladders, power tools, groups of guys with hats on backwards, joking, riding shoulder to shoulder. A sense of having soiled himself with Adrian grew in him as he traveled home.

Now that he was alone, Adrian walked around until he found a place to sit and study physics, facing a pair of females, who were sunning on the grass.

Occasionally, as he studied, a girl turned over, presenting a different portion of her body to the sun. Adrian adjusted himself beneath his textbook, which was resting on his knees. Sailboats continued tacking back and forth soundlessly on the water. An hour passed. A female wearing a baseball hat stood up, bent down, picked up her shorts, and wriggled into them, getting them above her hips. Toting her shoulder bag, she walked his way, looking at her phone, sport sandals slapping the path, bracelets jingling.

As she passed him, Adrian said something to make her look. He had removed his penis from his shorts. When she turned, he spread his knees and made sure she saw it. She was wearing sunglasses. She kept walking without changing her expression.

Her friends were waiting some distance away.

"Where?"

"Under the tree." She pointed. Her friends looked at Adrian, who pretended to study. They turned away as a group and went off wherever they were going. There was some laughter. Adrian watched to see what they would do, but they did nothing.

When they were gone, Adrian shut his book. He yawned again and stretched.

He crossed the bridge to MIT and set out across the athletic field, in his tight shorts and combat boots. The field smelled like cut grass.

On the other side, there was a space-age building with hexagonal windows. The lobby was air-conditioned. It had soaring walls of high-gloss white and geometric designs—simple Euclidean shapes—triangles, circles—in primary colors. Daylight coming from the windows created a greenhouse effect. A security guard walked out from behind a steel staircase and it was Leonard.

Adrian followed him downstairs.

"The best thing happened today!" he said when they were in the basement. "But before I tell you, you're going to want to know: I saw your son. We had a nice long conversation. I got him to talk about you. He told me . . . " and Adrian began painting Corey's admissions to him in vivid terms. "He sees you as this giant monster, which he's powerless to defeat, so he has to kill it. He has homicidal feelings towards you."

"He said he's going to kill me?"

"Not verbatim. But the homicidal ideation is clear. I know that from my own feelings of rage."

Then Adrian told Leonard his good news.

"I was studying on the Esplanade and there was this chick sunbathing on the grass, showing off her body, using all her sexual power to dominate me. She was showing me everything I wanted and I couldn't have. Well, I gave her a show of my own. I took my penis out of my shorts and when she walked by, I made her look at something she couldn't have!"

"Did she do anything?"

"That's the thing: She didn't do anything! She didn't say a word."

"Are you sure she saw you?"

"Oh yeah. I could tell from her face. She couldn't miss it—trust me."

"She might not have seen anything, if she wasn't looking."

"No, I know she did. She had these friends and they all started laughing about it together."

"They were laughing?"

"Yeah, it was great."

"You're lucky nothing happened."

"No. She was happy. She was laughing about it with them. I bet it made her feel important. She's probably going to get herself off tonight thinking about me. It completely proves my theory that women are just as aroused by seeing a dick as I am by seeing a pussy."

Leonard said, "Sometimes people laugh when they're afraid."

16

Cherry Pit

Late that night, Corey was awakened by the sound of tires stopping on the road outside his house. An engine died. Then the front door opened. A switch snapped and a line of light appeared under Corey's bedroom door.

He got up, put on his grappling shorts and went out to the living room. The living room was empty. Leonard's black zippered cop bag was lying on the floor. Corey went to the kitchen and looked around the corner. His father was standing under the fluorescent light, facing out the window. He was wearing a nylon jacket that said POLICE on the back and he was staring at the marsh.

"Dropping by?"

Leonard didn't answer.

Corey went back to the living room and, after a moment's thought, began to move the furniture. He moved the coffee table, then began opening the futon, controlling the mattress so it wouldn't flop and slam the frame into the wall and wake his mother, who was sleeping in the other room.

"Bed's all set up for you," he said. There was no answer from the kitchen.

He waited. He was so awake, he thought he could hear his mother's respiration through the bedroom door. Total silence came from the kitchen.

He went to the kitchen and looked inside. Leonard had turned around and was looking at him with a blank expression on his face.

"What's going on?" Corey asked.

"I know everything about you."

Corey went to his room and closed the door but did not go to sleep.

He determined to respond. When Leonard next dropped in, this time at an earlier hour when it was still light out and Gloria was awake and eating dinner, Corey walked up to him and declared that Muay Thai can beat boxing and jits can beat wrestling. He looked his father dead-on, then slid his eyes up and over Leonard's head to indicate there were bigger things than him. He addressed the air, the pocket of emptiness above the man's shoulder.

"If you're a cop, how come you smoke weed?" he demanded.

"I don't smoke weed."

"The fuck you don't." And: "If you're a cop, where's your gun? I never see you with a gun. You sure you have one?"

But Leonard had his own way of punishing Corey. He began making Gloria cry.

"If you make my mother cry," Corey said, "we're going to have a problem."

"Oh really?" Leonard said. "What kind of problem are we going to have?"

Gloria begged the two of them not to fight. "I can't take it!" she screamed.

The Fourth of July is a good time out on Houghs Neck, a time of families, barbecues and beer, and fireworks popping up in the ocean sky above the woods, celebrating the American war against the British. The Goltzes passed the holiday in their small house, isolated from these celebrations but aware of them.

A week into July, Corey heard Leonard in his mother's bedroom speaking to her in a way he didn't like. Corey knocked on their door and went in. He saw his mother standing in the bathroom in just a T-shirt, balanced on her walker. Leonard was sitting on the toilet seat behind her holding a tampon applicator.

"I need help," she was crying. There was blood running down her leg.

"What's wrong, Mom?"

"He's hurting me!"

"I'm telling you to lie down so I can do it, Gloria," Leonard said.

"Leave me alone!"

"I'm telling you for the last time, Gloria. I'm warning you."

"Leonard!" Corey screamed. "Get the fuck away from her!"

"Let me tell you something, Corey. If you lay a hand on me, you're going to go straight to jail for assaulting a police officer. And then nobody will be here to take care of your mother."

Corey rushed over and grabbed Leonard's wrists.

"I'm not assaulting you. But you're not touching her."

They struggled. Leonard broke free and shoved him. Corey lost his balance and fell into his mother. He knocked her over and barely managed to catch her before she fell. He was left holding her, half sliding down the wall, the walker tangled in his legs.

He slid all the way down to the floor. With his mother lying on him, he turned himself sideways so he could get on one knee, stand up and pick her up under the arms. They stood there a minute, his arms around his mother's waist, her T-shirt riding up, Corey holding her and gathering his strength. One of his feet was through the walker still, and the walker was trapped in the doorway. It would be easy to trip. A shelf had collapsed. The tile floor was a mess of combs and spilled green shampoo. The only light was coming from the bedroom. He reached out and snapped on the bathroom light and stepped carefully out of the walker. He felt his mother getting her feet under her. He relaxed his hold on her waist and pulled her shirt down. Leonard had disappeared. With one part of his mind, Corey listened for him in the house.

"Are you hurt?"

"No."

"I'm going to get your walker."

While continuing to hold his mother, he bent down and picked it up. Unjamming it from the doorway was a bit of a puzzle. He had to breathe and calm himself to do it. He righted the walker and his mother put her hands on it. They began walking out of the bathroom, one foot at a time. She led the way to her bed.

"Get a towel."

He ran back to the bathroom, got a towel and put it on the bed for her and she sat down on it.

"Do you need a doctor?"

"I don't know," she said. "I don't think so."

"Should I check you? I don't want to, but should I?"

"If you think you can."

He went to the bathroom, got a wad of toilet paper, wet it at the sink, and blotted her, and showed it to her.

"Are you okay?"

"I think so."

She told him to get her a pad. He found her sanitary supplies in a white wire basket by her bedside. He peeled the backing off a Lightdays pad, pressed it down on the old stained cotton liner of a pair of her underwear, and fitted her feet through the leg holes one at a time and pulled them on her, and put her back in the bed.

He brought her her laptop, but she had trouble touching the mouse.

"Did you get hurt when you fell?"

She had. She had hurt her wrist.

He began cleaning the bathroom, picking up combs and toothbrushes. The shampoo sudsed up when he tried to wipe it up. He got in the tub barefoot to rinse a towel, twisting it over and over again. He took the broken shelf out of the room and leaned it against the wall. He found the tampon applicator under her sink and threw it out.

He opened her bedroom door and looked around. The house was empty. He went outside and looked up and down the street, but saw no one.

"Do you think I should call the cops?" he asked his mother.

"No."

He went to sleep on her futon, but all night long he kept smelling Leonard in the cushion and waking up, feeling himself in mortal combat with the man. At two in the morning, he woke again.

He'd had a nightmare. The dream was so real that Corey got up and crept to his mother's room and made sure she was breathing. Her room was warm. The sound of her snoring came from her bed. He went out to the living room again. A tiny bit of light here. Enough to perceive the room as a black-and-gray painting. Shapes and masses, shadows and squares. A window with a night sky behind it. He checked that the door was locked. He spread the blinds and checked the road.

Leonard stayed away for nearly two weeks after this conflict. The second night he was gone, Corey took the train to MIT and began walking around looking for him, circling the edges of the campus as the sun went down. He hiked alone through the soviet-sized emptiness of Kendall Square, dwarfed by the huge geometric research centers, which reflected the gold sky in the west. He passed the open bay of a loading dock and heard the whistling of a magnetron. The sun slipped under the horizon. He walked for hours—in and out of East Cambridge, to the Galleria and back—back to the train tracks that cross Mass Ave and the giant redbrick warehouse that looks like a castle. He saw a herd of MIT students leaving the Infinite Hallway and dispersing like shotgun pellets across the avenue and into the trees beneath the amber safety lights.

He walked for hours in a fog. He passed a group of young people standing outside a bar, smoking cigarettes. By now it was nearly midnight. The T would be closing. The drinkers were getting on their phones calling Ubers. Corey was wearing baggy jeans and a black hoodie. He had an urge to say something impolite to them. He saw an MIT police cruiser and thought, What if he really is a cop? What if I did something out here and he arrested me?

He took a side alley through black trees and dumpsters to the Central Square T station. From a long way away, he saw a man coming towards him. They were the only two people on the street, but instead of making room for him, the man was walking an undeviating path straight at him. Corey spread his arms. The man made the same gesture back at Corey, as if this was a game. There was a weave in his step. He had been drinking. He was a big, well-built guy in his twenties. He walked straight at Corey with his arms out and stared down at him from an inch away. He had black curly hair and he looked amused.

Corey punched him in the jaw with an uppercut, and the man collapsed on the sidewalk.

The man lay on the sidewalk without moving. Corey was afraid to leave. Sixty seconds went by. Ninety seconds. Two minutes went by. Finally, the man's head came up and he let out a groan. Corey fled down the block to the T. On the train he wondered if the man was paralyzed. He had lifted his head as if it was the only thing he could move and he had wanted to see his feet. It would be months before Corey again set foot in Cambridge.

Alone with his mother, Corey demanded: "Is he a cop or not?"

"No, he's not."

"I knew it. Why didn't you tell me sooner?"

"I didn't want to run him down to you."

"Why the hell not?"

"It's not good for you to hate him."

"Why the hell not? Do you know how strange that is, that he lies?"

She didn't answer. He shook his head. "The physics professor. I can't believe I fell for that . . . That bum. He's a rent-a-cop."

"Afraid so."

"He's got problems."

"Well, maybe he does."

"I'd like to go see him at his job. I'd like to join the police force and go see him in my dress blues. I could be a cop, if I wanted."

"Sure you could—you could be anything, Corey—but why would you want to do that?"

"To stick it in his loser face."

"Oh, come off it. It's no skin off your back."

"What are you defending him for?"

"So he's a security guard. He's the one who's got to live with being a loser."

Corey looked at his mother's thin-nosed, delicately aquiline German face. He was going to ask Gloria why she had gotten mixed up with his father.

"That bastard's more than a loser. He's rotten and screwed up."

"You think I don't know that!" she cried.

Since Leonard had been gone, it had been unseasonably, autumnally cool for several days, but now there was a resurgence of the summer heat. Now the noon sun was glaring down on the old red car, turning it into a hot box outside their door. The shadow of the car fell directly on the salt-white asphalt. The shadow shrinking under the metal chassis, growing inside the house—the shadow of the blinds on the dusty wooden floor—the bars of sun, which began as planes of gold in the morning when they shone in from the ocean, having withdrawn across the splintered decking and vanished beneath the sills, the entire house steeping in glowing gray shadow, trapped heat, the green marsh soughing and rustling—the silence from his mother's bedroom where she had been taking a nap.

Corey went in to ask her if he could get her anything and found her awake.

"No," she said.

There was an intricate tapestry of the Tibetan universe on the wall. The figures of peasants, monks and deities were rendered in black outline on a tomato-red earth, the boundaries of which were ornamented with designs that could have been breaking ocean waves, blooming flowers or billowing smoke and fire. The tapestry hung above his mother's dresser. It was littered with the jewelry she used to wear to represent her allegiance to Asia and Africa and South America. She had put her pipe away; she owned a phallic glass pipe for smoking marijuana, and it was out of sight now, in her drawer, a forgotten embarrassment, one of the many things she'd rather not remember. Her books on art and health lay in a corner. Her closet was open and some clothes lay on the floor. Her hippie dresses, thrift-shop dresses hung flat and drab from the hangers. She lay on the bed on her side, facing out the window with her back to Corey. One couldn't see out the blinds, but the sun slanted in and one could hear the leaves in the marsh and the birdcalls and feel the air coming in. Her small round head, like her son's but smaller, lay on the mattress. She was in her clothes, a long, body-hiding dress that she could put on without asking for help. Her feet were tucked up and hidden. The walker stood next to her bed on its own lightweight aluminum legs with rubber feet.

Corey went back to his room in the depressive summer heat.

That same afternoon, he asked Eddie's permission to train with the fight team.

"Fighting's a forty-hour-a-week commitment."

"I understand."

"You're gonna have to get here five, six days a week."

"I will."

"Okay. Go get changed."

To pay for the extra gym time, Corey cleaned the bathrooms and mopped the mats after training. He picked up the kickboxing gear and put it away on the shelves at the end of the night. When he was alone in the gym, he lifted kettlebells and climbed the hawser rope that hung from the ceiling.

Leonard was gone, but he'd be back.

School resumed. Corey was a senior now. He had been passed into the next grade despite his bad performance in the spring. At the first assembly, the gym was filled with excited kids, many of them suntanned like himself. Gregorio gave a speech from the center of the basketball court that was impossible to hear over their rowdiness. Eventually, the principal told them they could go. Corey moved out with the crowd. In class, he sat neither at the front nor at the back but by the window, gazing out at the sun on the clean concrete sidewalk. In the cafeteria, he tried sitting with people he had known, but an alien nature had crept into them over the summer. It had used to feel as if he had enemies; now everyone was simply a stranger. Molly was gone. He wondered why he was here at all, other than the fact his mother wanted him in school. He waited for the day to end. When it ended, he hurried outside and drove to the academy.

As the term got underway, he did no homework. On weekends, he did the Craigslist hustle: painted fences, raked lawns, moved boxes from basements to attics, making twenty or thirty bucks a job. Gas was up to four dollars a gallon due to refinery shutdowns. To get cheaper lunches, he went online to student@quincy.com and applied for reduced-cost meals, which allowed him to pay $0.75 for school breakfast and $1.50 for school lunch.

One good thing happened. The first week of school, at another assembly—on college admissions—Corey was sitting near a girl in the bleachers. She turned around and looked at him. He spoke—he said something to her—he wasn't sure what—and she replied in a strangely natural way as if they were longtime acquaintances. He asked to see her after the assembly. She said yes. His heart was beating out of his chest. They met and went down the stairs behind the door which let out to Faxon Field. He didn't know what was going to happen—but he knew. When they were alone, he reached out to her. She reacted as if she had been waiting for him and they kissed.

He felt drunk afterwards. He walked her back to class with his arm around her waist. If her body had been water, he would have been drinking her dry. She disengaged and said goodbye. He spent the day in a desperate, drunken state of mind, thrilled and agonized, knowing he'd met the girl of his dreams.

For several days he pursued her. He found it harder and harder to get her alone. She relented and went with him twice more. But each time she was less willing than the first time and acted more distant afterwards when she was straightening her clothes. He was pouring out how beautiful he thought she was and all kinds of personal details, telling her about his mom, how bad it was—and how happy she, this girl, made him. She didn't say, "Darling, I feel the same." Rather she changed the subject to—he couldn't tell what—superficial things. She talked by making noises he couldn't quite understand. She wasn't saying "I love you." It took him a little while of her ignoring him, shrinking away as if he were uncool, pointedly showing attention to other guys, and denying his requests to go back down behind Faxon Field for him to figure out she wasn't interested in going on with him.

"That hurt," he said. The incident slapped him—it got through his guard like a punch in sparring.

But it was a wonderful moment, that first stunning moment when she had taken her shirt off and there were her breasts.

For a long while afterwards, at night, lying in bed, sore from training and thinking about fighting, he tried to deduce what he had done wrong with her, and sometimes he fantasized he would not only win a fight, but in so doing, would win her back as well, and then she would confess her love, telling him she had only been testing him and she had loved him and wanted him all along.

By now, Leonard had reappeared in Quincy. Corey had heard him come in in the middle of the night. He had fried a steak at three in the morning, filling the kitchen with smoke. In the morning, Corey had seen his greasy plates and pans in the sink, the bloody stinking wrapper the steak had come in in the trash like a maxi pad. The linoleum floor was grease-slippery. Leonard wasn't anywhere to be found. But a few days later he had showed up again. Throughout the fall, he continued dropping by their home in the same random way that he had been doing right along.

After Leonard's return, Corey had a dream: The kitchen floor was covered with late-summer cherries, thousands of glossy black cherries covering the linoleum in an edible layer, and Corey was trying to scoop them up because he needed the nutrition. When he finished gathering them, however, there were only a few cherries left out of the thousands there had been. Almost all of them had been reduced to handfuls of dead stems and slimy red pits by someone who had gotten to them first.

17

Protein Polymer

In September, MIT held a fair for new freshmen. There were white tents on the grass. Young people followed their phones around like divining rods, which led them to their friends, whom they embraced. A sign asked, "Do You Want to Live in a Carbon-Free World?"

Adrian arrived in his black leather jacket. He stood stock-still in the center of the lawn.

After getting his possessions from his mother's minivan, he went to his dorm, which was at the corner of the quad. A line of sycamores marched past it, creating a stony shade, like a quarry in the woods. Access was controlled by card key. Adrian did not let his mother follow him inside.

He went upstairs, carrying the Everlast bag on his shoulder. He lived in a coed pod, a set of rooms that shared a kitchen and a shower. He entered his room. There were two sets of furniture, two beds. His roommate hadn't yet arrived. Through the walls came the sound of furniture moving, students moving in. He chose a bed and dropped the punching bag on the bare mattress. Female voices murmured throughout the building. He closed his door.

Adrian's roommate arrived, struggling with enormous duffel bags full of clothes, and discovered Adrian sitting shirtless at his desk, doing physics problems. "Aren't you going to get enough of that? Classes haven't even started yet!" He introduced himself to Adrian and started unpacking clothes, computers, sports equipment. To beautify the room, he tacked up posters and set out plants—a peace lily to purify the air.

The posters were M.C. Escher prints, elaborate pencil drawings that played on optical illusions. One showed a Möbius strip stairway that somehow climbed underneath itself.

The term began. Adrian sat in physics class, up in the stadium seats, at a high angle, up by the audiovisual equipment that was recording the lecture. From where he sat, one could see a downward-sloping field of heads, and, at the bottom, the instructor, a graduate student, who was wired with a microphone. She was describing how gravity warps space-time and makes light rays bend. She had glasses that magnified her eyes. The blackboards behind her spanned the width of the room. She drew planets and erased them, leaving a messy cloud of chalk on the slate surface. Her voice was nervous—the first week of class. She left imprints in the clouds with her sweating hands.

When the lecture was over, the class stood up, shouldering backpacks fitted with water bottles, carabiners clipped to key rings, as if they were going camping.

Adrian walked across the campus in his thin-soled wrestling shoes, his large head down, the gravity book under his leather arm, to the athletic center. A pixyish brunette scanned his student ID. She wore pancake makeup, had a Massachusetts accent. She offered him fresh white towels.

"Oh, no," he said. "I'd just make them feculent."

"Have a great workout!" she told him.

Wearing the same clothes he wore to class—leather jacket, sweatpants, knee pads, groin protection, wrestling shoes—and still carrying his textbook, he entered the quiet, clean, modern fitness room—kettlebells, battle ropes, big soft yoga balls in candy colors—found a chin-up bar and began to chin himself in a state of frenzy, wrenching his body up and down with such force he could have ripped it out of the wall—as if he were being electrocuted—as if a carnivorous animal were tearing at his legs.

At mealtimes, he sat alone in the cafeteria in his leather jacket, filling himself with food, eating piles of chicken, flicking the skin away with his fork, making a hill of bones and skin in the gutter of his tray. Late at night, he hung his heavy bag in the girls' volleyball court and hit it with devastating punches.

In the day, as the fall progressed, he moved steadily around campus, from classroom to lab, in the tight-fitting motorcycle jacket and thin-soled wrestling shoes—always dressed the same, regardless of the temperature.

He had no friends, but he was noticed. From a distance, class-mates saw him climbing the steps of the neoclassical building, three at a time, as an exercise for his knees and legs, and disappearing down the Infinite Hallway.

Midway through the fall semester, a pair of Adrian's pod-mates met in the common area to discuss him.

"He nailed *what* to his wall?" exclaimed the boy.

"A burger," said the girl, who was standing by the refrigerator with her arms crossed. She wore a plaid shirt. With her wire-rimmed reading glasses, she looked like a preacher at a West Virginia mining camp. The boy she was addressing had slender, almost translucent fingers and sculptural hands, and a tuft of hair on his head like a paddock for grazing horses.

"That's so weird," he said.

"Ajay wants me to go to the dean about him. Apparently, he's done other bizarre stuff."

"He's not in there now, is he? Listening to us?"

"Oh my God, that'd be freaky." She knocked on Adrian's door. "Is anyone home? Hello? Nobody's answering. He can't be there."

"Unless he's in there pretending to be asleep."

"Don't say that!"

The pod door opened with a click and they started.

"It's Ajay," Robin said. "Hey, Ajay, come here for a minute. Tell us what's been going on with your roommate."

Ajay was a six-foot-tall youth—boyish, soft-skinned, serious. He carried his book bag on one shoulder. The weight of his bag was pulling open his MIT warm-up jacket, popping the buttons open, giving him the half-dressed just-rolled-out-of-bed look of a genius hacker who slept late and had to run to work in the morning to report to a job where his true identity was unknown and his true abilities unguessed at. He walked up, looked at them expressionlessly and let loose a gush of speech, which he had been holding in for hours.

"The hamburger? He puts this burger patty on the wall. I'm like, 'What's that for?' He tells me it's an experiment."

"To play devil's advocate, could it have been for class?"

"I'm like, 'Okay, if it's an experiment, what're you testing for?' I actually asked him, 'What's your null hypothesis? What's your control?' He had no answer."

"I'm not in chem. Is that, like, a dead giveaway if he doesn't know that?"

"That's the deadest giveaway in chem. In any empirical discipline. In anything. The case is closed. He's just putting rotten meat in the room for its own sake."

"Did it smell?"

"Hell yeah, it smelled! It's gross."

"I can verify it smelled. I walked by Ajay's door a few times when it was open, and I definitely smelled something weird."

"He's always working out, he doesn't wash his clothes, and he doesn't like to shower. He brags about being dirty."

"Why don't you tell him to cut it out?"

"He's a little intimidating. He bench-presses like five hundred pounds. I don't bench-press, but I know that's a lot of weight!"

"That'd be like a world-record bench press if he could do that. If that's true, he could lift all of us at one time. Add it up. I'm one-sixty. Ajay, what are you? One-eighty? Robin's like . . . ?"

"I'm not telling."

"What? This is for math. Like one-ten? One-twenty? I don't know! Tell me! I don't know what girls weigh! Like, one-twenty-ish? That's five hundred. He could totally lift all of us!"

"What happened when his mother came by? Did he really lock you in his room?"

"Yes! His mother barges into the pod last week when I was studying for my computer science test. I'm like, 'Adrian, your mom is here.' And he barricades us into the room."

"What for?"

"She wants to give him a cheese basket. Wait, let me back up.

This is the story. First of all, his mother was calling him all the time, and it was getting him really upset, to the point that he stops answering his phone and he's just letting it ring constantly while I'm studying. He tells me it's because she's pressuring him about getting a girlfriend or something. So he picks up the phone and tells her that he's not interested in the opposite sex anymore, to shut her up. Basically, he claims to be gay. Then she—apparently she has some kind of background in the sciences—she thinks his body isn't making enough testosterone to allow him to get aroused. His body fat is too low. This part is semi-legitimate physiology, at least. So she brings him a cheese basket to raise his cholesterol, cholesterol being a precursor of andro-steroids."

"And he locks the door on her?"

"Not only does he lock the door and refuse to accept his mother's cheese, they have this ten-hour hostage negotiation through the door. She's like, 'Let me in!' and he's like, 'Just go away!' While this is going on, he picks up a whip—I shit you not—that he keeps under his bed, and he starts whipping the door."

"He's whipping the door while he's talking to his mother?"

"Precisely."

"And you're . . ."

"Cowering in the corner. I went on Twitter to post a cry for help."

"Do you want to show us the burger?"

Ajay unlocked his door. His room was a rectangular box with a modular closet unit in the middle, which divided the living space in two. The far end of the room belonged to Adrian.

Adrian was sitting at the far end of the room. His desk lamp was on. The rest of the room was dark, and he was framed in darkness.

"You were here?" Robin said.

Ajay flipped the light switch, and the overhead light came on. Adrian turned.

"Do you want something?"

Shirtless, his torso looked like a Roman gladiator's anatomical breast plate. His chest had two U-shaped slabs of muscle on it—his pectoral muscles. The U's were rounded at the bottoms in a way that recalled a childish two-dimensional drawing of a woman's breasts—a strangely shaped musculature, thick as porterhouse steaks lying on his rib cage. He had no fat. His skin followed the contours of the structures under it. His stomach muscles—a rack of iron cannonballs. A Texas-shaped region of black hair grew in the center of his chest. There was hair on his shoulders. His arms didn't bulge: the bicep and tricep looked like blocks of wood. His body fat was so low you could see the grain in his muscles even at rest. Red pimples dotted his shoulders, skipped over the smooth, thick column of his neck, which tied into his clavicle, and reappeared on his sweaty oily forehead above his glasses. Some of him was beautiful and smooth, and some of him was dirty, pungent, rashy and unshaven.

Robin called over her shoulder, "Jeff, could you join us in here for a minute? I'd like a witness."

But Jeffrey, the boy with translucently delicate fingers, said, "This is too weird for me," and left, which left her and Ajay confronting Adrian. The room was sour and pungent.

Robin said, "Hey, Adrian, we wanted to talk to you. Do you think you could put your shirt on?"

"Why?"

"I'm asking you to."

"Why?"

"As a member of your community, I'm asking you to, to respect me."

"Just do it, man. Put your shirt on. She's asking you to."

"You should give me a reason if you want me to do something," Adrian said. "The whole point of everything we're learning at MIT is to use reason. What if I said, 'Take your shirt off to respect *me*'?"

"Okay, Adrian. Whatever makes you happy. I was going to say this nicely, but since that's the way you want to be, we're here because everyone can smell you."

"Let me see." Adrian picked up his shirt and crushed it to his face. "Aaahhh! That's ambrosial."

"You have to wash."

"I do?"

"Yes."

"Or what?"

"Or we'll go to the dean. Do you still have a hamburger on your wall?"

"No."

"Yeah, he does. It's right there." Ajay pointed over Robin's shoulder at a grayish disc of meat nailed to the wall next to the row of books standing upright on Adrian's desk.

"What's that?"

"Let's see what it says. Hmm. It's my protein polymer experiment. My *long-chain* protein polymer experiment."

"Why do you even have that?"

"Maybe I want to see it grow."

"You're going to have to take that down."

"Why?"

"You're not allowed to take food out of the dining hall. It's not very nice to Ajay."

"That's not nice to me. You've got your posters. I don't have anything else on my walls."

"It's got to come down."

"If I have to take it down, then you have to take something down too, something that's special to you. Think of something that's special to you, and then we'll trade."

"It doesn't work that way," Robin said.

"It should," said Adrian.

Despite this controversy, which provoked a letter to the dean, a round of meetings, and a formal apology from Adrian, it seemed that no one had yet noticed Adrian's affinity for the basement of the dorm, let alone what it could mean. In general, the only people who went down there were the guards. The guards at MIT worked for a rent-a-cop company, utterly distinct from and not to be confused with the MIT Police, who were a genuine police agency. The police uniform had red piping on the trouser legs; the guard uniform had blue. Guards had no special skill or training. They didn't carry weapons—at least, they weren't supposed to. Most were not intellectuals or even intelligent. A social barrier obtained between them and academic people. Generally, a guard passed his shift in solitary silence. When a student swiped in, her face came up on a computer screen behind his desk. He could pass the time by reading a book or looking at the students' faces, except when he left his post and did rounds throughout the building.

18

Body Puzzles

On the last day of September, Corey went to New Hampshire on the Concord Express bus out of South Station. His teammates sat behind him, reclining, listening to Beats headphones. Corey sat in a window seat, watching the redbrick waterfront and long wharves below as they climbed the Zakim Bridge and took the elevated highway north.

Soon they left the city behind, started coming to strip malls, big signs on super-tall poles that could be seen for miles: Nissan, Wendy's, Best Buy, Mobil. The buildings shrank to the ground, the trees rose up, and the highway became a broad channel into the woods. The entire way, he could feel them traveling uphill, up a slowly rising mountain. He heard it in the engine.

After an hour, they exited. The driver took a long, disorienting turn, a seemingly endless, swinging turn, past a needly wall of pine trees an inch away from the windshield, and let them off at a brick building by the highway cloverleaf. There was no town, only a huge expanse of churning gray sky, the tan road curving like a child's racecar track through the rolling hills, pine trees at the horizon, and Corey could contemplate what the world meant this far away from Boston.

They checked in at the Travelodge, and Eddie took them, walking as a team, a mile down Policy Road. Coming out of the woods, they saw a mall, which looked like a formerly grand hotel, and on the other side of it, the casino—a dirty white swan sitting in the great lake of a parking lot.

The lobby was empty. They entered through unattended turnstiles. Banners billed tomorrow night's fight as "The Combat Zone." They went through a vast amphitheater with floor-to-ceiling windows overlooking an overgrown racetrack like an air traffic control tower. Gamblers hunched at airport-lounge-type tables, watching miniature TVs tuned to races occurring somewhere else. Everyone was smoking cigarettes. Junked furniture was piled behind betting counters: "Cash/Sell—All Bets." Pillars held up the ceiling like an underground garage. In their tracksuits and hooded sweatshirts, the athletes walked through the smell of rotting carpeting, must and mold and years of cigarettes. Outside the chained-shut doors at the end of a hall, one saw cracked asphalt and nature taking over.

They followed Eddie to a doctor's scale in an upstairs room. The athletes took their clothes off. An athletic commissioner, wearing a gold badge on a leather wallet flipped out of his breast pocket like a sheriff, watched the weigh-in. A referee with slicked-back hair manipulated the sliding weight.

Corey had been dieting for weeks, taking one slice of bread off his sandwich every day at lunch. Three times he had reached for a piece of carrot cake with cream cheese frosting in the high school cafeteria, and three times he had pulled his hand away. After practice, he put peanut butter on his dry skinless chicken—anything to get his protein up. If he got hungry at night, the only thing he could eat was a can of tuna fish with the oil drained out. Before practice, he drank Gatorade and ate a gummy protein bar. He had gotten to the point where he could feel exactly what was in him. Every day he had gone to the locker room and weighed himself on Eddie's scale. The fat under his skin had disappeared.

But the thought of losing muscle had troubled him and late at night when he couldn't sleep because he was worrying about the fight, he had gotten up and gone out to the kitchen in the dark and eaten his mother's protein powder, which tasted like vanilla.

Everyone but Corey was on weight.

"It's his first time," Eddie said to the ref.

"It happens."

"How long does he have?"

"I don't want to see anybody forfeit, but four thirty's the latest."

"Can you cut the weight in four hours?"

Corey had never cut weight before. "Yeah," he said.

"Get him on weight," Eddie told Corey's teammates.

"You're just wringing water out of a sponge," they told him. "Zip up everything and get moving."

Corey zipped up all his clothes and ran out across the parking lot. The northern sun was shining. It was warm for late September. His hood was cinched tight, leaving a tiny circle for his eyes. He cut through the mall and lost his way in the empty atriums, the loud pop music, all the girls in store windows folding jeans, dodged around families drinking smoothies, broke outside again into the lot, so huge it took minutes to jog across—a bundled figure in the warm day, sweat blotches appearing on his sweatpants.

He pawed up a grassy incline, crossed a major road, forcing traffic to wait, stumbled across another fringe of grass and burst into a gas station convenience store. The cashier and a customer—a guy in a Palmer Gas & Oil hat—both straightened up and watched him. Corey sprinted down the aisles, grabbing trash bags and duct tape and dumped them on the counter. He paid, and, right there in the store, while the men watched him in silence, kicked off his sneakers and pulled trash bags on his legs like trousers. He tore leg holes in a bag and stepped into it like a diaper. He pulled another bag over his head and stuck his arms through it. He had a sense of body asphyxiation, even though he could breathe—he tore a hole for his face like a knight's chain-mail hood. He taped his arms to his chest, his legs to his diaper, his top to his bottom, vacuum-sealing himself in. Covered in trash bags, his feet slipped back in his sneakers with frictionless ease. He pulled his sweatshirt and parka back on over his rustling plastic body and zipped up, banged out through the door and started shuffle-jogging back to the arena, his temperature skyrocketing, unable to hear anything but the trash bags on his ears, like a rumpled bedsheet sliding back and forth over a microphone.

At the casino, he ran straight upstairs into the men's changing room and turned the showers on hot. The air steamed up like a sauna. He jogged in place, varying his gait, skipping, his sweatpant-ankles heavy, swinging around his feet. After a while, a teammate looked in and said, "They've got a stationary bike set up, if you want."

It was the kind of bike where you rowed with your arms as well as pedaled with your feet. Corey got on and pedaled and rowed. He rowed into the sun, which was shining in his eyes. The wheel spun like a fan blade in a wire cage—a ratcheting and sawing of chains and flywheel. The window glass steamed up, as if he were breathing on it with a giant mouth. The sun moved. He turned his rustling body and checked the clock. He kept rowing until the hour hand moved again. His teammate came back and told him he was out of time. He climbed off, his ankles sloshing, took off his jacket, sweatshirt, ripped open his garbage bags like a present. Water spilled out on the floor. His soaking-wet sweatpants were loose around the waist. He pulled the drawstring and they dropped to his ankles. He was thinner. He wrestled off his shirt—suddenly cool—and stepped on the bathroom scale in his wet underwear.

"You there?"

"Right on it."

He made weight in the green room and tried to eat and drink all afternoon. That evening they went back to the hotel and he kept eating and drinking even though his body didn't want the food.

Eddie put out the lights, and the team lay in the dark, on beds and on the floor, which smelled like feet. Corey shut his eyes and imagined he could feel the protein he had eaten flowing out of his stomach and reassembling his muscles.

"You're not going to think about your fight," he told himself. "Everybody's in the same boat. You have to deal with it the same as them."

The next day they lay around not moving, like reptiles conserving energy. Around noon, someone said, "It smells like mad balls in here," and opened up the door, letting in the sun, and they started stirring, coming out of hibernation, getting up and walking back and forth, tossing out their hands, throwing punches.

"You ready to do this? Let's go." Eddie took them to the casino.

Carrying their gym bags, they went through the turnstiles and followed him upstairs to a room that said Fighters Only on the door. Inside, there was a mural of a jockey and a racehorse on the wall, and the room was filled with gangs of guys in team shirts—Sityodong, Bucket Brigade Fight Team, Destiny Boyz Wrestling Club, Renzo Gracie New Hampshire, Team Irish Fighter, Gorilla Crew, Cage Strikers Manchester, Team Havoc, Bearstrong—sitting in separate camps, welcoming their friends with handclasps and hugs, treating all others to silence.

Eddie checked them in at a picnic table. A young woman in silver hoop earrings found their names on a list. Upside down, Corey saw *Goltz, 154 pounds*, in blue ink, next to *Ochiottes, 154 pounds*, in red. The room was divided into two halves by a counter and a banner for Budweiser Select Poker. Opponents went to opposite sides like bride and bridegroom before the wedding. Bestway claimed a picnic table and dropped their gear. Eddie went downstairs to get a yellow wristband, proving he had a New Hampshire cornerman's license. Corey took off his clothes and put on his cup.

The athletic commissioner arrived, opened a briefcase and handed out badges on lanyards to the officials.

The referee with slicked-back hair called, "If I could get everybody down here for the rules meeting." The fighters gathered round and he started talking like an auctioneer: "Elbows to the back of the head: No twelve to six. Give me an angle on that. We're worried about the brainstem. Slamming: If you sign up for the ride, it's not up to us how you land. Vaseline: After you get your high-fives and hugs out of the way, then you do the grease. You're okay as long as you stick with the raccoon eyes. Groin and mouth protection: If your mouthpiece falls out, we won't stop the fight. In a choke hold, we ask for motion to show you're still awake. Move something for us. But don't let go of the choke to give us the thumb's-up."

His audience laughed.

"Eye pokes have been a huge problem in the sport. Don't stick that pitchfork in your opponent's face. Pros, if you don't want to tap and something breaks, that's up to you."

Eddie returned carrying a bucket of ice. He took out the top tray of a toolbox, loaded with tape, gauze, Vaseline, a single-use cold pack, rubber gloves, scissors. Sitting backwards on a chair, he wrapped his students' hands. Corey spread his fingers and watched Eddie winding gauze between his fingers. "Make a fist." Corey stiffened his arm, and Eddie slammed his palm into Corey's knuckles.

For the past hour, a crowd had been entering the turnstiles and going to the event room. By now, a sea of people was standing in every available space, stepping over folding chairs, eating pizza, drinking beer. One could smell the mustardy tang of the hot dog and pizza concession under the hot yellow lights. The room was airless and loud. Miller Genuine Draft and Pickle Barrel banners hung from the ceiling. People were getting drunk already. A biker gang, the Risen Dead, out of New Haven, sat at the best section of the bar—big bearded men with mean little eyes, wearing leathers. An army of cops in blue nylon jerseys was massed at the exit. Behind them stood a pair of EMTs, part-time firemen from Haverhill. Strapped to their gurney, instead of a body, were bags of medical equipment. In the center of the heaving room, under hot white lights, stood the cage.

The judges took their seats at cageside. A camerawoman wearing an orthopedic boot climbed a ladder one step at a time and aimed her camera down into the cage. The rock 'n' roll went off. The lights went off. An announcer in a tuxedo walked out under a spotlight. "Good evening, everyone!" he said. "The action tonight is brought to you by American Irrigation. Let the red, white and blue make it green for you!"

They heard him in the dressing room, which was connected to the event room by a tunnel.

The first fight was called. It was one of Corey's teammates, who put his mouthpiece in and went off down the tunnel, shrugging his shoulders and throwing uppercuts. Corey watched him go. The dressing room went quiet. A bunch of guys stared at a monitor on the ceiling. Suddenly, it was like everyone exhaled. Then Eddie and his boy were back and they were excited: He had won by knockout. Corey slapped him on the shoulder. His shoulder was warm. All the guys were excited. The victor posed for a picture with Eddie, who put his arm around him and held up a finger—number one.

"One up, one down. That's the way everybody's gonna do it tonight. This is our night, Bestway."

"Damn straight," the guys said.

Corey started bouncing in place. He checked his spot on the card. Goltz and Ochiottes were ninth.

The next bout went the distance. So did the next. Corey stopped bouncing and tried to meditate, without success. Around the dressing room, some fighters curled up like babies and slept. One lay in his girlfriend's lap while she stroked his head. They pulled their hoods over their heads exactly like depressed people, people at a doctor's office facing a grave diagnosis. A woman fighter put her face down on a table like a student who had failed her finals. Some shuffled around in sport-flops, sipping water. A few stalked back and forth with monster rock leaking out of their headphones, throwing combinations and snorting through their clenched mouth guards.

As the night wore on, out in the event room, the crowd got drunker, looser. The cops started drinking too. A fighter got kicked in the groin, and the ref gave him time to rest. He squatted froglike. The fight resumed. He wasn't local. He was up from Taunton. He got hit in the groin again—his opponent threw a lot of inside kicks. This time, he made a show of agony. A drunk kid in the audience yelled, "It's not *that* big, Taunton! Come on."

Eventually, all the Bestway guys had gone except for Corey. Eddie grabbed the pads. "Let's warm you up." He moved around him like a target in a shooting gallery. He flashed a mitt; the image triggered Corey's brain to fire a punch. Eddie beat Corey's fists with the pads. He made him kick. "Relax. Again. Better." He dropped the pads and dove into Corey, chest to chest, and they started pummeling. They swam their arms in alternation under each other's arms while slamming their chests together and switching their legs back and forth. The white towel in Eddie's waist whipped like a tail.

"Do you know anything about your guy?"

"No."

"Has anyone heard anything?"

"Who's he got?"

"Ochiottes."

"Do you know what school he trains with?"

"Sityodong, I think."

"Take him down. Get on top. Ground and pound."

The girl with earrings called, "Bestway, is that your fighter? I've been calling you!" The preceding bout had ended with a knockout. Eddie grabbed the ice bucket and said, "That's you! Got your mouthpiece? Come on!" They ran after her into the tunnel. She had a thick-legged, low-hipped frame, her Rockingham Park shirt untucked over khaki pants, which she wore low. At the final doors, she held up a hand and told them to wait as she listened to her earpiece.

"Are you scared? Run in place like this, like you're climbing a mountain."

Then the girl said, "Go!" and Corey went through the doors into the arena. Hip-hop was blasting. People were shouting and yelling and drinking cups of beer. He walked down a chute through the shadowy crowd towards the glaring spot-lit brightness of the cage. A woman reached for him and gave out a piercing scream. Guys slapped his hands as if they loved him. A bodybuilder in black rubber gloves stopped him and patted him down as if he were checking him for weapons before letting him into a club. Corey closed his eyes and someone greased his face. He stepped into the cage.

There was a Budweiser King of Beers advertisement on the padding. There was Vaseline in his eyebrows. He saw stains on the canvas and felt the heat of the lights. It was beach-hot under the lights, like being on the shore in August.

He sensed a turbulence in the outer darkness coming this way. As it got closer, it became a person with red gloves taped to his hands. Behind him came a group of unshaven men in ball caps. One looked directly at Corey while speaking to this person, who nodded. The fighter took his sweats off and held his arms out. The bouncer frisked him, and a moment later he bounded up into the cage, opposite Corey.

Eddie banged the fence. "Hey, Corey! Hey! Listen up! I just heard, this guy's a grappler. You're gonna have to watch out with him."

"What do you mean, watch out?"

"He's a purple belt."

"But what do I do differently?"

"Keep it standing!"

But Corey didn't hear him, because someone else was yelling, "Give it everything you got! Don't quit! Just do it!"

And the ref was shouting, "Blue fighter! Turn around!"

Corey turned around, and the bell rang.

The two young men went towards each other like two arachnids in a terrarium. Ochiottes caught him in a front guillotine choke while they were standing, jumped guard, pulling him down, and made him tap in under a minute.

The mechanics of it were: His opponent's legs weren't holding him and he thought he might get free. But then Abel kicked him off and figure-foured his arms around Corey's head when they were on their knees, then rolled on his side taking Corey over with him. The ref moved in to watch. Corey tried to grab his opponent's hands. But you can't untie a knot behind your head unless you know how it's tied. Abel caught him with his feet and pulled their bodies together, folding Corey in half, compressing his neck. Corey's face turned the color of a raw steak. He tapped Abel's arm. The ref lunged down and pulled Abel's arm off Corey's neck. Abel's corner jumped up in celebration.

Abel's corner ran in and hugged him. Corey went over to shake hands. Abel's unshaven coach gestured that someone was behind him. Abel turned around, glanced at Corey, said, "Good fight," and turned away.

The ref grabbed Corey by the wrist and dragged him to the center of the cage. The announcer said, "Ladies and gentleman, we have a winner." The ref raised Abel's hand and held Corey's hand down, as if he was afraid Corey would try to take credit for a fight he hadn't won. Corey went to the dressing room and found someone with scissors to cut his gloves off.

It was almost midnight when they left the arena. Corey hadn't eaten anything. One of his teammates had had the foresight to get two slices of pizza and a hot dog to celebrate his victory before they closed the concession. Now all you could get was beer.

The fighters and the fans were dispersing. A crowd remained in the event room, drinking and talking, the music still playing: *"I want to rock and roll all night and party every day . . ."* But the carpeting was littered with ticket stubs and napkins. The garbages were full. The exit doors had been blocked open so that people felt encouraged to leave. Drinkers pissed with the restroom doors open so they could shout to their friends. In the cigarette-musty betting room, the horses were galloping on the TVs—bringing their front legs and back legs together like hands frenetically grabbing more life, grabbing more life. No one was watching any longer. The spotlight over the cage went off. The event staff started folding up metal chairs and stacking them in the back of the room. The rock music went off and left the room silent with just the clattering of the chairs.

People streamed from the casino's half-moon lobby out into the night. Engines revved, headlights came on. You heard cars ripping away and laughter in the dark.

Bestway struck out for the hotel, carrying their gym bags. They argued about the way and got lost trying to circumnavigate the mall. Corey brought up the rear in silence. They walked back through the ankle-tickling grass on the side of Policy Road. Cold emanated from the countryside. The windows of roadside houses were as opaque as cataracts. A chittering echoed from the towering trees and deep weedy grass. There was a great three-dimensional space around them and it was full of insects.

When they got back to the Travelodge, one of Corey's teammates threw his bag on a bed and said, "I won. I get the bed tonight!"

Corey went out to the snack machine. He bought a pack of Oreos and called his mother on his cell.

"Hey, Mom."

"Hey, Corey. How're things?"

"They're okay. I lost."

"Well, I'm sure you'll do better next time."

"I know. I will. Are you okay?"

"About the same."

"Is anyone there with you tonight?"

"No. Just me and my lonesome. I watched a science program

I think you would have liked about the brain. They were talking about all the things the human mind can do. It was just magnificent. They had a pianist hooked up to a machine, and you could actually see the nerve impulses coming out in waves together with the music when he was playing. It was the most amazing thing I ever saw. They said he had trained from the time he was seven. His whole body had become the instrument. I thought, Corey'd love this, because he had your discipline."

"I don't feel very disciplined tonight."

"It's just one little night. You've got the whole rest of your life to be great. I'd give anything to be your age, Corey. I'd give anything not to be facing this."

"Mom—"

"You asked me how I am, Corey. I'm sad. I'm sorry, I'm so sad."

"Mom . . ." He kneeled in the parking lot, hunching himself over the phone. "Mom, it's okay . . . It's okay . . . It's okay. I'll be there soon."

He wiped his eyes after getting off the phone and ate the Oreos. The trash can was in the motel office. He threw the wrapper out. The night clerk was out of sight. He went back to his room. He told Eddie he was thinking about going to the bus station and getting the next bus home right now.

"You can't go there now. There're no buses now."

Corey lay down on a bedspread on the floor. "I'm taking the earliest bus tomorrow."

"What does he want to go home so badly for?" one of the guys asked. Another said, "Shut up. Let it go," because Corey was the only one who had lost.

The next morning, Corey left before the others and caught the six a.m. bus back to Boston. At South Station, he transferred to the T and stared at the subway tunnel walls.

The T rose out of the tunnel. Now he was looking out over the water, the sun in his eyes and the shore going by. Then they sank into the concrete cut between the houses. He got off in Quincy and went to Grumpy White's and ate a chicken parm, fries, a milkshake—near a thousand calories.

When he got home, it was noon. His mother had been alone all morning while he had been feeding himself. He put down his gym bag and made her lunch.

． ． ．

But once he had fought, it changed things at the gym. Scott the fireman tried to rough him up and, while not his equal, Corey was relaxed and unafraid of him and able to neutralize much of what he did. Furthermore, he didn't tire.

The fireman flopped on his back and groaned.

"What's the matter?" Eddie asked.

"This kid's annoying me today. Nothing's working on him."

"He fought on Saturday."

"I should have known."

He decided he would get his gear, his game, his life in order. Rather than taking his mother's protein powder, he bought Gaspari and Xtend at GMC and set them in his room with his board shorts, bag gloves, rash guard, jump rope, mouthpiece, kneepads, cup and hand wraps—all laid out so he could see them day and night. He'd learn to box you on the feet, using timing and angles, punch his way into the clinch, hit his favorite takedown, work his knee-slide pass, his Leo Vera, punch you from the top, ride you, hunt a choke, use leg-weave passing. His life would be devoted to solving body puzzles. He saw future contests in his dreams. If he lost position, he'd shrimp his hips away or Granby and recover guard and immediately go to mission control or the London and work between an omoplata and a triangle. He'd learn to ping-pong between positions, stay one step ahead of his opponent—to never get guillotined again. It suddenly seemed possible to do everything in life the way it should be done. Sometimes Eddie stopped him as he left the gym and shook his hand.

He bought his own gear. Did his laundry. In October, he turned seventeen. Balanced job, gym, mother—even school—for a little while at least—in the lull after his first fight.

The only signs Corey saw of Leonard during this period were his dirty rumpled clothes, bags of toiletries and jars of pickled garlic. The futon remained folded up. He almost dared to think his father had gone away. But one day, on his way to a Craigslist job in Milton, Corey smelled something in the air. He went into the kitchen. A great mass of Leonard's dishes was drip-drying in the sink: pots, pans, plates, spoons, tongs, his green enamel skillet, his canary yellow butcher knife.

Corey checked the trash. He found onion skins. The window had been left open to the marsh. His father must have cooked, but he had washed his dishes.

He knows I'm fighting, Corey thought. He doesn't want to play with me.

His eye fell on the dish soap, a 28-ounce bottle of Palmolive he had bought on sale at Stoppies only days before. It had been full this morning; it was almost empty now. He looked in the sink again. The dishes were covered in unrinsed soap foam. There were mountains of soap foam billowing out of the sink. It was so full of foam you couldn't see the bottom.

He stared at Leonard's message to him.

In Milton, he went to a woman's basement and hooked up her dryer to the gas, a simple procedure, connecting the silver exhaust hose to the vent. She lived in a dark house and Corey thought that she was very strange.

❧

In early November, Corey stayed home from school to take his mother to her clinic day at Longwood. It took a long time to get her to the car. He did up the buttons of her navy pea coat while she stood with her arms at her sides. A wind was blowing on the shore. She wore her sweatpants, white socks and white sneakers. Corey put her hat on her head—a knit hat with a pompom.

"Am I Santa?"

It started raining, wetting the black asphalt. He helped her into the hatchback and buckled her seatbelt while she stared out the window at the rain. Her hands in orthotic braces lay in her lap. She had orthotics on her feet. He put her walker in the trunk, the cold metal wet on his hands, and got behind the wheel.

They were due at Longwood at three o'clock. He drove them north along the shore. She sat next to him with her arms in her lap, bundled into her navy coat, the pompom bouncing on her head with the breaks in the road as the rain came down. The windshield wipers were sluicing the rain off the windshield. They were driving along the line of white houses and the gray ocean shore, heading north into the gray sky.

They drove up onto 93 and promptly hit traffic. It was already 2:40, and he was watching the time. At 2:47 they were getting off 93, driving down Huntington Ave. He braked for a red light and they waited, the stick in neutral, surrounded by idling city traffic. The wipers worked across the glass; his turn signal tick-tocked. At 2:52 they were turning south, past townhouses with limestone angels.

At 3:00, they reached the wide modern road flanked by towers like giant books standing on their ends. He turned into the Beth Israel driveway, paved in glazed brick. He waited for the machine to give him his ticket. The barrier went up and he drove down into the underground garage.

He parked and jumped out and opened the trunk and unfolded his mother's walker, unbuckled her seatbelt and let her lift her legs out by herself, "under her own steam," as she put it. When her legs were out, he lifted under her woolly arms and helped her stand. He put her thin weak hands on the walker. They felt like two thin fillets. She couldn't squeeze him back. He stepped out of her way and let her push the walker forward. She took a high slow step, the toe of her sneaker pointing down, and set her foot on the concrete floor. A ventilator roared. The garage smelled like diesel fumes. She took a step with her other leg, another high slow step.

He closed their car door and checked by feel that it was locked. He didn't take his eyes off her while she was moving. If he had to look away, he kept his hand on her back to feel her balance. He was ready to catch her under the arms if she fell. In wrestling, this was called the cow catcher. He could never be farther away from her than the time it would take him to catch her before she hit the ground.

She pushed her walker forward and began taking another step. He followed behind her, not touching her, but waiting and ready. She had fifty feet to go to the elevators. He checked the time. They were going to be late.

They took the elevator to the neurology department. Medical personnel in white coats and blue scrubs got off at an intermediate floor and hurried away, holding their clipboards to their bosoms like schoolgirls holding schoolbooks. The doors closed, and Corey saw his and his mother's reflections in the polished metal: his mother, now shorter than he was, her spine humped, leaning on the four-legged walker.

The neurology clinic smelled like antiseptic and human beings. Corey went to the counter to check them in.

"You could call next time," a scheduling nurse told him, a plump woman with bangles and painted-on eyebrows. "I'll have to tell the doctor to come back."

"I'm sorry," Corey said. "It's not my mom's fault. I hit traffic in the rain."

The waiting room had a plate glass wall that looked out at the gray sky. They were on a high floor and there was cottony fog swirling around the top of a neighboring office tower, so it was almost like they were in the mountains with the clouds.

His mother took a seat to wait. The sealed room was hot and stuffy. Corey took her hat off and began unbuttoning her coat. The banks of seats faced each other.

Across the room from Gloria, there was a woman lying in a wheelchair, a massive mechanical contraption. Complex supports held up each of her limbs. Her deformed neck twisted sideways like a vine. Her head resembled an orange at the end of the vine, and the headrest had to be off-center and out of true to support her. Long bolts stuck out from the headrest like torture devices that screwed into her head.

"I wish I'd brought a book for you," Corey said.

"Can you show me something on your phone?"

"Of course. What do you want to see?"

"Show me anything."

He went through his pictures. "Here. Look at this. This is a mandala."

It showed the Tibetan universe, a central mountain peak surrounded by the continents with uncountably many worlds bubbling into existence all around them like fish eggs foaming in the sea, teeming with black- and red-skinned gods and demons in gold finery with elephant trunks and tusks, white-skinned maidens, and various hells. In the upper world, farmers worked and prayed with their families by the river shores for healthy crops and healthy children. In the hells, scowling priests tore victims' legs apart and disemboweled them. The Buddha sat above the mountain peak, enthroned on a cloud in Suyama Paradise. His hair looked like the overlapping leaves of an artichoke. His cone-shaped head rose to a point, which ended in a jewel of flame. His soft earlobes hung down like dewdrops. His cheeks were soft and hairless, as if plumped with estrogen, and he levitated on his lotus cloud at the center of the cosmos but outside it—smiling, sexless, all-powerful and calm.

His mother looked at the image on his smartphone. Come on, Gloria! she thought. Breathe! She raised her aquiline face, her narrow nose and jaw, and closed her eyes, as if she were basking in a joyous sunlight coming from the clinic's ceiling and hearing beautiful music.

The nurse with bangles called Gloria, and she went in to see the doctor. He reviewed her progress and told her it was time to go down to the basement.

There was a workshop in the basement that looked like a lost-and-found for canes and crutches. Women who were both therapists and mechanics were waiting for them. Corey saw a box full of foam rubber, sheets of different thicknesses and densities. The therapist-mechanics had a workbench, plastic templates, a T-square, compass, cutting tools—shears, matte knives; and a wheelchair seat supported on a horizontal axle, whose height could be adjusted. They asked Corey to help his mother sit in the chair, then began to make adjustments to her height. They slipped a sheet of foam rubber behind her spine and asked where she felt the most pressure on her skin. They added inserts to the foam. It was like building up a contour map: concentric islands. They did the same beneath her backside. Finally, they arrived at this solution: a piece of stiff white Styrofoam with oblongs cut out for each of her hip bones and foam rubber artfully cut to fit inside the oblongs.

All the pieces would have to be glued together to fabricate a custom cushion for Gloria's body. They would install it in Gloria's wheelchair and ship it to her at home.

"They're gonna make this just for you, Mom," Corey said.

One of the women was the physical therapist who had given Gloria her dumbbells. She wore olive cargo pants with the ankle ties untied and had a winter tan, as if she'd spent a month out west hiking. Squatting, she put a wheel on the mock-up wheelchair with a socket set.

Corey asked if she was a cyclist.

"Sometimes," she said.

"Do you need any help with that?"

She answered by putting her wrench back in its case and spinning the wheel—it gave out a fast, well-oiled ticking against the bearings—and asking Gloria if she liked the angle she was sitting at.

On the drive home, Gloria didn't speak.

"It's just a bike on four wheels, Mom," Corey said. "We'll go anywhere you want."

We're Going to Have a Problem

He was standing in the parking lot outside the Quincy Center T the Saturday after taking his mother to the doctor. The sky was overcast, he was wearing sweats beneath his parka, a gym towel around his neck, there was a blue knuckle mark under his eye. He was handing out flyers to a cage fight.

Molly came off the T, carrying a shoulder bag full of textbooks. He hadn't seen her since her graduation in the spring. She had a gray wool band around her head—like a scarf for the ears. Her coppery hair hung down her back. She wore purple tights that hugged her legs so tightly she looked like a marble statue that had been spray-painted at an auto body shop. They were infused with violet light like an airbrush sunrise. Out of modesty, she had a sweatshirt tied around her waist.

"Is that you, Corey?"

"Molly, hey!"

"What're you giving away here? Your next rap album?"

"No, this is for an athletic competition."

"'An athletic competition.' Let me see. 'The Brawl at the Palladium.' What is this, backyard wrestling? Oh, it's ultimate fighting. Is that why you look like a battered wife? Is this what you're doing?"

"Yeah," he admitted.

"You nut."

"How's college?"

"It's a lot of work." She was home for the weekend and had a paper to write and was going to the café to work on it. Corey asked to walk with her. She went to Gunther Tooties. He followed her inside. She stood in line and bought a coffee. While she was waiting, she checked her phone. He got the impression she didn't want to talk. He said he had to hand out the rest of his flyers. "Good luck with your paper." He left.

An hour later, the door opened and he came in again.

"Mind if I sit down?"

"No."

"Mind if I close my eyes for a minute?"

"No. You must be tired from getting black eyes."

He pulled his towel over his face. With his eyes closed, he could hear her typing. He could feel her when she shifted on the couch.

"I'm sorry about last year," he said from beneath the towel. He took the towel away and looked at her. "I'm sorry."

"Don't worry about it."

"I was stupid, and I'm sorry."

"Everyone makes mistakes. Don't worry about it. Go back to sleep."

"What's your paper about?"

"Psychology." It was her major. She had planned to major in small business administration. "My dad used to work for this really small company, like one guy and a van, and they laid him off when the recession hit in 2008. Now, you know my dad: He's way too proud to go on unemployment."

"I never knew he got laid off."

"That's because he didn't tell anyone. So, we were like, 'What's going to happen?' I thought he should go into business for himself so nobody could lay him off."

"Your dad's my hero."

"Every guy says that. I'm like, 'You're not living in his shadow.'"

"I'd love to live in his shadow."

"Well, he doesn't talk much."

"No, he's old school."

"He has no idea how to talk to me. I used to be mad at him, now I just feel sorry for him."

"Do you wish you'd had a mother?"

"Yeah, of course," said Molly—and that was all she said about it.

An hour passed. He'd fallen asleep. He woke up and blinked and saw Molly checking her phone. The laptop was off. The café was about to close. The last of the shiny cards his coach had had printed up at the printer's lay on the table. Corey asked Molly if she wanted to see a fight. To his surprise, she said yes. She closed her laptop and put her things away and stood up and shook her hair out and refitted the woolen band around her ears. "Let's go."

"You really want to come with me?"

"Yes, nerd. Get your car."

On the drive to Worcester, she described her college as being out in the middle of nowhere. They had genuine farm girls there whose idea of a joke was to pronounce *pasteurized* "past-your-eyes." They'd take a glass of milk and swing it by your face. For the first time, Molly had heard the ad for a country dating website, FarmersOnly.com: "City folks just don't get it." The campus was surrounded by woods. She ran cross-country through miles of trees. At night, she saw the stars.

But usually she was too busy to look heavenward. She had to keep her grades up, she had a scholarship, she played two sports, she worked, and UMass was party central. The drinking was on another level. She had broken up with her shot-putter from last year. As she said this, she looked out Corey's windshield. They were tunneling down the Mass Pike in the darkness. She said she'd met some asshole guys.

The campus was big and industrial—a concrete factory in the middle of the woods. Soviet-project-sized dorm buildings. A matrix of tiny fluorescent lights in a giant cement slab in the freezing black New England night, one of them her room—hers and the girls she roomed with and the bottle of vodka and the chocolate cake they ate for comfort. Going to the yellow gym to watch squeaky-shoes basketball. Betting online on a website hosted in Costa Rica. Thinking what would they do for spring break if they had no money. Joking about UMass's isolation. Her best times as always came when she was running for distance and playing soccer—she was a halfback—and she got her instep on that ball.

"I bet you'd kill someone if you took Muay Thai."

"Muay Thai: What's that?"

"A martial art."

She said she didn't remotely have the time.

They reached Worcester and parked in the square lot out-side the Palladium. The building looked like an old New England textile mill, like the ones in Lowell where Tom, her father, had worked as a young man. Molly had been here before to see My Chemical Romance on their Black Parade Tour. They waited in line, got wristbands and found seats inside with a view of the as-yet-empty cage.

Molly took out her phone and looked at Facebook. "How long will this be?" Her girlfriend wanted to meet her back in Quincy later. "No offense," she said, but to her, the ultimate smackdown stuff was just brutality. If you wanted to give blood, play hockey.

"Hockey's a combat sport," Corey agreed.

The rock 'n' roll came on, the stadium filled up with athletes and their mothers, fathers, brothers, sisters, coaches, friends and training partners wearing fight academy T-shirts. The round card girls came in and sat on folding chairs. One was a blonde, one was a brunette, they were wearing matching strawberry spandex jog bras and shorty shorts and sneakers without socks, and when they sat down, they crossed their legs the same way. Molly rolled her eyes. "Who're they? The Doublemint Twins? I get why you like this."

"I never noticed them before."

"Sure," she said. "I'd destroy that little outfit if I tried to wear it."

"Me personally, I think everyone should be big—males *and* females—with tons of muscle."

He excused himself to say hi to a few fellows from Bestway he'd seen across the stands. "Back in a minute."

"Don't worry. I'll be fine." A crew of big good-looking men in cammie hats, drinking beer and dipping chew, had just taken seats next to Molly.

When Corey was gone, the brunette round card girl turned around and waved. One of the good-looking guys climbed over the seats to her and gave her a respectful half hug. He was neatly dressed, manly and self-possessed. His black hair was combed on top and trimmed short on the sides, revealing his big clean ears and handsome neck. The girl talked in his ear. Her round breast was an inch from his chest. One could feel their bodies straining together. Under the cover of drawing him close to speak to him better, she placed her hand on his ribs.

They hugged again, and he climbed back to his friends, other wide-shouldered guys in hunter's hats drinking beer and spitting chewing tobacco in plastic cups.

"Oh, of course," Molly said, watching this spectacle.

By now, Corey had returned. "What is it?" he asked.

"Oh, nothing."

The lights went down, the rock went off, and a man in a sharkskin suit and a black-on-black dress shirt entered the cage and grabbed a microphone and said, "Hi, everybody. Thanks for coming."

"Yeah, sure," she said. "No problem."

"We welcome our first fighter to the cage."

The music kicked on and a girl walked out to the cage under a spotlight.

"Is that a girl?" Molly asked.

She was white and had her hair done in cornrows. Behind her came her coaches, men with full-sleeve tattoos. They took her black silk robe when she removed it. She was scrawny and flat-chested with a short torso and long arms, wearing a sports bra and big shorts emblazoned with Thai script, which looked like a chain of *m*'s or elephants. Underneath, she wore knee-length silky spandex bike shorts in pearl gray. Her legs were a contrast to the rest of her. They were glamorously long and strong with long-bellied calves like a dancer. Ankle wraps covered her insteps and exposed her white heels.

Next, her opponent marched out of the wings to the sound of military drumbeats: a glossy brown-skinned Dominican woman from Lawrence, with a fierce young face. Confident, good-looking and bursting with aggression, she had biceps, her shoulders were capped with epaulettes of muscle, and she had heavy legs and hips. She was wearing royal blue bike shorts. Her African hair was twisted into a pair of short pigtails and bobby-pinned to the back of her head like two sausages. She ran up into the cage clapping her hands and gave her opponent a smile in which one could feel the bad intentions.

The guys near Molly said, "This is going to be nasty."

As soon as the ref said, "Fight!," the women started throwing full-force punches at each other's faces. The entire room reacted. Everyone could feel the fighters getting brain-damaged, the egg yolk commonly cited by scientists sloshing in the skull, rupturing and leaking into the white. "Sweetness!" somebody yelled. "All night long!" Blood was running out the white girl's nose. She had a bloody mouthpiece. She kicked the Dominicana in the lower belly as if she wanted to destroy her reproductive organs. She pulled her head down and threw a knee at her beautiful face.

Corey twitched as if he were in the cage with them. "Gotta have more head movement!" He ducked punches in his seat.

They learned the fighters' names, when, at the start of the second round, the fighters sallied forth with their fists up to meet again in the center of the canvas and half the crowd began chanting, "Let's go, Rachel! Let's go!" and the other half of the crowd began cheering for Alayah, the Dominican. Her supporters shouted, "Mama says knock you out!"

"Come on!" screamed Molly. "Both of you! I'm rooting for you both."

The women fought through a second round and then a third. Rachel was repeatedly staggered by her opponent, but eventually the more muscular Alayah began struggling against fatigue. They fought until the final bell. No one gave in. The ref had to separate them when the clock ran out. The audience was applauding and cheering. The guys in camouflage hats put down their beer cups and clapped and whistled.

"That'll be fight of the night! Hands down!"

The announcer declared the winner by decision, and the ref raised Alayah's hand. She crossed herself and pointed up at God and said, "Thank you." Her corner went wild, pounding the apron of the cage. The two women hugged each other tightly. A wag in the audience whooped, "Oh yeah!," precipitating a bit of laughter.

Rachel's coach embraced her. The top of her head came up under his chin. "Sorry," she said. "I tried." She seemed not to take the loss too hard. She left the arena, high-fiving members of the audience who reached out to congratulate her. The sound system played "Hit Me with Your Best Shot" by Pat Benatar.

Molly kept saying, "God. Oh my God." She turned to the guys next to her. "That was balls-out!"

"Totally," they said. They recognized Corey. "Didn't we see you fight in New Hampshire?"

"Yeah, you did."

"You getting in there tonight?"

"Not tonight. And, hey, this is Molly, by the way."

"Hey, Molly-by-the-Way."

She curtsied—"Charmed, I'm sure." And the men said, "So are we!"

After the card was over, Molly and Corey sat in the hatchback, talking, while everyone else drove away from the Palladium. He was explaining martial arts to her. He'd been explaining it all night long and if she gave him another few hours, he'd explain the rest. There was a lot to cover—boxing, kickboxing, the clinch, trips, throws, takedowns, the ground game—Muay Thai, which he'd mentioned earlier—he was getting there—but she had not been bored, had she? It was a real sport, as real as hockey, wasn't it? Wasn't she glad that she had come?

"Yes—oh my God, those girls were tough."

"I'd *be* a girl if it'd make me tough as them."

Molly gave him the old sneer. "You're still weird."

"Come on, I've gotten better."

"You have. I'll give you that."

"I owe you for everything."

"For what?"

"Last year when I was fucking up, your father talked to me."

"That's not me, that's him."

"No, it was you too. He told me about you playing basketball, dealing with your coach, the one who said you were slow . . ."

"Oh, that."

"That. Yeah. That made me change my life."

The car fell silent.

She said it was about that time. He drove her back to Quincy. When he let her off, he asked if they could hang out the next time she came back from school, now that she didn't consider him too weird.

She said, "Yes, you geek, we can."

⁂

On Saturday nights, when the rest of the student body was at a cappella or watching Monty Python, Adrian was making his way across the long dark athletic field to the edge of campus, through a dead zone of industrial labs and into an enclave of private homes, public art and quiet parks near a Trader Joe's that faced the river. Among the private homes of Cambridgeport, there was a redbrick house, a dorm, that belonged to the university, which Adrian had begun to visit.

It was a house of many rooms, an old colonial structure, shabby and cavernous inside, with steep staircases, flaking plastic walls, and a multitude of corridors and closets. Upstairs, there was a common room, which was hung with tapestries. It had French doors and curtains and a TV set that no one watched. Adrian would take a seat on one of the soft, well-used couches or easy chairs and turn it on. If anyone else was there, he would encourage them to leave by talking to the TV, farting loudly, whooping with laughter. After they were gone, he'd shut the doors and draw the curtains, turn off the lights.

Tonight, as soon as Adrian arrived, the students in the common room, a pair of girls, got up and left. He sat in an easy chair in his wrestling cup and kneepads, and watched *Saturday Night Live* alone.

After midnight, footsteps came up the stairs and Leonard came in in uniform. He closed the French doors and adjusted the curtains. He sat on the couch, turned down the squelch on his radio and set it by his side. Adrian rose, inserted a thumb drive in the TV. A movie began to play.

"Oh, nice." Leonard glanced over his shoulder to see if anyone was coming.

"You won't get in any trouble for this, will you?"

"Nah. You will," Leonard said.

"If anyone complains, we'll tell them it's educational."

They fell silent watching the movie. Adrian had the volume turned up high. The characteristic porn movie soundtrack was audible through the doors and curtains in the outer hall.

Adrian pointed out what one of the actresses was doing onscreen. "See how she's trying to destroy his cock? That makes me so mad."

A female student passed on the other side of the French doors. The lights were out in the dormitory and she went by like a shadow in the blue darkness of an aquarium. Leonard, silhouetted by the movie screen, his glasses picking up the images of flesh, looked at her and she swam away.

They had been meeting like this for weeks. They didn't always watch pornography. Sometimes they simply watched TV and analyzed the ads. They discussed physics, society as Adrian saw it, and human nature. Adrian would begin by talking about the advances he had made in his studies and would end by talking about his mother. Sometimes Leonard's radio squelched and he got up and disappeared and returned much later, having tended to his rounds. Adrian would stay to talk until two or three o'clock before leaving. He would descend past the unmanned guard post with its still-burning desk lamp and head back to campus through the blacked-out streets, the klieg-lit research labs, strangely buzzing or crackling in the silence, and cut across the playing fields, the frozen cold coming from the river, having left Leonard upstairs in the cavernous house full of sleeping students.

Tonight, after the movie, they discussed what they had seen.

"I have this nightmare," Adrian said. "I'm lying in my bed and I see this thing looking at me in the doorway. There's nothing I can do. It starts coming closer and closer and I can't stop it. And I get so mad and scared, I can feel my muscles jumping like I'm hooked up to a car battery."

The thing had been a rubber monster mask with eyeholes, the kind you pull over your entire head, for Halloween.

"Was someone wearing it?"

"My mother. She was angry because my dad had just divorced her."

"So, this is not a nightmare; this actually happened."

"Yes, unfortunately."

"How old were you?"

"Like five. My parents had just got divorced. I guess I made my mother mad."

"So she put the mask on . . . ?"

"To punish me."

"How did she do that?"

"She came into my room and acted like a monster."

"But she did something else, didn't she? Something physical. What did she do?" Leonard pressed.

"She had a pair of scissors."

"What did she do with them?"

The physics student sighed.

"Does it depress you to talk about it?"

"It's not happy. It's a bummer. I mean, I'm mad. I could kill her."

"Well, she did something . . ."

"I have homicidal thoughts about her."

"Just to be clear, she had a pair of scissors, and she threatened you physically. She threatened to . . ."

"To castrate me, yeah."

"And now you wear a cup and have nightmares to this day."

"Yes."

Adrian felt boundless gratitude to Corey's father for eliciting this tale of childhood trauma. He was better than a trained psychiatrist, Adrian insisted.

Later that month, a group of female students were gathered in the common room behind his back making comments Adrian was meant to overhear. One said, "That guard's a creep." The young man turned around and replied, "No, he's not. I think he's a saint."

❧

The team's hardest conditioning workouts were led by a former college wrestler. He had a crewcut with a slice in it, a coiling dragon on his arm. His front teeth were missing, and when he didn't have his plate in, he looked like a vampire. He said to start the running. Their bare feet pattered around the mat. He called for bear crawls. They hit the deck and scrambled on all fours. Corey ran on all fours, seeing the heels of the man ahead of him.

The wrestler's drills were based on lifting your opponent off the ground. When you weren't lifting another man, you were lifting yourself. He had them doing jumping split lunges, bunny hops, springing down the mat throwing Superman punches, leaping up and throwing jump knees. "Ong Bak that shit!" He was a small-framed man, but he believed in strength at any cost, even if you had to take steroids to achieve it. He was the athlete of power, the antigravity fighter leaping off the earth.

Corey had to give a piggyback to a full-grown heavyweight wearing a compression shirt with a dagger of white silk-screened down the front and a bow tie at the throat like a tuxedo. It was mechanically impossible to lift the man's legs high enough to get his feet off the ground; Corey needed higher shoulders. The heavyweight raised his feet himself while Corey ran. No sooner had Corey dropped him than the call went out for High Crotch Carries. The guy said, "Let's go, pick me up," and swung himself sideways into Corey's arms. It was like running with a fire ladder. The man's weight pressed on Corey's heart. His body slopped with sweat. The hairs on his shins were plastered to his skin in patterns left by running water, like fossil traces in a riverbed. The man did the work of hanging on to him; Corey's biceps failed. The second lap he had to walk. When he dropped him, the heavyweight stepped out of his arms with his long legs and walked away, a much bigger life-form leaving a smaller one, who was bent and gasping.

Sparring turned ugly all the time. Real fighting was encouraged. You had to wear a mouthpiece. You had to wear a cup. The wrestler, who had been in combat sports since childhood and was working on a pro career, said that one time he forgot to wear a cup and someone kneed him. Later in the shower, he felt a sting. The end of his penis had been split.

"I woulda healed up faster, but I had to get me a little somethin'-somethin'."

The listeners, who were fighters, winked. Corey tried to show the right reaction, which was no reaction.

A blow to the groin could result in injury to the genitals, rupture of urethra or testes. A hard enough blow can smash a testicle, render it necrotic. One could get Thai-kicked in the leg so much in a bout—think of a leg being smashed over and over with a baseball bat, inflicting hematomas and then bursting these same bruises—that a gap opens in the flesh, the entire thigh fills with pus like a rotted orange—this is called compartment syndrome—and has to be drained. One could get a finger in the eye, deep in the eye, fingernail tearing the cornea; a torn cornea or detached retina. If you were mounted and punched with your head against the canvas, your skull could absorb impacts in the neighborhood of a thousand foot-pounds, depending how hard your opponent hit. Broken nose, jaw, orbital. You could get heel-hooked and wreck your knee. You could get double-leg slammed or suplexed, land on your head, and break your spine. Taking repeated blows to the head could cause dementia pugilistica or, as has been coming to light in football, make one prone to a neurodegenerative disease like ALS.

For all these fears, you wore a cup, you wore a mouthpiece, and moved your head. You tried to be skilled. As for your opponent, there was not so much you could do about him. You didn't know how good he'd be until you felt him in the cage.

There was one thing you could do. You could ensure you were in fighting shape, which meant you were conditioned to struggle even when your air was being taken away.

Green wind feeding red muscle in a never-ending Taoist cycle—Corey thought. Red muscle making motion. A calligraphic line cooling into green. A body swirling to arouse the wind—a Wu Li dancer, a flashing quantum body breathing air. He had strange thoughts in training when he was being crushed and couldn't breathe: "I'm dying into being Vairocana," and, when he had held out long enough to break free of a bad position and reverse it: "Break through and go the distance—out of chaos—the Grand Tour!"

"Okay, ladies," said their coach. "Get a drink and get your gloves." The young men ran for their gear. "You have one minute."

The bell rang and sparring started. A fight broke out between Robert, the tuxedo wearer, and a visitor to the gym, a pale fellow with a deep voice, it was said, from Macedonia, who spoke plodding English. He swung his fist like a bolo at Robert's head. Rob leaned back and kneed him in the stomach. The Macedonian instantly fell on the ground and made a sobbing noise. His diaphragm was in spasm. The point of the knee had hit him in the solar plexus.

"World Star!"

Corey put his hands down, thinking they should see if he was okay. The coach said, "Keep fighting, ladies! The round's not over."

Tonight, Corey's sparring partner was a twenty-five-year-old named Francisco, a recent immigrant, now living in Plymouth, who had trained in jiujitsu back in Brazil for the last ten years and had a brown belt under one of the leading São Paulo schools. When their bout went to the ground, Corey received a merciless grappling lesson. No matter what he did, Francisco slid over him like an anaconda, squeezing his ribs, riding his abdomen, asphyxiating him before he even got to his neck. To get starved for air when he was working as hard as he could—when he had just done the equivalent of sprinting up four flights of stairs with a human being on his back—was excruciating. Corey's lips turned blue. He gave up submissions just to make it stop.

By the end of the night, he could barely function. His face had been scraped raw by the man's stubble. The bridge of his nose was bleeding. His arms and legs appeared fragile, as if he'd used his body up. He was five pounds lighter, bruised all over. When he peeled off his kneepads, his knees were skinned and macerated. He stank like kerosene, ammonia, aldehyde, sweat. His waterlogged clothes looked like he'd been dunked in the ocean. Foreign hairs from the mat were sticking to his skin. His arm was hyperextended. His toes were jammed. There was a pull in his back. His head ached. Water nauseated him, yet there wasn't enough water in the world that he could drink to satisfy his thirst. His brain had shrunk inside his head. He could hardly think or talk.

Francisco slapped him on the arm.

"Keep it up. You should fight."

"I will. I am."

Corey saw Adrian after signing the contract for his next fight, which was going to be held early next month. As soon as he had signed the contract, he wanted nothing more than a vacation from fighting; so, for a vacation, he called Adrian. His friend agreed to meet him that Saturday. Adrian suggested they meet at Boston Common, since it was closer for Corey than going all the way to MIT. But the real reason, Corey realized later, was that Adrian liked the Park Street–Downtown Crossing area—there was something there that attracted him, though Corey never knew what. And there was the Common itself, which, like the Esplanade, was a park. Even though it wasn't sunbathing season, Adrian liked to walk around the park, in among the trees and benches, inspecting things and laughing.

When Corey met him, this is what he did—wandering in willful-child fashion hither and yon, directing Corey's attention to details that had meaning only to Adrian and connecting them to the abstruse subjects he was taking at MIT.

Tiresome as this was, it took Corey's mind off his fight. It wasn't as unpleasant as what could happen at Bestway on any given sparring night.

But after an hour or so, Corey would take no more. It was late afternoon. Dusk was setting in. By now, they'd walked over the bridge to Cambridge and had arrived at MIT. He hadn't been here since his friend had started college and was curious about the place. He asked Adrian to let him see his dorm.

At first, Adrian didn't want to take him, but Corey goaded him, saying, "What are you afraid of?" Finally, Adrian gave in, but he wasn't happy. He insisted this was a bad idea. "It'll be fine," said Corey.

They were walking towards his dorm when Adrian stopped in his tracks.

"Oh no."

"What is it?"

A woman in a wig was coming towards them.

"Adrian," she said, "you haven't been answering your phone."

Adrian went to confront her, saying, "Now just a minute. What evidence do you have?" He parleyed with her in the cove-shaped parking lot from a dueling distance of ten paces beneath the security lights, not letting her approach.

She said, "I had radiation. You're not allowed to ignore my calls."

Corey backed away. Snatches of their discussion reached his ears. Mrs. Reinhardt wanted to take her son to dinner at Red Lobster. Adrian said he was busy. "With what?" she asked. He began listing his courses and assignments.

"I have your schedule, Adrian. Don't lie to me."

Adrian headed into his dorm. His mother made a move to follow.

"I thought we agreed on boundaries."

"Oh, Adrian!" She tried to hug him.

"Stay back," he said. "You're radioactive."

He disappeared inside. Mrs. Reinhardt vanished too. Corey saw her getting in a minivan. Annoyed and bothered by the episode, he went home to Quincy.

The event had a postscript. Days later, when Corey was icing his arm—he'd tweaked it during training—Adrian called him to complain, again, about his mother. Corey realized his friend was somehow under the impression that he took his part. He decided it was time to set him straight.

"I don't care what she's done to you. She's your mother. You don't call her radioactive."

Adrian said Corey had no idea what he was talking about.

They wouldn't talk again until April after that.

⁂

Gloria only left the house on five mornings that November. On each of these mornings, Corey helped her get dressed. He fit her skeletonized hands into the orthotic gauntlets, strapped them tight, strapped on her ankle braces, as if readying her for a Thai fight; then put on her hat and boots and winter coat and walked her to The Ride. Her disability had come through from the state. Under its terms, she would receive full pay for working forty hours a month. She was finally on her way to being liberated from her job.

At her office, they allowed her to sit there and do little. Her employer, having no choice under the law, assented to this arrangement but was unhappy with it.

If she was staying home, Corey poured her coffee, plugged in her laptop and then he left her.

"I'm going to learn something today," she said as he was leaving. "I saw a Sanskrit course online."

He wore his hat, gloves, winter parka, sweatshirt, long johns, double socks, drove to Quincy High and sat through class with his gym bag between his legs and thought about his mother.

Once, he had a fear premonition and went outside and called her. The call was disconnected. He hit redial. No answer. He was about to drive home. Finally, she picked up.

"Are you okay?"

"I'm fine. I just had trouble with my hands."

After school, he drove to the academy, wrapped his hands, put on his headgear, groin protection, mouthpiece, shin guards, and got in the cage to spar. At five, he took off his gear and rolled with the jiujitsu class, and at six he put the hand and foot wraps back on and trained Muay Thai. Twice a week, he stayed late and lifted weights—a conditioning circuit whose goal was to make him throw up. Sometimes it was successful. Lying on his back, he performed leg raises while someone smashed him in the belly with a Thai pad. Every weekend, he took a long slow run along the shore, wearing his down coat, his body getting leaner and lighter under his sweats. The ocean detonated on the gray beach. He listened to it as he jogged. He ate tuna fish and frozen broccoli and weighed himself.

His skin burned constantly from chafing, and he went to Walgreens and bought skin lotion and it relieved him. At night, after training, he soaked his board shorts and compression shirts in white vinegar and hot water to kill staph, ringworm, herpes gladiatoris, and on weekends he took his and his mother's laundry to the coin laundromat next to Point Liquors and washed their clothes in Era Plus. While they dried, he fell asleep. He took them out of the dryer, cleaned the lint off the filter because he liked the soft, warm feltlike feel of the lint, and carried their clean clothes out in a plastic hamper to the old red hatchback, which his mother had started driving when she was a kid at Lesley College.

One of his Craigslist jobs took him to Central Square, to a residential development not far from MIT. He assembled Ikea furniture for a pair of girls who lived in a brand-new three-floor house with hardwood floors and a brick patio in the back. One girl had a conference call with a finance company, which she took in the bathroom, while he was working. She was still there when he was leaving. He flagged down her roommate, a blonde in her pajamas. "Oh. You need to be paid." She got her purse. "It was twenty, wasn't it?"

"Actually your ad said twenty-five."

Riding home on the T, for the hundredth time, he thought about quitting high school and getting a full-time job.

Every morning he woke up, the fight was a day closer. His opponent was with the Gracie Barra fight team. Corey looked him up online, saw his record. He didn't want to think about him any more than he had to. Once a day he thought whatever was going to happen in the cage would eventually happen no matter what he did and then it would be over.

While he was away, Gloria, alone in their house in Quincy, put aside her online Sanskrit lesson and left her bedroom and used her walker to make her way to the front door, which she somehow managed to open with her gauntlets. She stood on the top step of the stairs outside her house, which she was unable to descend on her own, and stared out at the seawall, clutching her walker.

The fight was going to be in his mother's hometown of Springfield, Mass. Three days beforehand, on December fifth, an arctic wind raced down from Canada and crashed into a warm surge boiling up from the Gulf of Mexico. Low, dark clouds rushed across the skies of Boston. Within minutes, the daylight world turned eerily black and a storm hit. Hurricane-force gusts bombed through the streets. Hail drove down violently. Trapped in the house in Quincy, Corey felt like a sailor on a tiny ship at sea. Beyond his windows, he could see nothing but a churning, impenetrable darkness that blotted out everything and had a frightening sulfurous cast.

He let the blinds close and went to the bathroom and found the clippers. While hail rattled the windows, he buzzed his hair off. Shorn and tense, he looked in the mirror.

"Ding!" he said. "The bell rings. I come out, I take my time . . ."

He moved through the house, throwing punches in slow motion.

"What do I do if he gets my back?"

He got down on the floor and bridged. "Handfight, handfight, handfight—respect the choke—kick the leg out—free that leg—don't let him mount—turn into him—payback time."

While he was twisting on the floor, his mother's wheelchair came by UPS. The weather had abated just enough for trucks to drive, but the driver and the shipping box still got soaking wet. Corey ran out to help the driver get it up the steps. Rain flew in when the door was open. He broke the box open with a razor-knife. The chair was folded. He pulled the sides apart and locked the bolts in place with a wrench and fit the custom-made cushion in its sleeve.

His mother was distressed. She had him hide the wheelchair in the corner and drape it with a bedsheet.

Corey put on a slicker and went up to the city, to the North End, the old Italian neighborhood. He bought her a license plate that said Mafia Boss and brought it home and wired it to the axle.

He knew it would offend his father. That may have been why he did it. The next night, his father walked in just after dinner. Corey heard him talking to his mother as if they were still a family. When Corey came out of his room, he saw Leonard sitting on the futon, reading a Committee to Protect Journalists book called *Attacks on the Press*, and Corey knew he'd seen the license plate.

Sure enough, a few minutes later, Leonard looked up from his book and said, "It'd be interesting if you met a real gangster someday, Corey."

20

Springfield

The next day, Corey drove to his mother's hometown and weighed in. Saturday morning, he drove through Ludlow and looked for the house that she was born in. In the evening, he sat in the dressing room underneath the armory that had housed the original Springfield rifle and got his hands taped up.

Upstairs, workers finished assembling the cage. They tightened turnbuckles under the canvas to achieve the proper balance of springiness and give. The black cage sat in the middle of a floor made of long, polyurethaned boards with an antique orange cast. The vast, churchlike interior of the armory rose up overhead. Giant banners, like models of blue whales in a natural history museum, hung suspended in the shadow up above, announcing basketball games and rock concerts.

Then the music kicked on, the audience came in, the announcer came out, and down in the dressing room, under the stage, competitors started hearing their names. They went out one by one. A lightweight in camouflage shorts went out clapping his hands and screaming, "Let's fucking do this!" The cheering echoed down into the subterranean corridor. Corey broke a sweat. An hour went by. Then it was time.

He walked out to "Welcome to the Jungle," wearing Bad Boy vale tudo shorts and a steel cup, swatting hands as guys high-fived him coming down the chute. He grimaced at the official. There were fangs painted on his mouthpiece. Veins stood out on his white biceps. He rapped his crotch. The towering bald man pointed him theatrically up into the cage as if it were a world of wonders.

His opponent, Jack, had broad shoulders and a big face like a TV personality, an older man's face, as if he had spent his young life working on an oil rig. His long shorts hid his knees and fore-shortened his legs, making him an oversized barrel-chested torso planted onto a set of knotty calves and big feet like a cholo gangster.

"Corey, you need this fight to be on the ground. You need to be on top," Eddie shouted. "Don't take bottom!"

The bell rang, and the two men ran at each other, and Jack dropped Corey with his first punch. The audience saw a white body fall under Jack's knee. Jack's fist was rising up and swinging down on a blond head. The crowd realized what was happening and its screaming turned deafening. "Roll out!" Eddie bellowed. Corey turned himself upside down and tried to roll. He kicked his legs up and rolled out from underneath the knee. Jack fell on him. Their bodies looked like two logs bouncing up and down, hit-ting each other. Both logs flew straight up off the ground, against gravity, and Corey picked up Jack, said, "You motherfucker!" and body-slammed him. Jack dove up and took him down. Because the action happened so fast and Jack wound up on top, the specta-tors saw *him* body-slamming Corey. Corey opened his legs like a crab and shut them on Jack's head and tied his legs in a knot. Jack stopped trying to hit him. The ten-second clapper sounded. Corey was straining to hold the knot shut. His leg came off Jack's shoulder and hooked over the side of Jack's face. Suddenly the ref ran over and grabbed Corey's legs and pulled them off. The bell rang. Corey let go and Jack turned away, holding his arm. The capsule of his elbow joint had popped. Eddie was on his feet yell-ing and cheering. Corey jumped up and screamed with a bloody mouthpiece.

The ref called him to the center of the ring and grabbed his wrist and lifted his arm. "The winner, by arm-bar submission," the announcer said.

Corey's body ran with sweat. Sweat was gathering in his eye-brows. His face was sunken, and blood was running out his nose. He took the announcer's mike in his gloved hand and said, "I want to dedicate this fight to my mother, Gloria. She's the only real gangster I know."

He climbed down from the cage and went back to the locker room barefoot, carrying his pile of clothes and sneakers. Guys leaned out of the audience to slap him on the back. He went directly to the bathroom stall and threw up. There was blood in his ears. The medics came and looked at him. His eyes had red rings around the pupils as if he was turning into a werewolf. They took his blood pressure and held a bag of ice on his head. He told the female EMT she looked pretty. She seemed to have a negative opinion of anyone who would fight, on the grounds that it was an irresponsible risk to take. Eddie sat with him and took the ice from her and held it on Corey's head. They asked him if he wanted to go to the hospital and he said no. Jack came in grinning, holding an ice bag on his swollen elbow, and shook his hand. Corey sat up for him. The EMTs packed up and left. Jack said goodbye: "I'll be back to training soon," and flexed his red wet swollen arm. He left too.

"Nice job, beautiful job," Eddie said. "You can't teach that."

Corey got his gloves cut off, leaving tape and gauze on the floor, and changed and left the dressing room and limped out to the bleachers and watched the rest of the fights with Eddie. Eddie said, "This is how it begins. You've got a career in the making." Eddie was wearing a shirt that said *For he to-day that sheds his blood with me shall be my brother*—the quote from Shakespeare's *Henry V* before the Battle of Agincourt. "The promoter talked to me. He wants to see you back here. We'll look at what he says. We'll move you up the right way. Depending on what you want. If you keep working like you have been, you could go somewhere with this."

They went to an after-party at a bar—a dark, overcrowded scene of confusion and noise, backslapping and shouted conversation. Corey appeared carrying his gym bag on his shoulder, wearing a sweatshirt, jeans, parka, and black sneakers with white soles, which looked like black boats with rubber gunwales. His close-cropped blond head stuck up from the puffy navy and black padding of his coats. The thick column of his neck held up his bony cranium. He had a flare of blue under one eye as if he hadn't slept with that one eye for quite some time or had applied vivid eyeshadow to it—a bruise. His ear, already cauliflowered from training, looked like a purple balloon tied in complex and painful knots. It shined with blood swelling. The bridge of his nose had a dark shadow on it. Had someone dipped a finger in charcoal and brushed it over the bridge of his nose? But this was another bruise. His nose had been fractured. His lower lip bulged. The red striations of his teeth and mouth guard had been imprinted on the inside of his lip. His cheekbone and forehead had the kind of marks you associate with rashes and acne. But they were a stippling of purple and red knuckle marks. The side of his head was swollen and mottled pink and purple from the temple to the jaw. The promoter came over in his slick gray suit and shook Corey's hand.

"I'm going to see you again, right?"

"Wild horses couldn't keep me away."

"Wild horses? I like you. You did great, fantastic. Help yourself to whatever you want. We got vodka, booze, schnapps. It's all on the house for you guys. Oh, you're too young? Then Eddie, you drink up for him! Eddie, my man, the living legend."

Back at the motel, he slept for an hour before the pain in his head woke him up. He hobbled to the bathroom and checked his phone. He had a message from his mother. She had called him hours ago and he hadn't heard it.

"I hope it went well tonight. I'm praying for you."

In the background of the voicemail, a voice was saying, "Gloria, I'm telling you for the last time, get off the phone."

Corey listened to the message twice. Then he flipped on the room light and started gathering up his things. There was no aspirin that he could find anywhere. Stepping back in his shoes and grabbing his bag, he left the hotel room and pulled the door shut after him, leaving the card key on the dresser. The hatchback was cold. He started it and drove slowly around the parking lot until his headlights picked up the driveway leading out of the hedgerow. On the street, he put the clutch in and glided towards the black hump of the forested hills, looking around for a landmark. A green reflective sign appeared in his headlights. He took the turn and came up on the highway. He let the clutch out and started speeding east.

As he drove, he stepped outside himself mentally and said, "You're getting yourself worked up for nothing. You *want* there to be a crisis with your father. There's nothing going on. This is dumb. Don't crash the car."

Twenty minutes later, the sky began to lighten. The hatchback was going east on 90 with trucks. He stopped for gas in Framingham as the sky was turning orange. He started to compose a text to Eddie—"I had to go . . ."—but deleted the words and got back on the highway.

He drove through Watertown, passed a steak house, sped along the concrete channel under Fenway Park and into the amber-lit tunnel to 93 South.

When he popped out of the tunnel, the flaming sunrise that should have been there had disappeared. The shore was gray. The sun was up in the heavens somewhere. Different ships could see the sun from different latitudes by spying into the heavens from other points on the surface of the earth, but it was invisible from this latitude and longitude at this time of the morning on this date in Quincy, Mass.

He spun down the off-ramp and wheeled past Grumpy White's. The sky had invaded the town with its dreariness. Going downhill to the water, he saw the houses sitting in their beds of marsh grass, an unfinished carpentry project in a yard, a board across a sawhorse, a circular saw left out.

Then he saw his mother's house and Leonard's car, and he drove up behind the Mercury right on its bumper and pinned it in. He threw the brake, jumped out and jogged up the wooden stairs of his home. The stairs were painted robin's-egg blue like the ladder of a boy's bunk bed. He was trembling and light-headed with fear as if he were getting into the cage. Without any good reason, he knew something terrible was happening. The fear was so stupid that he stopped where he was with his hand on the doorknob and took a breath to control himself.

Another part of his brain was anticipating how embarrassed he was going to feel explaining his sudden disappearance to his coach.

When he opened the door of his home, he knew something was wrong after all because the Buddhist tapestry had been ripped down off the fake wood wall. His hope died instantly, and after that he stopped thinking entirely.

He ran into her room and saw Leonard shouting at her. His mother was lying on the floor. Her walker had been thrown across the room. Her TV lay on its face, having dropped headfirst off the shelf. Its screen was smashed. Leonard was calling Gloria a bitch. He was telling her over and over to make sure she heard it. Gloria was lying on the bathroom floor, her head towards the toilet. She was crying. Her head was next to the toilet brush.

Corey advanced on Leonard, shouting, "Shut the fuck up or I'll fucking kill you."

Leonard was in an entranced state of anger with Gloria. When Corey shouted at him, he twitched and appeared to come out of it. He walked out of the room.

Corey picked his mother up. He asked her if she was hurt. "Just my head. I hit my head." He picked her up and looked for somewhere to put her. The only place was her bed. "What are you doing?" "Nothing." He kept his voice calm. He set her in the bed, put pillows behind her. "Are you okay? Would you excuse me?" He began to leave the room. "Corey!" she said. "What are you doing?" "I'll be right back." "Corey, no!" He ran outside and shut her door. He saw nothing. The house was empty. He ran to the kitchen. He ran to the front door and looked outside. He saw no one towards the water. He looked up Sea Street and saw a figure going up the hill. He ran after him. Halfway to him, Leonard looked over his shoulder. "I'm warning you. If you get anywhere near me, you're going to jail. Right to jail."

Corey caught him up. "Hey, buddy. Going somewhere?"

"Do you know what would happen to you in jail? It would be like putting you in a meat grinder."

"I figure you and me have got to talk."

"The only talking you're going to do . . . Don't play with me."

Corey put his hand on Leonard's shoulder. "Hey, old pal." He gripped the back of Leonard's neck. "You gonna try and stab me? You want to scare my mom? Look in my eyes, bitch. I'll fucking murder you. Yeah, I'll fucking murder you. Test me. Test me, bitch. Bitch. Youse a bitch. Not her. You. Bitch. Punk ass. Punk-ass motherfucker. Give me a reason. Give me a reason. Touch me, you bitch-ass motherfucker. Dude, you ain't shit. You pick on women. What does that make you? I've dealt with men out here. Men. You ain't nothing. Yo, the only reason I'm not murdering you right now is I gotta get home and take care of her. But you and me ain't done. If I see you, if you come here again? I'll kill you without a second thought. Pussy motherfucker. Pussy. Yeah, eyes down, bitch. Pussy-ass cop. Fake-ass scientist. Loser."

Leonard kept his head down.

Corey jogged back down the hill to his house. He told his mother he was home. She had somehow crawled out of bed and gotten to her walker and was standing on her walker in the middle of her room. She had urinated in her pajamas and she was crying.

"Everything's okay, Mom," he told her in a strangely bright sunny tone as if he were taking mood drugs and there was nothing behind his eyes but high-tech chemistry acting on his neurons. "Everything's okay. It's just me. He's not coming back."

"Did you do anything?"

"What? To him? No!" he exclaimed, as if the idea were unthinkable. "I'm just gonna change the locks. You'll be fine."

He took her to the bathroom, walking by her side as she took slow steps, her toe in its small white sneaker hanging down like a pointer dog every time she raised it. They moved at a processional pace to the bathroom. He sat her on the toilet and changed her pants. She needed to be showered. But they had never gotten the shower seat that would allow her to clean herself. She smelled strongly, his mother. He helped her on with her new pants and asked her where she would like to spend the day. She asked him to take her to the futon. He used pillows to build up a seat for her and support her back, because it was becoming difficult for her to sit normally without support. She couldn't hold herself upright anymore. He got her comfortable and put the laptop on her lap on top of a book so that the heat from the computer wouldn't cook her legs.

But she had seen the ripped-down Buddhist weaving. "Give me a second, I'll hang that up again." She tried to tear it the rest of the way off the wall. "Get rid of it! I don't care. Throw it out." He couldn't calm her, so he took the hanging down and folded it and put it in his room, telling her he'd hang it up for her later.

She cried again when she saw the TV was broken. He picked up the glass and vacuumed the rug. It was noon, and it was gray.

Her hair was unwashed and needed combing. She asked for her glasses. She sat reading on her laptop and radiating severity and silence.

He spent the rest of the day making things right, cleaning up. He made macaroni and cheese and served his mother. She said she wasn't hungry. He ate the entire pot himself. Long-suppressed cravings hit him. He had been dieting for his fight for the past six weeks. He went out and bought a twenty-two-piece chicken nuggets and a block of carrot cake with cream cheese frosting and a Coca-Cola at the general store and had them for a midafternoon snack. A friend called him on his phone to congratulate him on his fight.

"What's the matter, man? You don't sound happy."

"Oh, I'm happy. How're you?"

"I'm fine!" The caller laughed.

Corey hung up. He began trembling all over again with fury. He began looking around the house for anything that belonged to Leonard to destroy it. He spied Leonard's cop bag. "He's not getting that back." He took it to his room and dumped it out. There were several pairs of uniforms in it. Corey tore the clothes apart with his bare hands. His mother asked him what he was doing from the other room. He carried on a calm conversation with her. "I'm making rags for the gym," he said. He strained, pulling at Leonard's collar, and the threads popped and the shirt ripped in half down the back, leaving Corey with rags in each fist. She heard the ripping in the other room. Neither of them spoke. He stepped on the trousers and pulled the legs apart. He wished he could burn them. He had an overwhelming desire to obliterate anything that had ever touched his father and absorbed his smell. If his mother hadn't been here, he would have started a fire and burned everything, he knew.

There were other items in the bag—two large nightsticks of different sizes, two sets of handcuffs locked together.

"You ain't getting none of your shit back, you motherfucker," Corey said. He spat on the bag, but he did it silently so his mother wouldn't hear the telltale infuriated sound of someone spitting.

He went to the kitchen and pulled open every drawer and cupboard until he found everything that had come from Leonard:

the items of designer kitchenware—skillets, pots, several kitchen knives. They bore antiseptic ceramic coatings in interior decorator colors of dandelion yellow, sage green—Ikea colors. He put them in the gym bag with the truncheons. The bag was now so loaded with wood and steel it made for heavy carrying. He opened the kitchen window and lifted the heavy bag, filled with sharp implements, over the sill and set it outside the window. He crawled out after it and took it across the backyard to the marsh grass, which stood nine feet tall, the hollow stalks dry and yellowed, the chlorophyll leaching out, the leaves turning to the texture of corn husks. He tossed the bag into the rustling weeds, which snapped and broke when the bag fell into them.

Back inside, he kissed his mom on the head. "Everything's fine. Just getting organized."

In the course of hunting around the house, he found a pair of Leonard's special glasses. At four o'clock in the afternoon, he took them outside and stomped them on the asphalt sidewalk. He went over to the Mercury Sable and put them on the hood.

He tried to get in the car, but it was locked. He stepped back and kicked the passenger-side window with four gradually harder front kicks until it popped like a lightbulb and rained down in a rattling waterfall of green glass. Far down the street, a man putting boards in the back of his pickup looked at him. Corey reached in and unlocked the car door. From a distance, he felt the witness watching. He looked inside the Mercury, made a half-hearted effort to break the rearview mirror, felt self-conscious and increasingly scared of the consequences of his actions and closed the door and went inside.

He called a tow company to ask if they'd tow a car away from his house. They told him it would cost a hundred fifty dollars. "Never mind," he said. The crime had made him shake a little. He hung up and called a locksmith and asked how much it would cost to get his house locks changed. The locksmith told Corey he could change the locks himself. A new Schlage, a medium-security lock, cost only thirty-five dollars.

"God bless you," Corey said.

The Home Depot was in Quincy Adams. He was about to leave when he heard a knock on the door. It occurred to him that for the past several minutes, he had been hearing vehicles idling outside and the sound of voices talking. The door opened and a number of state troopers walked into the house.

"What's your name?"

"Corey Goltz."

"Stay sitting. Is this your mother?"

"What's happening?" Gloria asked.

"Are you his mother?"

"Yes."

"Did you know your son was vandalizing property?"

"Wait! Please listen. This is a more complicated situation," Corey said.

"Is that or is that not your car out there?"

Corey started to stand up because he wanted to tell the policemen his mother was sick, but he wanted to take them aside to do it; he didn't want to say it in front of her.

"Don't move," they told him. "I'm handcuffing you for our own safety. I'm not placing you under arrest at this time."

"Thank you, officer. I just wanted to explain what's going on here. My mom is innocent in all of this. Please be nice to her. That's all I ask. Please be nice to her."

"He looks like he's been in a fight," one of the troopers said.

"I fought at a mixed martial arts competition last night."

"Oh, how long you been doing that?"

"Like, six months."

"Do you mind if we search his property, ma'am?"

"Yes!" Gloria cried.

"Is that his room? For our safety and yours, we just want to make sure we're not going to find any drugs or weapons in the house."

The cops went into Corey's room wearing rubber gloves and lifted up his mattress, opened his closet, looked in his tub of Gaspari protein powder in case he had contraband in it.

The police radio sounded. "You're a popular guy today," one of the troopers told Corey. "We got two calls about you. We got a call that somebody was running around the house with a knife."

"That's completely false. I came home this morning and found my biological father abusing my mother. She was knocked down on the floor and he was screaming at her. I threw him out of the house. My mom has a walker, officer. She was on the floor. He was screaming at her. I told him—I'll be honest—I told him, 'I'll fucking kill you!' This is just payback for that."

"He says you threatened him with a knife."

"I never went near him with a knife. I never even punched him. I never even touched him."

"He says you've got a drug problem."

"Me? I train all the time. I've spent the last eight weeks training for a fight. I live totally clean. I don't do anything."

A team of paramedics from the fire department on Hancock Street came in. A paramedic in a navy uniform kneeled in front of Corey and put a blood pressure cuff on his arm and listened to his pulse.

"Who's the president?"

"Of the United States?"

"Yeah."

"Obama. Barack Obama."

"What day is it?"

"It's—it's—sorry, I had to think about it. I was at the competition last night; today is Sunday."

"Do you know the date?"

"It's December. I went to Springfield on December seventh, so today is the eighth."

"Today's actually the ninth."

"Oh, I was thinking of the weigh-in. The weigh-in was the day before the fight. Never mind."

"What's your name?"

"Corey Goltz."

"Can you spell it?"

He spelled his name. The paramedic ripped off the blood pressure cuff.

"What are you doing this for?"

"We want to make sure you're not hyper."

The paramedics picked up their gear. They consulted with the troopers and left. Motors idled outside. The dusk was falling. The door kept opening and law enforcement personnel kept coming in in shiny leather boots. Corey, whose hands were cuffed behind his back, tried to sneak a look at his mother.

"Hey, Mom. Hey."

She wouldn't look at anything.

The troopers had made a decision. They were going to take Corey in. Corey knew what they were going to do. He heard them discussing it in front of him. "Officer, if you take me away, nobody will be able to take care of my mother."

"We'll call someone to take care of her."

"Please don't do this."

"I'm placing you under arrest for vandalism and malicious mischief."

"Where are you taking him?" Gloria cried.

"Bye, Mom. Mom, I'll come back as soon as I can. It'll be okay."

A policewoman wearing sky-blue rubber gloves said, "Someone will be called to take care of the house." She walked out after Corey, the last person to leave. On her way out, she reached inside and turned off the light switch and pulled the door to, but not all the way, so that Gloria was left in a dark house with her door unlocked. The police could be heard lingering, talking in front of the house. And then, as an afterthought, an unseen hand yanked the door all the way shut.

Gloria sat in her position on the futon. The pillows her son had placed under her were hurting her back now. She was at an angle that made it difficult to stand. She couldn't rock herself to her feet. Headlights glared through the blinds. They moved across her wall towing a train of blackness. The police had driven away. She couldn't reach the lamp. Her fingers wouldn't have been able to turn the switch anyway, which was the type you twist. She stopped trying to stand. She stopped crying out for someone to hear her. Her eyes adjusted to the shadow. She closed her eyes and breathed. She wanted to make a desperate move, to throw herself sideways because she was so uncomfortable. She breathed until she gained some control of this desire. It would have been unwise. She might fall on the floor. She felt for the cell phone at her side.

The troopers took Corey to a military barracks—a decaying brick building on Furnace Brook Parkway. They photographed and fingerprinted him. A stern professional sergeant ran things— a big, gray-haired, permanently sunburned man. On the wall were pictures of wanted men and women; in the corner, the flag of the Commonwealth of Massachusetts; overhead, the state police bulldog mascot—spiked collar, interlocking teeth, the gray-blue color of its hide the same as the troopers' uniforms, the same as the gray on their two-tone navy-and-gray vehicles.

They gave Corey a desk appearance ticket and temporary restraining order ordering him to stay at least one hundred feet away from Leonard Agoglia until such time as a judge ruled otherwise, and then they let him leave.

He walked home on the Furnace Brook Parkway. To protect himself from the cars at night, he climbed over the guardrail and walked in the woods. A gully ran through the trees. A stream ran in the bottom of the gully. The trees arched over the stream creating a tunnel, which traveled deep into the west, rising as it went, up into Quincy's granite mountains. The marsh expanded to his right, picking up the lights from the shore. Beds of black grass gave way to water. He came out of the trees and smelled the sea.

At home he was reunited with his mother. In her desperation while he was gone, she had overcome her pride and called Joan, to whom she hadn't spoken in many years, and left a message. She didn't know if she had gotten through.

21

The Year of Joan

The Monday after his arrest, Corey stayed home from school and his mother stayed home from work. At seven thirty, the driver from The Ride honked outside. Corey went out in the gray cold morning and said, "She can't make it today." He tried to apologize. The driver put up a hand to stop him talking, as if to say he didn't want to hear it, he had troubles too, jumped back in his car and drove away, grizzled, red-faced and bleary-eyed.

Back inside, Corey faced his mother. She finally admitted she was too weak to go to work at all.

"I just can't do it," she wept. He went to her side and embraced her.

But she blamed him for fighting with his father.

"Look what's happened! When we needed him! You couldn't keep your temper in check."

He took his arm back.

"What can I do to fix things?"

"You could begin by calling him and telling him you're sorry. That way at least maybe he'll drop the charges."

"I'm not calling him. If you wanted me to kill him, I'd kill him. But I'm not calling him."

"Oh, give it a rest."

"And another thing: I can tell you right now, I'm not going back to school."

"Oh, God," she said and began weeping again. "I curse my fate."

For once, he watched her impassively. "No, it's a good thing. I'm not going back. I feel much better making that decision."

"You're foolish."

It was ten in the morning. The commuting hour was over, that brief time when cars streamed past on Sea Street, and now the silence of the shore reigned supreme, a near-total stillness. Within that stillness, one could subconsciously detect the presence of those people in neighboring houses who stayed home during the day, but they were a small population spread over a wide area, and their presence was like that of insects in an open field or crabs in the tide washing over a jetty. The vast space over the bay and rock-strewn beach gave forth a whispering sound, which surrounded their house, as if they were living in a conch shell.

Corey went to the kitchen and made coffee. When he returned, she was trying to put her reading glasses on and he helped her. He put the cup in her trembling hands, she took a sip and steam flamed up on her glasses.

"Do we have any money?"

"Not really."

"Where are we on food and rent?"

"See for yourself."

They looked at the laptop. She had the online banking page open.

"You *are* going to have to work. You're going to get your wish."

He got his spiral notebook, turned to a new page, and made a list of things to do. The first was check the cupboards in the kitchen. He shook a box of cereal to estimate the contents. He went to his room and checked his money drawer and counted up his dollar bills.

He had an idea. He called Tom. Voicemail picked up and Corey left a message.

"I might be on the way to figuring things out," he told his mother.

He glanced in the mirror at the bruises on his face and wondered if Tom would be impressed. He took a shower, grim daylight filtering through the frog-covered shower curtain. He scrubbed his short hair and said, "I can do anything!"

He yanked his jeans on and, while waiting for the phone to ring, ate the last of their cereal with the last of their milk, sitting in the kitchenette, tapping his bare feet on the linoleum floor.

At 11:30, his cell phone rang and he snatched it up.

"Tom!"

"Hey, what's up. I got your message. I couldn't call you right away."

"That's fine—thank you for calling!"

"So, you're looking for work?"

"Tom, I'm looking for work. I quit school; I'm totally available—twenty-four hours a day. I have to make a living for my mom; I'm gonna be our sole supporter. I'm ready to do anything, anything it takes. There won't be any bullshit like before. That crap is in the past. I'm not going to lie to anybody. I'm a different person. If you give me a chance, you'll see."

"Well, I'd love to help ya, but I can't hire anybody right now. It's the middle of winter and this is our slow season. I'm having to send guys home as it is. But hold on a second. One of my guys was telling me there's a local that's hiring. Wait a minute. Hey, Joe! Come here for a minute. Who did you tell me was hiring? The caisson builders. They're doing the bridge over by MIT, aren't they? What are they, Local 151 or something? Corey, my guy says there's a union over by you that's hiring. They're in Quincy, Local 133. I hear they just hired fifty new guys, and they're hiring guys without any experience. They're on Washington Street. Call over there today and see if you can put your name in. Those guys do pretty good. If you can get on with them, it's union scale. They might start you as high as twenty an hour. I don't know."

Corey started thanking him profusely. "Tom, I will never disrespect your name again. I'll never embarrass you about knowing me. When things are better, we'll have a beer and I'll buy you a hundred rounds . . ."

"That's fine," Tom said. "I gotta go."

Corey called the union and learned they were no longer hiring. He'd missed the last day while he was weighing in at Springfield.

He spent several more hours calling around to different construction companies until someone finally told him to get in touch with Labor Ready, a temporary employment agency for the construction trades. In the afternoon, he went to a dilapidated house in Quincy Center across from Family Dollar. The office had brown vinyl walls. There were giant posters setting out the labor law in minuscule fine print. Behind the counter, a white-haired woman was doing clerical work. An unshaven guy in construction jeans and boots—they were brand-new and hadn't been worked in—was talking on the phone with his feet on a desk. Seeing Corey, he took the phone away from his ear.

"What're you looking for? A little demo? We'll hook you up. Go to our website and fill out the application. All our policies are there. Don't show up drunk, don't show up high. We need a clean driving record. Make sure you click the thing saying you've read it. Make sure you give us a working phone number. If I call you, answer your phone. Make sure your ringer's on. What happened to your face?"

"I did a cage fight."

"My boy does that. He's like ten-and-oh. You heard of Bobby Shephard? You should check him out."

"All right. I need a job."

"Just keep your phone on. I get these guys bitching at me they didn't get a call and their phones are off."

He went back to his phone call.

"Wait a second," Corey interrupted. "Just so I understand: I'm filling out an application; does that mean you're hiring me, you're not hiring me, you're going to think about it—how does that work?"

"We just need your number so we can call you."

"Can I fill it out here since I'm here now?"

"Hey, Mags."

"What?"

"Can he fill out his application on your computer?"

"Can you kiss my ass?" the white-haired woman croaked. "I need my computer to work."

"You're gonna have to fill it out at home."

He did. He got his first job almost immediately, but it was

only for a day. He had to drive all the way to Medford, to a retail space that was being renovated—an old store being superseded by a Walgreens or CVS. The stock was gone; only the shelves were left. He and another teenager took them out and threw them in a dumpster. It echoed like a bronze drum when they dropped the metal shelves. A foreman, who worked for the general contractor, sat in his pickup, wearing a hunter's ball cap, eating a rotisserie chicken while they worked. Christmas decorations hung above the street. The other teenager walked slowly back after each trip to the dumpster; Corey jogged, seeing his breath in the air.

"You must have benefits," his workmate said.

Gloria had him move her to the wheelchair. He took the sheet off and helped her sit. He tilted her to ease the pressure on her spine and turned the chair so she was facing the sunlight in the window.

"Does that feel better?" he asked. "Is that, like, cheerful lighting with the sun?"

The neurologist was giving his mother L-Threonine, a white, crystalline amino acid that looked like cocaine, which she had to take with Robitussin. He drove to Walgreens to buy a case of Robitussin. Someone called the manager. They thought he was a tweaker robotripping. Corey explained it was part of a regimen to treat muscle cramping in ALS. The manager said he could buy one bottle at a time. Corey protested, "We're going to go through that in a single day. Every time I drive out here burns gas." The manager said he was lucky they weren't calling the cops. Corey drove home with a single seven-ounce bottle of cough syrup.

He needed gas for the hatchback, but the bank account was under a hundred dollars.

He got home and his mother needed the bathroom. He took her one slow step at a time. Labor Ready called and asked if he was up for work right now. "Mom, can I leave you?" He told them he'd call back. He left a message with Dawn Gillespie—"I need help"—then left and ran to a demo job on Hancock Street, scooping up rubble.

He worked in his winter coat in a room lit by a halogen lamp, dust swirling in the light beam. The foreman signed his time sheet:

four hours at eleven bucks an hour. He would submit his time on Friday and get paid the week that followed, which was Christmas.

The next day, he wasn't working. He got his mother up and in the wheelchair and poured her coffee and set her up with her laptop in the sun and went out by himself on Shore Road with the cell phone in his hand and waited for a call, too stressed to see the sea, the expanse of saltwater that rolled against the beach. The pale sun was in the south. He was alone with the jetty. The frigid wind buffeted his ears.

In another month, he would have to go to court to answer Leonard's charge.

He went home and got a call from Dawn. She went over their situation. A church, Quincy Reform, was paying a percentage of their rent. Disability paid certain medical costs but only after a complex reimbursement process. They received a check for $200 a month. Their food was partly subsidized. Corey was expected to work, but the state put a cap on how much he could make before he started losing benefits. He wasn't anywhere near the cap. His mother had to make $700 a month.

"My mother can't work at all."

"The *family* needs to contribute seven hundred dollars a month." If not, Gloria would go to a state-run home.

He called Labor Ready. The dispatcher said they might have night work for him; they didn't know yet, try back later.

His mother said, "Son, I hate to bother you, but could you make me something to eat?" For that matter, Corey was hungry too. The refrigerator was empty. He was afraid to shop and afraid to drive. He dished up applesauce for them both and put the spoon in his mother's hand while he made mac and cheese.

She needed him to take her to the bathroom. The door was too narrow for the wheelchair. She stood up and used him as a walker. Each step she took, he waited and he held her. He helped her turn for the toilet. He pulled down her sweatpants and lowered her to the seat. He waited while she went. They developed a procedure. He put toilet paper in her hand. She blotted herself. He helped push her hand between her legs while looking away. She had a distinct, non-male smell that came from her anatomy. He flushed for her, picked up her pants, and helped her walk back to her chair.

Labor Ready called back. They had the night work. He said, "Thank you, God!"

But they said, "Wait, you're only seventeen. You can't do it."

"Why the hell not?"

"Labor laws. You can't work at night until you're eighteen."

Gloria told him to take her credit card and get them food. He drove to Star, grabbed groceries and hurried back. On the way, he stopped for gas. He swiped her card and put the nozzle in the tank and watched the numbers climbing up and up and up until the eight-gallon tank was full and the pump in his hand clunked off.

The undergraduates went on Christmas vacation. Leonard continued working at MIT, guarding buildings that had been left vacant by their absence. He spent several long night shifts in the marble-floored halls of the main building and several more doing rounds in a near-empty undergraduate dormitory. He sat at the desk, reading *Dreams of a Final Theory* by Weinberg, which talked about the origin and fate of the universe. Christmas passed like any other workday. He spoke to no one but the 7-Eleven guy from whom he bought coffee at the end of his shift, and then drove home in the early morning with the fresh light of a new day on the brick buildings of Cambridge, traces of frost on the asphalt. In Malden, he returned to the burrow of his house, slept and woke refreshed at nightfall, except for a few nightmares. Upon waking, he spent several hours reading, browsing the Internet. Then he fixed dinner: meat and sauce, a lot of onion and garlic. The loss of his best knives interfered with his cooking. He calculated the cost of what his son had taken from him. At nine thirty, he put on his uniform, packed his book in a plastic bag because his son had taken the good bag, the paramilitary bag that expressed so perfectly what he wanted to say about himself, got in the car and drove through working-class Malden towards the lights of Boston and the gleaming commercial and technological utopia of MIT. There, he ensconced himself at his post and passed another night.

Around midnight, he was in the main building and encountered Adrian coming down the Infinite Hallway. He'd come back to school early to avoid spending the vacation with his mother.

They went upstairs to a professor's office—a windowless attic crammed with paperbound science journals on a half floor between the engineering and chemistry halls. The security guard and the student talked for several hours about families, mothers, women, the social meaning of Christmas and its hypocrisy. Adrian said that Christmas brought out the worst in people. He did most of the talking while Leonard sat with his feet on the professor's desk and his two-way radio on the green felt blotter. Around two a.m., Leonard did reveal one thing: He said that, due to his son Corey's violent, out-of-control nature, he, Leonard, had recently been forced to stop taking care of his mother, and that sooner or later, something would have to be done about it.

∻

On a desolate day just after New Year's, Corey was sitting on his bed, taking off his boots, having just returned from work. He had gotten a long-term job at a Target in a dying mall in Braintree, next to a Loews cinema with blacked-out windows and a Starship *Enterprise*-style roof, which cars could drive beneath. A red sun hung above the evergreens that fringed the colossal parking lot when he arrived at work in the mornings. He put up steel shelving in the northwest corner of the store with a gang of temp workers. They held the vertical rails; he worked his way up a ladder, banging the shelves in with a hammer.

He tossed his boot to the floor. It landed by his hammer and a cheap new leather tool belt from Home Depot. The bruises on his face were fading. He took his sweatshirt off. His stomach muscles had lost their definition. His hair had grown and there was stubble on his chin. He unfolded his time sheet and laid it on the other time sheets, which he kept pressed like flowers in the notebook he had used for martial arts.

He straightened up and listened: There was someone knocking on their door. He went out barefoot through the cold-floored living room, where his mother was sitting in her wheelchair, reading an article on the laptop in her reading glasses.

He opened the door—and found himself looking at Joan.

She had arrived at their moment of greatest jeopardy. It didn't seem real. Corey hadn't seen her since his elementary school days. She looked great.

"I do karate," she said. She was wearing white jeans and a bomber jacket. They hugged. She said, "I'm afraid to come inside. I don't know if your mom wants to see me."

"Of course she does. Mom, look who's here!"

Joan put her arms around Gloria, who started crying.

It was only at this point, by overhearing the two women talking, that Corey learned his mother had called Joan.

"Could I use your bathroom?"

She came back with her eyes red but dry. Corey asked if he could get her something. She looked in their freezer to see if they had any vodka. When they were in private, she hugged Corey with her whole body pressed against him, which confused him because he liked it.

Gloria didn't want Joan to stay, but Corey said they needed help—*he* needed help. When he asked if Joan would stay, she said, "Sure," just like that.

She'd just gotten kicked out of another house—and another relationship (don't ask)—but that wasn't why she was here. "I've got a lot of love in my heart for your mother. It breaks my heart to see her in there. She was always my good girl, my blondie. I would've thought with all the grievous things I've done, the risks I've taken, that it would be me like that, dying young."

Corey made up the futon, but Joan spent the entire night in Gloria's bedroom, talking. In the morning, Corey got up and made coffee for everyone. He hung up the mandala once again where it belonged.

Joan's return ushered in a period of new hope. There was love and humor, as there hadn't been with Leonard. Joan was a joker. She brought relief. She was the ally they'd always needed—good and loyal.

She had a job with Enterprise Rent-A-Car, vacuuming out the vehicles for the next customer. She went to her job in the city and slept with them at night. Corey temped for Labor Ready. They split the groceries and set the house up so Gloria could survive alone, each day leaving her a prepared meal that she could open by herself. Corey wrapped tape around the handle of a fork like a prison shiv so she could hold it.

With two women in the house, Corey sensed vortexes of emotion he didn't understand. Hidden turbines spin like a stack of washing machines under every wave traveling across the ocean to the shore: Thus were the currents of love between Gloria and Joan. Sometimes, Corey was sure he felt rancor in the air, only to see them talking like old friends. He was often confused.

By the same token, when Joan first arrived, Corey felt a strong attraction to her—a burst of lust, programmed into him in early childhood—and he was sure it was reciprocated; he could hardly sleep the first night she spent in the house, and he imagined a hundred times running into her coming out of the shower. But after she had lived with them a few days, he noticed a reserved and businesslike tone in her voice when she spoke to him and a brusqueness that warned him to not even fantasize about her, that to do so would be as unthinkable and perverse as it would be to proposition his own mother, and in such moments he felt appalled that he had ever lusted after her and mortally afraid of being found out.

One day, Joan asked him what his mother thought of acupuncture. Corey said it was a scam. "Oh yeah," Joan said, "I get that. Send nine-ninety-five. I'd be the type to give away my life savings. But, on the other hand, what if—ya know? Isn't that how the Egyptians healed wounds, with mold?"

Weren't there things they only knew about in China? People scammed, but where there was smoke there was also fire, and under every little come-up was a secret that even the scammers themselves were unaware of because all they saw was twenty dollars. It took the wise bloods, the stubborn old women whose periods had stopped, to restore the wisdom. Had he ever thought of that?

Corey didn't know.

"You're like, 'What's she talking about?' It's 'cause you're a guy."

For Corey, the month passed in a state of engagement, as things do when they are new.

. . .

Gloria sat propped up in bed with pillows. Joan was sitting with her in the dusk. Through the window blinds, a small orange sun slipped below the rim of the world. The land was black, the sky was purple. The room was gray, as if filled with seawater. The women were alone. Both had been crying off and on. Joan was wearing jeans, which were tight on her. She sat with her knees bent, her thick brown arms on her knees, and the meaty part of her pudenda outlined in tight denim. She rubbed her wet eyes and nose and shook her coarse mop of black hair. Her breasts were still full; she needed a bra. Next to her, Gloria lay sallow and deflated, her blonde hair gone gray. Her skull was childlike and small. Her narrow, Northern European nose and sharp cheekbones and hard triangular jaw showed clearly under her vanishing flesh. Her thin hands lay on her belly like a Knight Templar in a coffin. Unconsciously gesturing, she raised them with effort, like a ninety-year-old, and let them settle again. Usually she was matter-of-fact and war-weary from her disease, but when a wave of grief hit her, her face contorted and her eyes squeezed shut as if she were about to cough up chunks of her heart. Then the wave passed. She was settling now. Her eyes were closed. She had turned, as much as her paralyzed body was able, into Joan, who gathered her in. Now Joan sat with Gloria's head in her lap, cradling her in the position of the Pietà. Lines of tears were drying on Gloria's yellowed cheekbones. Her eyes were closed and her face was bizarrely calm as if she had taken morphine.

"I feel like this is all a great comeuppance."

"Sshh. Hey."

"Thank you for holding me, Joan."

"He's worse than a bum. He's a creep. You're better off without him."

"I know that's how Corey feels as well."

"There's no excuse. I've seen a lot of men who've had harder lives who haven't turned out like that. I know this one kid from the projects. He has no teeth, because they don't get good medical care. But he's the nicest kid. And to top it off, he's got MS. He never had any breaks. He's from Southie. So you're gonna tell me people from East Boston have such a harder life?"

"He hasn't done anything with himself, and neither have I."

"Yeah, you have."

"He could have done more."

"Poor him."

"Don't worry, I'm done worrying about his tragedy. I've got my own grief."

"You know, I never thought he was such a genius. I just think he has an ego."

"The ego is the great enemy. I wish I could let go of my fear."

"Is there anything I can do to help?"

"You're an angel for being here."

"No, I'm not. More like a devil."

"I'm sorry for hurting you."

"No, Gloria, don't. Hey, blondie. Hey. I'd been dumped before."

"Joan, I'm such a fool."

"Your son's probably worried I'm gonna dyke out with you."

The two of them laughed and blew their noses.

"I'm not gonna say it didn't hurt. For years, I looked for somebody to replace you, Gloria my darling."

"Oh, Joan."

"One time, I was dating this dude, and the whole time I was scheming on his ex-girlfriend."

"Sounds like trouble."

"It was. He got jealous and threatened her with a gun. So I said, 'If you're gonna be a fuckin' animal, I'm gonna go.' So I said sayonara and got the fuck out of there. And I was imagining if I was like a super-cool dude in the movies, I'd be like, 'Hey, there's room in my car,' and she'd jump in with me. But my car had all my shit in it and there wasn't room for anyone else, so I never got to say that. So I left, and I drove away crying, because I was imagining them having super-hot sex when I was gone. I'm crying and turned on and jealous. And I got so mad I thought about driving back there."

"Only you, Joanie."

"I know, right?"

❧❦

Two days before his court date, when he got home from Target, Corey found out his father had come to the house while he was at work. Gloria had told Leonard to stay out, he had tried to come in anyway, and Joan had blocked him at the door.

"He was surprised as hell to see me," Joan said. "He was all like, 'I should have known.' I'm like, 'Known what? That Gloria's got friends besides a creep like you?' Then he gets all crafty: 'Joan, you know me from the old days. Let's handle this like two adults'—blazzy, blazzy, blah. I'm like, 'If you know me, then you know I'll never let you in.' When I wouldn't let him in, he was fuckin' ripshit. What'd you take from him anyway?"

"His pots and pans and knives. I threw them in the marsh."

"Whatever it was, he wants it back pretty bad. You sure it wasn't a diamond?"

"No! I wouldn't steal from him."

"I wouldn't care if you pawned it down the block."

"I don't want anything of his. If he had a diamond, I wouldn't take it. All I wanted was a little justice for him throwing my mother on the floor. I tore up his uniforms. His handcuffs, his cop-stick-thing, his little cop bag—I threw all that shit out, plus his skillet, his fancy cooking knives. And I busted his car window and his glasses."

Joan remarked that this sounded like quite a lot of property.

There were different penalties under the law for property crimes, based on the value of the things involved.

"I won't be facing a felony, will I?"

"Probably not. I'm sure they'd let you plead it down."

On the morning of January 27, Corey reported to the Francis X. Bellotti courthouse. A handful of people were milling around the front steps. They were about the same people who hung around the T. An armed officer opened the door and told them to form a line. The line moved inside slowly, through a metal detector. They all went into the same courtroom.

The judge arrived, a rigidly decent woman in her fifties with glasses and a Boston accent, and the court began its day's work. Corey showed his desk appearance ticket to a clerk, who told him to wait for his attorney.

Almost that same second, a man in a tan suit came in, looked around and asked, "Are you Corey Goltz? I'm Shay. I'm your defender." He wore a red tie, his top button was undone, he had a sharp Adam's apple, and he was carrying a briefcase. All of his curly sandy hair grew on the top of his head, as if his head were a flowerpot and his hair was the plant life coming out the top.

As Corey would discover, Shay was a hardworking, cocky but nice young jock who, over the course of his association with him, would mention going to the gym in every conversation they had; he was either going to or coming from—or regretting having missed—the gym that day. His sports had been basketball, base-ball and hockey. For Corey, he would attain the same status as an Eddie. He was extremely diligent. Eventually, he would visit Corey's home and become a true ally after meeting Gloria and seeing her condition. He would try to file a counterclaim against Leonard for domestic abuse.

Today, Corey's name was called within minutes of Shay's arrival. They went to the front of the courtroom. Corey stood next to his new attorney. The judge wanted time to consider the case. They agreed on a date with the prosecutor, and Shay led the way out. He walked fast, hauling his briefcase, one shoulder before the other, as if he were lugging a bag of hockey equipment to the rink.

Outside on the steps, Corey asked where he'd gone to college.

"I went to Suffolk."

"Is law school hard?"

"Pretty hard. I didn't sleep for two months." Shay had worked his way through school, at the paint department at Lowe's and tending bar in the city near the Wang Center.

"I hear bartenders do well with girls."

"There's some truth to that. Some girls do like a bartender," the lawyer said. "So, the judge just continued the case. That means you're going to be back here on the eighth . . ."

"You're not that much older than me," Corey interrupted.

"Ten years."

"It just seems like you got a really good start in life."

"Not that good. My family lost our house when I was ten. I wanted to play hockey, but I had to work. We didn't have groceries until me and my brothers started buying them. It sucked."

"Where are you from?"

"Dorchester."

"We used to live on Washington Street. Was there a lot of shady shit?"

"My best friend robbed a liquor store."

"But you got out of there. You showed a lot of discipline."

"When things are tough, you confront them. Maybe it's where I'm from, but I've always been that way."

"I don't want to be in this situation, here in court. I never want you to have to see me again—professionally—as much as I like you! I want to just get to work and make something of myself."

"You're all right, Corey. I'll tell that to the DA. This is what we're telling them: This was a first offense, you've learned your lesson, and you need to be at home taking care of your mom."

"But it's true!" Corey insisted. "We don't have to make it up."

Shay was just waiting for him to finish talking. He said, "See you later, buddy." He stuck out his hand at Corey and Corey shook it. He went home.

At home, he thought of the courtroom. It was airy and white-walled. The high windows let in the winter sky. You saw treetops, rooftops, snow. The furnishings—the judge's podium, the corral, the wooden pews where people waited to be called, the massive tables for the prosecutor and the defendant with fat lathed columnar legs—were in good repair, made of blond wood. He had almost enjoyed court, the atmosphere of civilization—tradition, common sense, the slight flavor of scholarship, of college in the background. He admired Shay.

After court, he drove to the academy. The sky above the highway looked like the Arctic Ocean seen from underneath by a diver looking for a gap in the ice. When he arrived, he found the parking lot full of trucks. Inside, the gym was hot. He unzipped his coat—his work coat, covered in dust, a nail hole in the sleeve. Training was in full swing: twenty students paired up on the mat, grappling silently, seized in suspended animation, I-push-you-pull, cancelling each other out, moving slowly with one limb, trying to solve a leverage puzzle. A focus of concentration like a library. The sound of breathing. Occasionally, a scramble would break out and two guys would roll around each other and wind up in a new position, one man now pinning the other. The bottom player's stomach rising up and down in his rash guard, breathing, gathering strength. Hoping to defend, but in a worse position. The beginning of a slow relentless end, unless he escaped. They squeezed each other and sweat poured out of their black rash guards like sponges.

Eddie was going around from one set of trainees to the next, giving instruction. He saw Corey and didn't speak to him. "Make sure you stay tight. Take away all the air," he told one of his students, a burly, pockmarked guy with the bruised-looking eyes of a person of Mediterranean ancestry, who looked as if he had been jolted by an unforgettable vision of evil.

Corey waited till the end of class and went over to shake Eddie's hand.

"You take a break?"

"I should have called. I'm sorry. I had some stuff going on."

"You back now?"

"Not exactly. That's what I wanted to talk to you about."

Eddie didn't give him a private audience. Corey found it hard to discuss his personal situation with others listening. He said he had "some legal shit." Eddie didn't look impressed.

"Thanks for understanding," Corey said.

Eddie turned away in the middle of their final handshake to talk to someone else.

Corey hung around a few minutes longer watching the guys roll, then got back in his car and drove away.

"It's over for me," he told Joan when he was back in Quincy. "This is my fight now—" looking at Gloria in her wheelchair.

"Hanging up your guns."

"There's no time for it. You can't do it halfway. If you're not training every day and you go in there and meet somebody who is, something bad is going to happen."

"I guess that's how it is for you. For me, it was different. I didn't have a cage. You couldn't tell when it was gonna jump off. I had to be ready all the time."

"You can't be your best like that."

"No, you can't. I fought a girl when I had the flu. Congestion. I couldn't breathe."

"She jump you?"

"She called me out. I said, 'Bitch, I ain't afraid a you!' I was scared out my damn mind. She was big."

"What was she mad about?"

"Her boyfriend was talking to me. She called me a chink. I said, 'Bitch, I'm gonna—a-chew!' I sneezed my ass off. I lost. But I gave her a bloody nose. If I get in a fight, I always try to make 'em bleed."

In the mornings, he got up at four to go to a new assignment, in South Boston—on the harbor. He set up his mother's coffee, Robitussin, L-Threonine, orange juice and protein. It would precipitate and be clumped on the surface of the juice by the time she drank it. He put it in the fridge, turned off the kitchen light, took his tool belt, sandwich, a book to read on his break, and left. Through the wall of his mother's bedroom, he heard the thump of Joan's heel in the tub as she was showering. He hurried to the hatchback and drove into the city. Soon, before he was fully awake—and before the sun was up—he was standing in a bare white room that smelled like plaster, under a blazing fluorescent light. A supervisor was telling him to take a portable drill and install a mirror in the restroom down the hall of what was to be an office.

In the afternoons, he enjoyed the great reward of construction work: the early liberation that goes with the early start—and he drove home with his time sheet signed and saw his mother. The now-empty glass, rimed by a silt of protein, waited on her wheelchair's tray top. He set it in the kitchen sink. She was listening to NPR on her laptop, wearing a loose South Asian dress.

On Super Bowl Sunday, he saw Molly at the Half Door. She had a sort-of boyfriend with her, another large individual like her shot-putter from the year before. Corey watched the big game with them. The Patriots won. He told her about his fight. She knew that he had quit school and was working. When he headed home, a homeless drunk guy camping out in the Bank of America ATM across from Acapulcos raised his hand from the floor and gave him the thumb's-up.

22

Between Us

Court wasn't as pleasant when Corey returned to it in March. His father was there with a lawyer, a balding, goatlike, oilily smiling man in a brown suit. Leonard was wearing his trademark fedora and a brand-new pair of tinted sunglasses. He pushed through the waist-high swinging gate and took a seat in the wooden pew behind the assistant district attorney and watched her with his arms folded and an air of vindication. His smiling advocate gave papers to the clerk, who gave them to the judge. Shay went up to see what was going on. Shortly, Corey learned that his father was accusing him of threatening him with a knife.

If the judge believed the accusation, this could significantly change the way she handled Corey's case. He was old enough for her to treat him as an adult. The ADA stood up and said she was extremely concerned that the defendant was a violent person. She cited the cage fighting. There was a discussion of sending Corey to a court-appointed psychologist to evaluate how troubled he was. The judge continued the case again—this time until April. Shay said, "Thank you, Your Honor," and led Corey out.

"They're lying," Corey said. "I never went after him with a knife."

At home, his mother started getting phone calls. He knew they were from Leonard. His mother revealed that Leonard had said something ugly to her. She wouldn't say what, but for days afterward she seemed to sink inside herself. Corey started answering her phone. The next time Leonard called, he cursed the man. Joan egged him on. The phone kept ringing all night as if the caller enjoyed being called a piece of shit. But once, Corey heard someone else's voice, as if Leonard had gotten a confederate to call for him.

At the April court date, Shay was angry. "Did you make a harassing phone call to your father?"

"No."

"Because he's got a recording of you threatening him."

The ADA was calling the tape disturbing. The court was renewing Corey's restraining order. He wasn't allowed to talk to Leonard at all under any circumstances ever again.

Shay told Corey to wait outside the courtroom. Leonard and his attorney were lurking in the hall. Corey moved away from them. He put his earbuds in and tried to lose himself in music. He nodded to the beat, hooked his thumbs in his pockets, drummed his fingers on his legs. He risked a glance down the hall. His father and his lawyer were laughing at him, imitating him, bobbing their heads up and down.

I'm going to get back to the gym, and I'm going to kill him, he thought.

Shay came back. Fortunately, the judge wasn't going to listen to the recordings. Shay was vexed with Corey and seemed to have lost faith in his judgment and character.

A week went by after court. Leonard kept calling. "Corey, put your mother on." Corey would hang up. He did this five times one night. Leonard said, "Corey, you're going to be sorry. Put your mother on the phone or I'm going to have the police over there so fast it'll make your head spin."

He held the phone to his mother's ear.

"What do you want, Leonard?" Gloria asked.

Leonard said he wanted an apology for having his glasses smashed.

Corey took the phone away from Gloria and told Leonard to go fuck himself and hit the End button.

The phone rang again immediately and Joan answered it.

"Don't yell at me," she said. Leonard could be heard threatening her with legal action.

Gloria told Joan to let her talk to him. Joan put the phone against Gloria's ear.

"Leonard, can we calm down?" Gloria said. "I'm asking you as a mother. Please. I know you're angry, but he's angry too. I understand you lost your glasses. He'll pay for them, Leonard. Give him a chance. I know they weren't cheap. Well, I'm a party to this too. I'm sorry, but I've got my hands full. Can you do this for me? Is that too much to ask? Are you so full of hate? Is that all there is, this shit between us?"

Leonard began to seethe. He told her, "You never would have given me the time of day if you hadn't been a fucked-up person yourself. Death would be better for both of us."

Corey and Joan could hear these outrages.

"Tell him you can't talk to him!" Corey pleaded.

"This is bullshit," Joan said. She took the phone and told Leonard, "She's not alone here. We can all hear you." She ended the phone call and turned the phone off.

An April night. Corey was driving north along the oceanfront. Dark sky. Gray beach. Street lights. Then Dorchester. He was on 93 without a plan. It had rained and the car was wet. He went through the glowing amber tunnel and came out in Boston, and then the hatchback was flying by the CITGO sign in Kenmore Square and the Doubletree Hotel at the entrance to the Mass Pike.

He crossed the river and found a place to stop. Once again, he was just outside MIT. He didn't know why he was here. As he sat in his car on Memorial Drive, the spotlights above him shining on the high granite walls of the university's Olympian buildings through the trees, which were just beginning to bloom, Corey took his cell phone and dialed Adrian, with whom he hadn't talked all winter. The river reflected the moonlight. He didn't expect Adrian to pick up, but he did.

Corey said he was nearby and at loose ends. Adrian invited him to his dorm.

He waited downstairs in the lobby. His friend came down to meet him. Adrian appeared from the stairwell, his hair sticking up, his forehead studded with red pimples, his extraordinary muscular torso exploding through the thin tight fabric of a yellow-stained undershirt.

He greeted Corey with a revelation: He'd been upstairs studying so intensely for so long that he'd gone into an altered mental state.

"It was like I didn't know where I was! My mind got in this groove. I could see all these equations in my head and how each one was related to every other one in this giant network, and it's like my brain could convert these complex things into each other in the blinking of an eye—it was so incredible."

This had been going on for, like, fifteen hours straight, Adrian said. He hadn't wanted it to end, but he needed a study break. He'd almost been in danger of not feeding his muscles.

They went to the dining hall, which was in a white rotunda. A cashier was waiting at a register. A kitchen worker was replacing empty pans in the steam table. It was ten of nine and there was no one there, but they were still serving.

Adrian went to get food. Corey took a seat at a table in the seating area. He stretched his legs out and leaned back. The ceiling was very high. It looked like an eggshell with soft hidden lights glowing inside it. A trio of college women paid the cashier and came his way, carrying their trays, salads, waters, smartphones, wallets, keys. He straightened up and pulled his legs in and made a gesture that meant "there's room here." They went past him and sat by the tall black window, which was starred with amber lights.

Adrian got back from the food line. His tray was piled with baked chicken. Corey watched him eat.

"Is it weird I'm here? We haven't talked in a while, I know. Maybe things were a little tense the last we spoke. You wouldn't believe what's been going on."

Adrian was tearing the skin off his chicken and eating just the meat. "Yes, I remember the last time we talked. I sensed all this oral aggression coming out of you. It was like your limbic system was firing overtime."

It wasn't his limbic system, Corey said. He described the continuing state of warfare with his father. Everything had blown apart. He'd dropped out of school.

His friend laughed. *"I'm not crazy, you're the one that's crazy!"*

"Well, I don't think I'm crazy."

"Of course you don't."

"So how have you been, Mister Studying-eighteen-hours-at-a-stretch-without-leaving-the-room-and-never-washing-my-shirt?"

Adrian said everything was fine in his life; everything was working efficiently. "Let's see: I've been studying general relativity; I've been lifting—that's going well; I'm actually bench-pressing more; and, let's see, what else? Chemistry is going well. I'm taking math; math is going well; I just learned a new way to take the gradient; I'm becoming more efficient. And, let's see, I haven't seen my mother in . . . one, two, three, four—like six weeks. That's good. And as far as making friends and getting along with people, MIT is really great. There are a lot of really cool people here. They're really down-to-earth. If you don't understand something, they'll take the time to explain it. They're into ideas."

"And how's the girl situation? Is that going well?"

"I think I've solved the problem of women."

"How'd you do that?"

He gave a very complex answer, which went over Corey's head, but, on further questioning, it boiled down to his having discovered a place where women would do anything for money.

"What place is that?"

Adrian wouldn't say.

"What's it called?"

He couldn't remember.

"Where is it?"

A long way away.

"How do you get there?"

It wasn't easy.

"Then how'd you find it?"

He'd gotten lucky. "You'd be so jealous," he told Corey.

"I don't think I'm jealous, I'm just not going to believe you unless you tell me where it is."

Adrian said it was too hard to describe. He actually didn't know because he hadn't gone there on his own; he'd been driven by a person with a car.

What person?

Someone. A person. Someone Corey didn't need to know.

A girl? Had Adrian met an older woman?

No. A person who was really wonderful. Someone with incredible abilities, who used their mind to solve problems.

Was it a man or a woman?

A man, said Adrian. Yes. A man who understood women. He knew everything about them. He knew how to talk to them. "He gets them to do things you wouldn't believe. He knows exactly what to say. He told this one girl she had nice eyes and—boom!—she let him feel her tits. I've learned more about women from hanging around him than you can believe. You'd really love him."

"So why won't you tell me who he is?"

"I've told you everything you need to know about him."

"I just don't get it. What do you think, I'm going to steal your friend?"

"Let it go."

"Are you making up the fact that you have a friend?"

"No. He's a real person."

"Tell me one thing about him so I know he's real."

"I already have."

"Is he old or young?"

"I can tell you that he's young."

"Is he a student at MIT?"

"Maybe."

"Is he a physicist?"

"No."

"Is he my father?"

"No. I said he was young. Your father wouldn't be young, would he?"

"Yeah, but you could be lying."

"The fact that you think it's your father shows your paranoia. Why would you ask me that? I'd have to be a pathological liar to be friends with him behind your back. What does that say about our friendship that you believe something like that about me?"

"So it's not my father?"

"If you ask me that again, I'm going to consider our friendship nullified."

"Is it or isn't it?"

"Look, I've given you an ultimatum, I've set my terms, and you are choosing to violate those terms. This conversation is finished."

"It's not finished. I've got a right to ask you. If you're such a great friend, what are you so secretive for?"

"An individual doesn't have the moral right to demand to know everything about another person. That's a basic moral principle."

"I don't disagree."

"In asking all these prying questions about this other person who I'm friends with, you're violating that principle. You're flying directly in its face. You're flagrantly violating a basic human right."

"That sounds a little overboard."

"We know you're this super-aggressive person—"

"What?"

"You've been in street fights, you've been arrested, you've fought in cage fights. Let's look at the salient facts and assess what's going on here. You're in court with your father, who you drove out of your house. By your own admission, you needed him to help your mother. What did you do? You chased him away and destroyed his property. You've admitted to me that you sucker-punched some poor guy in Cambridge and knocked him out cold. He could have brain damage because of you. I'm two hundred ten pounds and I work out all the time and I'm afraid of you. I feel like you could just flip out and start destroying things. Most people would be afraid of someone bigger than they are; you show no concern about what would happen to you. Sure, I talk about violent ideas and stuff, but they're symbolic messages to my own psyche to help me do better at my studies, but with you, you're willing to actually attack another person, almost like a wild animal. You used to care about ideas and conversations, and now it's like that's totally out the window. You've dropped out of school; all you want to do is fight, work at a construction job, and—I don't know—probably vote for the next Republican candidate who's going to get our country into wars. You're going to wind up like a caricature of a dumb, uneducated redneck who just runs around getting drunk and raising hell."

Corey stared at Adrian. Then both of them started laughing.

Adrian stood up to dump his tray, loaded with chicken bones and skin, and farted loudly in the center of the dining hall. The three young women by the window looked at him. Corey hurried away in mortification.

"What did you run away for?" Adrian asked. "Oh, I get it! Everyone runs from my power."

❧❧

The cold, gray, sometimes wet days kept rolling on and on. There was no early spring this year. He saw Molly one-on-one when she was back in town later that month. They met in the same Irish bar, the Ash, drinkers framed against the stained-glass windows of white and green. Hooded in a heavy sweatshirt, snowy with plaster dust, cowhide gloves sticking out his pocket, he rested his boot on a table rung. She sat on a high chair, purse in her lap, drinking beer. He tapped her bottle with his fist. She'd offered to buy for him since she was older, she rarely got carded, and if she did she had ID—it was known between them he was still something of an innocent.

"How's school going?"

"The same. Lotta work. I thought I was going to the nationals this year, but it looks like that's not going to work out. Coach says I've got some work to do. There's next year. I'll be fine. I'm a freshman and it's pretty good I got as far as I did with it. But it would've been badass to go. Whatever. It's not like I don't have ten thousand hours of homework to keep me busy. The nationals for track. I thought you knew. I run the quarter mile. They're going out of state too. I so wanted to go."

"How fast do you run a quarter mile? I don't know anything about track. I have no idea how fast I could do it. I don't think I'm in the best shape. I'm probably creeping up on 168. All I do is eat."

"Aren't you working?"

"Working makes me hungry. It's the weather too. It's gotta warm up."

"At least you don't drink."

"How's the party life out there?"

"Off the chain. Girls in my dorm get more wasted than I've ever seen. Last weekend, I woke up with such a bad hangover, I was like, never doing that again. That was after I found out I wasn't going with the team. I'm over it now."

"I've been to court like three times since we talked. There's been a lot going on with my father. He's telling the court I pulled a knife on him."

"You didn't, did you?"

"No, I didn't. What does that even mean? Pulled a knife and did what? Poked him with it? Buttered some toast? Where did this happen? When did it happen? What was I trying to achieve? It's a total fabrication. As far as *would* I pull a knife on him, I'd just as soon knock his head in with a hammer—that's the point I'm getting to. But that's *would*, not *did*."

"Come on, Corey. I don't want you knocking his head in with a hammer."

"Why not?"

"Because then you'll go to jail—that's why!"

"Oh yeah. Well, jail's not that scary. When I got arrested, I didn't see anybody impressive."

"All right, all right."

"No, seriously. The scariest people are young people like you and me when they're in top athletic shape. We can do the most damage. You think some old guy has your wind? Your cardiovascular conditioning?"

She was letting his comments pass.

"You know who's scary?" he continued. "I've got—I don't want to say a friend—an acquaintance—who goes to MIT. This guy's scary intelligent and he's completely jacked. Benches four hundred. If this guy decided to hurt people, it'd be a problem."

"He would be a brainiac if he goes to MIT."

"Yeah, but this guy's unusual. We're not friends anymore because he's so unusual."

"What's unusual about him?"

"He's smart, he's strong—he's basically everything I want to be—and he hates his mother. I couldn't hang around him anymore. I just went to see him—"

Molly laughed.

"Don't laugh. I hadn't seen him since November and after this, I'm not going to talk to him again; he's too crazy. Really! I don't have time for his malarkey. I've got my mom to look after. But the guy interests me somehow, hearing his perspective, the way he'll take everything and reduce it to a rational problem. He's one of the most interesting people I've ever met. But what's crazy is—you know how my father works at MIT?—I started thinking he and my father must be . . . being friends."

"Well, that would be weird."

"I asked him and he won't admit it."

"Why do you think this? Do they even know each other?"

"They do. I introduced them. And then he was saying he had a friend who took him to strip clubs and my father popped in my head. Now I'm telling you and I don't know what to think."

"I can't see my father going to a strip club. Yes, I can. Probably when he was younger."

Seeing Tom's serious stoic face in his mind's eye, Corey said, "Your dad's a decent human being."

"Mostly."

"He's the man."

"You know, I wonder about you dropping out of school. Don't you want to do something besides construction?"

"Your dad's in construction."

"You're not my dad."

Corey said nothing.

"Don't take it the wrong way," she said. "All those books you used to read, the sailing bible—yeah, I heard about it—I admired you."

"That's funny. I admired you."

"I don't want you to be one of those guys, when I'm graduating college, you're stuck here doing nothing."

"I won't be. I'll do something. But I can't do anything now; I have to take care of things at home."

"You could be studying. You could take your GED."

"I gotta deal with this court case with my disgusting father. For all I know, the guy *is* friends with my friend behind my back. He's so devious, that's exactly what he'd do. But I have no idea. It could be true; it might not be. It doesn't matter. I'm cutting all the weirdos out of my life so no one can bother us again."

23

You and Me, the Labor

Corey's Labor Ready assignment was ending. The project was done. His super was having him clean the new windows with acetone. Landscapers were planting trees along the curbs. UMass was a Division One school and Molly was running in the postseason, thinking about next year. When she returned to Quincy to see her father, she was tan and conditioned and seemed to have been painted in brighter colors. Her long reddish-gold hair whipped behind her. She hugged her girlfriends and drove away with them amid a great celebratory energy. Hiking down the shore with his tool belt, Corey leaned in the window of their car and bumped her fist. He said his job was ending. She told him not to be shy about talking to her father. "Don't let him scare you. He likes helping people. You should call him."

"Think you can use me now it's getting warm?" he asked her father.

"To be honest, I don't know." But Tom offered to show him around his worksite.

He picked Corey up on Sunday. The snow-white Ford shone in the sun. Corey jumped aboard. A mug in the center console was filled with ballpoint pens and a bone-handled folding knife. A Navajo dreamcatcher hung from the rearview mirror. A die-cast skull was glued to the dashboard—a gift from Molly—her dad liked the Grateful Dead. Tom was wearing a do-rag and a lime-green safety shirt in double extra-large. His well-worn boot hit the gas and the truck sped away from the ocean.

They took the Yankee Division Highway inland past the South Shore Plaza, then the granite cliffs. They drove into a town. A white sign in Massachusetts style: Entering Dedham. The Ford roared along, the radio playing Neil Young. They were cruising by old warehouses on a country road—heavy construction equipment in dusty lots, blocks of stone, piles of lumber, hills of sand against a background of trees.

Tom was telling Corey how he'd gotten his job. "When I got laid off, I sent out my résumé. These guys called me in. They're the second-largest commercial HVAC company in New England. I'd subbed for them in the past. They knew me. They said, 'We want to give you what you're worth.' We shook hands."

After they'd hired him, he'd had to prove himself. He'd passed his licensing exam within a year. It had taken six months of studying at his kitchen table. Then he'd graduated to running jobs.

Tom pulled up outside an industrial hangar, turned the truck off and continued talking with his keys in his hand. He said they'd given him this vehicle that he and Corey were sitting in, and a laptop computer with Bluebeam on the hard drive, a type of software allowing him to size tin with the click of a mouse.

"They pay for my gas. All I do is turn in my receipts."

He got out of the Ford. Walking slowly, faded green tattoos on his arms, he led the way to the hangar. They were surrounded by rural silence, tall trees, sunlight. He entered the combination in the key case, unlocked the doors, let Corey in. The inside was cavernous and cold and smelled like wet cement. Construction materials were piled everywhere: iron I-beams, coils of cable, sheets of green glass, machines waiting to be installed. Tom pointed to a mountain range of silver ductwork.

They walked deeper in, stepping through the frames of uncompleted walls. Another room. A plywood board that lay across a pair of sawhorses. It said *Tom's Table* in Magic Marker. A roll of blueprints. Wooden crates on the floor, mock-ups for his rooftop units. Tom got down on his knees and demonstrated how, by measuring carefully, he laid them out on the floor exactly where they would go on the roof above their heads: blue tape for cold air, red tape for hot.

"Want to see what this place'll look like when it's done?"

They left the site and drove to a sister factory, which was nearing completion. When they went inside, the lights came on, illuminating a pristine white-walled stadium. The machines had been assembled into a series of production lines. High overhead, Corey saw Tom's ductwork in the ceiling—high pressure, medium pressure, low pressure—coming through the walls, dividing and subdividing in perfect lines like the complex of pipes in a pipe organ, a giant system that descended in scale down to the registers in the clean rooms.

There were no doglegs.

"No," said Tom. "It's got to look perfect and it's got to work perfect—or you're going to have to have a tech come out every weekend."

The project above their heads had taken fifty man-years of labor, counting all the men and time. Tom had gotten it done ahead of schedule. The owners had a blackboard in their office that showed everybody's jobs. He'd seen it. "If you're in the black, it means you're on-budget. All these guys are in the red, but I'm always in the black."

The plant was going to manufacture powdered substances for the vitamin-supplement industry like Gloria's vanilla protein powder or Corey's Gaspari muscle-builder shake from GNC.

"I've tried the chocolate," Tom said. "It tastes good."

They went outside and walked around the hangar. "Construction is a stressful business. The numbers are huge. Each one of those rooftop units you saw is twenty thousand dollars and we've got ten of them." He walked slowly, head down in the sun, boots crunching in the dirt.

"Thomas!" someone called out when they were crossing behind the hangar. It was an electrician at work inside a caged area where high-voltage lines connected. They went over to talk to him through a fence.

"Working on a Sunday?"

"Wiring the boxes. We're putting the big switch in tomorrow. Who's your buddy?"

"This is Corey. He's interested in what we do."

"If you're interested in construction, stick with Thomas," the electrician said. "He's the man."

"I know he is," said Corey.

"I've been telling him we show up on time and get it done."

"That's what we do. That's why we can make it fun. We get it done, then we can have fun with it."

"We're always doing something. Remember the mug? We've got this mug we give people. It says Biggest Sanchez of the Year. A Sanchez is a guy who sleeps with your wife. He's like a Jody in the military," Tom explained. "And another thing is zip ties." As a joke, they'd zip-tie each other's equipment. They zip-tied each other's feet to ladders. If they didn't like a guy, they crawled under his truck and zip-tied his drive train. You'd see him go halfway down the street and stop. He'd think something was wrong with his transmission.

The men laughed. A short, broad man, wearing all his safety gear, fall-protection harness, yellow hard hat, cowhide gloves and safety glasses, his many tools kept neatly around his waist, the electrician, whose name was Victor, gave an impression of unusual competence and judgment allied with good cheer. The thing that rose out of the cage above his head resembled a cubist sculpture of a vacuum cleaner several stories high. It drew air out of the factory and ran it through a filter and, if necessary, shut down power to the entire plant to prevent a dust explosion. The high-voltage lines six feet above his head could fry you.

They took their leave of him. "Nice to meet you, Victor," Corey said.

"He's good people," Tom confided on their way back to the truck. "It's taken me years to get guys like him, guys who are reliable. They're not easy to find."

And Tom looked after guys like that and kept them busy. If he had to send a guy home, he bought him McDonald's on his own dime. He didn't like to send guys home, but sometimes he had to for the budget. "I see all the money on the job. You know what the cheapest part of any job is?" He poked Corey in the shoulder. "You and me. The labor."

"I'd do anything to work with you," Corey said.

They climbed back in the truck and drove out of town without talking. Tom picked up the highway. Corey looked out the window, feeling the strange high-speed sense of stasis, the hovering stillness in relation to the other traffic moving seventy, seventy-five miles an hour. They seemed to crawl beneath the Braintree cliffs as they headed for the shore.

Tom started talking again as they were driving into Quincy. He said not everyone loved him. A persistent issue was coordinating the elements of a major installation. Not infrequently, the other trades would fail to work with him. They were supposed to miss each other, but if a plumber didn't read the blueprints, his pipes would run into Tom's ductwork. In these conflicts, the other tradesman would lose. "I tell guys, 'Look, you can do your own thing, but you're only hurting yourself, 'cause I can't move my stuff. Look at the prints. I told you exactly where I was going to be, this many feet above the floor.'"

Due to his perfectionism, Tom said, he had fired a lot of guys. One day he had fired a weightlifter, a steroid head. "He was a bad electrician. He came back to the site looking for me. People said he had a gun."

Nothing had happened; the cops had taken care of it.

They were heading down the Adams Shore.

"Last fall, when Molly was about to go away," Tom continued, "we went to Walmart to get her stuff for school and we ran into this other guy I'd fired. He's this dirtbag who does meth. He was with his wife. He didn't see me, but she did. She goes, 'There's the asshole who fired you.' I thought we were going to throw down right there. I went to sporting goods and got a baseball bat and put it in our cart. Molly's like, 'Maybe you ought to calm down, Dad.'"

They passed the DB Mart. The ocean appeared. A minute later, they were pulling up in front of Corey's house on Sea Street.

Corey reached across the cab and shook Tom's hand.

"Thank you. It was great seeing what you do."

"I know you'll find something. You're a smart kid."

"I can try the union again."

"Something always turns up, usually. You just gotta be at the right place at the right time."

"It'll be fine."

"Molly was taking business administration for a while. She

wanted to start a business for me, so she could run it. She thinks if I'm not stressed out I won't drink."

Tom sat still a minute longer.

Of his daughter, he said, "Ya know, there's all kinds of extras you gotta deal with, even with the scholarship. I never went to college, so I didn't know what they were gonna be. Fortunately, they've given me a bump, so I can pay for whatever she needs. I tell her, 'You do what you gotta do and we'll work it out. The money'll be there for you. I guarantee it.'" He struck his *t* on this last word.

They climbed out of the truck. The sun was in the high blue sky over the ocean. Joan was sitting on Corey's steps in her white jeans, smoking a cigarette.

"Joan, this is Tom. He's like my uncle around here. Tom, this is Joan. She's like my aunt."

On hearing his name, Tom, who had been drifting towards the beach, made a show of redirecting his body's momentum and changing course for Joan.

"Hi," Tom said. "I'm his neighbor."

Joan stood up, tiny by comparison with him, and said, "How do you do?"

She stood erect and put her shoulders back and smiled under her black bangs. Tom looked away at the ocean and held his car keys.

"Working on a Sunday?"

"I've been showing him around my job site."

"What do you do?"

"I'm a construction worker. We got a couple of plants we're working on over in Norwood. Corey wanted to see what we were doing. I do the ventilation. Heating and air-conditioning. They call me a tin knocker."

"You get a lot of work making everything green nowadays?"

"You mean, environmentally friendly? Yeah, that's not what we do, usually. There are guys who do that. Like retrofitting. We're more like a new construction company, so when we build something, it's already up to what the government wants."

Joan cocked a hip and took a smacking puff off her cigarette.

"The politicians probably have all the technology already, am

I right? Every time they start talking about global warming, I keep waiting for them to do something. I thought we were gonna have solar-powered cars by now. I thought I'd be flying one of them fighter planes from *Star Wars*. Right? They probably have those, I bet. They're probably keeping them so they can go fuck up ISIS and not tell anyone."

"They've got technology they don't tell us about."

"They better. It's getting crazy out there."

"The question is, are the liberals going to let us use it? Not to get into a . . ." Tom looked at Joan. She looked back at him and laughed. He put his hands up. "I mean, I dunno what your politics are. His mom is probably pretty liberal. I don't want to start World War Three."

"Nah, I'm all about defending ourselves. We've got to."

Corey went inside to check on his mother. Tom and Joan stayed outside talking. Through the window, he heard her say she was from Oakland. She'd seen James Hetfield of Metallica in the early eighties when he'd been barely older than a kid. Hetfield had just been getting started, but he'd been wild and it had been something to see him rock.

❧

Mother's Day had passed. No card this year. It seemed better not to commemorate it. It was the second anniversary of Gloria's diagnosis, the beginning of the third year of her disease. Her physical therapist told her to get a lanolin sheepskin. Now Gloria spent her days in the black thronelike chair, wearing soft white pajamas, the sheepskin underneath her to reduce friction on her skin.

The social worker paid a visit at the end of May. Dawn sat on the futon with her folder and her purse. She wore a sleeveless turtleneck. Her spotted arms had meat on them. She saw the wheelchair's Mafia Boss license plate. "Good!" she said. "You're decorating. You're making it your own."

"That was my son's idea. He's at that age."

A nurse arrived while Dawn was there. She had come from Beth Israel to give Corey's mother passive range-of-motion exercise. She put Gloria on her back and lifted her legs one at a time. In shorts and sneakers, Gloria resembled a football player lying on his back on the sidelines getting his legs stretched by an assistant coach before going on the field.

The nurse turned her on her side and rubbed lotion on her back. She moved her to the chair and tilted it into a deep reclining position and hovered her hands over Gloria's face and body without touching her. There was total silence in the house. She was directing prana at the patient. The nurse was a burly woman with an accent—a Jew from the Ukraine. What she was doing made Gloria fall asleep.

Dawn finished shuffling papers and tapping the screen of her BlackBerry. She gathered up her things, her purse and folder. As she was leaving, she said, "I left some paperwork for her when she wakes up." The nurse turned on the social worker and put a finger to her lips.

The nurse had covered Gloria with a blanket, which hung down, hiding the chair, so she appeared to be floating horizontally with nothing under her, as in a magic trick. Corey began to ask a question and the powerful nurse silenced him as well.

He tiptoed up and whispered, "What technique do you use? Is it a form of yoga?"

"It's like that," she said.

The Ukrainian visited his mother periodically for a while. Then, for reasons he didn't understand, she stopped coming. She had a rare skill. Every time she came, she soothed his mother enough to let her sleep.

He went to one more court appearance before the summer. Shay had managed to convince the court how sick his mother was. The judge continued the case until the fall. When they met again, Corey would likely get a conditional discharge. Shay explained what that meant in the courthouse lobby: Stay out of trouble and the charge would go away.

"Go home, take care of your mother, go to the gym. Just don't break any more car windows. Stay away from your father."

❧

Adrian was sitting in the Mercury in his kneepads, his smell filling the car. They drove north out of the city, traveling over the water on the high iron bridge and exiting in Chelsea. They drove by docks and down an industrial road: train tracks, a power plant behind a concrete wall, power lines and capacitors. The road curved. Long low factory buildings, a meat-processing plant, refineries, diesel trucks. No skyline. A sign that said Topless. A cocktail glass with a woman in it. A concrete pillbox with no windows called King Arthur's Lounge. The establishment was Mafia-run, Leonard said. "You're going to like this." Adrian rubbed his hands. They parked in a car-filled lot surrounded by a rusted fence, corrugated sheet metal, dumpsters. The wind bore the scent of fuel oil. A beat came through the walls.

Inside, the club was drenched in red light. A fat white guy on a stage in the back of the room was rapping: "Get up on the mothafuckin' floor!" They paid the cover. A young girl with big breasts in a pink see-through nightie took Adrian's money.

"How are you tonight?" he asked.

She deadpan-stared at him.

"Do you not like talking to customers?"

"Do yourself a favor, go sit down."

"There's a part of the brain that controls anger, the cingulate gyrus. Yours could be getting too much stimulation."

"Get out of my face." She made a hand-twirling gesture as if she were pulling something out of her hair.

The bouncer had tanned Mediterranean arms, an anchor tattooed below his elbow, and wore pleated gray slacks and dress shoes. His wet hair had comb tracks in it. He asked the girl, "Everything cool?" She made a hand-chopping gesture and walked away.

Leonard and Adrian sat at the bar. Women were pole dancing on a stage behind the liquor bottles. Others were climbing on the bar itself, crawling from one customer to the next, squatting in front of them. The bartender was wearing a black brassiere.

A dancer stopped in front of Leonard. "Hey, what's up."

"The sky."

"Haha! That's funny."

Leonard held out a dollar to her and put it on the bar. She leaned over him and put her breasts in his hands while staring down at him.

"Hahaha!" She laughed. "You like that, huh?"

"How do you know?"

"I can see you do."

"Do you like it?"

"Oh yeah, baby."

He slid his hand up her leg to her crotch. She let him feel her.

"Turn around. Wink your ass at me."

"Haha! You're crazy in the head." She turned on her hands and knees on the bar. "Is it winking?" She looked over her shoulder.

"You did it."

"See? I can make it do anything I want."

He held her hand. "Would you like to take a ride with me after the show?"

"You know I can't do that."

"Take a ride with my young friend here."

"He's with you?"

"Take a ride with us, and we'll get you something nice."

"What'll you get me?"

"A party."

"I can't."

"Why not?"

"I can't just go somewhere with you if I don't know you."

She moved over to Adrian. "Your friend is sweet. He's so nice! Are you nice too?"

Adrian said, "I'm the mean one."

Since he made no move to touch her or tip her, she forgot him and cat-crawled down to the next group of patrons and performed for them. They were enthusiastic. She saddled her legs over one man's shoulders and he began to perform oral sex on her right there in the bar, while she smiled down at the top of his head and made eyes at other people in the bar's mirrored walls. When she smiled, wrinkles stretched from her jaw to her ear. She was missing a tooth.

Everyone watched silently, solemnly, in the loud music. The black-bras-wearing bartender watched. A spectator in the crowd stuck his tongue between two fingers and wiggled his tongue.

The man continued performing oral sex on the dancer. The dancer clapped and pointed her leg at the ceiling.

Adrian said, "I can't believe he's doing that."

A blow struck a wooden surface loudly. They turned: The bouncer had a nightstick—he had struck something. He was making a furious cut-it-off gesture and was shaking his head and pointing: "There's cops right outside at the fuckin' Dunkin' Donuts."

The bartender put her hand on the bar and slapped it to get the dancer's attention.

"Ya gotta stop."

The dancer took her legs off the man's shoulders.

The bouncer came over to the man, who had long sideburns, and told him, "No more."

Adrian looked at Leonard. "You did great with her. You almost got her in your car."

"Can you believe she lets strange men put their filthy hands on her?"

"I wish I understood why she was letting us touch her. You only gave her a dollar. It can't be the money. Or is it? I wish I could understand what makes a woman do that. Why is she willing to let you feel her up for a dollar, and another woman, I could take her out for a twenty-dollar date, and she wouldn't even think of letting me look at her naked? It just doesn't make sense."

"She's on something."

"Really?"

"Of course she is. Look how happy she is. That's drug-induced. Drugs change everything with a person."

"Why does she need drugs? Imagine being able to walk into a bar and have strangers buying you drinks all night!"

"That's the way it is for women."

"Maybe I can train myself to not want more than this," Adrian said, looking at the nude women standing above the men on the bar. "Yes, that's what I'll do. I'll be satisfied with this."

"You can have more than this. This is just the beginning."

The bartender approached and Adrian and Leonard stopped talking as she collected the money off the bar into a child's plastic bucket, the kind that comes with a shovel.

Later, long past midnight, they were sitting in the Mercury somewhere on the shore, the engine idling, the two of them staring out the windshield. The headlights seemed defeated by the darkness as if they were deep in the ocean, looking out a porthole, seeing nothing but flecks of plankton.

Leonard asked if he'd enjoyed his lap dance. Adrian said it had made him feel so much better. He was pleased. The evening had been a success. Not all his evenings had been so grand. He cleared his throat and employed his nasal voice to say, "I told you how I got the clap, didn't I?"

"Yes, you did. It's dirty in there. What were you thinking?"

"It's one of those things I had to learn." Adrian cleared his throat. "I guess my father wasn't the best friend to me. That's why it's so great I've met you."

⸎

In June, Corey got on a major construction project in the North End, thanks to Tom. It was going to be a high-rise. The pay was union scale, which meant Corey was starting at eighteen an hour. Tom would not accept a thank-you, just told him to make the most of it.

He got up early and drove into the city and parked at Haymarket. Guys were there already, trucks parked on the sidewalk, traffic cones on their hoods, pulling tools out. One took off Corey's hard hat and showed him how to adjust the band. The union men were simply looking for the chance to build something; they were poor; they had to pay for trucks and tools and buy their gas. It wasn't a way to get rich.

They lined up for an OSHA-enforced warm-up session. In boots and hard hats, they did stretches—tricep, hamstring. When it came to the splits, most could barely get their legs 30 degrees apart. They had to do the standing quad stretch. Guys were losing their balance, their butt cracks showing. The sun was up. It was warm and going to be hot. A breeze chased through the site, carrying the smell of coffee and bread from the North End. The site was in the middle of the street and the roads split around it going towards Charlestown. The city came to an end here and the road went around a corner and on the other side of the corner there were more sites. The whole area was under development.

You could see the ant farm of high-rise construction next to the TD Garden and the Zakim Bridge, men in hard hats moving on precast concrete floors, vertical framing, flyouts, a welder producing a smoking blue-white light.

For the first week, he spent most days shoveling dirt in a wheelbarrow and running it over a bridge of boards, which bent under him. He plugged in the lifts at night. He met a woman on the crew from Roxbury who had a gold nose stud and drove a Bobcat. "I show and prove," she said. She was another Joan—racially mixed, confident and well adjusted.

His first day, the heavy wheelbarrow flipped him off his feet, and he got thrown head over heels—exactly as if he'd been tossed with a judo throw. He landed on the concrete slab, his hard hat flew off, the wheelbarrow flipped and dumped out its mountain of dirt. He set it upright, shoveled the dirt back in, and carried on. No one laughed; everyone was working. The summer was coming, he loved the job and the men. The pay was a godsend. His mother thanked him.

Joan said, "I like him in his tool belt. I bet he gets the girls going. Hey, I think you dropped a nail. Why don'tcha bend over and pick it up there, blondie." She began calling Corey "The Workin' Man."

After his first check cleared, he went to Stop & Shop and bought spaghetti, ground meat, tomato paste and vegetables. Joan made a big pot of spaghetti and meat sauce and they all ate a feast together, gathered around Gloria in her chair. For each bite, Corey wound the spaghetti on his mother's fork and fed her.

He came straight home from work in the afternoons, bringing the vigor of the construction site home with him. He got his mother up and out of her chair. He helped her go outside. She went for a short walk, one step at a time, with her walker. She went to the seawall and looked out at the beach, covered in smooth stones, wearing big sunglasses.

The wheelchair was supposed to be a way to extend the patient's range. It should have been there for her to sit in when she got tired. But Gloria's chair wasn't portable. It was big, heavy, hard to maneuver. One had to take off the leg rests, remove the special seat cushion, which had been laboriously constructed in the workshop at Beth Israel, and collapse the frame to take it outside. Even then, the task of fitting it through the doorway placed one at a mechanical disadvantage and required strength and balance. Corey prided himself being able to do it. (He was surprised to learn that Joan could do it too.) Then one had to carry it down the steps. Furthermore, it was fragile and expensive, which mitigated against rolling it on gravel.

Without the chair, his mother couldn't stay outside for long. She'd get tired and have to head inside. She'd be too tired to take the stairs. Corey would pick her up and carry her inside. But for her, it was humiliating to be carried.

As a result, for increasingly long periods, she was staying continuously indoors, seeing no one but Joan and Corey, the clinic staff on her monthly outings to Longwood, and the social worker. This was bad for her mental health, but it was a trend that would only continue as she got sicker.

In early summer, inspired by his construction job, Corey wanted to build a wheelchair ramp or a set of walker stairs outside the house. They'd be three feet wide with three-and-a-half-inch risers instead of standard seven-inch risers. He went to Lowe's and priced the supplies. But the project cost too much, plus he'd have to get permissions from the state. Dawn got involved, claiming she could get funding from Share the Care, but she wouldn't find an answer to anything until after the summer had passed.

To offset the monotony of her life, as the summer progressed, Gloria lived increasingly online. She spent entire days indoors sealed in with the air conditioner running, watching videos nearly around the clock. It was a model of addiction. It left her feeling empty and needing more of the same.

"I should pull myself out of this in the time I have left," she said. "Life is a gift. I'm not using it."

She made an effort for several days, but it petered out.

Corey said, "I see what's going on and I'm worried about you."

She became deeply upset. First she turned cold and told him sarcastically she couldn't be as good as he was. Then she grew silent and he could tell she was weeping. He kneeled by her chair and held her skeletal arm.

"I can't do any better! I tried! I tried!"

"We'll just get through it—any which way we have to."

At night, Gloria ate dinner in her Mafia Boss chair with her prison fork.

Joan came home after dark, and she'd sometimes sit with Gloria and go through her book collection, asking about books or CDs or paintings she used to have. "Do you remember that painting of the lady in the shower?"

"I lost that somehow."

"That was a good painting."

"Gone with the wind."

Gloria's physical condition remained the same throughout the summer, at least to the naked eye, though it had to be assumed that, at the molecular level, her motor system was continuing to deteriorate. Sitting in her chair in shorts, her exposed legs twitched as if hammers in a piano were striking the wires. But rather than reading about medicine—whether Western or Eastern or homeopathic—she looked at paintings on the Web. YouTube had slideshow videos of artworks set to New Age music, Gregorian chant, Sicilian folk music, Vivaldi and the like.

"Listen to that!" she said, her eyes closed, shaking her head with wonder, a feat she could still perform.

A night breeze came from the marsh side of the house, through the kitchenette window.

At this moment, she seemed to have stopped denying her fate. Nor was she angry. She was something else. One day, when Corey was carrying her downstairs so she could take a walk, she asked if he believed in miracles.

"I think anything's possible." He raised his chin at the ocean. "The fact that the universe is the way it is, that life is this way. Who could have predicted anything in our lives? Yeah, I think a miracle is possible."

"Do you think I could go into remission?"

The days got hot and muggy. At night they ran the AC on high in Gloria's room to keep her cool.

Even with Corey's paycheck, the electricity bill was hard to pay. They had another air conditioner in the back of his closet but didn't run it. Hers was the cold room. Everyone in the house went to Gloria's room for a drink of cool air. As she got sicker, Joan had stopped sleeping in the same bed with her. She slept on the futon—Leonard's old bed—with the living room window open, the rare car going by, lighting up the walls, then the crickets in the darkness.

For all he thought he was doing, he wasn't vigilant; he was failing to see everything he could do. He *could have* built the ramp, but didn't. It wasn't the social worker's fault he failed. He *could have* done yogic breathing and used prana to bring his mother peace.

Why didn't he? Good question. The disease, stress, arrogance, impatience, blindness.

24

The High Summer

A strange thing happened around the Fourth of July when the fire-works were going off on the shore. Corey drove out to the Neck. He thought he was going to see Tom. Along the way, he passed the Hibbards' neighbors grilling in front of their houses with their friends. The day was hot. He drove uphill into the trees with his elbow out the window of the hatchback. He was coming from work. His arm hairs held black iron dust from cutting rebar with a grinder, like the pollinated hairs on a bee's belly after crawling inside a flower. He could hear the birds and smell the woods. He parked.

The garage was open, but Tom's pickup wasn't there. Corey walked across the yard, cement on the knees of his jeans. The yard glowed in the sun. His boots crushed the grass into the warm black dirt. He knocked on the door and said, "Hello?" No one answered. He went around the side of the house and looked. In the semicircular hollow before the trees, he saw Molly lying on a lawn chair alone in the sun.

He said hello and she looked at him and said hi.

"Do you need anything?"

She said she was fine. He found himself walking towards her and when he reached her, he wasn't sure what to do. He bent down and hugged her. Then to be near her, he sat on the grass. She leaned back in her chair and looked at the woods lazily as they talked. He had a hard time thinking of things to say.

He reached up and played with her arm.

"Been working out?"

"No." She'd been lying here relaxing finally. It had been a busy summer.

She got up to get a drink. He followed her inside her father's house. Tools lay all around the carpet. The lights were off. The sunlight glanced past the roof and entered the abode by reflection. The shadows of trees mingled in the shaded rooms. She took a pitcher of water and poured a drink and set it on the chopping block. A fly flew past their heads. Her father had left out a pack of hamburger meat. "I should put that away," she said. "He's such a pain in my ass. Just kidding. I love my dad." She drank her glass of water.

Corey reached out and laid his hand on her hip while she drank. She was wearing a bikini. The burs of his callused hand ticked against the fabric. Across the border of the nylon, her skin was smooth as a space-age polymer. It was only possible to invent that polymer by playing with millions of atoms for millions of years.

She told him that if they did anything they could never be friends again, but that if he restrained himself their friendship could continue.

He petitioned her for mercy and asked her to believe that their friendship would only be improved if she were merciful in this instance. However, she remained steadfast. The choice was his; he could have the one thing but not both.

If she put it that way, he didn't think he could very well proceed, and he withdrew his hand from her hip.

Just at that moment, the door opened and Tom clumped in in his heavy boots and black wraparound safety glasses and beard. He greeted his daughter, who glided away to the backyard. He strode into his kitchen and got a beer. When he opened the refrigerator door, his hand, which held the handle, was an inch from Corey's chest—the kitchen was a small room—and Corey saw it in such high definition that he could see the cross-hatched crevices in that massive, thick-fingered rhinoceros-skinned extremity. "I saw your car," Tom said from inside the refrigerator. Corey mumbled that he'd just dropped in to wish him a happy Fourth. Tom came out with a beer. He uncapped it.

"How's work?"

"It's great. It's a lifesaver."

Corey pulled himself together and went home to his mother. The night came. His guilt-sickness eased. He left several messages on Molly's phone, apologizing. She didn't call back, so he contrived to see her the day after. "I really needed to apologize in person," he said. "For what?" she asked. She'd already forgotten. She made out the whole thing to be unimportant and talked to him in such a way as to give the impression that it had never happened.

Oh, he kept reliving the moment in her kitchen before her father came home!

Around the same time, one day after work, Joan put on a green mud face mask to cleanse her hormonal skin and went for a jog along the shore in the late-afternoon sun. She ran among the strange formations out on Houghs Neck. There were rocky cliffs and rusted iron railings to climb the stairs and jetties going out into the dark blue water. She came upon an empty sub-development like a vision from Northern Ireland—wooden houses, shuttered. A jungle gym, deserted. She jogged through, the road leading from one Norway-shaped peninsula to the next, the little penile Norways of the coast.

On her way back, she ran into Tom. His snow-white truck was stopped at the end of a dead-end street that met the ocean.

"Hey, what's up, guy!"

He was wearing black shades and a Harley-Davidson do-rag. He stopped in the act of pulling a tackle box out of his truck and said, "Hey." There was a bucket of seawater at his feet and a folding knife on the pavement. His fishing rod was propped against the railing and his line was out.

She had forgotten the mask. It was cracked and sweated through. Green mud was running down her neck into her cleavage. The roots of her hair were stiff with mud. Her fat, golden brown upper arms shone with sweat. A heavy metal guitar was wucka-wucking out of her earbuds.

"I'm the girl from Corey's house!" she shouted.

"I know. Of course. How are ya? What are you doing, jogging?"

She pulled her earbuds out. "Yeah. I'm getting this fat off from the winter. It's getting harder and harder to lose. I want to go to the beach without embarrassing myself."

"You're not going to embarrass yourself."

She put a hand on her hip, shot her hip out, did a fingernail display and head-shimmied. "Right?"

Then she saw her reflection in his truck. "Holy shit, did I leave my mask on? Is there green on my face?"

"It's fine," said Tom and waved away the subject. He was getting set to fish but could offer her a ride.

"That's okay. I need to get the miles."

"So, that's your thing? You're into working out?"

"Yeah, working out. Karate."

"No shit? Karate."

"I was never one to leave my fate in other people's hands. There's sick people out there, I'm sorry."

Tom listened to her talk about it. "I know," he said. "I've got a daughter."

"We understand the danger from growing up the way we did. It's like they don't get it anymore."

"Yeah," he sighed.

Her iPod was still screaming.

"Is that AC/DC?"

"I think so. Let me check. Most definitely. You recognize it?"

"Of course. The music of my misspent youth."

"Want to hear it again?" She held the earbud out to him.

The Hibbards became a subject of discussion in the Goltz household that night. Gloria said of Tom, "I'm sure he's very nice, but I met him once and thought he was bor-ing." Corey rushed to Tom's defense. He described the precision and complexity of the project in Norwood. "He's the man I admire most of all!" Gloria thought her son was cut out for more in life than being an HVAC installer. Corey said he didn't think there was anything more than that in life; it was one of many paths to glory, all of which were equal—scholar, fighter, builder, farmer, sailor, poet, monk. All were equally good ways of getting to Nirvana.

"Corey, I want you to go back to school and get your diploma and then I want you to go to college."

"Mom, I'd do anything you wanted, but I don't want to do that."

"Joan, can you tell him?"

"I dunno. I kinda always felt like school's for fools."

"Joan!"

"Mom, it's okay. Please—I understand. But I respect Joan's path."

Gloria was so adamant she risked offending Joan.

Corey tried to bring them all together: "Reading, doing art, doing poetry, thinking independently, living a life of independence: Isn't that what you've both done? That's what we all respect."

"But there's so much more!" Gloria cried.

Joan said, "I guess I'm gonna go smoke a cigarette."

When she was gone, Corey said, "I think you're hurting her feelings."

"Who cares? So what! For God's sake, this is your life we're talking about."

"Well, Mom, I can't just do what my mommy wants me to do. I'm seventeen. Let me figure it out."

Later, Joan remarked to Corey, "Your mother sure cares about you." Corey was mortified at the implication that he had an over-protective mother.

In the middle of a hot August day, a black Mercury, reflecting the sun, turned down the crooked street and stopped. Leonard and his passenger, Adrian, got out. The sky was blue. The block was quiet. The trees in the nearby park stood still; there was no wind. Leonard wore black trousers, an undershirt and carried handcuffs on his belt. His companion was wearing a black baseball cap, skimpy jean cutoffs, black combat boots, and no shirt, his torso so perfectly muscular it didn't look real. He gave off ripe body odor. The older man led him to his house and unlocked the front door.

"Gosh, I can't believe you'd take me into your confidence like this," Adrian said. "I know you don't like people."

"You were ready," replied Leonard, letting him inside where it was suddenly dark. "But this isn't my total confidence. This is one degree. There are further degrees. You're not seeing everything."

"I'm not sure I could ask for anything more than this. I love it here. Just to sit here and do physics—it's such a great place! I love the depressing neighborhood. It's so grim and nihilistic—almost like a chunk of uranium where nothing can live except me—without meaning—creating my own meanings, like Nietzsche says, from math and physics—just these perfect, precise facts of the universe that I can discover with my mental power."

"Well, that's Malden for you. It's a depressed area. That's mainly because of corruption, mind you. No one wants to commute from here, thanks to the tolls, so the property values crashed in the eighties. But there are some compensations. You never know who your neighbors are. Take a look across the street. See that house? The guy who lived there would interest you. He killed his girlfriend."

"He did? I'd love to talk to him and ask him what it was like!"

"You can ask me. He told me everything."

"You've got to tell me."

"We'll have to think of something you can do for me."

"I was willing to make those phone calls for you."

"And I was willing to get you the best lap dance in Boston."

"What do you want?"

"Don't worry. I'll think of something painless. I know you don't want to jeopardize your university career."

"And then you'll tell me? Is it good?"

"It's vivid."

"I can't wait. That'll be perfect for my psyche."

"You'll feel like you're there."

"That's how I want to feel! That's what I'm into: using fantasy and rationality to control the world, while minimizing risks."

25

Into the Throat

The morning slipped by like water, as it always did when he was moving. His super had him shoveling dirt. But when the job was done, the super was too busy to tell him what to do. Corey went around looking for an assignment. He offered to hold a sheet of three-quarter-inch plywood against a two-by-four while a carpenter hammered in toenails. Soon, they were surrounded by other low-level employees looking for a way to be useful. There are often more hands at a construction site than needed. Each held out a tenpenny nail, hoping the carpenter would take it. Redundant and stalled, Corey stewed in aimlessness and dissatisfaction. The journeyman carpenter hammered away, a well-oiled machine. He never stopped moving; his body and spirit flowed together.

At break time, instead of sitting with the rest of the crew on the sidewalk in the shade, Corey went to his car and ate his sandwich with the key in the ignition and the radio on, listening to NPR. Without meaning to—and without pleasure—he thought of Adrian, doing physics and punching his heavy bag with ever-increasing force.

As the summer ended, his restlessness did not abate.

The Friday before Labor Day, he went through the site until he found the female Bobcat operator working in an alley between two old North End houses, one of which was being taken down. When he found her, she was leaning over her controls, smoking

a cigarette, wearing her hard hat, reflective vest and dusty leather
gloves, surrounded by a rubble of bricks, which she'd been clearing. There was a vein in her bicep. He asked to speak with her. She
turned her engine off to be polite.

Now there was no cover for their conversation, and they weren't
alone. A group of guys was watching—all guys in their twenties
who knew where they belonged: right here, on the job. Everything
he was about to say to her he had to say with them listening. And
they all happened to be very big. Corey asked her out.

She told him graciously that she had a boyfriend.

"I get the feeling he's here right now."

"That's him." She pointed at one of the men behind her.

"I hope you don't mind me asking. I meant no disrespect."

"None taken."

He walked away under the eyes of the other men—and under
the half-built tower, which would soon be twenty stories high,
overlooking Boston harbor. He shouldn't have walked away from
martial arts.

September had arrived, the elbow of the year. The weather was
still warm; he didn't see birds flying south, not yet; but the angle
of the sun was different and the ocean was turning a darker cast
of blue. Molly was going back to college. He had just decided to
go back to Bestway when his mother's disease progressed to her
throat.

He wasn't ready for his mother's loss of speech. She sounded
drunk. He thought it was the Robitussin. But she was drunk the
next day and the next. She went from sounding tipsy to sounding
slow and stupid all the time. Then suddenly she began to drool.
It all just happened. "Mom," he said. He wanted to say goodbye.
They never had a last good conversation. The key moment just
got by him.

She cried out, "I'm having trouble talking now."

"I understand you fine. You sound great to me."

"I tried to talk to the nurse and she couldn't understand me on
the phone!"

"What, Mom?"

"She couldn't understand me on the phone!" The struggle

to speak made her stiffen spastically in her wheelchair. Her body straightened like a board and she slid down. She stared at Corey with desperation.

"It's okay, Mom," he said. "I understand you."

"What am I going to do?" Her teeth caught on her lip. She couldn't control her mouth, couldn't close it properly.

"We'll work it out," he said.

A Lucite board appeared, leaning against the living room wall. It had the alphabet printed all around it and a square hole cut in the middle, like a picture frame. Joan said Dawn had left it there. She showed him what it was for.

You held it up and looked through the picture frame at Gloria and said, "First letter: A, B, C . . ." Her eyes would pick the letter out. You'd say it aloud; she'd blink to confirm. Then you'd start around again, she'd pick another letter, and so on, until she spelled a word.

Insurance didn't cover an iPad with a voice synthesizer. Dawn told Corey to contact medical technology firms to see if they would donate one to his mother. He made some calls but gave up.

She didn't like the letter board and resisted it, preferring to talk—but all she could do was moan. Corey tried to develop a code with her. They never did. At a nurse's advice, he asked his mother yes or no questions. But her yes sounded like her no. The only way he could tell them apart was by guessing from her tone of voice and body language, but when she was in distress, these subtle signals were hard to read. In moments of crisis, they couldn't understand each other, which made the situation worse.

As her mouth and throat muscles went, she started losing the ability to chew and swallow. She started choking on her food. For reasons no one understands, even though her muscle mass is disappearing, the ALS patient needs more nutrition, not less. There's the danger of a deadly spiral: getting too tired to eat, eating less, losing weight and strength, getting weaker and more tired. The harder it got for her to eat, the more they had to feed her.

He made pureed peas with salt and pepper and a chunk of butter. They added butter to everything she ate, for calories. He set it on his mother's tray and put a dish towel on her chest and prepared to feed her. Slumping compressed her stomach. He tilted back her chair to free her abdomen from her body weight and help keep food in her mouth.

He fed her a spoonful of puree and she swallowed it. He fed her another and she began to choke and cough. Peas slipped out of her mouth.

"Water?"

She nodded. He gave her a sip. Water ran out of her mouth. He wiped her chin clean. She opened her eyes and nodded for another bite.

He gave it to her, and a cough erupted out of her, spraying peas from her mouth. Her legs kicked out rigid. Her throat was blocked. She wasn't breathing.

He jumped up, ready to give her CPR, watching her color. Dawn had brought them a donation from a medical equipment manufacturer, a suction machine: a steel box that sat on the floor and plugged into the wall socket. When he switched it on, the motor began grinding like a compressor at his construction site. A clear hose ran from the housing to a plastic wand used to suction excess salivary secretions from Gloria's throat.

"Suction?"

She squeezed her eyes in a way that might mean yes. He kicked the motor on and put the wand inside her cheek, vacuuming out the material she was eating. The machine spat it into a clear plastic receptacle attached to the housing, filling it with mucus and pureed peas. Her saliva snapped and rattled in the hose.

She started breathing. Corey emptied the receptacle in the kitchen sink, rinsed and reinstalled it.

Joan was unusually good at handling mealtimes. Maybe the secret was that she had been inoculated against stress by the chaos of her life—the recurrent breakups, job losses, evictions, periods of homelessness, legal dramas, traffic accidents, friends who OD'd or who went to jail, break-ins, robberies, feuds, workplace harassment, you name it—she'd had it all. She had a happy star-child way about her, where she would sit for hours cross-legged on a bed looking at the album covers of vinyl records, examining the symbolism of angels smoking cigarettes on Black Sabbath's *Heaven and Hell*.

She could get carried away by a whimsical thought in the middle of a house that was falling down and let out what she was thinking in an unchecked stream—the monologue of a plucky, self-consoling street kid who'd spent her life without security but had a knack for creating it out of thin air—a what-if?/didja-ever-notice? kind of stargazing.

So she'd talk to Gloria while feeding her, laughing at her own ideas—almost having a two-part conversation, as if she were gossip-ing with herself, the emotional pitch rising and falling with expres-sions of outrage, streetwise realism, innocent wonder, X-rated sex talk, a burst of bathroom humor. She was an engine that would run of itself. But the beautiful thing was that this was not a one-way soliloquy after all. The two women were actually communi-cating, Corey saw; Joan was saying something and, with perfect natural grace, she was picking up on Gloria's reaction by looking at her eyes.

She stayed loose and laughy, showing no annoyance at being interrupted when Gloria had trouble swallowing. She talked about sexual, biological things in all their grossness, telling a story about how once, when working in Methuen as a dishwasher, she'd been on her period and her white pants had gotten wet and her period had soaked through her pants all down the back of her legs, with-out her knowledge; and all her coworkers had known about it before she did.

While telling the story, she farted. "Oh, sorry," she said with-out embarrassment. It did nothing to diminish her in Corey's eyes. She had an untouchable charisma.

MassHealth started paying for a home health aide to assist them 30 hours a week. The other 138 hours Joan and Corey divided between themselves. They tried to have the health aide cover times when neither of them could be at home. In mid-September, the agency sent them a woman up from Brockton, next to where

Corey had taken martial arts. She wore dark dresses like a Muslim or a Caribbean Christian, and her name was Hattie.

A week after Hattie started taking care of Gloria, Corey worked an overtime shift and Joan got home before him. His mother told Joan to take off her pajama bottoms, and Joan found bruises on her thin white legs above the knees.

How did this happen?

Hattie had given her a bath.

"I'm going to talk to her."

Gloria looked at the letter board.

Joan fetched it and Gloria conveyed the following message: *She did it on purpose. I asked her to stop. She knew what she was doing. I said, "I hope you're enjoying yourself," and she said, "Yes."*

By the time Corey got home, Joan had kicked Hattie out of the house and the incident was over, but it reinforced his picture of the world as a place with no rules except those that good people managed to enforce on their own.

He immediately told his super that from now on he'd have to leave work at a fixed time every day. His super, an Irish-Italian from Dorchester with a white skunk stripe in his dark gray hair, met Corey's request with silence. He said construction "doesn't work like that."

Quite soon he showed what he meant. The next day started badly. Corey and two other laborers had to break up a concrete slab that had been incorrectly poured. To coordinate with other trades, it had to be removed as fast as possible. The men took turns jackhammering and using the chisel end to pry up chunks of rock. The pneumatic hammer weighed some eighty pounds. A demanding job at any time, to do it at a sprint was backbreaking. To make matters worse, Corey's mother had had a bad night the night before and he hadn't slept. He couldn't maintain the pace of the others. The super shoved him out of the way and snatched the hammer. "My five-year-old kid could do it better than you!"

The day went on as it had begun in a state of perpetual crisis and pell-mell activity. By quitting time, it hadn't abated; a trench had been cut to the wrong depth, and it was clear that the laborers would be getting overtime. They stood in their reflective vests, muddy sweatshirts, yellow hard hats, leaning on their shovels, waiting for the super to tell them what he needed. Mindful of his mother alone with another home health aide, Corey spoke up and said he had to leave. The super, who was bent over measuring the trench, yelled, "Shut the fuck up. You're gonna stay here until I'm done with you."

"No, I'm not," Corey said, and walked off the job site.

Quitting his well-paid construction job couldn't have come at a worse time. On top of everything else, his court case had just been resolved after nine months of continuances and he had to pay his father $400 in restitution for smashing his glasses.

Leonard had petitioned the judge for the specific figure of $1,257.32, which he had itemized in a matrix format: Sunglasses (1), Car Window (1), Cost, Tax, Time, Pain and Suffering. In a rather striking omission given this appetite for every penny, Leonard had said nothing to the court about his multiple law enforcement uniforms, butcher knives, batons and handcuffs.

"I quit my job. I'm terrified to tell your father. This is the second time I've disappointed him. He'll think I'm no good. Please don't tell him."

"I won't."

"It's not that I want to hide it."

"Don't worry about what he thinks."

"I guess I worry."

"You're fine."

"Thanks. I thought you were mad."

"Why?"

"Over the summer."

"Oh, that. You're just a guy."

"I'll stick with being friends, if that's still an option."

"It's still an option," Molly said.

She told him she was coming to town that weekend. When the weekend came, he put his coat on and hiked up to Quincy Center. There was litter on the street outside the Family Dollar and Irish fiddling coming from the taverns. He went into The Stadium. The room was packed and loud. Guys in football jerseys, their hats on backwards, stood around holding beer bottles while the game played on scores of TVs. In the crowd, a copper-gold flash of hair caught his eye. He worked his way over and found Molly carousing with friends. "Heyyyy!" she exclaimed and embraced him. He reached through the palisade of beer bottles on the table and shook her friends' hands.

Together they watched the game.

He said he had to go at halftime. He hugged them all goodbye. He kissed Molly on the cheek.

"Tell your dad hi for me."

"Sure."

He left the bar. Behind him, a receiver caught a pass and the bar cheered. Across the street, a Quincy construction guy, a bodybuilder in patent leather shoes with the red beefy veiny neck of a bull, skipped by, escorting a petite woman with high heels, round breasts and a cascade of silvery blonde hair into an Italian restaurant on the corner called the Alba—through the window, a scene of candles and white tablecloths, black dresses and dark wine bottles. The evening was just getting started for some people. Corey hurried home to his mother.

During the day, now that he wasn't working, he had to drive to Star, buy food, prepare it. Strip the sheets, drive to the laundromat, do the laundry. Feed his mom. Give her fluids. Wash the dishware. Take her to the bathroom. Change her clothes. Bathe her. Comb her hair, brush her teeth. Pay electric bill. Gas bill. Phone bill. Get a letter from insurance and not know if it was a bill. What was a claim exactly? Must it be paid? Who to ask? Not know this either. Get email from MassHealth saying they had exceeded their allotted home health aide coverage and would be billed. Know this was a mistake. Not know how to fix it—and nor did Joan who was leaving now for work. Find out they were paying for Gloria's Robitussin when he had thought it was covered by insurance. Check the bank account and see it was lower, much lower, than he had thought—the effect of debits he had not foreseen. Get a statement from a credit card he was using to buy the groceries. Go in the other room to call the ALS Association and try to reach the care services coordinator. Leave a message asking about Share the Care. It was a nice idea, but who did you share it with?

The weather darkened. The autumn days got shorter. He chained himself to the house. His birthday passed: He turned eighteen. He saw no friends at all except for Joan. He added butter to his mother's peas and dreamed about the world out there.

When Joan got home from Enterprise, no matter how late, Corey took the baby monitor out to the kitchenette and sat with her and talked to her, listened to her tell him about the outside world, about her job and the people she'd seen.

"How's work?" They spoke in whispers.

"Fine." She lit a menthol. "You think she'll freak if I smoke in here?" She got up on her short strong legs and went to the window. He took the screen out for her so she could sit on the ledge with one knee up and blow her smoke out, her sock foot resting on the sill.

"I'm so lonely for like a girl," he said.

She bounced her eyes at him and formed a sophisticated smile and dropped the subject and moved on, all in the space of a second.

"You're growing," she said—returning to it.

For a few hours on certain evenings when they had a home health aide he could trust, Corey worked at a liquor warehouse on the Southern Artery, cutting open delivery boxes, taking out the bottles of wine and liquor, and putting them away in the storage shelves under the store. The basement floor was raw concrete with a glaze of shellac over it, a sealant to keep out the damp. He stomped the empty boxes flat and put them in the machine, which whipped a loop of bailing wire around them so that the recycler could take them away.

Putting Gloria down to sleep was getting harder every night.

For all these nights, she was lying, unable to move, in vary-ing degrees of discomfort—a state of minor annoyance that would become steadily intolerable. She couldn't say, "There's a single strand of hair that's tickling my cheek that's going to keep me awake. Can you brush it away please?" She couldn't say, "Please bend my knees," "My hand's trapped beneath me and losing circulation," "In the process of moving me, my underwear has gotten wedged in my crotch and is making me uncomfortable," or "The fabric of the bedclothes has gotten folded underneath me." All she could do was moan.

Through trial and error, Corey had learned the basic things that Gloria wanted. She wanted to lie on her side with her legs bent and a pillow between her knees so her bones didn't rub together. To keep her from rolling, he tucked a pillow against her back. He put another two pillows under her head to support it at the same height as her spine. A special danger area was her bottom arm: He had to make sure she wasn't lying on it. Generally, he brought the elbow forward, bent the arm, and let her hand rest on the pillow near her face. Her top arm rested along her top side, the hand laid flat on her hip.

He would begin the night by trying to arrange her in this position. Sometimes she would accept it and the night would get off to a good start. Other times, her body would resist it.

She'd roll out of position in protest. She couldn't cry, but she looked as if she were crying.

This whole time, he'd be saying, "I'm sorry, let me try again."

He would try and bend her legs, but they wouldn't stay put; they'd resist him; the spastic, perpetually rigid muscles would straighten out again. Her legs were wrong and her pillows were wrong. She'd roll away. He had to re-tuck the pillows under her head, between her knees, under her back.

"Is that good, Mom?"

Yes, she moaned.

He drew a blanket over her, put on her baby monitor, turned out her light, and kissed her head and went out to the kitchen. At intervals all throughout the night, Gloria would need to be moved again. As soon as he was asleep, he'd hear her on the baby monitor, a sound from her vocal cords. He'd get up in the darkness and fumble his way to her room.

He'd have to go through the same process all over again. He

had to re-tuck the pillows under her head, between her knees, under her back. The time he spent in the bent-forward care-ministering position started to tell on him.

In wrestling, you move the opponent by fitting your body to his while maintaining a position of mechanical advantage; you disrupt his balance while keeping your own. In moving his mother, he gave up all advantage for the sake of being gentle with her. The simplest movements became surprisingly hard, all the patient's weight on the small of his spine.

Sometimes he was able to make her comfortable. Sometimes not, and that was bad. "This is hard," said Joan. "We'll get it, Mom," he said. They tried again. "Mom, the problem is, I don't know what you're trying to tell me." It was the third time they'd readjusted her that night. "Are you okay?"

Yes, she moaned.

And he'd take the baby monitor back to bed. He never slept fully and, in the morning, the bleary day would start all over again. This routine went on with no beginning and no end and created an endless trance state in which the sun was never fully up. He was awake so much at night during this stage that he thought of it as Night World.

One night in the kitchenette, Joan told him that once, when she was a teenaged girl, a guy had chased her with a steel whip. Corey wanted to know why. Joan said they'd been at a rock concert and the guy had gotten mad because she'd turned him on.

She looked at Corey with her brown eyes. He wanted to say something, but didn't know what.

He told her he'd had a friend who wore a cup seven days a week, three hundred sixty-five days a year. He told her about Adrian's eccentricities, his intense determination to improve himself, his enormous physical strength and training in math and science.

"Worried about his jewels, huh?"

"He's scared his mother's going to castrate him."

"If I were a boy, I think I'd be afraid of that too."

"What's any girl going to see in him?"

"Besides an intact set of nuts? You never know who a woman's going to pick."

"I don't know why my mother picked my father. If I was a woman, there'd be no way."

"She thought your dad was interesting."

"I think he's a worm."

"Love is blind."

"I guess it's not my business, but I wish she'd stuck with you."

Joan made a sound between Oh and Aw.

"Love you, Joan. Always have."

"I know you have."

Corey stood up.

"No. Sit down."

"You sure?"

"Sit down."

"It's hard to sit down."

"I bet it is. No. Sit down."

"Are you sure you're sure?"

"Do what I tell you."

"All right. All right. I'm sorry."

"When I say something, I mean it."

"I apologize."

"I'm not going to do anything with you."

"I apologize, Joan. I'm sorry. Can we put things back the way they were?"

"You ought to be ashamed of yourself, coming on to your mother's girlfriend."

"I was wrong."

"You're a perverted one. You're sick and twisted. I should've known."

"I didn't mean any disrespect."

"That's okay, you're going to make some girl very happy some-day with your pervertedness."

"I'm not perverted, Joan, I swear."

She stubbed out her cigarette in the sink.

"Your mother's going to bite my head off for smoking in her house."

He listened for any sound from the baby monitor. If the smoke had reached his mother's nose, she would've moaned. The monitor was silent.

"Can we forget this happened, Joan? Please? You know, you're a big person to me. I've had dreams about you all the time. The dreams took over."

"It's forgotten."

"I have these dreams from back in Cleveland Circle. You and me saw *Billy Jack.*"

"No doubt. '*One tin soldier rides away.*'"

"Was that the song?"

"That was it."

"The drugstore scene when he stands up for the Indian kids: 'I just go berserk!' He puts that motherfucker through a window."

"A classic."

"I remember the Freedom School. The blonde woman getting raped out in the desert."

"You remember that? I'm surprised you knew what that was. You were really young."

"I still see it in my head."

"What else do you remember?"

"I remember you bought me a book for my birthday."

"That's right. You were this little blond kid. Your mother used to read to you. You were like, 'Why's this book about girls?' I was like, 'This kid's gonna be a little sexist when he grows up, like his father.' Ha-ha," Joan laughed. "No, you were cool. But your father wasn't. He kept coming around the house, night after night, to kick his little rap to your mother."

But, a thing she didn't discuss with Corey:

Joan recalled, at the turn of the millennium she and Gloria had been in love. Having learned of their affair, Corey's father had begun to call on them persistently, demanding their attention at every turn, teaching Corey pig Latin and lecturing them on the game of chess. Joan had understood what he was after—Gloria. His ego had been injured. He didn't love her, but he wouldn't be satisfied until he got her back.

One horrible day, Gloria had finally agreed to go camping with

him. Joan had fought with her, crying and wretched. But Gloria
had resolved to go with Leonard. She was going to make up with
him because he was Corey's father.

Joan had stormed out. Then she'd turned around on her heel
and stormed back in and snatched Gloria's birth control. During their argument, Gloria had claimed that she didn't want to
sleep with Leonard. Joan yelled, "If you're not going to sleep with
him, then you won't be needing this!" And then she'd stormed out
again and slammed her door—a bang to wake the entire building.
Smoke had seemed to curl in the air as after a gunshot. Choking
back her tears, she'd run down to her car—a Saturn twin cam in
those days—and driven through Boston recklessly to relieve her
broken heart.

Seventeen hours later, the next afternoon, she'd called up Gloria and told her, "I'm sorry. I guess, I've got a temper. I guess I
should move out. Can I at least take you out for a sandwich? Can
you see me?"

The day soon came when Leonard arrived for Gloria, driving
not his usual car but a dirty old van, which none of them had seen
before. He didn't want to take Corey on their weekend, but Gloria
insisted—he *had* the room—and then Leonard said, "Maybe it's
not such a bad idea. Both of you get in."

Joan helped Gloria pack a picnic and carry the cooler downstairs. She felt as if she were giving her away. But she hid her sorrow and her hatred and pretended to be perfectly happy, so as not
to allow Leonard any reason to gloat.

He sat behind the wheel, rushing Gloria and her son to get
inside the unfamiliar vehicle. Joan approached and chatted him
up. "You picked a nice weekend for it. The weather's supposed to
be great." She said she'd been out to Provincetown a while back.
And then there was Maine. She was trying to feel him out about
where he was taking Gloria. He wouldn't say. Joan made an issue
of it. She stuck her head in the window of the van and said to
Gloria, "So, do you know where he's taking you? Because he won't
tell me."

"Where *are* we going?" Gloria asked.

Leonard didn't want to be forced to say.

But Joan made Leonard tell them what he had planned. He

was taking Gloria to Harvard, Mass.—a small town west of the city past 495. A friend was lending him a cabin.

And the van departed, leaving Joan in Cleveland Circle.

Halfway through the weekend, Gloria called Joan. She said the weekend wasn't going well, this had been a mistake. They weren't in Harvard, but in Ayer—in a trailer in the woods. She had gotten disoriented on the trip and wasn't certain where they were. It would be hard to find. She'd seen a lake where they had turned. She described the trailer.

She gave Joan enough to go on, and after driving around for six hours, Joan had found her, had seen the van through the trees. Joan drove up and honked the horn. Leonard opened the door.

Joan wouldn't leave until Gloria came out with Corey. She kept her distance from Leonard, yelled to him, "Mikey DePaolo and Justin and Terry all know I'm here."

Gloria and Corey got in her car, and she drove them back to Boston. As she backed away from the trailer, Leonard had looked at her, his eyes reflecting her headlights, no expression on his face.

26

Gelato

In his second year at university, Adrian had undergone a transformation. In September, he had arrived at school with a mountain bike, a Habit with out-front steering geometry, full suspension, and eighteen inches of travel, which he rode across campus to his independent project, an internship at a research lab in the Polaroid building, on the geometric image of a photon. The mountain bike, which retailed for two thousand dollars at REI, sliced along the winding paths trod by quiet academics. It was powered by Adrian's bulging legs, fitted into clean tight-fitting denim.

He had gotten rid of the motorcycle jacket, the sweatpants, kneepads, the tattered wrestling shoes. Outside a steel and glass, corporately donated research facility, beneath a twisting modern sculpture, he secured his bike with a Kryptonite bike lock and went into the lecture hall, carrying on his shoulder a new backpack from Eastern Mountain Sports, dressed in clothing so unremarkable and inoffensive that one couldn't say what he was wearing. Quietly, he took his seat and seemed to vanish among the other young people facing the front of the auditorium.

In stark contrast to his freshman year, he gave a general impression of a mature young man leading a highly scheduled life, moving in duty-bound fashion from one commitment to the next, turning in assignments when they were due, meeting with his study group to work on problem sets, communicating a machine-like responsibility and task orientation. He had taken to wearing a pair of horn-rimmed glasses.

He had grown a partial beard and bought a pair of leather dress boots from the New York Lug Company for the weekend nights when he went out. He'd gotten a fake ID. On a typical Saturday night, he went to a bar in the Fenway, wearing his high school letter jacket for wrestling, which had white leather sleeves, and when asked "What'll it be?" pressed two fingers to his lips and said, "Hm . . . I think I'll have an IPA."

Those who knew him included Ajay Singh, his freshman roommate. Ajay would report that Adrian had a new interest in evolutionary biology, which he was using to try to understand women.

"He was getting better about his mother," Ajay would say. "He had a plan to go to grad school at Caltech. All he had to do was finish MIT in excellent fashion in the next three years, and he'd be free."

In October, just after midterms, Adrian was at a dorm-wide meeting when a chemistry major from another wing of the building made a pass at him and invited him to her room. She was a loner herself—a short-haired woman with a cold, strong-jawed face, who led an adult social life without sentimentality. In her room, Adrian removed his cup. She reportedly said, as she took hold of him, that he had a beautiful cock.

They were seen together around campus after that—not holding hands, but trading looks with one another while they locked up their respective bikes—she had one too.

Adrian was very pleased about the affair, according to those who knew him. Athena—the chemistry major's name—was very interesting intellectually: "She thinks just like a man. She's even turned on by other women. She's perfect for me."

One night at the peak of the affair, Adrian went out to Red Lobster with his mother. His mother bought them daiquiris and asked about his girlfriend. He told her he didn't want to tell her— but he'd tell her a little. His mother picked up a spoon, rubbed it and hung it on her nose.

"No fair!" he said. "You're cheating!"

"You try!"

He took her spoon and set it on his nose. His mother smiled.

When he got back to the dorm that night, he was seen walking up and down an imaginary line on the floor like a tightrope walker, arms out, the spoon, which he had kept, balanced on his nose.

Ajay asked what he was doing. Adrian said he'd been to dinner with his mother, he'd had a couple daiquiris, he felt as gentle as a bear.

❧

They started Gloria's dinner around five and it took until eight o'clock to get it all done. The day got harder as it went along because everyone, Gloria especially, was getting tired. A great deal of the time, she seemed to be displeased with everyone around her. The house swam in unhappiness and dissatisfaction, the same emotions that an overworked person brings home every day from a hated job. The job was her life, the job of existing in this wheelchair. She wanted to be left alone with a glass of wine in her hand, perhaps. But she could never do that again. And she was always closed in with people, locked in endlessly prolonged interactions over putting a spoon in her mouth. She had to absorb their energy too, just as they had to absorb hers. It had to push her beyond patience. She couldn't talk about it. She couldn't go for a walk by herself. She couldn't pick up a book and forget it. No, the only thing she could look forward to was being put down on her bed and having the lights turned out on her.

As the evening turned sour, Joan, who had a temper and who wasn't immune to having moods, went out to the kitchen to wash the sippy cup and the Tupperware, smeared with pureed squash, and put the wet dish towels in the laundry basket by the dry gray mop in the spiderwebby alcove that housed the boiler. She went outside, squatted compactly on the steps and smoked a menthol, shook her head and said, tearfully, "I'm not a fuckin' doormat."

She wiped her eyes on her brown hand and said to no one, "I know it's hard for her, but my heart's not made of gold but it's not made of leather either."

One night not long thereafter, Corey was sitting in the kitchenette listening to the baby monitor. He could hear his mother's breathing the same way he could hear the night sky when the window was open.

"I wish she'd never had anything to do with him."

"You mean you don't want to be alive?" Joan asked.

"I don't know why she ever liked him. I wish you were my dad."

Joan knocked the ash off her cigarette. "I'm not perfect either, you know, my dear."

"What's wrong with you?"

She shook her head.

November. The North End was strung with thousands of red, white and green lights and banners for a saint's day, Saint Therese of Lisieux, patron of the little flower. Local tourists—Mass. residents who had driven in from Peabody with their families—crowded the narrow sidewalk, big people, their small sons carrying a football. They walked in front of Corey. The dad said, "Why don't we go in here?" and pointed to a pastry shop. Mom, strong and fat in tight-fitting jeans, her hair in a sexy ponytail, pivoted on the ball of her Under Armour sneaker and went in, her purse over her shoulder like a rifle sling, calling back to her girlfriend, passing the word back. The girlfriend was the wife of another guy and they had kids and friends too. The families were chained together in a great united clan.

They all entered the shop, enveloping Corey like an amoeba, carrying him along. The women wore baseball hats and their ponytails fed out the hole above the adjustable plastic hatband like a horse's tail coming out the back of a ceremonial saddle in a parade. The boys played together; the men stood with their hands in their pockets and their sunglasses over the brims of their ball caps, looking over everyone's heads at the loaves of bread. An aging yellowed hue to the shop's interior. Glaring fluorescent lights like a public school built in the 1950s. Industrial gratings. Statuettes of the Madonna. A photograph of "Our Nonna" signed "with love from all of us." The antique kitchen in the back. Corey waited in the crowd. It was like waiting for tickets at Fenway Park, the customers forming into several lines to get to the women behind the counter who were like moving ticket windows—pale Old World women with brown and blonde hair and oval faces—Italian, Slavic, Albanian.

The mothers and dads ahead of him were joking. "Mike's getting her a cannoli." "I'm putting out an Amber alert." "Why does he take her out on a Friday night? He's setting her up for Saturday." "He should pay for her hair. He works at the beauty parlor. Let her get a cut and color." One of the boys tossed the football to his brother. It missed and Corey picked it up and gave it back. The father: "Thanks. He drops things."

He reached the counter and bought his mother twelve dollars' worth of gelato in three flavors—hazelnut, chocolate and vanilla. Leaving the store, he passed a church with a white plaster Madonna in the front yard, her robe rippling and draped against her legs, as if it weren't made of stone. She was a figure you had seen a thousand times through a spiked wrought-iron fence. Tilted head, downcast eyes, ritual pose.

Across the avenue, the construction site where he had worked had grown into a tower thirty stories high with a crane parked next to it, reaching skyward in the darkness.

He got on the T and left the city, riding south through the tangled black trees of Dorchester, the nightscape opening up and panning by as they roared above the water, the treetops dropping away, the shore spreading out, lit by distant industrial lights.

At home, Corey told his mother, "We'll have a party." He set out the gelato and lit a candle like a single Italian light. She made a moan of surprise. He thought he understood her. "Thank you for getting me a present, Corey. This is fun." She closed her eyes and leaned against him. "Thank you," she was saying. It was just the two of them. Joan wasn't there. Gloria might have been crying, he couldn't tell.

Joan did not show up the next night or the next. She called instead. Corey held the phone to his mother's ear. He translated for her when she wanted to talk. He found himself in the middle of a conversation he didn't understand.

"I'll try to be there tomorrow," Joan said, "if I can make it."

"My mom says, 'Don't worry about it.' Just a minute."

He got the letter board.

I forgive her.

"Tell her that?"

Gloria moaned.

"She says she forgives you."

The phone went dead in his hand.

"What just happened? Did she hang up on us?"

His mother said, *She isn't coming back.*

Corey thought that was impossible.

Gloria said, *You'll see.*

He called her in secret when his mother was asleep. He hid in the kitchen and talked to her, as far as possible from his mother's hearing, his voice lowered, just as he had when she was here in person. On the phone, her speech was colorful as always, but she never said how she could leave like this. So he called her back at Christmas and asked her why she'd left—was it because of him? She intimated that it was.

"Joan, this is my mom we're talking about. I can control myself."

But she did not return. And he wasn't brave enough to tell her, "You can give me any reasons in the world, but this is wrong. What about that woman dying in there? You call yourself *her friend*?"

She'd fled to Dorchester, apparently—or so she'd said. She'd moved in with someone—man or woman, sex unknown—who lived on a Haitian block. She'd lasted a year with Gloria's disease.

❧

By the end of fall semester, Athena had dropped Adrian for a girl, a female student who was as innocent as Athena was sophisticated. This new partner had floppy limbs and looked like someone you could unfold. Adrian saw them walking around campus arm in arm, whispering and laughing. He told a classmate he was used to using his rational mind to deal with rejection; he was back to being "a proud, lonely boy."

Over Christmas, he went to stay in Cincinnati with his father.

Mr. Reinhardt was prepared to let his son stay over, but wasn't prepared to feed him. The elder Reinhardt was sharing his home with "his new playmate," as he described her—a petite young blonde named Sheila, who drove a black sports wagon, wore sunglasses, short skirts and played tennis in the summer. The only thing Adrian was allowed to touch in the kitchen was the stove. Frank and Sheila's groceries were off-limits, so Adrian lived on black-eyed peas, which cost 89 cents a dry pound. He made pounds at a time, soaked them overnight in a ten-gallon pot, boiled them for hours, filling the tall-ceilinged kitchen with steam, and stored the giant pot in the refrigerator. When he was hungry, he ate the cold congealed peas directly out of the pot, without seasoning, up in his room.

He ate and studied at the same time so he didn't have to take his eyes off his physics. The peas gave him gas, and he lifted up one buttock and farted loudly. His father on a lower floor said, "Adrian, you're disgusting."

"I know," said Adrian. "That makes me so happy."

The big, dusty house had four or five floors, a winding central staircase, which switched directions like a snake at each landing—the kind of house that cost a million dollars, but there'd be rusted nails sticking in a closet door or broken glass shards in a window frame and old wires wrapped in gummy black electrical tape jutting from a light socket. The large windows in Adrian's room didn't have shades or screens.

Sheila and his father were eating dinner in the kitchen. Adrian walked in to get his beans, and Sheila remarked she'd come across a photograph she thought he'd want to have: It was of Adrian in the woods carrying a deer across his shoulders.

"No, my dad wants that. That was from our hunting trip together."

"No, I don't. You can keep that," Frank said. "Sheil', you want to know the story behind that picture? Adrian's fourteen. We bag a deer, and he wants a picture of it on his back. So, Mister Show-off, he picks it up. But it was a buck, and he didn't know it. Its penis went in his ear. The weight compressed the bladder and it pissed in his ear!"

"Oh, Adrian!" Sheila laughed. "Didn't you see the horns?"

A few weeks later, the vacation ended and he went back to MIT. He did well on his highly difficult exams.

Over intersession, the period of independent study and self-renewal between finals and the start of the spring semester, he lingered in the dining hall, eating copious amounts of ground meat and rice long after the kitchen closed. A classmate who sat with him one day learned that Adrian was teaching himself the crystalline structure of metals, a subject that interested them both. They fell into conversation. Adrian revealed that his vacation had been marred by an incident in consequence of which his father had told him that the only women he was ever going to get were "gas station women and nigger whores."

Adrian's listener was shocked. He thought people only talked like that online.

"Yes, it's damaging to my self-esteem. But," said Adrian, "I've accepted what I am."

Suddenly, he put on a whiny falsetto: *"A-drian, I don't like what you've become!"*—and laughed. His mother's cancer was getting worse—that is, she was *claiming* it was worse. She was simply angry, he explained, that he hadn't spent the holiday with her.

It was around this time, in early January, that other residents of the dorm noticed Adrian's renewed affinity for the basement.

Adrian said he was having certain ideas in his head, things he had to tell someone.

Corey's father said, "Come with me." He picked up his radio and led the way downstairs into the basement. It was long past midnight.

They came to a locked door at the far end of the basement. Adrian thought they'd have to turn around, but Leonard had the key and they passed into an old tunnel with two-tone painted brick walls: a fallout shelter from the Oppenheimer days, the subterranean rock so thick it blocked all frequencies and sounds. You couldn't use your phone down here.

"Now you're in the catacombs," Leonard said.

"I love this!"

"What's on your mind?"

"I dream about hanging up a live deer on a tree like a heavy bag." Adrian began throwing pantomime punches from his hyper-muscled torso while staring far away. "I'd have my hand wraps on. I'd be wearing nothing but my kneepads and my cup, so it couldn't kick me in the groin, and I'd start smashing it. I'd break its ribs. I'd beat it until I popped its organs and it exploded. I'd put my fist right through it. Then I'd take it down and put a condom on and fuck it while I was punching it as hard as I could. My body would be completely covered in its blood."

"And?"

He wished his penis were made of steel. He fantasized about ramming his hips into a woman until he had smashed her womb into a bloody pulp—into taco sauce.

"And you feel like there's something wrong with you?"

"No. I feel like something's right."

Leonard held silent.

"It's like a prison down here," Adrian observed. "Sometimes I've thought jail would be perfect for me. I'd lift weights all day and wouldn't have to worry about room and board."

"The end of all worries."

"One time, my mother didn't want to pay for me to join a gym, so I found this cheap place to work out, the Y in Central Square. It's like this halfway house. All these guys were ex-cons. I met this one dude who had gone to jail for statutory rape, and I asked him about it."

"Did his alleged crime bother you?"

"Well, let's look at this. Here's some woman who's been having sex since she was twelve, she's fully developed, she lies about her age—if you ask me, the real crime is putting him in jail. He served like ten years. They ruined his life! And he had this great attitude: He was philosophical about it. If that happened to me, I'd be so angry. I'd be looking for revenge after I got out."

"What would you do?"

"I'd find that girl."

"And what would you do to her?"

"I'd file a sexual harassment lawsuit against her."

They laughed.

"But then you'll never know what it's like to do certain things."

"Yeah, but I don't actually want to go to jail."

"You don't have to. FBI statistics say there's about a hundred serial killers in the U.S. at any given time. That's an estimate based on the number of unsolved homicides, the key word being *unsolved*. Nobody has to go to jail. There're a lot of people who are gonna die anyway."

"But a lot of people go to jail for murder."

"Not everyone." Leonard gazed at Adrian from behind his brown-lensed glasses, which protected him from cosmic rays. "Not everyone gets found. Decomposition can be catalyzed."

"Yeah, but the human body is like ninety percent water. You need a super-high temperature crematorium."

"You've heard of a pot roast, haven't you? You cook that in a household oven."

"Oh. Like Jeffrey Dahmer?"

"The biggest bone in the human body is the femur. You could have it in a bag of golf clubs in your closet. Then you got the skull, the spine and pelvis. You can do different things with each one. You could have a cop over to your house and serve him coffee in the skull of some unlucky individual and he'd never know it."

"I guess there is something kind of primitive and special about eating someone."

"It's the ultimate in domination."

"Yeah, but isn't it gross?"

"No. I mean, yeah, it is, obviously; it's sickening, but that's illusory. Once you get past the societal prohibitions, you're dealing with the meat. You're handling it; it's up to your standards of cleanliness."

"I don't know. I tried eating this whore's pussy over Christmas and it made me throw up."

"Why'd you do that?"

"I wanted to get good at it. I wanted her to have a good time."

"You could catch something like that."

"I dipped my tongue in Clorox afterwards."

"Did she like it?"

"I don't know if she could enjoy it. She told me when she was a kid, her stepdad used to come home drunk and make her sit with her legs spread open on the kitchen floor, and kick her right between the legs with his boot. But I could sort of tell when I was doing it right."

"I'm surprised you fool around like that given your experience with gonorrhea."

"It was a great experience for me. I went out there every night. She was blown away by my physique. I was the best sex she's had— and she sees tons of men all the time, so she has her pick of the litter. We basically started going out. It was just like being boyfriend and girlfriend."

"How much did she charge you?"

"I didn't pay a thing. I took my stepmother's credit card and used it at the whorehouse. When the first charge of five hundred bucks came up, my stepmother was like, 'What's Starlight Entertainment'? I was like, 'I have no idea.' So she called the card company and stopped payment and they cancelled the card, but the whorehouse didn't figure it out until the charges got declined. By then, I'd had like all these times with Tricia. When she found out, she was pissed. She said I owed her two thousand dollars and she was gonna send these corn-fed guys out to my dad's house to do a job on me. They had the address off the credit card."

"They show up?"

"Yeah. They threw a brick at the house. I called the cops."

"Look, kid, if you want to have a good time without paying, all you gotta do is slip the girl a mickey. You give her a date-rape drug, and it's your word against hers."

27

Night World

Winter. The social worker visited in her red turtleneck one day while his mother was sitting in her chair, to talk about end-of-life planning. Gloria was having her morning juice. Did she want radical measures taken to keep her alive? Would she want to be kept alive on a ventilator? Did she want a tracheotomy? Did she want a feeding tube, a PEG? If she couldn't make decisions, did she want to create a medical power of attorney?

Gloria said yes, to this last question. She wanted Corey to make decisions for her if she couldn't make them for herself.

What about the breathing tube and the feeding tube?

No, she said. Not yet.

What about later?

She writhed in her chair and made a sound of aggrieved protest.

"My mom doesn't want to talk about this now, I don't think," said Corey.

"Doesn't she have anyone but you?" Dawn Gillespie asked as he was showing her out.

When Corey was a child, when he and Gloria were living in her car, they'd traveled out to Springfield to stay with her parents, he recalled. His memories were vague. He believed they'd spent a night with them, but it might have been a week. It hadn't ended well; he had an impression of his mother, her thin cheek flushed, suppressing tears as they were leaving—and then the stress as she had stopped at gas stations and argued with a clerk for change and made calls on a pay phone to try to find them somewhere else to stay.

"Why don't we go back?" he'd asked. She'd said, "They don't really want us."

A clapboard house, a yard inside a wire fence, dull and quiet— these were his snapshot memories of his grandparents' home. A blue dining room where he ate a bowl of Rice Krispies. His grandfather putting a spoonful of sugar in the milk. His grandmother making meatloaf in the oven. A ketchupy aroma. The Revolutionary War–themed plates that she collected. Helmeted men on horseback, brandishing sabers: Hessian horsemen. A country landscape, plumes of smoke from flintlock pistols and muskets, the horsemen leaping stone walls.

There'd been two sides in the Revolutionary War. The Hessians were Germans. He hadn't known which side they'd fought for, American or British. He hadn't known if he was allowed to like his grandparents.

It had all been new to him; he hadn't minded it; he'd thought of Springfield as the country. Years later—last year—when he'd returned to Ludlow to fight, he'd realized it wasn't the country, but a small economically depressed city in the foothills of the mountains.

His grandfather had fabricated mechanical parts. The parts went in machines, which went in factories, which produced more machines, possibly cars, possibly something else like lawnmowers. In a shed outside his plant, there'd been a row of drums. The workmen spent their day grinding and polishing parts, then came outside in machinist's aprons and dunked them in the drums and shook the liquid off. They'd worn rubber gauntlets. The chemicals were toxic, his mother claimed. Corey remembered his mother telling her father not to touch her son unless he washed his hands first, and both his grandparents—especially grandma—getting angry.

His grandmother had worked in the plant office, as a secretary. Both she and granddad had worked there over thirty years.

Corey's grandfather had died of heart disease during Corey's childhood, but he'd been expected to die of cancer. It was possible that the chemicals he had put his hands in had affected his DNA, causing him to pass something on to Gloria that had made her prone to ALS.

Gloria hadn't gone to her own father's funeral. When she'd come down with her disease, Corey recalled her saying that her disease was her comeuppance.

Corey wished they had family to help them now, but, either because Gloria didn't invite her or because she held a grudge against her daughter, Mrs. Goltz did not appear.

During the day, he fed her and gave her oxygen, and at night, after her feeding, he took her to brush her teeth. They had invested in an electric toothbrush. Gloria stood balanced at the sink in her white pajamas and sneakers, seeming to float, due to the involuntary tension of her legs and the fact that she was losing weight. Corey held one arm around her, ready to catch her if she fell, and prepared the toothbrush.

Loading the brush with toothpaste one-handed was a delicate task. He laid the electric toothbrush on the edge of the sink and squeezed out toothpaste on it. The weight of the toothpaste would make the brush roll over, and the dollop of Crest would fall off in the sink. There were too many things to hold for the number of hands he had, and he couldn't leave Gloria unsupported, even if she seemed to float. His hands could be no further from her than the distance they could travel in time to catch her if she started falling. He had learned to rest his leg behind her so that it became a third arm while his hands were occupied. With it, he could sense if she began to lose her balance.

Once he had made the toothbrush ready, Gloria wanted to be the one to hold it. He took her hand and moved it to the brush and put her thumb over the button. He held her hand on the brush and raised it to her mouth, making sure the toothpaste stayed balanced on the bristles. You had to fit the toothbrush in her mouth without smearing the toothpaste off on her lip or teeth. He had learned to try to seat the toothpaste surface of the toothbrush against her back molars. "All set?" he asked. Yes, she said in her way. She moved her thumb to the on-off button. He pressed the button with her thumb. She would keep control and guide the brush around her teeth. His job was to follow her energy while providing support.

She spat in the sink, he gave her a sip of water to rinse and walked her back to bed. Now it was time to take her sneakers off because her day was over.

Corey held her hands. Gloria's hands had shrunk until the phalanges of her fingers, those tiny bones, resembled beads on a string. You could see the radius and the ulna and the dent between them. There was no increase in thickness from her wrist to her elbow. Tiny guitar strings flickered under her skin, the last wires of muscle. Her head felt damp, hard and bony, hair damp with sweat. Her cheeks were thin. Her jaw had trouble working. It hitched sideways when she moved it.

The flesh had melted off her legs like cheese in a microwave. Her bones rose up out of the ocean and the sand poured off them. The skin draped over her thigh bones. He could see the basket of her pelvis in her pajamas—that U-shaped boat where his life was launched.

He made her comfortable and tried to leave the room to get her dinner only to have her call him back again. She was getting bedsores. A nurse came and peeled up the back of her shirt and rubbed lotion on the knobs of her spine.

Sometimes Joan called and asked how Gloria was doing.

"I'm thinking of her, you know. How're things?"

"The same. All right."

Corey lived with his mother around the clock. When the home health aide came, he ran out to the library on Albatross Lane, grabbed adventure books off the shelves and returned within the hour. Quincy was gray and the sky was gray and the sea was gray and white.

He stumbled across a Navy man's memoir from World War II. He read it sitting at his mother's bedside or in the kitchenette, listening to the baby monitor, as the night deepened. He read *Lone Survivor, Service,* and *No Easy Day.*

One night, Corey was trying to make Gloria comfortable and they had terrible trouble communicating. She became mutely hysterical; she rolled her eyes and begged the world to kill her with her eyes.

He applied a great deal of force to her legs in order to bend them. He lifted her head and restuffed the pillow forcefully under her cheek.

"Are we good?" Perhaps he had hurt her. Who knows? His mother was quiet.

He looked up and thought he saw Joan looking at him from the doorway.

"How 'bout now?"

But it was his imagination. She wasn't there. All he had been seeing was the Buddha on the wall.

He got his mother in position, drew the blanket over her again and went back to his room to sleep, taking the monitor with him. While his mother lay in the dark, he prayed, "Please stay quiet."

The body of the sleeper lying on the bed under blankets. The sound of her breathing. Light snoring. The smell of her macerated skin, her unwashed body and hair. The cups all over the bedroom from last night's dinner, the residue of powder in the cups. The wheelchair like a black torture device with a bolt to screw into the back of the invalid's head—actually just the adjuster of the headrest. The levers to tilt it, a barber's chair of death. The dim gray light from the seashore. The sleeper's breathing faded and returned, harsh. He sat and meditated in the dreary room. He tried to count his breaths. But his spirit wasn't calm enough. He lacked the patience to discipline himself to this. He just wanted her life to be over. Depression followed his shameful thought. The gloom was unrelenting.

When she was asleep, he dreamed about leaving home. Her unconsciousness was deepest in the morning. For a few minutes, he thought, This will all be over someday and then . . . ! I'll go back to my adventure . . .

She blinked. The rest of her paralyzed body couldn't move. She had opened her eyes. He saw the two dark dots, looking at him. She had been awake, but hadn't called him. Had she sensed what he was thinking?

"Mom, do you want to get up?"

She made a vocal sound. She was saying yes, meekly.

He hurried over and kissed her head good morning. He got her up.

One day, Leonard called. It was gray, the house was filled with gray, his mother was lying in her wheelchair in her pajamas. There were dishes in the sink. Corey was out of shape, soft around the middle, under-slept, unshaven, living in his bedclothes. He held the phone and heard his father's voice.

"What do you want?"

"I want to speak to your mother, Corey. Put her on."

She made a childlike, inarticulate sound that meant "Who?"

"It's Leonard, Mom. He wants to talk to you."

She moaned.

"Are you sure?"

She closed her eyes.

He put the phone to her ear and held it there until she let him know that her conversation with his father was over and he could hang up now.

He looked through the blinds and thought ahead to his mother's death. He looked out at the ocean. While a home health aide fed his mother in the other room, he sat on his bed and watched a movie called *Act of Valor*. In it, a SEAL team rescues a woman who has been tortured. As she lies in an assault boat headed for medical evacuation next to a warrior who has been shot in the head and clings to life, his comrade says, "It was not for nothing." She reaches up—her fingers have been drilled through with a power drill—and her savior clasps her bloody hand.

Corey watched this scene and broke down weeping silently in his room.

. . .

Sometime later, Leonard called again. He asked Corey how he was faring, with seeming care.

Corey closed the door so his mother wouldn't hear him lie and told his father he was in training for a fight, which he was going to win.

"That's wonderful."

"You don't have to believe me."

"But of course I do. Why wouldn't I?"

"You're not my father," Corey whispered. "My father's name is Tom. He's a construction worker. Your most hated enemy. He gives me jobs. He looks out for me. He's a fuckin' man."

"This is all too wonderful. I'm so happy for you."

"I bet you are. And I'm marrying his daughter."

"His daughter?"

"Yes, his daughter. She's a track star at UMass. You can look it up."

"And what's her name?"

"I'm not telling you."

"When's the wedding?"

"Do you think I'm lying? Do you really think I would lie about loving someone?"

"I think you'd say anything to me."

"You're gonna feel so stupid. Her name's *Molly Hibbard*. Get a pen."

The bills came in the mail. The church visited. The Faheys didn't come, and Corey thought bitterly of the two of them, father and son in their docksiders. The home health aides trooped in and out. He napped on the futon when they were here feeding his mother. The social worker visited in the afternoon and saw the blankets he had been sleeping in, the bills on the coffee table, the dishes in the sink.

"Where's Joan? She isn't helping anymore?"

"She's been gone forever."

The rent was unpaid. The social worker checked the refrigerator and the cupboard. She told Corey that he was at the point where he was going to have to accept more help from strangers.

"I don't trust anyone else around her."

"A nursing home is not unregulated."

"I'm not doing that to her."

"The patient is running out of food. That can't happen. So, unless you can find some other way to turn things around, that's likely to be her best bet."

"I don't want to give up on her."

"It's not giving up. You're tired."

He let her tell him what he wanted to hear. She took charge and went in and talked to his mother.

The ambulance traveled with its lights on, but without a siren. Corey followed in the hatchback. They passed an umbrella-drink Chinese restaurant, the North Quincy T station's stadium parking lot, an urban high school with grilled windows, a McDonald's, a shopping plaza with a Dollar Tree, and turned seaward, down Commander Shea Boulevard, onto the Squantum Peninsula.

The home was hidden in a lonely place between abandoned concrete structures attached to the roadway and the shoreline. The ambulance stopped and turned out its flashing lights. Corey parked and hurried over to help unload his mother.

He walked with his hand on the rail. The attendants pushed his mother's gurney through the electric doors. The lobby resembled that of a hotel or conference center.

A gaunt woman in a nurse's blouse asked, "Who is this?"

She marched off and struck the elevator button. Once the bed was loaded on, he, the attendants, and the nurse all stood close together without speaking.

"Are you okay?" he asked his mom.

She closed her eyes at him.

They reached her floor and wheeled her to a room. The staff, composed of men and women, argued about who was going to make up the room. Gloria was transferred to another bed. The attendants took their gurney out and left. Gloria's room was blue. The window opened on a black expanse.

· · ·

The day after his mother moved in, he asked the staff how she was doing. They said they couldn't tell him; it was a HIPAA violation; he'd have to ask her next of kin. He said he *was* her next of kin; he was her son. They said they didn't know that. Could he fix this confusion? They offered no answer, so he suggested one: "Should I get in touch with the social worker?" You might do that, they said.

He called Dawn Gillespie and couldn't reach her but left a message, and later in the day, no one opposed him when he went back into his mother's room to sit with her, so one might conclude that he had been officially recognized as his mother's son; but when he tried to confirm that he was legitimately here, the staff only shrugged as if they didn't know this for certain and still suspected he was taking advantage in some way. An air of mistrust hung over the home; he seemed to be trespassing at his mother's bedside.

He spent five days sleeping on chairs in her room, keeping an eye on the staff.

"Who are you?" the night staff said on the sixth night.

"Her son."

They told him he had to leave.

"I just want to spend the night with her."

He knew she was dying. Still they insisted he leave. When he protested, they threatened to call security. He said goodbye to his mother and went home.

The next morning, instead of going to her immediately, he went for a jog on the beach, came home, picked his way through the messy house. The day went by. He told himself he would go see her that night.

When Corey was gone, a nurse went into Gloria's room, rolled her on her side, while holding a conversation with another nurse who was changing the wastebasket. She folded the sheet in half under Gloria's shoulder, went around the bed, pushed her the other way, and pulled the sheet off. She shook out another sheet and rolled Gloria two more times to get it under her.

Gloria lay in her hospital bed, a hose taped into her throat, painted with betadine. The curtains were open enough to let in the cotton-gray sky, a colorless glare. The trundling of a food cart, the clattering of trays, the squeaking of the mop wringer and the sluice of dirty water. People's shoes, walking away. A distant thundering echo of a steel door swinging shut in a tiled hallway, and silence. She lay breathing imperceptibly through her open mouth, her eyes closed.

As she lay in her final coma, This is it, she thought.

She was remembering things she hadn't thought about in years.

The autumn day had been crisp as an apple when she'd met Leonard. And he had lied about his name. When she'd found out the lie, she hadn't cared—not then—because she'd believed he would save her.

She'd believed in him with all her heart.

He had given her pot to make her a better lover. Their love life had gotten off to a fast start. He had wanted her to use a sex toy. He had insisted on penetrating her with larger and larger objects. When she'd told him this wasn't fun for her, he had disappeared.

A year later, he showed up at a coffeehouse in Central Square where she was working in an apron. From across the counter, he'd acted kind and calm—as if he had grown.

"Look, I was never fully trusting. I didn't think we would last," he told her on her break. They were having cappuccino. She noticed his new affectation, the fedora, and decided to see it as charming. His speaking style had changed. The very blue-collar Boston way he had talked—*fuckin' Revere, fuckin' Malden, fuckin' winter's long as fuck*—the sharp jabbing *fuck*s—had gone away. Now he talked deliberately and colorlessly, which reassured her.

He seemed to have undergone some kind of enlightenment while they were apart. She wondered what he could have experienced to make him change. She was jealous of his spiritual alignment. Over the year they had been apart, her intellect had stalled. His had rushed ahead. He said he was doing an important dissertation. She imagined nights with him, the two of them writing.

He didn't mind that she was seeing another man. In fact, he even walked her to that man's apartment on Commonwealth Ave.

It was a twenty-degree winter's evening. Brick and limestone architecture, the trolley running down the avenue, frozen air, the burning orange sunset, a frigid cosmic fire, the sense of distance, the turrets of the apartments, the courtyards, gates and gargoyles, the wealthy, the hints of a Jewish presence near Newton, of European immigrants, bookstores and secrets. Parting from her, he said, "I'll be thinking about you up there with him."

He picked her up afterwards and took her home. The physical evidence of her first partner didn't bother him.

She left her boyfriend, who didn't care about losing her anyway, and committed herself to Leonard—if that was his name. Her whole life was in this transfer of herself. Only then did she tell him that he had made her pregnant the year before and that she'd had it taken care of.

She moved all her chips onto him. Her parents meant nothing to her. The sheer daring of the move meant it had to pay off.

But it didn't. He broke her down without building her up. He worked on her and worked on her until she quit school. Only too late did she realize it was because he hadn't gone himself.

One day before the end, Leonard took her to his house in Malden. She'd been here before and knew about the murderer he had told her lived across the street. In the kitchen, Leonard rewarmed some pork. She thought he was being sweet. He had nice wood floors. Curtains on the windows. Sun coming through the glass. People were playing in a park outside, littered with soda cans and bits of trash—skinny loud boys, burly threatening men. They congregated on a porch a few doors away. Yet she couldn't hear them, as if the glass were soundproofed. She let the curtain go. The apartment was quiet, perfectly quiet, she thought. Leonard's house was big enough for three. "This place is really nice," she said. "You ever think about fixing it up?"

It was utterly bare except his room. Of all the rooms in the house, only one had Leonard's things. A mattress on the floor, a desk, a book or two. A closet he opened briefly and shut again. It contained his uniforms on hangers. She knew he was in law enforcement in *some* capacity at least. She wandered around a part of the house he didn't use and saw old portrait photographs in sepia—family figures, various women and men, Italians. A wooden cross leaned on the mantelpiece. The diminutive body of Christ, realistically carved, displaying his interlocking ribs and abdomen, loincloth, tender legs, the expression of mournfulness.

They ate in the barren kitchen. A single cheap pot with a black handle sat on the drain board. He had a white Formica counter flecked with tiny leaves of gold. She knew she was pregnant. She was wondering what she was going to do now that she had dropped out of school. He told her he was going to be accepted on the force at a police agency, maybe even the Staties. His physics studies were on hold. "I've been dealing with too many mundane things for far too long." When he had his career settled, he was going to return to the dissertation he was writing and transform physics as we know it.

She remarked that it was unfortunate for them to be paying rent on two different places. His house was really huge. She was preparing to tell him she was pregnant.

In the middle of their lunch, he told her, "I've seen a girl who looks just like you go from being alive to being dead."

"Yeah right," she said.

"Get down on your hands and knees," he told her. He wanted to have sex. She complied.

During sex, he said, "How would you like it if I killed you?"

Afterwards she asked if he'd been joking and he said of course he'd been joking.

Shortly thereafter, back home in the city, she called him in Malden and told him she was pregnant and was wondering what to do with it.

"If it's mine, I expect you to keep it."

"Of course it's yours. Stupid. That's why I'm calling you."

She'd had a breakdown after that. The Friday night before Mother's Day, she started acting strangely. Her Mission Hill roommates finally called the Boston PD. She argued with a cop while his partner stood out in the hall. She picked up a ruler and threw it and the cops restrained her. She screamed hysterically—as if in a vision of horror—when they handcuffed her. Paramedics carried her out of the four-story walkup strapped to a white stretcher. She screamed the whole way down, begging them to not restrain her.

She spent ten days in a locked psychiatric ward and another

ten days on a lower floor of the building with fewer restrictions after she had contracted for safety with the staff. In the dayroom, she played checkers with a strong broad-shouldered girl with a big jaw and a large beautiful aggressive face with vivid eyes and dark eyebrows and the clean, glowing skin and ponytail of an athlete, wearing a blue hospital gown, yellowing bandages taped around her wrists. At night, she slept so hard, she thought she had been surreptitiously drugged. When she asked one of the nurses about this, a polite burly man from down South, he told her that no one was ever drugged without their knowledge. She named him Bear because of his curly beard.

She sat in group and declined to say anything besides her name and listened to a young man, who had gone psychotic, say that he could see a bouncing yellow ball.

She put off calling home until she'd had a chance to see the head doctor, a tall man, who would give her her diagnosis. Carrying a clipboard, the tall doctor led her down the hall to his office, where she took a chair and he sat facing her from behind his desk. The first thing that occurred to her when he asked her to tell him what was wrong was to tell him that he was making her feel like she was in trouble, that this situation was threatening, like she was a little kid who had been taken to the woodshed for a scolding, and that it made her frightened and upset. She satisfied herself with saying that she "just felt bad." Protectively, she folded her legs up onto her chair seat and sat with her arms hugging her shins, and she adopted a cynical stance with him.

He said, with her permission, he'd like to keep her a little longer and talk again in a few days. "Try to talk in group," he said. "See what happens."

Over time, she relaxed her view of the doctor, coming to feel that he was a lovely man, caring and humane, and she told him that she had "thought-slash-dreamed" of seeing him for coffee when she was out and healed, to show her gratitude.

"Absolutely no thanks is necessary," he said. "It's its own reward to see you doing better."

She called home from a pay phone, and her mother asked if she had a feasible plan to pay back the part of her hospitalization cost that was not covered by insurance. During the phone call,

Gloria broke down in a tearful rage. "Sure, Mom, don't worry!" she sobbed. "You'll get your money."

And for years, until she had come down with ALS and was forced to confront another authority, the one that lived inside her biochemistry, she had held on to the bitter view that a human authority was hurting her mercilessly.

After she had gotten out of the psych ward, after the summer, in the fall, she'd had Corey at Mass General. School might have been over, but she'd been so in love with the child, had never felt closer to anyone in all the world than when she was giving it her breast.

⁓

In the late afternoon, a woman called Corey on his phone. "Mr. Goltz? She's gone."

He went to the home and saw her. He lifted her up in the bed where she lay. Her corpse was so light. What had happened to that backbreaking weight he'd had to wrestle with? It had been the magnetic tension in her spastic muscles. Now she was all gone, consumed. Grief burst out of him at the evidence of what had been done to her. It was precisely the kind of flowering at the crown that he had sought in enlightenment.

"Mom, I'm so sorry!" he cried out, holding her.

He felt possessiveness over her corpse. He thought he should have the right to take her from this room and dispose of her body as he saw fit, to create a private ceremony of honor to her. He imagined stealing his mother's body, taking it by force.

At the same time, in mid-grief, it occurred to him that the corpse in his arms was not his mother. The thing in the bed could have been a doll. He realized the falseness of embracing this thing and talking to it as if it were his mother. Her mouth was open—like a roadkill racoon. His mother was gone from the earth.

He put her husk-light body down and stopped his crying. The nurses were appalled, shaken, maybe moved by his outpouring. He felt that he had attracted their attention through the door. Some were scared of him. Some were angry: He was too loud, he had grieved wrong. But some were sympathetic. As he left with his head down, he was aware of a nurse controlling her tears as she and a coworker whispered together. A security guard escorted him down in the elevator, standing with his hands gripped one over the other and his chin up, neck expanded, gun on the hip, watching Corey from behind, watching the numbers of the floors. But halfway down he cleared his throat and asked Corey, "Do you want a glass of water?"

"No, thank you." And he left the hospital.

He drank himself sick drunk and threw up and woke up the next day in a house that stank of vomit.

28

The Nationals

Two or three days later, he got an invitation to his mother's funeral in the mail. The card was printed but wasn't signed. His first thought was, How did someone get her body? No one had talked to him. He flipped the envelope and checked the return address: Springfield. So it had to be her mother, who had not been there for her in life.

On the appointed day, he drove out to the forested western part of the state and into the gray, low-income city with its low profile of low buildings constructed in a river valley that looked up at the highway.

He waited at a stoplight at an eight-lane intersection with one other car to keep him company. It was raining. The light changed and he drove on. He found the cemetery, went through the iron gate in the stone wall and parked under the overarching trees.

He crossed the field of headstones on foot. At her grave, twenty or thirty people he'd never known existed were sitting beneath a tent, white-haired senior citizens, men in khaki pants and blazers. "Are you her son?" they asked. They had reserved a chair for him. It took him time to figure out that the elderly individual sitting by his side was Gloria's mother.

"We didn't think you'd make it," she said.

The rain, which had waned, came back again, pattering on the tent.

Someone introduced him to a person in a black-and-purple robe—the priest. "You're the son?" The priest was narrowly built and had well-trimmed fingernails.

"Gloria was my mother, yes."

"Do you have any special recollections of her?"

"I remember I was really young and we were crashing in somebody's house. We didn't have anything of our own and she somehow got me a TV to keep me company, because I was sick and she couldn't be there because she had to work, and she put up prayer flags over me. I don't know if you know what those are . . ."

"Prayer tags?"

"Tibetan prayer flags. It's a Buddhist thing. Do you know anything about Buddhism?"

"No."

"It was to pray for my health. She hung them up for me. And they worked, by the way. I was lying there watching TV while she was gone and I got better. And I've never forgotten what I saw while I was lying there. It was—"

He was about to mention Action Man. His story got interrupted. A stranger came over and the priest turned away. Corey took his seat.

The ceremony began. The priest began by welcoming Mrs. Goltz, the mother of the deceased. Mrs. Goltz pressed a handkerchief to her face, held it wadded in her fist, while the old women around her patted her hands. The priest recognized all of the departed's family. He pointed around the audience. "Her cousin from right here in Chicopee . . ."—a woman in a hat dipped her head—"her son from Boston . . ."—the priest's eyes skimmed over Corey.

"So many people remember Gloria," the priest continued, raising his eyes to the tent roof and cooking up a smile, "for the joy she brought others." He began to throw out Gloria anecdotes. "Her cousin remembers ice-skating with her as a girl . . . Her son remembers special times in front of the TV . . ."

Corey hadn't been warned that his remarks to the priest would be used as material for a hastily thrown together eulogy.

The coffin rested behind the priest, a giant wooden piece of carpentry that weighed so much more than the body in it. Corey saw that Gloria had been embalmed and dressed formally in a navy dress and a blouse with a bow. She looked mature and formal, like a young woman of a bygone era going off to college.

They buried his mother on a hill.

On his way back to Boston, he stopped in a valley and shadow-boxed by the roadside while the cars blasted by him in the dusk.

After the funeral, it rained. He was alone in the house, wondering what to do with his day. As he listened, the downpour became a storm. Through the blinds, he watched sheets of rain bowling down the street, hitting the window an inch from his eyes, turning the concrete seawall brown. He stayed inside, listening to the wind pry at the roof.

After several hours, he tried Molly's number. When she didn't answer, he went back to wandering around the house from room to room, listening to it rain.

The rain stopped for a little while on Monday, but he didn't go outside. No one called him back. The entire day went by.

That evening, he tried her one more time with no success.

He finally called Tom, who asked about his mother.

"We had her funeral out in Springfield. I was right next door to Amherst."

Tom said his daughter was away with her track team competing in the nationals in Texas. Corey took this to be the reason he couldn't reach her.

❧

The night before it rained was Saturday, March 21. On Monday, on the UMass Amherst campus, Molly's psychology class met in Tobin Hall, a concrete block with a honeycombed appearance, which strongly resembled a criminal justice building in Boston's Government Center. The psychology instructor wondered aloud if anyone knew why one of her students had missed that morning's test; she had been doing well. Someone said she was at the nationals in Texas. But one or two young people who were present, who knew members of the track team, had heard otherwise. Someone texted Molly's roommates and reported that they hadn't seen her either: She was neither here nor in Texas.

The instructor said maybe one of them "ought to contact someone." She never clarified if this *someone* was the police. Presumably, it was someone other than the professor.

That afternoon, Molly's classmates told the dean of students that a sophomore girl was AWOL. The dean emailed back that if this was an emergency, they needed to contact the police. Her friends weren't sure: *Was* this an emergency? If it wasn't, should they *not* contact the police? The dean's response left them confused about *what* to do. It was written in such bureaucratic language, so heavily reliant on subjectless verbs in the passive voice, that they didn't know *who* should do anything.

A rumor began going around campus that a few impulsive girls on the track team had pooled their money to go on a last-minute spring break trip before the NCAA championships; Molly had gone along with them to Mexico and gotten left behind.

The members of the UMass women's track team, deplaning now in Texas, were under a different impression altogether. They thought they were going to have to do without one of their better sprinters because she was sick at home in Massachusetts, having come down with a sudden illness during their weekend celebration.

The source of the sudden-illness story was Amanda Fiorelli, a hurdler from Dracut. But no one, including the coaches, had been able to confirm it by speaking to Molly directly.

Molly's roommates, Danielle Baskys and Heather Bishop, hadn't seen her since early in the weekend when she had gone out for pizza with her team. Since then, her dorm bed had been empty and unslept-in, as far as they could tell. If she was sick, she hadn't told them. They hadn't been worried by her absence, because they had known she was going to the championships in Texas.

But on Monday night, after she was supposed to have left with her team, the roommates noticed that the bag she'd been packing for the trip was still in their room.

. . . .

The coach of the UMass women's track team called Molly's father, from Texas.

"Are you Molly's dad? Can you fill me in on what's going on? She didn't fly with us today and I didn't have your number. One of my assistant coaches is telling me she's home, sick."

Tom strode across the kitchen with the phone to his ear and looked in Molly's room. He opened the garage and turned the light on, seeing bugs and cobwebs around the lightbulb.

"She isn't here."

Coach Kershaw said, "This is unusual. I hope she's okay."

Tom found himself reassuring her. He knew his daughter would be okay. "She uses common sense."

After talking to Kershaw, Tom tried to call his daughter. She did not answer. He told himself she might have lost her phone. He tried to go to sleep.

A few hours later, while it was still night, he got up and drove his route to work. He sat in the long white truck outside the plant in Norwood in the dark.

At four a.m., he was hunched over the iPhone, listening to it ring. Rain was spattering the windshield. The lot had turned to mud. The phone rang and rang and clicked and went to his daughter's voicemail. "It's your dad," he said. "Call me."

He reached down with his powerful finger and delicately touched the red Disconnect key and remained staring at the phone, which, along with the magnificent truck, had been a gift from his bosses.

When the men arrived at daybreak, Tom got out and walked with his head down through the drizzle to the hangar. He worked the morning, directing technicians on a snorkel lift.

At lunch, he went outside again. The rain had stopped and the sky smoked and boiled. He made his way through the wet mud to the truck and called the college. An administrator told him that, due to privacy rules, she couldn't talk to him about his daughter.

Tom hurried to his truck when the men went home and started driving and drove without intending it all the way to Amherst. He steered through the town with its quaint, ski-lodge-style chalets and onto the state school campus. A hockey player let him into his daughter's dorm and led him to her room—Tom had never been here before—and eventually, after waiting ninety minutes, he managed to speak with Molly's roommates, who told him that they hadn't seen his daughter.

"Do you know where she is? Did she say she was going somewhere?"

"We thought she went home. We figured she had a personal issue." A whippet-thin girl, Danielle Baskys wore pancake makeup and hunched when she talked. Heather Bishop parted her hair with a barrette, was short, had a childish face, and her blouse was covered in embroidery. "I tried to text her," Heather said. "Both of us were worried. We told the dean."

At eight o'clock that night, Tom made the decision to call the police. When speaking to the dispatcher, he stipulated that this *was not* an emergency.

An Amherst police car met him in front of Molly's dorm. Students in Minutemen sweatshirts stopped to watch their classmate's father being interviewed by a young patrolman.

"Has your daughter run away before?"

"She's never run away before."

"What was the name again? Hubbard?"

"*Hibbard*." Tom spelled it. "Do you want my number so you can reach me?"

"You can give it to me," the officer said.

The policeman went away, the onlookers dispersed, leaving Tom alone amid the playing fields, in the middle of the campus, against the black backdrop of the woods. He checked his phone: Still no word from Molly.

He got in his truck and drove back to the shore.

The next morning, the cold woke him. He had fallen asleep in his clothes. He got the iPhone and looked up the number for the UMPD, called and spoke to Police Officer Jessica Ventra and said he wanted to report a missing student. Ventra said that a report had already been taken.

Two days later, News Center 4 reported that the UMass police were declaring Molly Hibbard a missing person and the detective bureau of the Amherst Police Department was investigating her disappearance. Tom called Officer Ventra to ask if he should give his statement to a detective. Ventra told him to call Amherst Police Detective Dale Herrick. Tom did so. Herrick said he wasn't in charge of the case; a detective named Paul Costa was. Tom tried to reach him, but Costa didn't answer his phone, so Tom left a message. Costa didn't return his call.

The next night, upon returning from Texas, Kershaw led her fellow coaches and her athletes out to the residence houses to request volunteers for a campus-wide search of the university in conjunction with the UMass police. Their search failed to turn up any sign of the missing athlete.

Corey heard about Molly's disappearance when it was reported by the news. He thought of the last time he had uttered her full name—when he had claimed he was going to marry her—to his father.

Detectives with the UMass police went to Molly's residence and searched through her belongings. They learned her class schedule, her track and field events. They bagged up her toiletries and makeup. They learned she had a work-study job at the Sylvan Snack Bar. She was an America Reads tutor for kids sixteen and under. She had student athlete financial aid, which depended on her grade-point average. Her major was psychology. She had taken Social Psychology, the Psychology of Sensation, Child Behavior, Primate Psychology, Development and Personality. Detectives looked for evidence of sadness, stress, drug and alcohol abuse, a boyfriend. They asked about her friends and grades, her followers on Facebook.

Investigators spoke to Heather and Danielle. Molly's roommates described her as a responsible person who liked to joke about being irresponsible and wild. She had joked about making money as a high-priced prostitute—or, with her luck, a low-priced one! Her roommates had been in stitches. She was very funny. She didn't joke about her sports performance. Where men were concerned, she had been vexed. Earlier in the winter, after an unhappy one-night stand, she had forsworn them altogether.

Her swearing-off had been tongue-in-cheek of course. After-wards, she had started getting weird phone calls, her roommates said, from a blocked number.

Investigators located her one-night stand, a Minuteman foot-ball player with a pigeon-toed walk and bisonlike legs whose shoulders were humps of muscle. He came from New Haven, Connecticut ("the hood"); was white, rough, of below-average intelligence. On weekends, he got drunk ("You know how it is"); on the night in question, he and Molly had both been drunk to the point of madness. He did not like to learn that she had been upset afterwards, especially when the detectives made it clear that she was missing now. And he got angry when it dawned on him that he might have let his team down through this stupid drunken conquest. But he readily gave them permission to check his phone records. The police verified that he had never called her.

⁓

Amherst, like everywhere, is a somewhat divided town. It's sit-uated on the Connecticut River, near Mount Holyoke Range State Park, a short distance north of Springfield and roughly thirty miles east of the border of New York State.

One of the most attractive features of the town of Amherst is the loveliness of the state park, which offers grand views of the val-ley from its promontories—a hiker's paradise.

It may be thought that the individual—and women perhaps especially—can find themselves in nature here. There's a flavor of benign mystery in the air in Amherst—in the postcards of long-haired girls holding hands on forest paths among old stones, by a creek, their leafy natural temple graced by a beam of dreamy sun-light. There's the Emily Dickinson Museum in a yellow house, the high ground of Holyoke, the trees on the edge of the Connecticut River like a rolled seam in green velvet, sown fields radiating later-ally in serried rows away from the banks.

At the Beneski Museum of Natural History, the dinosaur skeletons look like devils—tusks, ribs, huge skulls with teeth, big crouched leg bones, claws, leather wings. Next door, there's a café with salmon salad.

There's free Wi-Fi in downtown Amherst. The title of a lecture at a local bookstore: "How Not to Think in Terms of Race, Gender, and Class." On the college website, we see, first and foremost, a young black woman, seated in a coffeehouse, working at her laptop, partaking of a cappuccino—she is slim and elegant—and she is first—and everything around her, everyone but her, is out of focus. The next image is a pair of young white women, laughing over coffee. Links include Student Life; Our Community; Health, Wellness & Safety; Federal Policies; Transgender Rights; Queer Resource Center—Proud, Vibrant, Caring. In "Housing," we see two women in a dorm room; a white girl is sitting in a chair looking up, a black girl is sitting on a desk above her, laughing down at her. It cannot be but that these tableaux have been artfully designed with the humane ambition of correcting the historical past by symbolically humbling the descendants of the Anglo-European colonizers of the Americas.

UMass has 23,373 students. A Division One party school, its nickname is Zoo Mass. The football team is called the Minutemen. They play Coastal Carolina, Georgia Southern, Brigham Young, FIU and Temple.

After games, UMass students have rioted, clashing with police.

The Amherst police log is public record. Typical arrests are for speeding, unlicensed operation of a motor vehicle, DUI, destruction of property, unlawful noise, liquor possession by a person under 21, open container, no seatbelt, Class C drug possession, trafficking in marijuana.

Less typically, a man who might have been in the Latin Kings was shot in the townhouses on Route 116. He was helicoptered to Springfield and died at a trauma center there.

Cops, courts, social services publicize efforts to keep at-risk kids off the streets and out of gangs. Around Amherst, the backbone of these efforts seems to be a team of women in pantsuits with tired faces—judging by photos on the district attorney's website. Topics of current concern are the opioid crisis and sexual assault on campus.

The bars in town include Rafters, Bistro 65, the Olde Town Tavern, The Spoke, and Stackers: "Watch Every Game Here." The patrons—townies, college kids, and those just passing through—come for the pitchers and pool tables. They come for the Rolling Rock and Rubinoff.

Besides beer and pot, the drugs are 2C-T-7, also known as Lucky 7, Beautiful, Blue Mystic, PT-DM-PEA, Red Raspberry, T7, Tripstasy, Tweety Bird Mescaline, 7th Heaven, 7-Up; AMT (or Spirals); BZP (also known as Nemesis or Frenzy); Foxy; Fentanyl; DXM; GHB (code-named Great Household Bargains); Jimsonweed; khat; ketamine; OxyContin; Rohypnol (Circles, Forget-Me Pill, Lunch Money, Pingus, R-2, Roachies, Reynolds, Wolfie); Salvia divinorum; Soma (or Soma Coma); Triple C; Yaba (which means "crazy" in Thai, a mixture of caffeine and methamphetamine); synthetic marijuana, a.k.a. Spice, K2, Blaze, Red X. Dawn, Blizz, Bombay Blue, Genie, Zohai, Black Mamba, Cloud 9, Yucatan Fire, "incense," "potpourri"; and bath salts or Flakka.

Even in an enlightened place like Amherst, it's possible to see surveillance footage of persons possessed apparently by the devil, tearing their clothes off, sprinting full speed through a parking lot and smashing headfirst into a car, shattering the window, falling down—and jumping up again and running away like a werewolf—naked, berserk and impervious to pain.

※

To qualify for the nationals, Molly's track team had beaten Rhode Island, a victory they'd celebrated on Saturday. After morning practice and a team meeting at which the coach reminded them how to approach the upcoming national competition—by fighting their utmost to win, hardening their collective will, banishing the thought of failure while remaining ever ready to learn from their mistakes—the girls went out for beer and pizza despite the rain in Amherst. The weather was going west to east.

As they set off, the coach enjoined them not to eat or drink too much or do anything that would take away from their performance in Texas. They mustn't drink and drive. She expected the more self-disciplined girls to lead by example. There would be time later for unchecked celebration if and when they won the national trophy, which she expected them to do. Outside the coach's earshot, some girls voiced dissatisfaction with her advice. In a parody of her warning, someone said: *"Go have a good time! Make sure you don't have fun!"*

The team broke apart into several groups, because they had

different notions about where to go in town. A line of girls linked their arms together and began trooping along past the clapboard houses, singing Rihanna songs, loosely followed by a cluster of others laughingly and loudly declaring, "We don't know you!"

Amanda Fiorelli would tell police that she was standing next to Molly when they disowned their exuberant teammates. Both she and Molly were in this more cynical faction, which was bringing up the rear.

At 6:55 p.m., the sun set. The moon, which was in its first quarter and waxing, had risen earlier but had remained invisible behind cloud cover until now. It would reach its zenith in three more hours. The temperature was in the mid-fifties. There was a hole in the rain. Fog was coming in at midnight. Then the moon would set.

In the morning, Quincy would wake up to rain. For Molly's father, the day would pass without a call from her. She had spoken to him a few days earlier to confirm that she was going with her teammates to the nationals. They had talked about money—he was helping pay her credit card this month. Their conversation had been tense, Tom told investigators. She had accused him of being angry about money, which he had denied. When she didn't call him, Tom said, he was not alarmed.

Law enforcement concluded that no one had seen or heard from Molly after the night of the twenty-first. Somewhere in the course of that night, the girls had gotten separated. Everyone was drinking. At around nine o'clock, a witness saw Molly in Stackers Pub with a drink in her hand, talking with someone at the bar. The witness was looking through a crowd and couldn't see this other person. An hour later, a local woman, who had stopped in to ask about a waitressing job, may have seen Molly in the parking lot. She had noticed a tall, well-built girl with reddish-blonde hair, wearing jeans and a short down parka, staggering, as if heavily intoxicated, away from the raucous noise of the pub and out into the darkness.

Ten days after Molly was declared missing, News Four reported that a clerk at a Mobil station off Route 116 some miles north of Amherst had found a pair of woman's jeans rolled up in the dumpster behind the bathrooms. The clothing had been thrown out before the police could secure it as evidence.

Tom thought back to the last time he had seen his daughter in person. He'd been asleep when he'd heard her coming home late one night from college. This had been many weeks ago, back when the winter had felt like it would never end. Through the wall, he had heard her talking on the phone, getting ready for bed. In the morning, he had gotten up, fixed a cup of coffee, seen her Uggs outside the door of her room. Her laundry basket had been resting on top of the washing machine. He had gone to the garage, fired up the truck, gone to work. It had been a good day. He'd seen her in the afternoon. She'd sat next to him on the couch, manipulating her smartphone, figuring out her evening. The next morning, she'd made eggs and bacon and pancakes—the bowl smeared with raw batter in the sink, eggshells in the sink, batter dripped on the stovetop, a tray full of hot scrambled eggs, thick-cut bacon done in the oven, grease in the paper towels, the sticky syrup bottle, a real feast washed down with orange juice. Father and daughter drank black coffee together afterwards—two big individuals in a sunny house in their pajamas. Then she'd disappeared into her room while he'd sat on the couch and watched TV. He'd heard the shower. She'd come out an hour later, a new person, a woman dressed and in makeup, her travel bag on her shoulder, heeled boots clopping the floor, and she'd gone back to school. Somehow before leaving, she'd magically done all the dishes: His old-man's kitchen was clean and bright.

    The weekend before she went to Texas, when she hadn't called, he'd gone to work as usual and put in his eight. After work, the yellow sun had painted the trees and houses and the road beneath him in shades of gold when he was heading home. He'd had a Sam Adams in front of the TV. He'd seen a reality TV show about a father and his sons living in the wild. The father sent the boys off to spend the night alone. They built a shelter in the snowy woods and slept with their .22. At twilight, he crept up on them, like a hunter. The boys heard a twig break but failed to take action.

Their father stepped out in the open, revealing himself. He warned them: "Next time, trust your gut. I could have been a predator."

Tom had woken up. He had fallen asleep. His empty beer was in the cup holder on the arm of the couch. The house was dark, but the sky was light—a strange effect. A slice of blue-gray illumination cut across his wall. The TV continued to warp and ripple and flash and implode with advertisements. A truck chugged uphill like a rhinoceros against a scene of brilliant skies and tall trees. The intimate chummy TV voices cajoled him to come on down to his local Chevy dealer. He muted them. The house was empty. His daughter was at school. Then the sun went down completely.

He hadn't worried until Kershaw had called from Texas. Now, as his worry turned to dread, he looked back on that moment on a Saturday night at dusk, when his only act had been to mute the TV and get himself a fistful of pretzels from the cupboard, and wonder—what had been happening to his daughter at the same time he had been eating pretzels in the dark?

29

Girl of the Long White Limbs

In the black hours of the night, a little south of Amherst, a park ranger was patrolling a seldom-traveled road that penetrated into Mount Holyoke State Park. The forest here was very tall. The land swelled like a giant wave in the misting darkness. The unpaved road led uphill into the high land. He drove slowly, bumping over rocks. His headlights picked up something white at the base of a tree. He approached, then stopped and backed away and called the police. A state trooper drove to the scene at midnight. The ranger in his green coat stood by, holding his radio. The oceanic darkness contained the glow of their flashlights, revealing the profound massiveness of the landscape as it unfolded around them, miles of trees, descending in tiers and waves. The ranger said, "There," and pointed at the naked white form that lay beneath the leafing tree.

It was the kind of instant frame you could get at CVS—a translucent plastic cube into which she had slipped her pictures. The cube rested on the dresser in her room at home along with makeup she no longer used and an old hair dryer whose cord was wrapped around the handle. Tom picked it up, felt its weight and scrutinized it. The photograph she had put beneath the plastic glass was one that he had taken. It dated back to her time in junior high, when he'd been unemployed. It showed his daughter running track with a number on her chest. She was in motion, coming out of the woods, mud on her socks, one knee rising, the other foot kicking off the sod—a competitive moment. She was in a thinning herd of other runners, all young.

When the call ended, he put the Lucite block down on the dresser. He texted one of his crew and told them what he needed them to do today. He would not be coming in. Then he drove to Boston Medical Center. He found himself in a desolate area of unoccupied brownstones with boarded windows and no stores but liquor stores and a soul food restaurant. The hospital lobby was a vast modern cavern of soft gray light and quiet sounds.

The detective put a hand on Tom's arm—"Let's go down here"—and guided him to the silver elevator. They went downstairs. He told him to stand outside the window of the morgue while the orderly, a tan quick-moving man with a lined, sunspotted forehead, on the other side of the glass lifted up the sheet and displayed the girl, her reddish-gold hair cascading over her white shoulders on the steel table and her mouth open.

Tom identified his daughter. The detective took him back upstairs. The father went outside and sat in his truck and looked at the Grateful Dead skull she had given him, a plastic skull glued to his dashboard—while the city traffic fled by, car after car after car.

Corey watched the breaking news on the minimart's TV. A wooded mountainside filmed from a helicopter, a winding dirt road cutting uphill through the trees, strewn with chunks of tumbled rock: The missing student had been found. His mind asked, Can that really be her, the person that I know? How can she have flown away from here and alighted on that mountain?

The victim's body was processed in the gleamingly modern Boston Medical Center. An orderly took the white-sheet-covered cadaver downstairs in a freight elevator and rolled it into a tiled room in the basement. There, a forensic pathologist, wearing a wet green rubber butcher's smock, scrubs, goggles, gloves and face mask to protect him from flying infectious biomatter, his torso crossed by straps holding his air tank and bone saw, hoisted the woman from the woods onto an inclined stainless steel table with a drain in the footwell. It was a loud dirty setting that more resembled an auto body shop than one's image of a hospital.

Her body was 5 feet 10 inches tall. Her rigor mortis had broken. The skin on her face looked granular, yellowish, crusted, infused with a flush, which was turning purple—a mixture of human clay and blood. Her tongue was grayish purple. The papillae stood out like the grit on heavyweight sandpaper. Purple stippling showed on her cheeks. The pathologist folded down her eyelids and discovered bright red bleeding—a common sign of strangulation. He noted severe contusions encircling her throat. The bruises overlapped, as if the same hands had let her go and repositioned—almost as if she had been strangled by many hands. She had bleeding in her eyeballs. Her eyes were cloudy. The pupils had turned black in the air. She had what looked like a sprinkling of parmesan cheese at the corner of her mouth: blowfly eggs. On her lower belly a greenish blue streak was beginning to spread. Her intestines were liquefying. Her cadaver gave off the smell of methane, putrescine and cadaverine.

Her back and shoulders looked as if she had been lying on a stove: Her skin was a deep brick-red color, like a bad sunburn or the purple hide of a rhinoceros—postmortem lividity. The examiner pressed the redness with his finger. It did not turn white but remained red. Her red blood cells had seeped out of her veins into her skin, permanently changing her color. In the redness, there was a muddy greenish-brown scaling. There were two sweaty white patches on her back where her weight had lain. They resembled hives. The sweatiness was the beginning of skin decomposition. Mold was growing on her skin.

The pathologist took out her lungs, heart and liver and weighed them. When he cut open the top of her skull to inspect her brain, he saw a highly visible dark purple mass, like a black plum, in the middle of her red-and-white brain—evidence of intracranial bleeding. He flayed open the marbled meat of her upper body and found dark red bruising in the strap muscles of the neck. In the soup of blood of her larynx, he found the hyoid bone broken.

The pathologist X-rayed her for broken bones and foreign objects and took samples of her blood, urine, vitreous humor—the fluid from her eyes. She had multiple bone fractures. She had alcohol in her system, which had decomposed to aldehyde and sugar. He took her hair. He swabbed her body for sperm and prostaglandins. He fingerprinted her. Under her fingernails, he found shreds of bloody tissue, which he sent for DNA analysis.

Leaving her on his steel table beneath the roaring vacuum hood, he unhitched his breathing apparatus, peeled off his gloves and went upstairs to his computer and began to write.

Her death was a homicide. She had died from blunt force trauma and strangulation.

Her toxicology report detected chloroform.

Her funeral was held at an Irish funeral home down the street from a car care center. A crooked sidewalk went by small houses, brick stoops with loose mortar, and scraggled hedges to the wide white sign and black script, like a letter written in 1776 with quill and ink. It faced the redbrick Quincy firehouse. Tom wore black shades at the service and stood with his thick hands clasped one over the other beneath his belt buckle. His graying hair hung to his shoulders. The coffin that Molly rested in was made of mahogany, planed, finished, inlaid with gold. The well-designed lid created a hermetic seal according to the funeral director. It stayed closed. Underneath it, a soft silk lining pillowed her body. Tom spent over fifteen thousand dollars on her funeral. His relatives came from New Hampshire. Women in his extended family brought yellow flowers shaped like trumpets. At the end, he was one of the six men who carried out the heavy shining coffin to the hearse.

Corey hadn't been invited. From across the street, he watched them carry out the coffin.

The news reported that a cell phone had been found lying in the trees off Route 116, less than two miles from Mount Holyoke State Park where Molly's corpse had been discovered. The police recovered the SIM card. Valuable information was on the card. They wanted to know who had called her. It led them to a Cambridge man named Adrian Thomas Reinhardt.

The Massachusetts State Police homicide unit attached to the Hampden County District Attorney's office was handling the investigation of Molly Hibbard's murder. The district attorney and his investigators appeared on the news and said that they were moving forward.

But nothing happened next. As the weeks went by and April became May, the case vanished from the news and the drive to prosecute it seemed to stall, leaving everyone who cared about it in a state of suspended animation. A popular theory for why this happened was that Reinhardt was a wealthy kid from Cambridge who was taking nuclear physics at MIT, while the victim was a Quincy sheet-metal worker's daughter.

The papers said that MIT was expelling Reinhardt pending the outcome of his case and that his mother had retained a criminal defense attorney to defend her son.

In a statement to detectives, which the public didn't hear, Reinhardt claimed that any record of a call to Molly Hibbard's number which had originated from his phone was either the result of a misdial or had been made by someone else.

Any idea who? investigators asked.

Adrian said: A youth from Quincy, like the victim, who'd been obsessed with her, named Corey Goltz.

Ten days after the news broke of Adrian's entanglement in the case, one night quite late, Corey's phone rang when the lights were out and he was trying to sleep. Earlier the waves had been washing the shore, but at some point, the wind had dropped, the tide had turned, and now the house was silent. He picked up the buzzing Samsung. The voice on the other end began speaking without preamble.

"Who's this?" he interrupted. But he knew it was Adrian and sat up on high alert.

"I guess you don't remember me. I guess I'm pretty forgettable." Adrian's voice sounded strange, as if he had a cold or had been weeping.

"Why are you calling?"

"Oh, I guess I don't have an official reason. I could probably hang up again and the world would keep turning at the same speed around the sun."

"Where are you?"

"At school. It's going well. I'm still learning things. I'm taking gauge theory. I'm going to pass my finals. That won't be a problem. I'll probably be doing a summer internship."

It struck Corey that these were fantasies or lies.

"I've got a problem, buddy."

"Is it something to do with your mother?"

"Someone killed my friend."

"That sounds very traumatic."

"I got a feeling you know all about it."

"I can't know about something unless it's been communicated to me."

"It's been on the news, Adrian." Corey was standing in the dark, his heart pounding down to his legs.

"There must be a thousand things on the news every day that aren't true."

"Adrian! They say you're a suspect! You did something to her!"

"You have your facts wrong. If I were a suspect, I'd know it. The police have talked to me, but that doesn't mean they think I'm guilty of anything."

"So you *do* know what we're talking about!"

"As I was saying, they talked to me. They asked these questions: a, b, c, d . . . I said, let's look at these questions logically. Here's where there's a fact or phenomenon you may have missed—just like with any scientific hypothesis. And it must have convinced them, because obviously they're not going to let a murderer run free on the streets. It was just providing information. It's like in any scientific observation you can't gather enough information from one point of observation, so you have other points of observation, and then you check the data to see if it matches."

"This isn't science class, this is life, Adrian."

"Well, what use is science if it doesn't work in life? I mean, that's what it's for—using facts and data and reason and trying to invalidate or confirm a hypothesis. If anything, I'm thinking the cops are going to get around to talking to you."

"Adrian, they're not just talking to people at random. They're talking to people for a reason. They think you killed her. And that's because you did, didn't you?"

"I'm sorry you think that. Killing a woman, that would be immoral."

"You're a fucking liar."

"Let me think about this. No, I'm not lying. It would be immoral to kill a woman, just because—for whatever reason. I mean, we could debate about some counterfactual situation where she'd done something to you first, but unless it was like some really extreme case of child abuse, say, it's like, you're not going to justify that."

"Are you telling me the news is making up the fact that you're a suspect?"

"I'm not telling you anything. I haven't seen the news you're talking about. All I know is there's this crime—this tragic thing that happened—and the police are trying to figure out what happened. That's as much as I know. If anything, you probably know more about it than I do, since you knew her."

"What are you talking about?"

"She was your friend. That's why the cops are probably going to want to talk to you. It's like, who's more likely to kill somebody? It's somebody who knows this person, who has this nasty mixture of feelings of love and hate for them. What stranger is going to feel that way? Unless you're talking about a serial killer or something—like some guy who's been killing people for years, which is obviously not true in my case, and it's probably not true in your case, unless you've been hiding it really well."

"Are you saying the police were actually asking about *me*?"

"Your name came up. It only stands to reason. It's nothing you should be worried about."

"I'm not worried about it. I hope they do talk to me."

"What do you think you'll tell them?"

"The truth."

"It might be a good idea to have an alibi for the night this happened. You could tell them you were hanging out with me. That'd be a good idea! Think about it! We could tell the cops we were at your house in Quincy. If we both stuck to that, they wouldn't be able to do anything to you, no matter what evidence they turned up."

"What the holy living fuck are you talking about? I'm not going to lie to the cops. I don't need an alibi, I'm innocent. Innocent people don't need alibis. You're the one who needs an alibi. You killed her, Adrian."

"No, I didn't. My conscience is clean on that score."

"I know you. You did it."

"You're just jumping to conclusions."

"How else would you be mixed up in this? You had to have done it."

"Well, there is one other way I could be mixed up in it: if I knew someone who was mixed up in it."

"Who? And you better not say me."

"I wasn't going to say you. But it would explain it if something happened and I'm innocent and this other person is guilty."

"Who the hell are you talking about?"

"You're going to be mad, but it's someone you won't like. You'll probably feel that competitive jealousy."

"No, I won't."

"It's your father."

"What about him?"

"He would be the reason this happened."

"When you say this, you mean the reason Molly's . . ."

"The reason she died. Yes."

"Did you see him kill her?"

"No. I didn't see that."

"Did he kill her and he told you?"

"All I can do is provide the data that I can collect from my observation point, not the data from another observation point."

"Adrian, you better tell me."

"I can tell you that I was friends with your father for a long time, and if I owe you an apology for that—I guess I do."

"So, you and my father: What did you do?"

"I didn't say we did anything."

"Did you kill Molly?"

"I didn't say that."

"You didn't say you didn't either. So did you or didn't you?"

"I would ask you to stop trying to get me to say something that won't make any difference to a person if she's dead."

"You did it. Oh my God."

"I haven't confessed or anything. Those are your words. If you're planning on telling anyone about this conversation . . ."

"I'm not interested in telling anyone, you sonofabitch!"

"That's a noble response. I'd expect nothing less than that nobility from you."

He stared at the wall without seeing it. The lights were out in the house and there was nothing to see. He stood in the center of the house without turning on the lights, the phone dead in his hand, his head alive with imagery, the whole history of him and Adrian pouring through him like a river. And his commentary on that history going round and round in circles and following that river down a hole.

I was fascinated with him, he heard himself think. I admired him, yes. What did I want? Big muscles? A's in math? I wanted to learn his secret. He was outside the struggle of life like the Buddha in a flower. He pursued self-strengthening without anxiety, feeling only entrancement. I wanted his calm and blissful self-involvement. I knew, I knew, I knew he was playing chess with my father. And I ignored it, because I coveted a secret. A secret I have since learned doesn't exist. All because I was afraid to go to basketball practice like everybody else—like Molly. Who now is dead.

And Corey saw her standing in the cluster of athletes in the echoing court, breathing hard, wiping her face with a towel, reaching out to him with her sweating hand.

Another wave of loathing convulsed him for Adrian's cowardice and misogyny: He was a malformed male who aimed his rage at women. Corey swore he'd go to the police about him in the morning.

But Corey was a coward too. He was very afraid and horrified. The morning came and he didn't go to the police.

. . .

Tom had been drinking straight for days on end, going to work, drinking in his truck, drinking continuously and staying drunk as the days turned into weeks. His bosses told him he could have all the time off he needed. He said he didn't want any. They gave him paid leave; they let him keep the Ford. He had taken leave for his daughter's funeral. He didn't talk, he drank. He drank and was drunk behind the mask of his Viking-face, behind his black sunglasses, behind the straight line of his compressed mouth, his puffy dimpled cheeks and the gray biker beard that reached the chest of his Harley-Davidson shirt. He fell unconscious in his truck one night. He kept drinking when he woke up. His friends developed theories of how and why the DA was corrupt and spoke of advancing their theories in the media. "It's a buyout," they said to Tom. They spoke of how to get the bureaucrats to act: from threatening lawsuits to taking pictures of them cheating on their spouses. If they couldn't get the wheels of justice to turn, the next question was, what could be done to the guilty party, this Cambridge boy, to punish him in vigilante style?

Silent Tom kept pouring alcohol down his throat. One morning, when he was already drunk for the day, he broke his silence to call the state police and ask, "Why haven't you arrested this kid?" A detective told him they were working on it.

After work that evening, Tom and his crew parked their trucks behind a Dedham strip mall, sat on their tailgates, talking, tossing their words at the cinderblock wall like dice. Tom's big hands hung like deadweight in the belly pocket of his sweatshirt. Under tension, the fabric stretched down from his square shoulders. His beard thrust out from his chin like a plant that lived on runoff from the scooped stone of his face. He was wearing black wraparound shades, which doubled as safety glasses.

"You hear anything new from the cops?" one man asked.

"No." Tom stalked away and kicked his boot on the asphalt.

The talk lagged and resumed. A man came back from the liquor store with beer. Victor said he didn't want any; he was driving. The men shared out the beer. Tom took a flask out of his pocket and drank it off like water.

One man said quietly, "I'd be afraid to do that."

Tom said, "I'm not driving a lift. All I gotta do is stand down here and go 'Make sure it's straight.' And if they bust me, I'll accept the consequences."

"I'd hate to see you get in trouble. You're one of the good ones."

"One of the good ones . . . " Tom muttered.

"We don't want Vizzer running things. We don't want to get Vizzered."

"I used to drink my ass off and I always showed up in the morning."

"Vizzer took Sean on a job to Connecticut. They went to play Golden Tee Golf at four dollars a round. They were doing Guinness Nitros. He fires down a growler every time Vizzer does. He got so drunk, he said, he couldn't remember his own name."

Tom walked away and kicked his boot on the ground again. "Growlers. Uh-oh."

"Sean said he was so drunk he forgot his own name. He got Vizzered."

Tom circled over to an electrician who was smoking. The man palmed his smoke to him. Tom hit it and handed it back, palm up, at the level of his waist. Exhaling smoke, he went to his truck. The men watched him. Tom got the bone-handled knife out of the cup, cut a zip tie that was binding a coil of extension cord and kicked the cut plastic loop away.

"Let us know if we can do anything, Tom."

"We shouldn't let him drive."

He had gotten in his truck and was sitting, slumped behind the wheel.

Victor walked over to him, saying, "Thomas . . ."

"They're investigating," Tom slurred. "They're doing their job like we do ours."

Several weeks after the funeral, on an evening in May when it was still cold, Corey went out to Houghs Neck and knocked on Molly's father's door. No one answered.

He stood facing the door a long time. Dusk blurred everything around him.

Finally he went in.

A scene of clutter met his eye wherever he turned—washing machine, toolboxes, extension cords, rolls of sheet metal, fishing rods, cases of Dasani water, boot prints on the carpet, piles of clothes, a Grateful Dead ashtray cupping the butt of one of Tom's cigars, junk mail on the seats of chairs, beer bottles, CDs—Martina McBride's *White Christmas* on the kitchen counter. He found Tom sitting on the couch in front of the TV wearing old-man reading glasses, plaid pajama pants and a UMass sweatshirt as a memorial to his murdered daughter. His long, cinnamon Viking hair was undone. Shot with gray, it spread from his head out to his shoulders. The TV was off and the screen looked like a polished black gravestone.

Corey said hello, put out his hand and waited. Tom said, "Oh, you're shaking hands—okay." He reached up and shook Corey's hand and didn't break it.

"I'm sorry. I don't know what to say."

"Corey, it's a hard thing . . . I'll tell ya . . . the thing about Molly is, she was a good person. She was never mean to anyone." Tom began talking about having had to identify his daughter's body. "It's something nobody should have to do. They told me it was her," he said, as if he hadn't seen her body for himself.

"I'm sorry."

"Don't apologize. You've got nothing to say sorry for. I know you went through your thing too."

Corey moved a flashlight off a chair and took a seat and leaned towards Tom to speak to him. As soon as he sat down, Tom got up and went to get a beer. He opened the bottle with his Leatherman. He began going through the mail on his kitchen counter, throwing letters aside.

"This one's from her school. They want to let me know she's absent. That's a good one."

He tossed it at the trash can.

Corey got up and followed Tom to the kitchen. "Are the police going to do anything?"

"They know who did it."

"Are they going to put him in jail?"

Tom said nothing. He drank his beer off and walked back to the couch. Corey got out of his way. Tom's whole body seemed to sneer—a brooding, massive statue of a man who didn't speak.

"Who are they saying did it?" Corey asked.

"Some kid from MIT."

Corey watched as Tom pulled his toolbox over to the couch. It was unclear what he planned on fixing. He stirred his big hand in the tools and found a drywall knife and began to change the blade. He snapped in a new razor and screwed the handle back together.

"Was it dull?"

Molly's father didn't answer. The inside of the toolbox was reflective yellow, the outside black, nature's warning colors, the same pattern as a Gila monster. He tested the knife, pushing the razor in and out with his thumb, and dropped it back in the ballistic yellow tray.

Corey cleared his throat, "Tom, I need to tell you something. I think . . . I knew him."

"I heard he was a friend of yours."

"He wasn't my friend." Corey approached the older man. "Molly was my true friend," he said. "You were."

Tom stood up and walked away. Corey stayed planted where he was, looking at the dirty carpet. He heard Tom in the bedroom. The floor creaked. A drawer slid in a wooden track in a chest of drawers.

Night had fallen. The house was dark. Corey picked up the Maglite and clicked it on and off and wondered if he should leave. Something told him he should leave.

Tom walked out of the bedroom in work clothes, boots and jeans, Harley-Davidson belt, Leatherman on his hip, the UMass sweatshirt on his chest, his hair undone. He snapped a woman's elastic band around it and gave himself a ponytail on his way out the door. The Ford pickup vroomed to life in the garage. Corey went out to the garage with the heavy flashlight in his hands. The truck was idling.

"Should I come?" Tom didn't answer. Corey climbed aboard.

Tom put the truck in reverse, hit the gas and shot them backwards, bouncing over the curb into the street; braked—they jolted to a stop—changed gears, and shot them forward. They drove over the hill and down Winthrop, splashing houses with their headlights. The wide truck seemed to fill the entire road yet somehow didn't smash the rare car coming the other way, which slipped by like a skiff under the gunwale of a barge. Then they were flying through the open blackness of the seashore under amber lights set on high masts above the street.

They stopped in Dorchester and bought a case of beer at a package store. Tom opened it in the parking lot and handed him a can.

"To my daughter."

Corey thought they were going to drink together, but Tom poured his beer out, foaming on the asphalt, then crushed his can and picked it up and whipped it at a dumpster. The tiny discus disappeared into the night sky and somewhere distant clattered to the ground. He climbed back in the Ford and turned the engine on.

"Coming?"

Corey poured his own beer out and climbed in with Molly's father.

Now they were driving north on the highway, Tom drinking from another can.

"She never asked me for anything. I wanted to see her make the most of herself. And then this reject comes along and kills her, this Adrian character, this friend of yours."

Corey said nothing. He shook his head. They were coming up on Boston. They drove into the concrete tunnel under Chinatown, lit up laser green, curving like an endoscopic view. The truck got sucked through arterial ducts and came out on Storrow Drive. Tom took the bridge across the River Charles and now they were in Cambridge with the CITGO sign in Kenmore Square behind them.

They had started up Mass Ave. Corey saw the lights spreading their glow upward on the walls of the university's Parthenon-like main building.

"This is MIT."

"This place is a reject school."

"I could show you where he lives."

Tom didn't answer. They were tearing past the campus to the bars and art supply stores and dance academies in Central Square. They passed the Middle East. Corey looked and saw the homeless people sitting on the granite planters outside the all-night CVS.

Traffic pressure kept them going up Mass Ave. Tom blew a

light. Now they were coming up on Harvard. They passed the brick wall around the college.

The traffic slowed. They came to a stop a furlong from the square, facing the redbrick amphitheater of the T entrance, the illuminated shops, the crowds passing in front of lighted windows, the Coop with its crimson flag.

"I hate driving here. It's all one-ways."

They waited at a light, the big Ford idling.

Corey said, "I can show you where he lives. His mother's house is right down there on Mount Auburn."

When the light turned green, Tom hit the gas and hooked downhill, leaving the square, and turned up along the river.

"It's that way."

They accelerated. Corey saw Adrian's house go by and said they'd passed it.

They stopped at the edge of Belmont and drove back slowly.

"That's the house."

"The lights are out. No one's there."

"Look over there, at the traffic island." Far ahead up the road, Corey pointed at a figure in the trees.

"Is that him?"

"That's somebody."

Tom cruised past.

"That's him."

"I see him. He's hitting something."

"I know what he's doing. He's hitting a punching bag."

"He does it in the dark?"

"Yeah. He does it at night."

"Are you sure that's him?"

"I know that's him."

Tom hit the gas again and they were speeding up the road along the river, the white centerline disappearing under the hood. They took a turn and Corey fell against the door. Now they were racing back.

A block from the traffic island, Tom pulled over, turned his lights off and started crawling forward, looking in the trees.

The figure on the traffic island was tilting against a hanging, swinging object, which was swinging from a tree. It was too far to hear the impact of his fists, but he was hitting it. He and the object, the punching bag, swung together and apart like two pendulum-magnets in a physics experiment. Passing traffic caught the scene in their headlights. The forms went from black to color. The punching bag turned blue; the figure's black fists appeared in red boxing gloves.

"That's him for certain," Corey said.

"What is he, a boxer?"

"Not even. He just hits that thing because he's angry."

"What's he angry at?"

"His mother."

Tom looked over at him. "Let me see that."

Corey gave him the Maglite.

"A cop hit me in the mouth with one of these when I was a kid."

"Why?"

"I broke into a warehouse with my brothers." Tom hefted the flashlight. It was filled with D-cell batteries and heavy as a club. "I'm not a nice boy."

The two of them fell silent. Tom put the flashlight aside. He opened another beer and drank. A streetlamp cast a gray light through the windshield, painting the shadow of the dreamcatcher across his face, a leather trampoline.

"Do me a favor. It's time for you to hop out."

"I can stay."

"You know how to get home from here?"

"Yeah, I've got the T."

"Go home."

Corey got out.

"Is everything okay?"

"It's fine. Go home."

"I'll see you back in Quincy?"

Tom leaned over and pulled his door shut from the inside, leaving Corey out on the street looking at the idling truck. Released by distant traffic lights, cars drove by them in waves.

Tom touched the throttle and started rolling forward.

Corey backed away.

He jogged to Harvard Square and caught the Red Line to the city. After downtown Boston, the train went on, half-empty. A guy in a demo company shirt dominated one end of the car, standing with his foot on a seat, wearing his safety shades and flexing his arms from the overhead grab bar, as if he were about to do a chin-up, while Corey sat staring at the floor.

When they got to Quincy, he walked out through the portcullis of the station into the open air. A bus was leaving and he caught it. They went downhill past his high school. When he disembarked, he smelled the ocean. He went inside his house and shut the door and put the light on and kept it on all night.

Adrian untied the punching bag. It dropped to the ground on the tree's roots. He picked up the heavy, tight canvas and leather sack of sand on his shoulder and began picking his way across the dead grass to his mother's house.

The white Ford broke from around the stand of trees and shot down the roadway. The distance between the pedestrian and the vehicle collapsed: one Mississippi. The long gleaming body of the truck hit the curb and bounced like a crocodile leaping over the sand bank into the water: two Mississippi. The pedestrian sensed something and turned. The truck touched Adrian's body. At impact, the Everlast heavy bag jumped up and fell under the truck's front tire, which ran over it. At the same time, glass and plastic and halogen dust exploded from one of the headlights and spilled across the pavement. When the truck touched Adrian, he flew up in the air, cartwheeling, elongated by centripetal force. His sweatclothes pulled away to the extremities giving a flash of exposed midsection. His body flipped three times, flung in such a way that the legs flew up and struck the head and arms. It went through an arc as high as a second-story window at its zenith and a horizontal distance of forty feet in three-quarters of a second. Weighing two hundred pounds, he had absorbed the momentum of a three-ton truck traveling fifty miles an hour. Being thirty times lighter, he flew away from it like a jack-in-the box. His body hit the wall of his mother's house and dropped, falling into the path of the truck, which had kept coming. In the last instant of the crash, the vehicle struck Adrian a second time and buried him into the wall.

Tom's foot had been jamming the accelerator to the floor since the development of the crash. When he hit the wall of Adrian's mother's house, he was going even faster than when he had hit the boy, about fifty-five miles an hour. The six-thousand-pound truck plowed through the home's siding, which rolled up like a window shade. Foundation blocks exploded into rubble. The strangely shaped house caved in, and the roof dropped above the impact site. The vehicle hit the slab on which the raised floor was built and a pair of load-bearing beams, which took the impact and tore through the ceiling—like falling telephone poles—before the plaster, wiring, and insulation stopped them, entangling them. The entire house was knocked backwards, the internal wall cracked from floor to attic. The truck was decelerated from fifty-five miles an hour to rest in under a second. It transferred its momentum to the driver. Everything in the cockpit jumped into the air. The cup, the bone-handled knife, the dreamcatcher. Tom's body leaped out of his seat, hit the windshield with his head, fell back into his seat, and bounced forward onto the steering wheel.

Cambridge Fire Rescue found Adrian inside his mother's walls. Large fuzzy pink curtains of fiberglass insulation obscured his body. A fireman moved them aside and found the MIT student bent backwards with his legs pinned by the F-150's still-hot grill. His head was covered in plaster dust like a kabuki dancer's. Pink strands of fiberglass stuck to his whiskers. The top of his skull had ruptured. An oval of bone was missing from above his hairline, and a pink bubblegum-colored tongue of meat had jumped from his head—like a frog shooting its tongue at a fly. The meat was his brain and it had intestinal coils.

The rescuers lifted Tom out of his driver's seat and laid his large-framed body on a stretcher. He was pronounced dead at the scene. They covered him with a white Tyvek sheet.

Corey slept badly. In the morning, the sky was full of thick clouds, jockeying for position, as if a new order were being established in the heavens. He walked to the DB Mart. The bell rang when he went in. The paper was upside down; he saw the word *deadly* but missed the rest. He took a juice from the refrigerator. As he was paying, he caught a flash on the muted TV of an accident scene: a debris-littered sidewalk and police tape. It didn't look like Cambridge, therefore he was reassured. He climbed the hill, sipping his pint of orange juice. The mass migration of people going to work was draining the town. Soon, the only people left in Quincy were mothers going to the store and workmen driving vans. At ten, he went to the sub shop and bought a sandwich from the Greeks who ran it. The daughter wore an elastic headband like Molly. The mother had blonde hair and a large nose and spoke with an accent. The sandwich was white-meat chicken grilled on an open fire, wrapped in hot pita bread. The news broke in loud on the TV above the drink cooler. That was when he heard "deadly crash in Cambridge that claimed two lives." He put down his sandwich and picked up his phone to call Tom, and before he could push the button, he stopped himself. "I'm sorry," he said. He wrapped the half-eaten chicken in the tinfoil and threw it out. Keeping his head down, he went outside. By the end of the day, he had heard the names, Hibbard and Reinhardt, confirming what he knew. After that, he heard the story over and over on the news for many days.

The news came on the TV in the kitchen in Malden. The small television set was plugged into the toaster outlet. Leonard was sitting at his table eating crackers and some gravy he had cooked. With a spoon he dipped up minced garlic from a jar. The screen showed Adrian Reinhardt's face. Leonard put the cracker in his mouth and chewed. He prepared another bite. The report went to commercial. He forked up an anchovy and ate it with a cracker while the advertisement for car insurance played.

30

A Loser Who Kills Others

Sometimes it seemed that he had been locked indoors listening to the rain falling on the marsh outside his kitchen window for as long as he could remember. The oxygen machine in the corner. The suction machine squatting on the splintery wooden floor next to the black specter of the wheelchair. The bedroom smelled like his mother's skin, which had turned waxy and soaplike in her endless state of suspended animation. The house had absorbed her smell. The years had been so long. The Tupperware out of which she had eaten her last meals was in the sink, still unwashed, the residue of yellow powder having dried and petrified and turned brown. The shore had always been raining. Raindrops clung to his windows. They atomized on his screens. The trees staggered wet and black on the roadside going uphill to town, past Albatross Lane, the asphalt wet and black. A gray light in the bathroom where she had fallen. The whole world through a plastic shower curtain, cloudy, filmy and mildewed. The rain kept dripping on his roof, working away at the timbers. The books all around absorbing the dreary twilight, too heavy to move, too many words, too much work to understand.

His litter of clothes and possessions—the remains of his obsessions—ropes, pulleys, boxing gloves, the term paper on ALS somewhere in the drawer of a secondhand desk his mother had gotten for him when she was well—the gangster license plate, the newsboy hat in the closet with his skateboard, the eyebolt hanging half ripped out of his ceiling—there was shame and sorrow in every square foot of the house. He lay on the futon with a T-shirt over his face, the marsh seething in his head.

When he couldn't stay at home anymore, he began spending days away, wandering through Quincy, going for miles up and down along the shore, past the New England churches, below the granite cliffs, the old, dark brown terraced condominiums, the rocks wetted as if a giant had urinated on them after the rains—eating at convenience stores, drowning out his thoughts with music. Sometimes, he sat alone in Quincy Center by the T.

One day, after Tom died, he saw Stacy Carracola getting off the train, wearing nurse's scrubs. They looked away from each other by mutual accord.

Not long after, a drug dealer, a filthy, shirtless tough in a backwards Bruins hat, circling the parking lot on a child's dirt bike with a cigarette behind his ear, rolled up to Corey and asked if he wanted to score.

"You straight?"

"I'm fine."

"Then how come I see you every day?"

Corey got up and left past the granite war memorial to Quincy's Men of Honor.

He followed gravity downhill to Braintree and looked out at the water. He saw that he was close to buying opioids. He might wind up living in a halfway house with other addicts, spending his life overdosing and getting revived repeatedly with Narcan, whiling away the days talking about the unforgivable failures of character that had brought him to this.

There was a marina on the Braintree Landing. He went in and asked about a job, thinking at least he'd be on the water. They shrugged and gave him one.

He got a tour from a man in salt-stained shorts and wire-rimmed glasses: This was the boathouse; this was the dry dock; the channel was eroding. The Army Corps of Engineers was going to dredge it. The tidal current went down the middle road, carving its way in the silt. Sometimes it flooded to the parking lot. Riprap covered the banks. A drawbridge spanned the river. Last year they'd had a jumper, an Irishman, here on a working visa, who had drowned over a love affair gone wrong. At high tide, you had to contact the bridge by shortwave radio to request an outbound opening. The bridge said "ten-four" and the highway broke in half and started rising like the letter *A*. A craft was motoring away, *Double Trouble* on the stern, water boiling around its twin Evinrudes, like a pair of eggbeaters. Out in the bay were two-foot rollers. This was a workingman's yacht club, the man told Corey. He could help them wash their sails.

He worked with a rigger named Ian, who stood six-foot-one and carried a stainless steel folding knife on a decoratively knotted lanyard. It had a locking marlinspike, which he used to pry apart knots by breaking their crowns. His purple hands were eagle-claw strong from ropework. Rope was *line*. Call it rope and he called you a *scumpuppy*. His lanyard had a Turk's head in it.

Together, they stepped a mast, walking it forward like the Marines putting up the American flag at Iwo Jima. The base fit into a socket in the hull, known as the step. Ian inserted a cotter pin. They secured the standing rigging to the rails. He learned how to put a screwdriver through the turnbuckle and twist it, tuning the shroud until it twanged. The tension had to be the same on both sides or the mast would bend. Ian sighted aloft and declared that it was true.

When the job was done, Corey celebrated by jumping off the dock. A boater in mirrored sunglasses called him a retard. Corey swam back through a rainbow film of gasoline. Seagull feathers and Styrofoam cups clung to him in the green sloshing sea under the pier. He kicked away from barnacled pilings, looking for a way up. Ian looked down at him.

"Do you expect to be saved?"

He dropped him a line and Corey climbed out, pulling himself up on the galvanized mooring cleat. His wet body ran brine on the planking. There was tar on his sneakers. Blood welled out of a slice on his ankle. Ian sent him to get the first aid kit in the shingled boathouse.

"I don't know about you. You must like splinters. Explain yourself, scumpuppy."

"I've wanted to do that since I was a kid."

"You must have had an interesting childhood."

The days were spent fiberglassing and power-sanding boats. In the middle of the summer, the rigger took him sailing on the bay. They seemed to be walking through the waves, against the chop, like farmers in a flooded field. Ian gave him the helm. The wind was blowing, the mainsail and jib were full, the lines that controlled them—known as *sheets*—were taut, creating airfoils that sucked the boat forward into the low-pressure zone beyond the bow. Telltales fluttered from the wire shrouds. The sun flashed on the waves, and the boat surged up and down like a skateboard doing ollies. Through his hands, Corey felt the balance of forces—wind from the side, low pressure from the front, the keel holding them in the water, the rudder pulling against his grip. He braced his sneaker on the deck and held his course for shore.

As the days went by, with Ian's blessing, he began taking out the dinghy on his own, one-manning it around the bay, doing ollies, getting sunburned, staying in sight of land.

But soon he thought of turning the tiller the other way and fleeing. He wondered if he had escaped the further consequences of the murder.

❧

The police investigating Molly's murder were contacted by a man who called himself "a sergeant at MIT." He said he was "on the job" and was going to help them "clear a case." He wouldn't give his name. They took several calls from the anonymous informant over the course of several days. He said he had important evidence to show them. The investigators, who were based in Springfield, traveled to Cambridge to meet him, a two-hour drive with traffic. They parked in front of MIT's main building on the evening of a late-summer day. Dark blue dusk lay on the Charles River. At the top of the steps, they were met by a sunglasses-wearing individual in a jacket that said POLICE.

"I'm your contact."

They followed him into the cavernous lobby under the domed ceiling. He led the way into a maze of corridors and stairs hidden inside the skin of the building, off to the side of the central Infinite Hallway, to an office with an antique wooden door, which he unlocked. It was a professor's private office filled with academic journals. The informant took the chair behind the professor's desk and the cops took seats in front of him like pupils. He said that now he could tell them a bit more about himself. He put his hands behind his head and talked.

Eventually, the investigators asked about the evidence.

He gave them a handwritten document. It read, in part: "*I can't reflect the colors of a rainbow when all that shines on me is darkness . . . Corey has become a black hole . . . I know what he wants is wrong. I've been asking myself if I should contact the FBI . . .*" The next sentence was highlighted: "*He wants to rape and kill a woman to know what it feels like.*"

It was signed *Adrian Reinhardt*.

The top of the page was torn where the salutation of a letter would go.

"Can you tell us how you got this?"

"I cultivated a rapport with him."

"And you did this because . . . ?"

"Because of my background in law enforcement. I thought there might be something there."

"When did he give this to you?"

"I don't remember the date."

"It looks like there's a part missing. There's no way for us to see who it's addressed to. Was this addressed to you?"

"It was like that when I got it."

The detectives didn't pursue this further. They wanted to know about the "Corey" in the letter. The informant revealed this was Adrian's friend, one Corey Goltz, last known address: Sea Street, Quincy, Mass.

They thanked him for his help and collected the document into evidence.

They figured out their tipster was Leonard Agoglia of Malden, Massachusetts, an hourly wage security guard working for a private company, Allied, which provided unarmed staff to sit at checkpoints and walk rounds at dorms and facilities on campus. It was decided not to confront Agoglia with any facts that might embarrass him, so as to keep him talking. Because of the avoidance of any subject close to the heart of who Leonard was, it took a while before anyone finally realized that Corey was his son.

A woman left a voicemail on Corey's phone. He called her back. "This is Corey." "Just a minute. My boyfriend wants to talk to you." She gave the phone to a man. "This is Detective So-and-So." Boston accent. No-nonsense. Not her boyfriend. They were cops. The reason for the ruse was to make certain that he called. There were some questions that needed clearing up.

"What kind of questions?"

"We just need your help. Are you at home right now?"

"Yes. Do you need me to come in?"

"No. We'll give you a ride."

He went to the door and saw a car that reminded him of his father's Mercury, only it was silver-gray, sitting in his driveway.

They drove him to the Quincy police station and took him through the lobby—low ceiling, dark glass booths like an aquarium where fish in uniform looked out at you, posters of sex offenders, trash cans, a bulletin board display of drawings by local school children. They unlocked a door and took him into a carpeted hallway that looked like a doctor's office and into a room the size of a large closet. There was a camera in the ceiling, which fed to computer monitors throughout the building. There was a one-way mirror, which now was obsolete—it was covered by a curtain like a motel window. The furniture was arranged in a specific way: a table surface and two chairs positioned, not across the table but to one side, so that there was no physical or psychological barrier between the interviewer and subject. There was a wall switch, which started the recording, and the detective flipped it on as soon as they entered. He offered Corey a seat and took the other. There was a remote fob in his pocket. Pressing it would mark the recording if Corey said something interesting so they could find it later when they reviewed the interview.

He put a form in front of Corey and handed him a pen.

"You don't have to sign this, but we can't talk unless you do."

Corey signed it and the detective gave it to someone else who took it and quietly closed the door. It felt like being in an examining room with a doctor.

The detective introduced himself again. He was with the state police homicide unit out of Hampden County. He was wearing chinos. He pulled his ankle onto his knee with both hands as if he were going to get into the lotus position.

"So, you know why we're here?"

"I'm not sure. Maybe you should tell me."

"Smart guy! I can't tell you how many guys think they're smart and then they sit there and just—they're not smart."

"I'm not trying to be smart."

"We're here about Molly Hibbard."

"I know her."

"She's the victim of a homicide I'm investigating. She was murdered on the twenty-first of March. You know about that, right?"

"Yes, of course."

"Hey, this is easy. Most people don't make my life easy. So, now we can get into this. I feel like you're a guy I can talk to. You're a pretty good guy, aren't you?"

"I don't know about that. I don't think I'm a good guy." Corey folded forward, covering his eyes, and tried to hold back a sudden urge to weep.

"It's okay," the detective said. A sharp-eyed look came over his face and he pressed the key fob.

When the interview was over, the detective let him find his own way out. Corey was unsure how long he'd been inside the closet. He was suddenly outside under the evening sky amid the sound of cars. It felt like years had passed. The whole universe had changed.

He contacted Shay for the first time since his vandalism charge and told him he had made a statement to the police.

"My friend was killed."

"Are you a witness?"

"I'm not sure what I am."

"What exactly did you say?"

Corey tried to recollect.

"Tell you what, I'm going to make a call downtown and see what they wanted with you," said Shay.

The next day, he called back.

"It sounds to me like you're a suspect."

"I didn't see this happening."

"This is why you don't talk without a lawyer."

Shay had him take the number of a defense attorney. Corey wanted Shay to represent him, but Shay said this man had expertise with major felonies.

The attorney's offices were located near Chinatown, near the dragon gate, old bars, and the major roads that converged at South Station bus terminal. Windows overhung the sidewalk like the high transoms of square-rigged ships. A buzzer entrance, an intercom, a room with a water bubbler, an oil painting, a high-backed leather chair. Corey sat. The attorney wore a pin-striped dress shirt with cuff links and a bright white collar.

The consultation was free. After that, his retainer was two thousand dollars.

Corey outlined his predicament. "Am I talking too much?" The attorney checked his watch. "Keep going. We've got five minutes."

He kept going. When he finished, he said, "I know this was a long story, but am I going to jail?"

"I hope not," the attorney said.

The forensic services division of the state police can be reached by traveling west on Route 2, past Lexington, Concord, but not so far as Harvard, Littleton or Ayer. It feels a long way from the shore. There is no ocean here. Driving this part of the state, one may have the pleasure of breaking out of light-dappling trees into the open vista of a cornfield, a farm stand selling pumpkins, summer corn or homemade pies. In the nearby town, there's a hint of quaintness, of the historic past preserved. A thrift store sells Indian clothing out of a seedy mansion on a tree-lined byway. But there are pickup trucks as well—and perhaps a sullen, townie character. Maynard bleeds away into the trees, running out along the roads away from its own center, fleeing itself. The forensics office is in a plain brick strongbox of a building off the highway, behind a concrete wall.

Within this rural bastion, so far from Boston harbor, a forensic specialist had processed the blood and skin found under Molly Hibbard's fingernails, to reveal a genetic sequence that matched one person in 360 million—the one person in North America whom she had clawed as she was dying: Adrian Thomas Reinhardt. Corey had admitted to police that he had been his friend.

The attorney repeated this over and over, in a phone call a few days after their first face-to-face meeting, as if awakening to the realization that Corey was going to be a more-difficult-than-expected client.

The police had wanted to search his mother's hatchback for forensic evidence. The attorney had told them no; they had promised to get a warrant, which led him to believe they had probable cause.

"They have these things you said. I don't want to repeat them."

"What are you talking about?"

"I wish my penis was made of steel, so that when I fucked a woman I could destroy her pelvis," the attorney said.

"I never said that."

"The district attorney read it aloud to me."

"Something's wrong here. I never said that."

"They have you on tape, I'm told. This is not made up."

"I'm telling you, there's a mistake. I never in my life said that. What tape are you talking about?"

The attorney confirmed that the police had spoken to his father. His father had played them a recording of Corey threatening him in violent language on the phone. The DA had heard it and come to the conclusion that Corey was a sick and dangerous young man.

The police brought a tow truck to the marina and hooked up his mother's faded hatchback. Corey put down his sander and walked up the ramp to see what was going on. A woman with a pistol on her hip was filling out a form. She pointed: "Watch him." A patrolman turned to face him. Corey stopped and put up his hands, which were white with dust from sanding. They gave him paperwork and drove away.

They kept the car five days. When they finished searching it, they notified him. He went on foot to the police station, where he paid a fee at the window. It came to twenty-five dollars a day, but they only charged him for three days. They gave him another form to take to the tow truck company's lot and reclaim his car.

"Did you find anything?" he asked.

"I don't know what they found," said the cop behind the window.

"They won't have found anything. I'm innocent."

"Have a nice day."

"What happened?"

Corey stopped in his tracks. He had a centerboard in his arms—a sheet of reddish steel. "What happened with what?"

"The other day when the cops were here. They were looking for you, weren't they?"

"It's a misunderstanding."

"That must be some misunderstanding." The boat owner, wearing a sun hat tied under the chin, was carrying a canvas tool bucket down to the flashing water. "They had the SWAT team here for you."

"Is everything okay? They're not going to fire me, are they?"

"You're getting paid to do a job. Nobody wants you bringing your problems to the workplace."

"Should I try and explain? The problem is I don't know where to begin. I had a friend who got murdered by someone that I knew."

"That's not my department. That's your business."

"All right."

Ian was waiting on the dock, belly thrust forward, forearms ruddy-tanned, a kerchief around his neck, the stainless knife hanging on his chest. Corey walked down to him and laid the rusted board on the planks at his sandaled feet.

"Ian, can I talk to you a minute?"

"I don't know. Can you?"

"Did you notice the cops were here the other day and took my car?"

"I did happen to notice that."

"Is everything okay after that? Is my job okay?"

"As far as I know."

"Do you have any questions?"

"Questions?"

"Is there anything I should tell you about?"

Ian shook his head as if he'd never heard anything more absurd.

"Your timing's good. I was about to call you."

Corey said, "We need to get in touch with the police or the DA or somebody and tell them everything."

"Well, that's not going to happen," replied his attorney.

"That's exactly what should happen."

"That's why you don't have a law degree."

"I've got information they should know."

"What information do you have, Corey?"

"I think my father is trying to frame me."

"That's unfortunate."

"Aren't you supposed to defend me? Why wouldn't you be interested in what I'm saying?"

"It surprises a lot of clients when they find out that their lawyer doesn't do everything they say. I have to explain this to people sometimes. It's the lawyer's job to keep you out of jail. You might think it's my job to do what you want. If I did that, I wouldn't have a practice. Now, listen, Corey, here's what I want you to do. We're going to have you see a psychological counselor."

"What for?"

"So you can show the court that you're trying to resolve your issues and get some help."

"This doesn't seem right. I don't think I'm crazy."

"Nobody's calling you crazy. It's at the office of probation. You see a psychologist. He interviews you and prepares something called a presentencing report."

"Why would I want a presentencing report when I haven't even been sentenced, because I haven't even been found guilty, because I haven't had a trial yet, because no one's even heard my side of what's going on here—including you?"

"Call them and make an appointment please."

Corey hung up. A minute later, he called his attorney back and said, "I'm not doing this."

"Suit yourself."

"I think it's time I fired you."

The attorney laughed and sent him a bill for $2,000.

31

Route 2

He skipped work and called Joan for the first time since before his mother's death and told her, "My father's trying to frame me with the cops."

He had reached her at work, where she was vacuuming a car. "What do you mean?"

"He's telling the cops I did something I didn't do. A friend of mine got murdered. Maybe you heard. Remember Tom? His daughter got killed."

"You didn't do it, did you?"

"No."

"Just checking."

"I didn't have anything to do with it, but Leonard's saying I did. And what's worse, I think *he did*."

"Wasn't it some kid from MIT?"

"Yeah, but I think Leonard knew him."

"Are you sure *you* didn't know him?"

"What are you talking about?"

"Didn't you tell me about your weird friend at MIT?"

"I wasn't friends with him," Corey said. The truth was too much to admit.

"I thought you were."

"The person who killed Molly? I wasn't friends with him. That's what I'm trying to tell you."

"I must've heard you wrong. I guess there must be a lot of weird guys at MIT."

"I think Leonard was behind this thing for real."

"How do you know?"

"The things he's saying to the cops. He knows way too much about this thing. I think he's a murderer."

"That's devious and evil."

"He has no limits."

"I'd say I'm shocked, but I'm not. It's in character for him."

"If you look at how he treated my mother."

"This was bound to happen sooner or later. I always thought I'd hear about him on the news."

"There's nothing he won't do."

"The signs were always there. Your mother used to talk about how he was always driving."

"What does that mean?"

"That's how some guys look for victims."

"Oh. You think he's killed other people?"

"I'll tell you one thing: There was a guy in Malden who killed his girlfriend back in ninety-three. He lived right across the street and Leonard was his friend. He talked about him *all* the time."

"Really?"

"Like he idolized him or something."

"I can't believe this guy's my father. Why did my mother have anything to do with him? What is it? You're not saying anything. What are you thinking?"

"Did you know about his trailer?"

"His what?"

"He's got a trailer out in Ayer. At least he did."

"I had no idea."

"You were there once. Do you remember?"

"No. I don't think so."

"He took you and your mother for the weekend. You were four. Something happened—some kind of problem. Your mother called and asked me to come get her. I could barely find the place. It was way off in the woods."

"But what happened?"

"I beeped my horn and your dad came out and I told him I'm not going without you and your mom. It was a bad scene."

"Bad how? What was going on?"

"I don't know. They weren't getting along, I guess. Your mother never told me."

He wanted to see the trailer—he had to see it with his own eyes—he insisted—there was nothing so important.

Joan didn't know if she could find it again but agreed to meet him after work. He went to Dorchester to wait. He took Freeport Avenue along a strip of fenced-off beach and came to the International Brotherhood of Electrical Workers local in a brick building with a flag. The dead-end streets ended in graffitied walls and trees. Joan lived in one of the cottages. Since he was early, he went through an underpass. There was a shady spot under tall trees growing in front of Saint Ambrose Catholic Church. He saw a statue of a woman in a robe, her head covered, her hands out, open, her countenance a mirror of stillness. Further up the avenue, past wrought-iron lampposts, red fireboxes, the odd Irish bar in dark green clapboard, a Vietnamese bait shop, he found the road chockablock with cars: speeding, stopped, parked, double-parked, honking. Across from 7-Eleven and a dentist and jeweler in a black granite storefront was the community health center where his mother had worked. Corey stopped and looked. A couple women in black tights, red-and-white sneakers and multicolored do-rags were outside smoking under a sign that said We Keep You Well. It had mint-green railings.

Then on his way back, he noticed the strangest thing. Out front of the church, there was a sign with his father's name on it: Leonard Street. He imagined his mother would have passed it every day.

An hour later, Joan picked him up and they drove out of the city together. Soon they were on Route 2 in Cambridge driving west to Concord. They went uphill as if they were going into the sky. The road was beautiful. The sky was blue, the great tall trees were green, it was hot and bright in the afternoon. She drove fast, talking, playing the radio, the CD player, checking his seatbelt, checking him over now that his mother was gone and he was on his own. She was his and his mother's ally once again against his father, the way she always had been.

They sped west, Joan too tough, too urban, to be fazed by other drivers—forever at ease in the world in her armor of courage. The traffic was fast and impatient—intolerant of indecision. They passed Concord, the prison, Acton, Maynard, Littleton, kept west towards Harvard, Mass. The route grew countrified and wild. In Ayer, they passed a disintegrating gas station. Corey glimpsed a tiny road going into the woods marked Poverty Lane.

At a stoplight in the town center where there were a number of different roads she stopped and thought about what to do for a minute. Then she turned the wheel hard to the left and took them out of town—speeding on a country road, going long and straight in one direction. They passed a field. Joan started slowing down. She took a turn that he had missed. Through the trees he saw a pond as she steered along an unpaved lane into the woods. The pine boughs closed like fingers around the car. Surrounded by the forest she drove slowly onward. They stopped.

In the trees ahead there was a mobile home.

They approached. There were pine needles on the welcome mat. On the siding, there was a faded bumper sticker, barely legible, that said "Kiss Me! I'm Italian!" Joan knocked on the door. No one answered. Corey tried the knob, but it was locked. Joan peered in the window.

"Is this it?"

"I think so."

They looked around the side. Behind the dwelling, they saw an ancient, rusted GMC Vandura Starcraft that had once been white. Its license plates had been removed. The quarter panel was rusted through. A front wheel was missing, the chassis was canted over, and an axle rested on the ground. They circled, looking through the Soft-Ray, Safety AS-1, Flo-Lite, laminated Guardian windshield, taking in the decals on the glass: the noncommercial registration sticker, the East Boston inspection sticker, expired.

Joan opened the door, grinding on its rusted hinge, and looked inside the vehicle. There were bags of what appeared to be household trash stuffed between the seats, as well as lumber—boards, nails, rope, detritus in the cargo hold.

Out of the eight black leather seats, only one had been broken in—the driver's. It had been crushed by what must have been thousands of hours of solitary driving.

She checked the glove box but couldn't tell to whom the vehicle was registered.

"I think it's his," she said. "Want to try and break in his trailer? I've got a screwdriver in my car."

He put her on his shoulders and she jimmied the window. Then she crawled inside headfirst and let him in the door.

Inside, the dwelling smelled like a rotting mattress, like cotton turning to black dust after it had gone through the digestive systems of mites and had been expelled as powder. A wispy fungus was lifting off from the carpet, one of nature's strangely beautiful ways of spreading spores. Trash was strewn around—newspapers and magazines, the paper damp and mold-blackened. A ring of dried dirt in the sink. Leaves in the drain. A pinecone on the countertop. In the living room area, there was a ring of built-in couches, like the seats in a theater, and all the lines of sight shot from there, down the length of the floor, to the king-sized bed at the other end, with no barriers in between. The bulkhead dividers, which could have separated the different segments of the house, as in a bug's body, were folded back inside the walls. A series of plastic bubble skylights evenly spaced down the central axis of the domicile had been blacked out with layers of newspapers and aluminum foil and 3M packing tape. The arrangement channeled one's eye towards the dark end of the trailer where the bed awaited, like a raised stage at the bottom of a mine shaft.

Corey turned on the flashlight on his phone and played the light around the boudoir. He saw a closet with stained pine walls and a locking door. There were other closets and compartments. The refrigerator wasn't running. There were dead flies on the tray-shelves. He looked inside the bathroom, the shower curtain throwing a capelike shadow up to the ceiling when his phone-light struck it in the tight, rubber-floored space.

Joan went outside to wait in case anyone had seen them and called the cops.

Going through papers stuffed in drawers and cardboard boxes, he picked up a pile of junk mail and a stack of photographs fell out. The top picture was a blurry image of the woods taken on a gray day when the leaves were not in bloom. The one below it was a woman. Her face leaped out at him with lurid force. She stared unhappily at the camera. She was blonde. She had a narrow body. She was wearing pegged pants with room in the hips she didn't need. In her hand she held a can of Sprite. Corey matched the background to his surroundings. It had been taken here.

He shuffled to the next photo. It showed her sitting as before, legs crossed, drinking from the soda, staring disconsolately away. In the next, she was talking to the camera; in the next, drinking from the can again; in the next, not talking: lying down. In the next, her eyes were closed. And also in the next. Corey shuffled through the stack. He counted nearly thirty pictures of her sleeping on the trailer's black-sheeted waterbed.

In one image, she was lying by a boy of kindergarten age, who, like her, was blond. The date was stamped in glowing orange digits: 1999. It had been developed at CVS. Corey saw a glint between the boy's eyelids as if he had been watching the photographer while pretending to be asleep.

Joan said the woman was his mother and the little boy was him. The photographer must have been his father.

Corey was outraged. He wanted answers.

"What was going on? She's sleeping. Did he put her to sleep? What did he do to her?"

Joan said, "We don't have to go there."

She went into what was wrong with Leonard. (1) He was an asshole. (2) He had a small penis. (3) He was jealous that Gloria had loved her son and not him.

"He's not gonna get away with this. He's gotten away with it my whole life. It stops dead-shit today!" This was an expression Joan had used. She was given to tirades and Corey had studied her. He put on a Joan-style tirade against his father: He was going to fix him with the police! He was going to fix him on his own—in the streets!

He and Joan were standing on a corner in Dorchester by

now, the summer sun about to set. Concrete blocks, three-family houses, golden sun.

"I'm gonna hurt him up. If he thinks he can do this to me, he's a—and I'm gonna—" and so on.

Joan lit a cigarette. "Do me a favor. Don't fit this guy for some concrete shoes without talking to me first."

"Bet I can make him read my Nikes. Bet I can stick him somewhere they'll never find him: the swamp behind my house."

"I know you're mad, but if you go away for twenty-five-to-life, you might get to be my age behind bars and think it wasn't worth it."

"Oh, I know, no doubt . . ."

He squirted saliva on the sidewalk from between his teeth, the pictures in his pocket, Joan nodding, flicking ash from her cigarette, saying hi to people she knew, leaning on her car.

He went on punking and motherfuckering and punk-motherfuckering his father.

Joan nodded along. "So, what are you going to do?"

"I'm going to give them to the police. I don't need to go to jail."

"What do you think's going to happen?"

"He's gonna be up shit's creek."

"But it's not like he hurt her that I can see."

"He can't do this to somebody!"

"I'm not saying he can do it. I'm saying, I don't see what they're gonna do."

"They ought to put his ass in jail."

"For what?"

"I don't care for what. They need to just throw him in a cell. I don't care what you want to call it—child abuse, woman abuse, drugging somebody . . ."

"Hey, I understand you're angry. I'd be angry too if it was my mother."

"Yeah, I'm angry!"

"I'm just saying the pictures don't show anything."

"Maybe something was happening that they don't show."

"That's just the problem."

"But someone should see them. The sheer fact that he would take them."

"Why is a cop gonna care about that?"

"You could come to the cops with me and say you remember that night he had us there."

"I don't think so, Corey."

"Why not?"

"Because I said so. Because your mom's dead, Corey. She passed away, and there's nothing they can do about it."

"So, I'm not supposed to show them to a detective, say I think my father took them, I think he knocked my mother out with—it looks like he doped her with something in that soda can? I'm not supposed to do that?"

"You can do whatever you want. I don't see how it's going to help."

"You don't see that someone could look at these and draw the conclusion that whoever took them has something wrong with them?"

"I didn't say that. Hey, Corey, don't raise your voice at me. I'm trying to help you. I took you out there, and I'm getting tired of you getting lippy with me just because I'm not gonna do what you want. I don't know what the cops'll say. Maybe I feel guilty that I didn't do more to help your mother. But she wouldn't let me help her. I couldn't keep her away from Leonard. She made her own decisions, so maybe I'm not as worked up as you at this late date. She didn't have to get in the van with him, but she did. So maybe if she fell asleep, she was taking a nap and it had nothing to do with him."

Corey shook his head.

"And just 'cause you're upset, don't think you can scream at me."

"I'm not screaming."

"I drove you out there."

"Thank you."

"If it was my mother, I'd want revenge, so I don't blame you. But you're not the only one with a temper."

"All right."

He lay awake all night long in Quincy. Finally, he turned on the light. The first thing he saw were the photographs on his desk. He put them in a drawer so he couldn't see them and went out to the kitchen and sat in the dark. It was a hot night. Dawn was coming. He sat in the dark in a dreamy state.

After some time, his eyes turned towards the kitchen window. A breeze was coming through the screen.

He opened the window, climbed out, walked down to the marsh and stepped off into the water.

Under his weight, stalks of grass cracked and popped, the roots broke, snapped, gave way, and he sank in to his knees. He lurched. The mud sucked at his shoe. He yanked his leg free and stepped on something sharp. The brine stank. Leaves and insects were sticking, biting, tickling. He waded further in. He sank to his waist, plunged forward, slipping, sinking down to his chest. Clawing at the bank, feeling the firm ground with a hand, he reassured himself, if he had to, he could do a chin-up and drag himself out of the soaking, sucking muck. He crouched down in the reeds and plowed around with his hands, feeling inside the thicket of sharp snapping stalks. Something was crawling on him and he knocked a spider off his neck. When he crouched again, his shin touched something. He felt in the water with his hands. There was something down there. He grabbed his father's bag and heaved it up on the bank—soaking wet, immensely heavy and gushing water.

He climbed up after it onto the slimy grass, carried the bag back to his house and set it in the middle of the floor. The zipper was rusted shut. He pulled it open with a pair of pliers. The inside of the bag glimmered. He could see the knives in the dark water, rusted together.

As the sun came up, he sat on the futon, making the cushion wet, staring at the bag.

Corey went to the police station and waited at the window.

"I have evidence that could be evidence of something serious."

"What is it?"

"It's a bag with knives and handcuffs, a nightstick and a bunch of uniforms."

"What's it in reference to?"

"That's going to take me a long time to explain."

The officer picked up the phone, reconsidered, said to leave it in the lobby. Someone would collect it. Corey wanted to give it to someone personally; it was important. The policeman said they didn't just take things from people who said they had evidence; there was a chain of custody.

"That's why I don't want to just leave it on the floor. How will anyone know what it is?"

When the officer ignored him, Corey said, "This might involve a murder."

The man ordered him to leave his evidence where he was told. Corey didn't want to. He turned around and left. The cop came outside with another officer and a detective. One said, "You can be held if we deem you to have evidence pursuant to a crime. Where's the bag?"

Corey told them it was in the trunk of his car. They went over to his mother's hatchback.

"Are there going to be any surprises in that trunk?"

"Absolutely not."

They had him take his car keys and open it himself.

"Is that the bag? Why's it wet?"

"It was in the marsh behind my house."

They took it from him.

"You've got to test it for DNA," he said. They said they would, not to worry.

"I know you think I'm a kook."

The first cop said, "You must be a fuckin' mind reader."

"What are we supposed to do with this bag?" the detective asked. "What's in here anyway? How did it come to be in your possession? How do we know it's your father's? You come in off the street and tell us all this—you see the problem?"

"I do."

"We'll make sure it gets to the right people. Don't worry, we know who you are. We'll be talking to you again. The reason you're here, maybe it's because *you* feel guilty. That happens sometimes. Maybe you've got a whole lot more to tell us."

"I *do* have more to tell you."

Corey let himself be guided back into the police station. But because the Springfield detectives were unable to make it today and the Quincy detective had an urgent call, he ended up going home.

He called Joan and told her what he'd done. He got her voicemail. On the recording, he denounced the cops for unprofessionalism, for giving him a hard time when he was trying to do the right thing, was on the side of the angels, was trying to help them do their job. His mother had been drugged unconscious and no one cared. But that was fine. He had other methods at his disposal.

32

Polar Bear Swim

The weather remained pleasant after Labor Day, but the sky lost its richly saturated blueness due to the changing angle of the sun. They spent September pulling the boats out of the water with a Hostar hydraulic lift. The operator was crane-certified. A three-man crew made four with Ian. Corey was the helper. They brought the boats on land and set them on tripodal jack stands, then took out the docks and stacked the sections. The banks of the river were going to freeze. To winterize a boat they bent a long narrow rib of wood from bow to stern and stretched a skin of plastic over it.

Joan and Corey spoke again that month. He heard something in her voice.

"You're upset with me. What is it?"

"I wouldn't say I'm upset about anything."

"You are. I hear the anger."

She recalled Corey's mentioning of an individual from MIT who wore a cup at all times, last year in his kitchen. "So you *did* know the kid who killed her. And you *did* tell Leonard about her."

"I never said I didn't."

"I wonder what you said to him. I guess we'll never know."

"Joan, what are you saying?"

She said it was a damn shame Tom wasn't alive. She'd never

known his daughter, but Joan was sure she'd been a nice girl who hadn't wanted to lose her life.

"You weren't honest with me," Joan declared.

"Well, I'm being honest now."

"You didn't invite me to your mother's funeral. You should have."

"It was out of my control."

"I guess I didn't know you."

They finished winterizing the marina in October. Corey told Ian he hoped to see him in the spring. Ian said he was dreading it already.

"Then again, I might not be seeing you. I might be in court."

The rigger listened, curly head lowered, chin to chest, looking at his belly, iron-claw hands at his sides, as Corey talked:

"They think I killed a girl. She was my friend. I didn't do it."

"I don't know what to think of you."

"I understand. I hope you don't regret knowing me."

"It takes all kinds," Ian said and went back to work without inviting Corey to help him.

They parted.

Corey got a new job at a business that made kitchen countertops off Commercial Street in Weymouth. The stone came in by flatbed, the slabs leaning together like books on a library shelf separated by wooden spacers. The driver unstrapped it and they picked it up by forklift and drove it into the warehouse. Maneuvering granite was based on tilting, rocking and lifting together. Corey stayed off to the side. The men didn't know him. They cut marble with a circular saw and used water to wash away the slurry.

In his dreams at night he saw the murder.

Gray days, winter ahead. His depression returned. He turned nineteen. He went to work without enthusiasm. He waited for anything to happen—even to hear from the police.

. . .

On November 12, he was summoned to the office of the Suffolk County prosecutor, who was reviewing the Hibbard case because the alleged killer had gone to MIT, which was in his jurisdiction. Corey took the train to Government Center—that open stadium which looks like a massive skate park. There was a courthouse faced in marble with Egyptian friezes, clean, sparkling granite, new, bright, smooth, silent, sealed with green glass, running silent silver elevators. The prosecutor was around the corner in a structure without character, a narrow high-rise that could have been an apartment tower, scaffolding around the entrance.

A woman behind a bulletproof barricade buzzed him in. The prosecutor was a trim, short, white-haired man in his seventies wearing a charcoal suit. He was talking to a police detective in a belted leather jacket when Corey entered. The detective eased to the back of the room and everybody sat. Gold-framed oil paintings of Washington and Lafayette hung on the walls, these tall figures seeming powdered white and spot-lit against their dark backgrounds. Under the feet of Corey's chair, there was a woven rug adorned with fleur-de-lis.

The prosecutor looked at Corey from across his massive antique desk. "So here you are," he said. "On paper you don't look so good." He glanced at a folder on his desk top. "Vandalism. Harassment. Assault—that was dropped. Theft. Restitution. A restraining order. Did you deal drugs in high school? Never mind. I see you thinking about your answer. And now a suspect in a murder. How old are you?"

"Nineteen."

"And you're a high school dropout. That fits. Any idea what you've got planned for the next nineteen years? Want to spend it in MCI?"

"What's MCI?"

"Massachusetts Correctional Institutions."

"No, I don't."

"If you lie to me, that is exactly where you will go. Have you been advised of your right to counsel? You don't have to talk to me. You can walk out that door, but if you do, you're not getting back in. Now I'm going to ask you some questions and, so help me God, you better tell me the truth. Who killed Molly Hibbard?"

"I think Adrian did. He called me and admitted it."

"You and Adrian were friends."

"At one time but not when this happened."

"Did you plan it with him?"

"No. Molly was my friend."

"Did you go with him to see her?"

"No. Absolutely not."

"Why do we have this letter where it says you want to rape somebody to know what it feels like?"

"Those are not my words. Adrian wrote that."

"Your father is Leonard—how do you say his name?—*Agoglia*. Security guard at MIT. Gives us the letter. Says he's worried about you. Wants you to get some help. You were in family court?"

"Yes. He was phone-harassing our house."

"What's his role in this?"

"I don't know. I think he planned it."

"He says you, you say him."

"I say him, yes. I don't know how else Adrian would know Molly existed. I think my father told him to hurt her. I'm convinced of that. I believe that in my heart."

"So you gave—what do we have here?—pots and pans, knives—to the Quincy police and said they belonged to your father?"

"They *did* belong to him. That was his bag—I stole it—I admit it—and threw it in the marsh."

"Did he use these things in a crime?"

"I have no knowledge that he did. I just felt it was possible, based on knowing him. Did the police test them?"

"Test them for what?"

"DNA."

"I don't know why they would do that. Your father's not a suspect in a crime."

"Have you talked to him?"

"No, I haven't because I don't need to." The prosecutor raised his voice. "If I feel like talking to him, I'll get around to it. Right now, I'm talking to you. Problem?"

"No problem."

"Just answer his questions," the detective said from the back of the room.

"Fella, if you give me a hard time, I'll chase you out of here so fast your head'll spin."

"I understand," said Corey. "I'm not giving you a hard time."

"What happened in Cambridge?"

"Are you talking about Molly's dad?"

"I'm talking about Molly's dad and Adrian Reinhardt, who wound up dead of a collision. I want to know how that happened."

"I went over to Molly's house to see Tom. We got in the truck and started driving. I told him I knew where Adrian lived and we drove there. And Adrian was outside. I said, 'That's him.' Tom told me to get out of his truck and I did. I got back on the train and went home. I heard about it the next day."

"Did you know Tom was going to run over Mr. Reinhardt?"

"I didn't know what he was going to do."

"Did you talk about it?"

"It was in the air."

"What does that mean?"

"Nothing was said out loud. But I don't have a problem with the fact that Adrian got killed."

"That's not an intelligent thing to say to a prosecutor."

"I'm just telling you the truth."

The prosecutor looked at the detective, who said, "Just stick to what he asks you."

"You did or didn't know what Molly's dad was going to do before he did it?" resumed the prosecutor.

"I didn't know."

"Did you have a reason to want to see Mr. Reinhardt killed?"

"Yeah. He killed Molly, didn't he? Shouldn't he pay for that?"

"Do you have a problem containing yourself?"

"Sometimes."

"That's not a compliment."

"I'm sorry."

"What do you think of Mr. Goltz, Detective?"

"I'd like to see him take a polygraph."

"So would I."

"I'll gladly take one," Corey said.

. . .

He took the polygraph on November 22 in an interview room at the Quincy police station.

The day after he took it—Sunday—he woke up early and walked into town as the sun was rising. Everything was silent. The church bells hadn't rung yet. Orange light was flooding Walter Hannon Parkway.

In the plaza next to Star, he came upon a deep, first-floor warehouse behind a glass storefront. The door was open, but the lights were off; the place was strangely empty. The room was filled with iron barbells.

He moved through the silent field of weights. There was a heavy bag in back. A set of mismatched boxing gloves lay on the floor, one of them pink—a woman's. He put them on and tapped it with a jab.

After a minute, he began working around the bag—little patty-pat punches, as if he were tapping you on the shoulder, saying, "Hi, remember me?"—until the first light perspiration broke out on his head—then every fourth punch had a crack to it. A minute of this went by, then he pounded the bag five times in a row. The dam broke and he started beating the heavy leather methodically, burying his knuckles in it with every punch he landed, leaving fist holes in the stuffing—sweat from his face wetting his gloves, flying off in spray. He thudded and swatted the bag in violent furious mathematical-sounding bursts, which ended with a shin kick. His shin kicks detonated. The bag jerked and swung. The chains jangled like a tambourine accompaniment to his drum solo.

Drenched in sweat, he went to the parking lot, sat down in the cold sun with the rocky pavement under his haunches and the sun shining through the thin barrier of his eyelids, filling his head with light.

After a time, he went into Star and bought steak and charcoal and went back home and grilled it in the yard, the smoke billowing up in his face, his eyes on the flames, watching their little story unfold, the rich charcoal smell of the steak, the liveliness of this chemical process, the hot steak in his fingers and teeth—sucking up the blood-coal-juice-oil-salt, standing there in his winter coat as the grill died, the bone in his hand, black on his fingers, the sun in the sky, the slow fullness as the meat broke down in his stomach's hydrochloric acid and filtered fats and acids out into his bloodstream, his satisfied settled state.

And now to drink some water, something sweet, some soda.

He wondered what the prosecutor would decide and if he would end up going to prison.

He had always thought he was going to get back in the cage. A Brazilian jiujitsu school called Trifecta Martial Arts had opened above the Family Dollar. There was a basement boxing gym across the street, below an African hair-braiding stylist. He'd always figured he'd get back to training, eventually get back to Best-way and impress his old coach with a better, stronger version of himself.

But now, as he thought about Molly, he felt he had to do something bigger—something of which prizefighting was merely a subcomponent: warfare at its highest level—expeditionary, total, encompassing the realms of sea, air, land—even space—something so great it could kill him, forcing him to overcome with finality the inner weakness and self-regard that had allowed him to fail every-one around him—a path to honor, invincibility, pride and moral purity—where his father had indulged in scandal, obscenity and dysfunction.

The weeks passed—he went on cutting stone in Weymouth—then, a few days before Christmas when it was gray after a snow, he found his way to a back alley on an asphalt cliff above Star Market, above a loading dock protected by a rusted iron railing, where there was a single-story building like a postal substation with a poster on the door of young people in uniform gazing up at jets wreathed in the Stars and Stripes. He went inside and down a hallway, passing a roomful of men in faded camouflage fatigues and tan jump boots, all burned red, a shock of color in the barren whiteness of the office, evidently here from somewhere hot—Marines—and at the end of the corridor found the Navy.

The Navy recruiter was a hulk of a man with bulging biceps and full sleeve tattoos hunched over a laptop, hunting and pecking the keys. His room looked like a telemarketing operation—folding chairs and tables, landline telephones, pencil stubs, scraps of paper littering a desk.

Corey told him he intended to be a Navy SEAL.

The man looked up. "That's extremely hard. No one can guarantee you that."

He gave him a pencil stub and some pieces of scrap paper and had Corey take a timed, multiple-choice test to determine his mental and moral fitness for the Navy.

Corey went into his mother's bedroom on Christmas morning, took her reading glasses off the nightstand and looked through them. They made the venetian blinds sharply precise. He set them on the bedspread. He began going through the room, taking each thing of hers and putting it with the glasses—silver jewelry, elephant ornaments, woven purse, driver's license with the sad picture of her face—taken after she had been diagnosed. Discovering her phallic glass pipe, he hastened to throw it out. He kept cancelled credit cards, South Asian ornaments, clothbound notebooks she had used for shopping and to-do lists, written in what had used to be a beautiful hand.

He hadn't realized how beautiful her handwriting had been. A note said: "Application, three references, timing belt, inspection sticker, greens, onions, butter, poem." On the overleaf, she had drawn an abstract design of a flower and the words "I Can See It."

He found several messages she'd written expressing her hopes for him and bemoaning her struggle with herself—willing herself to struggle past her tendency to self-defeat. Then he found a letter she'd written after getting diagnosed. Like the others, it was addressed to no one. He didn't finish it. He folded it shut. Her writings got shakier over time. The entries grew shorter and shorter.

Most of what she'd done was beginnings without endings.

But he kept finding more beginnings. She'd written him a partial letter. The handwriting changed halfway and he realized she'd dictated it to Joan. It dated from his trouble with the law: "My dear son . . . I've got my eye on you . . ." it finished. He read it carefully.

She'd wanted him to not throw his life away. He put the letter in his room.

He took her mandala down and folded it.

The next day, Sunday, he went into her closet and took out her clothes, aware of their weight, smell, variety. The things at the back of the closet were different from the things at the front. She had more clothes than he'd ever seen her wear. In the middle of the day, he drove to Goodwill and gave them her clothes and drove away before they could open the bags in front of him.

The house seemed somehow messier when he got back. Everywhere he looked were medical documents, the endless forms and flyers, doctors' bills, laboratory invoices, insurance company mailers, notices from the state for disability, credit card statements, tax bills, *ALS: What It's All About*. He tore it all up—it made a sea of paper in the center of the floor—and stuffed it by the armload in the garbage.

He got his wrench and attacked the wheelchair, took apart the leg rests, broke it down and took it to the car. He unwired the Boss license plate and kept it. The oxygen and suction machines went next. He drove to a medical supply in Randolph with the trunk tied down with clothesline and unloaded everything on the sidewalk.

At home again, he vacuumed. Night was falling. He ate chicken fingers, drank a Mountain Dew and turned the lights on.

He was up all night again. Her books and papers, writings about art, society and the self, he preserved. Over and over, he found writings in which she reflected honestly on who she was, grappling with herself, exhorting herself to fight on and do something she could be proud of before it was too late. It had been the theme of her life for decades, long before she had gotten sick.

He saw *The Flower Ornament Scripture* in her milk crate. He hadn't opened it in years. He turned the pages—sutra after sutra—Sanskrit on the left, English on the right—Chief in Goodness, Purifying Practice, Super-knowledge, Ascent to Suyama Paradise, Eulogies, Awakening by Light.

On her laptop, he found an abortive essay she had been working on the winter leading up to her diagnosis: run-on word-jammed pages fragmented into stop-and-start ideas, author's notes: "Need to study French painters!" "Go back to the Greeks!" The last line

was "I've gotten some bad news. Can I use this?" He went back
to the beginning and read it. It didn't sound like her. It was by
turns highly technical—bristling with dates and specialized knowledge about Mycenaean friezes—nudes came flowingly to life in
480 B.C.—and polemical, strident, funny, interrupted by comic
interludes and aggressive flights of fancy. It was disorganized too,
a wild rough draft with long riffs on small points she built into bigger and bigger mountains—a Nietzschean expansion. There were
passages that had come out ringingly well. Most of it was finding
her way—and then she'd found it: flares of fire. Bigger, smarter,
meaner, surer—more daring—than the mother he'd ever known in
person. The start of a new person, but an unfinished one.

He preserved her writings in a waterproof plastic tub marked
"The Real Gloria."

In the new year, he moved out of his mother's house to a room in
town, a few blocks from Molly's bars. Parking was free. There was
an outside staircase to his floor. Women lived on the second floor,
men on the third. The rooming house was the size of a barn. He
kept the old hatchback downstairs in the snow. Two guys lived on
his floor, a landscaper who was always working and a pot smoker
who never worked, who woke up in the afternoon and played guitar all night. They shared the kitchen and bath. Corey had brought
nothing with him but his sleeping bag and his boots, a few books,
a towel laid out to dry on the radiator with a toothbrush and a bar
of soap. Everything else was in a storage unit behind a Master lock
at Quincy Adams.

In the winter mornings, he left the house before dawn when
it was all guys in pickups on the roads, listening to sports radio,
windows up, heaters on, eating sandwiches at stoplights, waiting
for diesel trucks to roll through. In Weymouth, a giant man named
Bench, the boss's right-hand man, was always there before him—in
mackinaw and rubber boots, picking his way around the stone in
the half dark. The daily delivery came in and they cut stone all day,
filling the drain with milky slurry, or went out on installations.

In the evenings after work, Corey went to Northeast Health
and Fitness and trained according to the guidelines from the Naval
Special Warfare website.

. . .

One night, instead of going to the gym, he ran from the city center all the way down to his mother's house, hopped the seawall and ran along the ocean.

Soon, he was going over the seawall, regularly, in construction boots, running in water, getting wet on purpose, doing calisthenics in the sand. The SEALs had a deck they called The Grinder; he had a grinder of his own—a spot where he did sit-ups on asphalt deliberately to lacerate his back. He sprinted, picked up lightning-scorched logs, so heavy his skeleton's integrity was in peril. Worried about tearing apart his shoulder, he cast the timber off and it thudded to the ground. It would have crushed his foot if he hadn't pulled his leg away. One night, wearing a sack of wet sand on his back, he toiled down the beach, running on his hands like a bear.

He was pushing against an internal limit, the selfish pain-fear boundary in his head, trying to move it. It was the heaviest log to move. Every day he pushed against it, and every night someone came along when he was sleeping and moved it back. His goal was to move it all the way to the horizon.

On the fifth of February, he drove alone to Wollaston beach and parked. On the ocean horizon, the clouds formed a stack of horizontal lines. The stratospheric winds were curling the top row of clouds, blowing them apart and driving them across the sky like suds in a pan. He was shivering in his clothes. He stripped, ran out and threw himself in the heart-stopping water.

33

Total War on Sea, Air, Land

It was snowing. The end of March. The recruiter was surprised to see him, it had been so long. Corey brought a copy of his birth certificate and GED, which he had passed. It was cold and white and quiet all around them. They spent the day filling out forms.

He called the prosecutor's office. The prosecutor couldn't take his call. He was put through to someone else.

"Detective Bellavia. Can I help you?"

"This is Corey Goltz. I came to your office months ago and I haven't heard anything. Is there anything going on?"

"If there's anything to tell you, you'll be notified."

"I took a polygraph. Nobody notified me of anything."

"You passed."

"I passed?"

"Yes. You sound surprised."

"I'm not surprised. Does that mean I'm in the clear?"

"I wouldn't say you're in the clear."

"But how come, if I'm telling the truth?"

"You can be charged with a crime even if you're telling the truth. If you come up to me and say 'I stole a candy bar,' that's a confession and you can be charged with that confession. Happens every day."

"Okay . . ."

"Makes sense, right?"

"But what is it about what I've told you that you're going to want to charge me with?"

"We don't have to tell you that. That's up to the prosecutor's discretion anyway. But I'm sure you can imagine."

"Would it be that I was in the car with Tom?"

The detective said nothing.

"Is it that I knew Molly? Or that I knew Adrian?"

"I'm sure you can figure it out for yourself."

"Does this mean you're going to charge me?"

"I can't tell you what's going to happen."

"All right. Well, at least now that we know I'm not lying, do you want to hear about my father?"

"If you want to tell me."

Corey spoke at length.

"It's not like I have proof of anything. This is just my impression of the man."

"That's quite an earful."

"There's just so much about him that nobody knows. I could tell you more."

"I don't really have time now."

"When you hear what I'm saying about him, does it show you that maybe somebody else is guilty besides me?"

"Obviously, if you're the one telling me, I have to take it with a grain of salt."

"But I *am* telling the truth. As best I know."

"You mind me asking what you're doing with yourself?"

"I just enlisted in the Navy."

"No kidding. I'll have to tell the boss. He's a Marine Corps guy, so he'll enjoy the part about the Navy. He asks me how come I wasn't a Marine. I call him one of Uncle Sam's Misguided Children. He calls me a Ground Replacement Unit."

"What does that mean?"

"A grunt. It just means he loves me."

"Were you in the Army?"

"For better or worse."

"I really wish I could talk to you a lot longer. I've got a lot of questions."

"Talk to your recruiter. But don't believe a word he says."

. . .

Corey had placed the call from his bachelor's room. The musician was sleeping. The smell of pot hung around the house. He sat on the floor of his room and stared out the white window at the snow.

According to the Naval Special Warfare website, he'd have to be doing 1,000 push-ups, 1,000 sit-ups, 200 pull-ups, and be running at least 50 miles a week to be ready for selection. He'd want to be lifting double his bodyweight, if he could, like an ant. He'd want to surround his shins with muscle to prevent stress fractures, because, at selection, they would run literally hundreds of miles, in sand, in boots, in life preservers, which were wet and heavy, and steel helmets, carrying boats on their heads.

Other injuries he could expect: tendon tear, cartilage tear, anterior cruciate ligament, inflammation of the knee, tendonitis, splitting the Achilles tendon sheath, sprained ankle, torn rotator cuff, chafing, staph infection, cellulitis, falling from a height, broken leg or spine, hallucination from exhaustion, falling asleep while running, hypothermia, lung edema, death.

No one who has gone to selection has ever found it easy. Training deaths occur. Some men commit suicide after failing. Some try again. It's more pain than most will take. He'd be competing against the toughest, strongest, fastest men from every state across the country. If he made it through selection and joined the Teams, he could expect to deploy. Special operations are at the forefront of the United States' current military strategy.

If, on the other hand, he failed, he'd spend his enlistment doing what? Menial work on a destroyer?

But if he did nothing, he would stay right here.

He imagined facing an enemy in a match without rules. He imagined facing them, exhausted, when he could no longer defend. He felt himself succumbing, the air being choked out of him, exhaustion consuming him. He could see what would happen if his enemy, possessed by fury, were allowed to strike him after he was spent, the horror of that—of dying like Molly in open combat without a referee.

If any enemy, no matter how powerful, had threatened his mother, Corey hoped he would have found it in himself to defend her. He could not feel fear where Gloria was concerned. But he did. He could imagine all too well those he was afraid to face. Could he overcome his fear of every monster on the planet?

Simply by running on a quiet road, he knew, if he exerted himself to the fullest, the sensation of drowning on dry land would soon grow so intolerable he would do anything to make it stop. All his resolutions were nothing next to the need for oxygen. If he couldn't overcome his desire to breathe when he was running unmolested, how could he stand up to a vigorous adversary without quitting?

One says "I'd summon the strength to kill for you." But could he summon the strength to fight anyone for her? Could he summon the strength to hold his breath for her? Could he summon the strength to die for her—not by a bullet but by inches?

And all this was far easier, it seemed, than the task of always treating her with patience.

Could he summon the strength to be a saint for her? Would he take her ALS from her? Would he trade places with her in that wheelchair?

The very thought was too much to consider. Corey knew he wouldn't do this for her. Her disease had terrified him. Which forced him to ask: Of what quality was his love?

The quality of his love was lacking.

To truly love someone, you must be willing to do anything for her. To do anything, you must be able to face any fear, any pain. Killing was easy, fighting was hard, sainthood was harder, ALS was the hardest of all, it was impossible—and yet his mother had faced it.

That evening he called Joan again for the first time in a long time and asked her how she was. He told her he was worried that Leonard was going to get away with everything.

Joan said, "The cops'll probably let him get away with it. Look at what they did for Whitey."

"If they would only talk to him, they'd see."

"That'll never happen."

"How can you say that?"

"Because they're all men. They don't care."

"You don't really mean that, do you?"

"Yes, I do."

"But some men *do* care, Joan. Not everybody's bad."

"Well, they *should* care, Corey. And I *do* think that men should protect women. And I *do* think that men who beat up on women aren't men. They should get paraded down the street in dresses like little fucking girls."

"Hey, I agree."

"And I think that if a man rapes a woman, he should get something stuck in him."

"No argument."

"A needle. In his dick."

Corey winced. Then the conversation took another turn he had not foreseen.

"You'd never hurt a woman, would you, Corey?"

"No. Of course not."

"It's funny, because I remember you telling me about your friend from MIT in your mother's kitchen on the day I turned you down. And then this happens to a girl you knew. And it takes you, what, six months?, to come clean to me that the guy who did it was your friend? So I gotta wonder what you're hiding."

"Joan, you're getting carried away."

"Maybe your father made you into a pervert. Maybe you can't accept it if a woman tells you no."

"Would you ease up on me? You're supposed to be my aunt. If any of that was true, would I be thinking day and night about taking the law into my own hands and doing something vengeful to Leonard?"

Joan agreed to change the subject. She began telling Corey how she had moved to a new house in Dorchester, which was beautiful and huge. She lived there with her boyfriend, a construction worker. Irish dude. Very young—Corey's age—she was robbing the cradle blind. Young but wicked mature. A plumber. He had no teeth, she said. He'd done time. "You would love him."

Corey said that was great. He said he'd like to meet him.

He revealed his military plans to Joan.

The military wasn't right for him, she said. She'd dated Marines; she knew.

"Joan, I've fought in the cage."

"Oh, that's right," she said. "I keep forgetting."

"What's wrong with you?" he asked, hurt.

Joan said, "I just don't think I trust you."

In the morning, he checked in with his recruiter, who told him that one of these Saturdays—soon—they were going to MEPS, the enlistment center, where Corey would officially enlist.

"You ready?"

"Yes, sir!"

"Hooyah! Be ready!"

Up till now, Corey had concealed the full nature of the legal and criminal matter that was hanging over his head, and the recruiter hadn't asked him for anything more than a superficial account.

❧

Less than one week later, he heard about the lawsuit.

It had been many months since he and Shay had spoken last. The April day on which the lawyer's call came in was beautiful and bright. Corey was sitting in the sun on the stoop of a boarded-up storefront next to the Brother's sub shop, having just bitten into a grilled chicken sub. It was midafternoon; he was done with work; this was dinner. It had been a day of sprinting and doing star jumps at the gym and carrying marble. He ate with his eyes fastened on the recruiting office, which he could make out above Walter Hannon Parkway. When he finished eating, he was going to take a shower and fall asleep in his sleeping bag listening to One Republic. His phone rang and he dripped tzatziki sauce on his boot toe putting down his sandwich to pull the Samsung from his jeans.

"Corey, it's Shay. How you doing?"

"Good. How are you? It's been a while!"

"You're good?"

"I think I'm good. Is something wrong?"

"What about your charges?"

"Well, yeah, what about them. I guess I'm kind of in limbo. Nothing's been happening that I know of. I ended up talking to the cops, and I feel like it kind of got us somewhere—a little bit— insofar as I told them my story and laid it all out there and—it's not like they heard it and decided to charge me. So, you know— it's not like they're going after my father, which is what I think they should do, but at least they're not going after me. At least not yet. So basically, I guess everything's okay. Sort of."

"I see," said Shay.

"Oh, the lawyer you sent me to—I didn't like him too much. He says I owe him two thousand dollars. Maybe that's not good. But he was not in favor of me talking to the cops, which was why I fired him. I hope you're not pissed about that. I just feel like he wasn't really representing me, like he wasn't on my side. I don't think he even thought I was telling the truth, which kind of pissed me off. If anything, I'd just like somebody to believe me. You were the best lawyer. We trusted each other."

He noticed Shay's silence and realized the man was waiting to tell him something.

"I heard you're being served."

"What's that mean?"

"You're being sued."

"By who?"

"You don't know anything about this?"

"No."

"The mother of the MIT student is filing a wrongful death suit against you, I heard."

"You mean Adrian Reinhardt who killed Molly Hibbard—his mother wants to sue me?"

"I heard your father was helping her. My info's a little vague. I thought you'd know more about it."

"I didn't know anything about this. You're telling me my father's helping her?"

"That's what I heard."

"My father?"

"Yes."

"And they're going to sue me?"

"Yes."

Corey laughed. "That makes perfect sense!" What better proof of his father's strange, malignant nature? There was something astonishing about Leonard, it seemed to Corey, but the more he said about it the less anyone seemed to get it, including Shay, and he finally shut up.

"I'm going to need a lawyer, aren't I?"

"Yes, you are."

"Would you be available for that?"

"If you get served with papers, call me."

The call over, Corey got up and went to his parked car, intending to drive home. But instead of going anywhere, he sat frozen behind the wheel.

Maybe, he was thinking, I could move without telling anyone so the process server can't find me. I could move to the woods. Spring is coming—I'd have mud to deal with—marshy mud and ticks. Get Lyme disease and you sleep all the time. I wonder if it gets in your nervous system? It must. There's insect repellant. What else? I could light a fire, put down a tarp, sleep in a hammock. But the ticks would come down the tree and up from the earth. You'd get the disease. If DDT works, maybe I could get by in a bag on the ground as long as I'm not in the brush. Then what? Hide the gear during the day and hike to work? Keep the car where? Are there woods in Weymouth? Yes, there are. There's a state park. Well, it's in Braintree. I'd live in the park—no, on a mountain—on rocks, away from underbrush and ticks. The Swingle Quarry. But then you've got skaters coming and finding your campsite and stealing your stuff. I don't have anything I care about. What about washing? I know what cold water's like. Because of my father, I'm going to wash in cold water? He's going to make me live in the woods? How about the sea? There's a boat problem: I don't have a boat. So I'll live in my car in the woods and lock my gear in the car and wash at the gym. But if I keep my job, they'll find me. How about out of state? Rhode Island? As if they won't look there. All I have to do is last until the Navy takes me. Then I'm out of here. Then he can't touch me. Or maybe he can. What if the lawsuit gets me barred from enlisting?

He had no idea about military policy and was afraid to ask his recruiter. He wished he could ask Joan, but after what she'd said, he couldn't call her.

Instead of going home, he started the hatchback and drove through Quincy heading north. He drove away leaving his sandwich on the stoop. He passed his mother's rest home, crossed over the Neponset, went around the circle and up on 93—elevated, speeding, seeing the wide marshy coastline meeting the blue ocean and the white-covered boats in the corner of his eye. He barely saw the traffic on the road. He played a game of dodging shadows with his lower nervous system. The rest of him was looking out the top of his head, up through the car roof, at scenes in the sky, which only he could see.

He was going to ask his father to drop the case. Or at least that was what he was going to tell people he had done.

So be it, he thought, and drove into the tunnel under the city of Boston for the thousandth time, but probably the last time. So be it, he repeated.

As he drove, he was imagining how to get his father down to the ground to rear-naked choke him. He watched the tunnel for the Storrow Drive exit while seeing he'd have to hit Leonard to drop him, and began thinking what to use—his fist or something heavier. A leftover piece of himself watched this thinking with disgust and despair. He knew if he was contemplating it this seriously and coldly there was something very wrong with him.

The Storrow Drive exit demands a sharp, almost ninety-degree turn into the wall of the tunnel, which can feel slightly impossible to execute under the pressure of following traffic. He missed the exit.

He told himself to wake up, you are doing something dangerous. Snap out of it and look alive.

Fine, he thought. You missed MIT. You'll have to get him in Malden. You'll have to find him there. He let the pressure of traffic push him out of the tunnel and north over the bridge onto the fragment of land that was Somerville and Charlestown. Cambridge was in the west. Then he rose over Somerville on the Tobin Bridge and went down the arc, seeing water and sky, slum and industrial buildings between rivet-studded girders. Trucks dived with him down the rattling chute of the ironworks under the flashing girders, which sent the speeding driver through hypnotic bands of shadow and light.

Find his house and wait for him and when he arrives, hold up your hands to show they are empty and say, "Father, I apologize. My heart bothers me. My conscience burns. That's why I have come."

He still won't let you approach. Tell him: "I'm depressed. I'm crushed. Everything I've wanted is gone, Father. Everything I've done has come to nothing. I was wrong. That is why I have come. I've come to beg your forgiveness. There was a time when you treated me as a son. Can you remember? Everything I've tried to build since then has collapsed on me for the eleventh time. I have sin on my head. I hate the sight of myself and the smell of myself. My soul is disaster. Everything I've done is disaster."

Leonard would let his guard down then and allow him to approach.

"Will you let me inside, Father, as a token of your trust?"

That is where he would draw back. The blitzkrieg would have to take place then and there on the street. The thing would be the uppercut, which he wouldn't see if they were standing close together. It had worked so well that night in Central Square. It was better than a haymaker, which he'd see. He'd see the shoulder moving and he'd flinch.

Corey was waiting for the light to change in Chelsea. The sign for Route 1A, which he planned to take to make his approach to Malden, was in front of him through the windshield; and he sat idling with all the other cars and thought:

I've worked so hard at nothing. I've lived in my empty room in that bad-smelling rooming house and cut marble and thought I was doing something special because I went to a gym. What total triviality! You thought you were going to be a shaved-headed saint who controls his breathing. You have been wasting the world's time. And he saw he was inferior to the occupants of all the other vehicles with whom he waited at the light. They were people coming home from work. They were not on their way to kill a parent.

In its totality, he saw his plan was to deck his father, rear-naked choke him unconscious, cuff his hands with his own handcuffs, drive him back to Quincy and throw him off the Swingle Quarry.

He pulled out of the traffic queue and off the road, stopping along a fence around a factory with smokestacks and a yellow gate. He wrestled out his phone, found the detective's number and started calling. No one answered. He kept calling, calling and hanging up every time voicemail answered. He hit the Call button some sixty times. The afternoon became the evening. He hunched in the front seat, calling.

Finally, someone answered. "Who's this?"

"This is Corey Goltz. Are you Detective Bellavia?"

"Yeah."

"I kind of need to talk to you."

"Is this urgent?"

"Yeah, it's pretty urgent. I think I almost got in trouble."

"Okay . . ."

"I got pretty upset. And I think I was going to do something that I shouldn't do."

"Is this something that's happening right now?"

"Well, kind of."

"What's going on?"

"Basically, I got very upset—I got some bad news—something that upset me—and I came out looking for my father. I drove out to MIT to look for him, but I missed the exit. And then I was like, I'll go to Malden to look for him. But I pulled over."

"Okay, so answer me very carefully. Where are you right now?"

"In Chelsea, I think. I'm in my car."

"Is anyone there with you?"

"No. I'm by myself."

"Has anyone gotten hurt today?"

"No."

"If I check with MIT right now, am I going to find out that something happened there?"

"No. Nothing happened. Like I said, I didn't go there. I was thinking about going there. I was going to go and do something physical to my father. But I missed my turn. And I'm sitting here talking to you, and I'm calming down."

"So you're giving me your word of honor as a gentleman that your father is okay?"

"Yes."

"You didn't do anything to him?"

"No. I didn't do anything. I haven't even talked to him."

"And nobody else is hurt?"

"Nobody else is hurt. I swear. All I did was I got upset and I called you. It helps me to talk to you. I'm all better."

"Glad you're better. Remind me, what kind of car you driving?"

"It's a red Toyota Tercel. This is not an emergency anymore. You don't need to come and arrest me."

"I'm not going to arrest you if you didn't do anything. But if you did something, you have to tell me."

"I didn't do anything. I was upset because I found out my father is bringing a lawsuit against me. He's supposedly teamed up with Adrian's mother, and they're suing me for the wrongful death of her son. And I'm like, these are the people who killed Molly, and I just went off."

"Well, if you didn't do anything, we're okay here."

"Look, Detective, I don't know if you can see your phone, but I called you like sixty times. I just feel like I need someone to talk to. It would make a difference in me not throwing my life away. I'd really give anything if I could buy you a cup of coffee. I don't have anyone else to talk to."

Detective Bellavia said he could meet him at a gas station in Revere.

Corey took Eastern Avenue half a mile north and hooked into a Sunoco. He recognized a man in a belted leather jacket getting out of a black car outside the police station on Revere Beach Parkway. The detective came across the parkway on foot and greeted him.

"Everything still okay?"

"Yes. Everything's okay. Thank you for seeing me."

"I was ready for a coffee. Want to grab one?"

"Can I pay for you?"

"No. I got it."

The detective led them into the Sunoco. Each of them made a coffee and paid for it himself. They met back outside and had their coffees standing a few feet apart, looking out at the parkway.

"I called you sixty times. I feel silly about this whole thing. I'm not a weirdo."

"You're signed up with the Navy, right? How's that going?"

"Supposedly that's going to happen. As long as my father doesn't fuck my life up."

"If anything, *you're* going to fuck your life up."

"I just lost my head."

"Can't do that. Guys who do that wind up in serious trouble."

"You got me back on track."

"If you do something stupid, there will be consequences. You'll wish you hadn't."

"But what about my father?"

"What about him?"

"He's getting away with a lot."

"And what are you? Judge, jury and executioner? How do you know what he's getting away with?"

"He's not in jail. He's not dead."

"Is that what's going to be enough for you? If another man is dead?"

"My mother's dead. Molly's dead."

"How about Adrian? Is he dead?"

"Yeah."

"How about Molly's father? Is he dead?"

"Yes."

"And you're walking around."

"I know. And I worry about being a bad person."

"Then don't be a bad person."

"I'm contaminated."

"By what?"

"By the fact that I'm alive and they're not."

"All the more reason to do the right thing."

"I want to do the right thing. But it's going to land me in jail if I go and smash somebody."

"That's not what I'm telling you to do."

"Don't I have a debt to people? Shouldn't I step up and do something if the law's not doing anything about it?"

"You don't know what the law's doing. I'm the law. Ask me. You think I'm sleeping on this? There's no statute of limitations on murder. If I find something out, whoever it is is going to get caught. It could be him. It could be you. It could be twenty years from now."

"Good. That's all I want."

"That's the way it is."

"So what do I do? Just go ahead and live my life and not worry about it?"

"Go ahead and live your life."

"Should I join the Navy?"

"Join the Navy."

"I don't know anymore. Should I?"

"Did you sign the contract?"

"Yeah, but should I go through with it?"

"You made a commitment, didn't you?"

"I know, but maybe I was wrong."

"Yeah. Well. Then don't. It's your life. But you made a commitment."

"I'm just confused. Job, school, take revenge on Leonard— I just don't know what to do."

"Keep your nose clean. Don't be an idiot. Pay your taxes. That's life."

"I guess I might wind up going to war."

"You might. I mean, I'm not telling you to go. I wish I hadn't done it. It's horrible. I lost men over there no older than you. Not one drop of their blood was worth the medals I received."

"So should I not go?"

"All I can tell you is there are some guys who find out it's right for them. I don't know who you are. And maybe you don't know who you are until you get over there and see."

34

Leonard Agoglia

The threatened lawsuit did not come that spring. Nor did any other legal sanction. As he waited for his recruiter to take him to MEPS, the new rumor Corey heard was that Adrian's mother was in Mount Auburn Hospital, her cancer having come out of remission. One day, heading to an installation job in Belmont, a marble countertop and backsplash bungee-corded in the back of the van, he drove by Adrian's mother's house. It had been repaired, and he wondered if she was alive and living in it or had followed her son into the grave.

He heard nothing from his father and resolved to forget him.

While Corey was forgetting him, Leonard was going to the doctor for his headaches, which were severe. He told a nurse who asked how he was doing that he wasn't doing well at all; he hadn't slept in weeks. She said she was very sorry. She had a white dimpled face, a ponytail, a high voice, and was wearing cherry-colored scrubs—a short, fast-moving girl in sneakers. They were standing in a black-floored hallway. He said he'd be fine, just fine, not to worry about him, he was a tough old cob. She put her hand on his black-sleeved arm. "See you next week."

"Not if I'm dead."

"Oh, stop!"

"They'd be doing me a favor."

He left the hospital and drove the Mercury the five miles back to Malden. The sunlight intensified into a gold fire from heaven. The city was empty. Only the trees were alive, blooming in the spring day.

He parked and went into his house, took his pills and tried again to sleep. At three p.m., unable to sleep, he got up and went to the kitchen and ate something and calculated the hours until he had to go to work. He walked around the house, going in different rooms, looking for a phone number to call the doctor's office to tell them the pills didn't do their job.

Not long thereafter, on another day, having yet again found it impossible to sleep, he got up from his bed in the afternoon and walked from room to room, finally coming back to where he had started, the bedroom, and, as he had done countless times before, spread the blinds with his fingers and looked out the window at the house across the street. It belonged to a notorious murderer—that was what he called him to everyone who entered this room.

Leonard had moved to Malden, to the house across the street from the murderer, before the crime he was accused of had occurred. Only later, the year he met Corey's mother, had the murderer become a murderer—albeit an accused one, a suspected one—but never one who was officially charged, indicted, prosecuted or convicted.

The murderer had never gone to prison. He had lived his life in Malden and now was most likely dead—no one ever saw him anymore.

But Leonard had showed him—his house, that is—to Corey's mother, and she had seen it. She had stood here in this room, in this very spot where he stood now, looking through the blinds. It had been at night. He had turned the lights out on her, perhaps as a joke. She had been quite unnerved by that—as if she'd been afraid of *him* and not the man across the street.

He, Leonard, was the one who should have been afraid. She was the one who got pregnant and out popped someone else— a creature he never had foreseen.

Gloria had been a beautiful girl. If he bothered to look, he had hundreds—maybe close to a thousand—pictures in his desk drawers of her sleeping. There had been a time when it had been of irresistible importance to him to take the photographs. The act of taking them was engaging. But his experience indicated that studying them afterwards was uninteresting. He wished he had someone lying here to take a picture of now.

He pulled out his fingers and let the blinds spring shut and drifted through the house again and stopped at the mantel in the unused room. On the mantel, there was a framed portrait of a woman seemingly dressed in the white robes of old Palestine, hawk-nosed, beautifully bird-of-prey-like, with furrowed brows and deep-set dark brown eyes, seamed and sunken cheeks, furrowed lips clamped together, jaw raised, casting a look of longing at the sky—the image of Saint Teresa, a twisted band around her white draped head, her robes so folded, thick and white.

It was a portrait of his mother, which she had posed for and had taken in 1971, the year his natural father died—of malnutrition and exposure somewhere out on the street in Eastie after two decades of using heroin. Leonard had been born in 1958, the year before the birth control pill had been invented and the intrauterine device.

He put the portrait back down on the mantel and went back to the bedroom and put himself back down on the bed but couldn't go to sleep.

🙝🙟

Leonard Agoglia continued working at MIT. He spent his nights reading at the checkpoint of a dorm. As in years past, the kids swiped in and out and all night long their faces appeared on the screen behind his book, shining with potential and intelligence, and then they went upstairs and eventually went to sleep.

35

Goodbye to the Flower Bank World

During the last phase of the spring, as he waited to enlist, his routine was to run each day to Braintree, past the cliffs to the marina so he could see if the boats were out, then back uphill as dawn broke, seeing in the twilight, set back in the trees, a Cambodian temple in a ranch house where a statue of the Buddha rested in the yard.

Still, from time to time, an internal voice told him that he didn't want to be a soldier who devotes his life to the service of his country. It seemed there was a thing in him that wanted to lay down his life for something else—for someone he didn't know yet.

But he was going to ship out.

Then something happened that surprised him.

He had put five hundred miles on his sneakers since the year began. One afternoon, he bought a new pair at South Shore Plaza. To break them in, he decided to run north. He thought he'd make it to Dorchester. He ended up running all the way across the city and didn't stop until he got to Harvard Square.

It was nighttime when he arrived, a lovely night. The air was feather-soft. Men and women swirled together in yin-yang spirals on the redbrick sidewalk of The Pit. Cars went around the square with their headlights on like torchbearers at a village festival. He stood in his new sneakers, blood humming, ears awash in traffic sounds, hearing the high notes of women's voices.

He saw an individual—there were people with her and he wondered, Why is she with them? He watched her. Maybe she wasn't with them, not really. The more he watched, the more he thought she was alone. Her face was uplifted. She wasn't speaking to anyone. She appeared to be a nun consulting a power above them in the sky.

When he looked again, she had wandered away to the entrance of the T. He went to her and—seeing a flyer, which proclaimed an instance of social injustice—had a flash of inspiration.

"Are you a Marxist?"

"What?"

"I'm just kidding."

"You had me with that."

"So, are you a Marxist?"

She just stared.

"I'm a capitalist. My name's Corey."

She shook his hand.

"Who are they?"

"Guys who wanted to talk. They're British."

"You know we kicked their asses in 1776."

She laughed. She came from Maynard—near Lexington and Concord, the cradle of the Revolution and the shot heard round the world, but not as rich.

Corey stopped a pedestrian and borrowed a pen and wrote his number on a piece of paper and gave it to her.

"If you ever want to have lunch with me."

"What's this?" She poked his chest. His shirt was plastered to his chest.

"I was running."

She turned around and looked at him as she was taking the elevator into the T.

The next day, she called him on the phone. He went to meet her in the same spot. She arrived and gave him a bunch of purple flowers.

He had never been in love before.

She walked with him past a café with brass hookahs in the window. Her clothes hung off her like a good witch, trailing down. Her hair hung down, in ringlets, as if it had been drenched by rain.

They went to the park and he carried her in his arms. She kicked her feet.

She never answered any questions.

They met at all the Red Line stops in Cambridge—Harvard Square, Porter Square where the commuter rail came in, Alewife station with its parking structure and open-air elevators, like successive waterfalls—trying to find somewhere to be alone. She drove from Maynard in a borrowed Honda Odyssey, and they used it to be alone in the Alewife parking lot. While they were resting from making out, she turned on the car stereo and played "The Queens of Noise" by The Runaways for him.

Something was weighing on his mind. He told her about his military commitment. He was going to have to go away. He told her a librarian had tried to make him go to college instead of join the Navy. She hadn't understood our country needs to be prepared for war.

The girl told him she was going away to college.

When?

Soon.

But still, did she have to go away?

She hardly spoke.

He warned her. She was going to have to be careful. It was dangerous. He told her what had happened to Molly Hibbard.

"It was a tragedy," he said.

But she was unmoved.

He gathered that his American girl didn't have a happy home. Someone in her family was on opioids. She was trying to engineer her own escape from Massachusetts.

"Everyone's got their own sob story," she said.

Being in love with her had made him rethink whether he wanted to ship out and go away for years. The chance that he would lose her was very high.

They drifted apart with nothing settled between them. But he was sure he'd see her again. But there was never a goodbye. He was almost lucky that he had signed a military contract because the tug to her was so strong he might never have left Massachusetts; he would have gone to find her at her college. Because of the contract there was no going back—he was committed.

His recruiter called him at the end of May and asked him if he was really ready to enlist. Corey said he really was.

The day before he had to leave, he decided to go down the hill to say goodbye to the boats. He jogged from Quincy Center. When he got to the cliffs above Braintree, he saw the Cambodian temple with the golden Buddha on a rock and started weeping. He ran over and pulled up fistfuls of flowers from around the statue and put them in his backpack, roots and dirt and all.

It was a year since they had all been lost. He went to Ian and told him he was leaving. He borrowed the skiff and took it out on the chop. Looking back at the shore of Massachusetts, he opened his backpack, took the flowers out and threw them in the water.

❧

What would be the legal outcome of his case? Was the prosecutor done with him?

The brown-haired girl wondered.

She feared she'd never know. He had said he was a witness in three homicides—this had taught him to be alert for evil people. But she wondered how he could have managed to be friends with both the victims and the killers without lying in someone's face.

Was he lying in hers?

He was alive and nineteen with life ahead of him. But his life was not worth more than Molly's or Tom's—or anyone else's—and they were gone—all people he had called friends.

Their story was so tragic!

The girl was fleeing Corey for a reason.

Maybe he *would* end up serving time in prison. There had to be punishment waiting in his future. She knew we all have to pay in equal measure, for that is how we learn. Until he saw what he was missing and repented, his girl would mourn him but never trust him, and he would not be welcomed back in her embrace.

36

O Gloria!

It was the promised Saturday. The recruiter was taking him to take the oath. Corey was looking at the ocean. They were driving up the Southern Artery along the marshes on the shore.

"Not getting cold feet, are you?"

"No," Corey said. "Hell no."

They crossed the river into Dorchester.

He thought:

Let's say you make it, get through Hell Week—and then the further training, where you're tested at every evolution, facing constant attrition, the constant pressure to wash out of the most ruthless meritocracy on earth (so-called by a former member); the hazing, the never-ending *eat-shit-new-guy* attitude, the training evolutions that send people to the hospital, the dives that kill people, forcing gases into their tissues, sending them to the hospital in comas with bloody brain swellings; the helo crashes, the quick funerals on deck and back to training, the unit brawls, the punch-outs in the confined space of a van on the way to a range, the coat hanger brandings, blood pinnings, young-wife-gangbangs and other rites that bring warriors closer at the expense of all else that is holy; not to mention the ever-harder training, the stress positions, the seven thousand flutter kicks in boots while being hosed down with ice water, the underwater blackouts and CPR resuscitations; the deliberate, planned, seemingly sadistic capriciousness of the instructors who are conditioning you to the nature of war, inflicting frustration on you to see if you break, compelling you to stand a microscopic inspection of your person and your gear, finding one speck of lint and failing you, trashing your entire room, dumping all your uniforms and equipment in the mud, including your personal effects, and forcing you to clean everything from scratch and stand inspection again—on no sleep, never any sleep, because war is a sleepless adventure—and on the threat of being canned from the team and sent back to the fleet, all your dreams over, to serve out your enlistment stuck on a destroyer, breathing diesel fumes, getting fat with nowhere to run or swim, wearing a Dairy Queen hat and bell-bottom jeans. Then you go home from that, work as a mechanic in a shitty garage, marry a woman who doesn't like or respect you, get even fatter, get cancer and die.

Let's say—and we know it's unlikely—but let's say he discovers he's one of the rare men who can get through Hell Week, and he finds himself on the team, six months into advanced training, swimming with a rebreather and laying mines on the hulls of sunken training ships in the vast green sun-dappled underwater realm— the sea warm at the surface, then cooling as he sinks deeper, big black hard rubber government-issue fins on his feet, giving him unexpected propulsion every time he kicks. He has seen the weird bubble of air and been tossed by the turbulence that results when you set off a mine underwater; all the men have. They've swum twenty miles between islands, pushed jeeps and logs uphill for exercise, killed wild pigs and roasted them on the beach for dinner. On dares, they've eaten raw snakes. He's here with them, in this strange place that no man belongs except a born soldier, and he's arrived here to earn the respect of new fathers—such as the stocky sergeant with a short mustache, who will say, "We're the baddest people around. I've killed, like, twenty people." It's the life of a man standing on a high wire, swinging his arms to stabilize his balance. How long can he last? Privately, secretly, he and others may ask themselves if they truly belong here. It is such a strange blue edge of the breathable atmosphere. But some men want to breathe it; they seem to show no fear of going even further, right out into space, where they know they will die.

By now he has experienced the competition and the likes and

antipathies of his comrades, and, like them, he lives with the constant pressure to perform up to expectations that are both ruthlessly, corporately professional—and primordial.

And, today, he jumps out of an airplane. In the air, he has the extraordinary sensation of jumping after feeling that it is both impossible and expected—one fear next to the other, the fear of death next to the greater fear, the greater impossibility of not doing what is expected—as one man after another gets slapped on the shoulder and told to jump out of the plane in his helmet (essentially a skateboarder's helmet) and goggles and black chute rig.

And so he's falling. It's terrible—like so many things they do. The body wasn't meant for this—the falling body keeps expecting land beneath it—but the body can be made to do it anyway.

The gale tears his cheeks away from his mouth, which he clamps shut. The hurricane wind flogs his dull green jumpsuit. It reaches its fingers around his arms and legs, which have been trained to do thousands of push-ups and lunges, and tugs them enough to remind him that he's tiny, that he can be pulled limb from limb by the sky. He's balanced through physical control on top of a column of air that could obliterate him.

He cannot move the world, but he can move himself; he can, to an extent, control himself—to a greater degree than he once thought possible—but not absolutely. Accidents will happen. He and others will make mistakes—flip in the air, get caught in turbulence—and have to right themselves using techniques the jump-booted instructors taught them: "You're gonna doggone spread-eagle your doggone selves and do a college-boy roll. Why? 'Cause college boys are smart. That's why."

They are taught to keep track of their fall, to count, and how to breathe.

For a few moments during his free fall, he's alone and can briefly forget the unrelenting pressure of his profession. Now, he gets to see the land and the curved horizon—from the viewpoint of a demigod or a man about to die were it not for his technology. It's much like the view from a commercial airplane. Even without the window glass between him and this bright cold world, even in the open air, the vista below looks misty and almost unreal. The miles of vapor in the air make the distant horizon look soft. The glowing sky ventures over the earth's edge onto the sea—a fuzzy golden peach about to roll over a blue table, crushing under it minuscule fishing trawlers and tanker ships. Meanwhile, the ocean's wave-scored surface drives out to the horizon and beyond, like an end-less conveyor belt set to death metal played by Viking berserkers, whipping their hair up and down.

He sees the blessed white line of the ocean where it meets the land; and he sees how the beach slides below the water and stretches out to sea, a downward-grading terrain, which appears turquoise until it drops away into opaque blue darkness. If you drained the sea away, you'd see the dinosaur hills and canyons of the Dakotas.

His eye takes in the land, which is in vivid, sharp relief. Plum-meting closer by the second, he's still ten thousand feet above it. The high definition of what he sees dizzies him: the super-clear rooftops and the man-made world of rectangular boxes—houses, hangars, storage sheds, trucks, containers; hoses, tanks, and pipe-lines; the violin wires of power lines strung for miles by human hands, by men on cranes and ladders in safety glasses, dealing with harnessed lightning, being very careful.

He sees the sectors of the land: the forest where they have trained to protect the country and its wealth, while getting eaten by mosquitoes; the open fields, one of which is the drop zone; and the farms—the entire economy, agriculture and power produc-tion, dirt roads leading to well-engineered highways, and trucks moving along them into the sun, shipping tons of frozen meat, oil and broccoli to people who will consume it.

The land is wealth. You can see this truth from the sky. It has been used and tended, divided into squares bounded by straight roads, trimmed, cultivated, watered, rid of pests, tamed and con-trolled through industry and hard labor. He sees a tractor working across it—from up here a tiny intricate toy that he would have never been able to stop studying if he had owned it as a child.

At the borders of the tended land, he sees more forest, wild areas, marshes and the saltwater curdling up in a scummy estu-ary inside a hooked finger of brown terrain where it wouldn't be wise to swim. He understands that when they are deployed this is precisely where they will go, trying to swim and run and maneuver while wearing protective suits, among rusting barrels of rotting sewage and nuclear waste. The muddy earth is going to peel open in his future and he's going to see rioters tearing buildings apart with their bare hands, ripping out the boards, smashing the windows, hurling the desks down marble stairs, scattering clouds of documents, flinging computers into walls, trailing wires—flinging a screaming woman bodily out into the street. They drag her outside in the stench and heat ripple of burning tires, pour oil on her, make her drink it, bring newspapers and tires and leaves from the underbrush and set her on fire, chanting and clapping, push her down into the ditch, and heap more burning trash on her. She cries and they laugh.

They drag a man out of the building in a tie and a Western dress shirt drenched bright red with blood and kick him in the back, knocking his glasses off, and throw him in the fire, saying, "Here's a man to keep you warm!"

And the brush crackles, burning. And the shouting boys with rags tied around their heads roll tires down on the man and woman, who suddenly comes alive, slapping at the smoke coming from her hair, before slumping and rolling down into the smoking leaves. The boys hit their victims with sticks, to discourage them from trying to beat the flames out.

He will attend a PowerPoint briefing on board an aircraft carrier. A man's face appears onscreen—a so-called high-value target, a rebel leader, an insurgent—a man from a different people, not Boston Italian but black and bearded—but hearing what the man has done, he'll recognize his father and say to the confusion of a colleague, "That's a Leonard."

The rebel leader comes from West African bureaucratic parentage and got his degree at Virginia Tech, where he felt alienated. He tells his followers to roast and eat the flesh of their victims.

"I get that," say the SEALs, because they are warriors too.

The politicals and the advisors come into the briefing room— a genderless group in suits. You distinguish them not by gender but by competence and sympathy, though most of them are somewhat muted, repressed and cold, by dint of corporate culture.

But the warriors are cold too, ice-cold professionals. They don't indulge in lightheartedness until they have a break in their crushing deployment cycles, most of them dealing with chronic pain, hernias, bad shoulders, stress fractures, tropical infections, STDs, nightmares they don't admit to, bad backs, lost wives, estranged sons, no cartilage left in the knees—especially the older ones—they don't laugh that much anymore. And the young ones are all ambition; they have nothing to smile about either.

A helicopter lands on deck, and our president enters the briefing room—our first woman, a woman from South Philadelphia who went to law school—and everyone stands up, and the team salutes their commander in chief. She listens as an admiral with short neat white hair and a wedding ring on his finger lays out the operation and predicts its probable outcome. She asks a question or two, nods, and gives the order to go ahead. She closes a folder, stands up and leaves, followed by an aide carrying a briefcase, and the rest of her core staff. The mission is a go.

Sitting in the briefing, he knows that, according to some, he and his team are there to project American power onto foreign lands and defenseless people. Probably it's absolutely true—even though it's complicated, too complicated to say for sure. They also want to help. But the government is enormous—it's far bigger than a couple of highly motivated guys who can swim for days and do a lot of push-ups—so who knows what it will accomplish in the end. Thousands of people with competing agendas are running it. Whatever he's a part of—call it war—it's going to eat up a lot of people—and their homes and land—and money, oh the money!, so much money, so staggeringly much money—and time and energy and paper and ink and electricity and gas and food and marriages and men—before anyone sees the humanitarian payoff. How you see the use of force probably depends on who your father is.

As they unfold, these events will be debated on the Internet. Much later, they'll be analyzed by a scholar who has studied the Greeks and Moghuls, working fanatically day and night at her laptop while listening to the Rolling Stones' "Street Fighting Man"—believing that her own sex and destiny is to absorb all of history, going back to the Stone Age, the age of cave paintings, and express in clear, forceful language the patterns she sees in human affairs.

My mother could have done that, he thinks. *She* could have overcome herself.

O Gloria!

And they arrive at MEPS and he goes inside with the Navy man and does what he says. There's a giant American flag on the wall. After stripping to his underwear and seeing the doctor who measures his arches, Corey lines up with the other young men and, holding his spine straight, swears in.

Acknowledgments

My thanks to my father for financial support I received from him during this project.

To Jordan Pavlin, my editor, for her masterful guidance. She had the ability to compress instructions into a few clear and simple bullet points, which, like the best athletic coaching, could be followed in the heat of the game. She was right about what this story should (and shouldn't) be.

To Amanda Urban, my agent—steady and shrewd, loyal and patient—and a captain in her industry. On the hardest days of this process, she not only picked up the phone but bought me a beer. I won't forget.

To Ellen Feldman, my production editor—a prodigious, industrious technician whose clarity and attention to detail have made a vital difference to our final product. It has been a rare privilege—and relief to the author who sees nothing but his own errors—to work with her.

To Paul Webster and Taran O'Leary of Viking Moving Services in Concord, Massachusetts, for your tremendous act of friendship when this book was on the ropes. You are not just experienced movers since 9 A.D., you are patrons of the arts, and I thank you from the bottom of my heart.

And one more time to she who was there when it all started and walked every mile of this journey on her own bleeding feet—let's bandage those wounds—to my true friend—my wife. Beth, there'd be no song to sing without you.

Long life to our Kentucky sprites, Pinky, Tux and Nell!